Terror Travels
The Devil's Highway

By Charles Redner

A Maggie Lopez, Border Patrol Agent Novel

Al-Qaeda terrorists travel from Afghanistan to the Philippines, Columbia and Mexico where along the way Islamic fundamentalists and drug lords are all too happy to assist. Their reprehensible mission—spread fear far beyond New York City and Washington DC on 9/11. To succeed they must navigate Arizona's deadly, Devil's Highway.

Published by

PUBLISHING

PUBLISHING

Published by Ri Publishing, USA, an imprint of Redner Investments, LLC.
Laguna Woods, CA 92637
www.charlesredner.com

Cover photo by dreamtime.com
Cover and book design by Ri Publishing

ISBN-13: 978-1463605650
ISBN-10: 146360565X

Printed in the U.S.A.

Terror Travels
The Devil's Highway

A novel

By Charles J. Redner

Chapter 1

The actress sprawled naked diagonally across the ten-foot wide, super-sized king bed. A satin sheet covered her body from just below the small of her back as she slept face down.

Some al-Qaeda missions were better than others, the man in the shadows mused.

The greenish glow from the digital clock showed 3:10. A clamshell-shaped night-light projected a small white semicircle above the receptacle where it was plugged, just inside the cracked doorway to an adjoining bathroom. Wide-open French doors led to a second story balcony. The rising moon appeared a diffused crescent through sheer curtains that gently swayed from a season-changing breeze. It was light enough to make out shapes but dark enough for the intruder to stalk unseen.

A lavender scent lingered from two extinguished candles on the dresser. Bonnie Becker wasn't just asleep, she had passed out. Maliq had watched as she had escorted a handsome young man out of the house an hour earlier. Maliq surmised that she must dislike the morning-after rituals of a one-night-stand. A near-empty magnum of Mumm's Grand Cru et Rose champagne stood upright on the plush carpeted floor near the head of the bed. Two wine glasses lay next to the bottle. The remnants of four joints mixed with cigarette butts in an ashtray.

1

Maliq could make out the slight rise and fall of her upper torso with each breath. He walked silently over to the bed and gently slid the sheet down, exposing her exquisitely proportioned rear end. He closed his eyes, exhaled quietly through his lips, and controlled the urge to run his hands over the perfect female shape before him. An involuntary smile crept across his face. He had seen that ass on the big screen last year, when Bonnie portrayed a good-hearted Las Vegas stripper. The movie was panned, but her bare bottom received rave reviews.

He took a last long look, then opened the top drawer of the night table holding the clock and peered inside. He shined a pen flashlight on its contents. The light revealed a jar of hand cream, a bottle of eye drops, and a half dozen loose Advil tablets. In the back of the drawer, almost covered by a silk scarf was a Rolex Cellini Collection coin watch. Maliq picked it up and carefully examined the expensive timepiece. Its face was a 50-pesos Mexican gold coin. Marie had reporting seeing it in this very drawer many times but she had never once seen Bonnie wear it. He placed it into his coat pocket and closed the drawer softly. He moved the light to the top of a dresser where it caught the sparkle of a behemoth diamond ring and a pair of matching teardrop earrings. Next to them lay a black pearl necklace. He scooped up all the jewelry and dropped the items into his other pocket.

Maliq was not a murderer, rapist, or thief. He needed the watch because he wanted it found in Marie's possession. When Bonnie awoke and missed the jewelry she would assume that an insider had burglarized the house.

He moved away from the huge bed. He had completed his task. The orders from al-Qaeda had been explicit. This was a reconnaissance mission. He had entered the home undetected, got to within easy killing range of the target, and now planned to leave undetected. He'd sketch a floor plan of the house from memory later.

Satisfied, Maliq retreated from the bedroom and walked quickly down the stairs of the celebrated actress' Aspen retreat. He stepped out the front door and strolled down the driveway, bordered by tidy, ornamental rocks, toward the open gate. One of the rocks had been dislodged from its orderly position. On impulse, he snatched it up, whirled around and hurled it toward a bay window. He had wanted to do that for months – a small demonstration of his contempt for American decadence.

The plate glass shattered. Immediately an alarm went off. At the gatepost Maliq entered the code that would close the iron fence behind him. He walked unhurriedly to meet Marie, tensely awaiting him behind the wheel of his Silverado. He slid into the passenger side and Marie accelerated toward Independence Pass, away from Aspen's center, where a private security firm's employee had just observed a blinking light on his monitor board.

Marie glanced sideways at Maliq. "Well, Pablo, did you see her?" She knew him as Pablo Flores, although she knew that he wasn't Hispanic. He understood a little Spanish, but spoke to her in English with an odd accent. He definitely was not a gringo either. They had lived together for two months before he arranged the job that required her to move into Bonnie Becker's Aspen home. On the whole, Marie knew very little about her recent lover. Pablo she reflected, not for the first time, was very secretive. Maliq removed his calfskin gloves reached into his pocket, retrieved the watch and dangled it in front of Marie.

Fear contorted her face. "Pablo! You said you weren't going to steal anything – you said that you just wanted to see Bonnie naked. They'll think I took it. I'll lose my job. Pablo, why?"

"Relax; you're not going back there. I'll get you a new job. I took the watch because I want you to have it."

"But why? Where we going, Pablo?"

"We're going to California, and Marie."

Marie caught her breath and her tension eased. "Yes."

"I did see her naked and know what?"

"What?"

"Her skinny, white ass could use a transplant. I like yours better."

Marie laughed. "Pablo, that's not true. You're crazy? I've seen Bonnie naked. She's got the body of a goddess."

Maliq laughed, leaned forward and laid a hand on her arm. "Marie, pull over."

Marie turned off to the side of the road. When the car came to a stop he clasped the watch around her wrist. "Now slide over here; I'll drive." She did as ordered, pausing to press her lips on his;

she ran her tongue up his cheek and lightly bit his earlobe as she jumped over him.

"Thank you. I love this watch so much." Marie brought the watch to her mouth, steamed the face and rubbed her sleeve on it. She sighed contentedly.

Maliq's assignment had been to gain access to Bonnie Becker's house, using Marie's position as a live-in domestic with lawful possession of the keys, and codes, for all of the doors, gates and alarms. Marie had lived in the house for four months before Maliq asked her for the keys and codes. She had given them to him without hesitation. She was in love with him – and besides – she would still be a prostitute in Juarez if he hadn't rescued her last New Year's Eve. Every prostitute wished for a prince to take her away from a miserable life on the street. Marie had actually found one.

Maliq's drive to San Diego was almost uneventful.

Marie's much-decayed body was discovered three weeks later on a remote trail just off US 8, a few miles west of Dateland, Arizona—a few hundred yards from the terminus of the Devil's Highway. The death certificate indicated cause of death, "unknown," and her body was turned over to the Consul de Mexico in Tucson. The tag attached to her right big toe read: "Juana Doe with Rolex."

When Marie didn't return to the Becker house, it was assumed that she had committed the robbery. The Aspen placement firm that sent her had unfortunately gone out of business a month before the theft, and so the police had no one to question. Marie's whereabouts was solved when an Arizona Border Patrol agent, Martin Fallon, from the Wellton Station called Bonnie. He informed her that a Rolex watch with her name engraved on the back had been found on the wrist of a deceased female. Presumed to be an illegal. He wanted to know if Miss Becker was missing a Rolex.

She hadn't missed the watch but a quick check in the night table drawer confirmed that it must have been taken along with the other jewelry she reported stolen during a robbery months earlier. Bonnie was shocked when she heard that a woman, presumably

Marie, was dead. She was not overly surprised when the agent informed her that no other jewelry was found with the body.

Agent Fallon said that he would arrange for the watch to be returned and thanked her for the name she provided: Marie Flores, even though in all likelihood, he presumed that it was an alias. After she hung up Bonnie reflected viciously that Marie had only gotten what she deserved.

Soon after Marie's disappearance Bonnie hired a new domestic. A movie director friend recommended that she contact Domestic Service International, a Hollywood firm that specialized in servants for celebrities. She took his advice and a sweet Jordanian girl arrived the very next day. The maid possessed a green card and was bonded. Never again would Bonnie use a local firm for domestic help.

Insurance paid for Bonnie's lost jewelry. She had hated the watch anyway. The rock legend that had given it to her turned out to be a junkie and a complete disaster in bed. She was glad to be rid of both. She had completely forgotten about Marie until the agent had called. The Rolex arrived a few weeks later, C.O.D. postage due.

After paying the delivery driver Bonnie walked into the garage and tossed the unopened box into the trash. Aloud, the actress vented her irritation at the whole sorry episode. "Why didn't I tell the border-guy to bury the damn watch with the fuck'n Mexican thief? Would've saved shipping."

Chapter 2

Khalid Sheikh Mohammed entered Osama's tent and bowed deeply. An imposing figure at six feet, six inches, Osama stood some distance away. Seeing Khalid, he placed his hand over his heart and quickly closed the distance between them. They embraced. Khalid kissed the tips of the fingers and touched the top of his head and bowed again. Osama turned and sat down on a Persian carpet off to his right. After coffee and polite talk Osama met and held Khalid's eyes.

"Khalid, I have approved your inspirational plan to hijack American planes and crash them into buildings. However, instead of ten planes, I believe, only four would be wise – all leaving from east coast cities with east coast targets. I have already put into action another plan to strike fear into the rest of the country. Revise your operation to hit the World Trade Center twin towers, the Pentagon and the White House." Osama watched Khalid's reaction. He deduced that he was not upset by the order to reduce the number of planes. "May Allah guide your way." Khalid was excused.

A few minutes after Khalid departed Osama summoned his "adopted" son, Maliq. The coffee and small talk ritual repeated, Osama once again became serious. He stood and addressed his lone guest who remained seated.

"The time will soon be near to execute the plan you rehearsed in America. Choose your men and begin training. Instead of Mexicans we'll have placed bereaved Arab women in all the targets' homes by the time you're ready." Osama reached down toward Maliq and handed him a folded paper. "Here, read this later, memorize, then destroy it. Go now. It's almost time for prayer."

Maliq rose up and walked hurriedly to his tent. Uncharacteristically, he skipped evening prayers. Alone, he anxiously opened the note and read the names: real estate mogul, Megabucks McDonald; New Jersey's U.S. Senator McGuire; famous authors, Bart Nancy and Steven Trent. Maliq grinned as he examined the next three names—the major news network anchors. Genius, pure genius, he mused. He realized the beauty of eliminating all three network news anchors at the same time—who would report the others assassination? The balance of the list included famous writers, television and movie celebrities. His smile grew even wider. He'd assign the actress, Bonnie Baker, to himself—her home's layout still vivid in his head after twelve months—as was the image of her lying naked on the bed.

Chapter 3

For Maggie Lopez, marriage and motherhood could wait awhile.

In high school she had been captain of the tennis team and helped win the state title. Voting her "class clown," the yearbook also stated that she would likely succeed in "show-biz."

Maggie worked-out three times a week, jogged every day, and loved it. Her job required that she take a tough physical test every year. She was a proud member of the U.S. Border Patrol, Tucson Arizona Sector covering the port of Nogales.

Stepping out of the shower, she dried off quickly, grabbed her terrycloth robe and headed for the kitchen. Coffee was her first priority even though it was nine-thirty in the evening. Maggie pressed the start button on her coffee maker having set it up before she had gone to bed.

She walked out onto her second story balcony. Inhaling deeply she surveyed the parking lot and surrounding area out of habit. Large ironwood and palo verde trees dotted the complex. Off in the distance, Maggie could see hundreds of bats diving and darting above a nearby shopping center, feasting on the insects attracted to the lights. Nothing seemed out of the ordinary.

The Old Adobe Apartments where she rented was a fairly new complex in the northwestern part of Tucson. Maggie liked the location because it was close by her parents' house and an on-ramp that led directly to Interstate-19 south for her daily commute to Nogales.

Her apartment was the two-bedroom model that supplied ample room for a single woman. Maggie was quite comfortable in the somewhat Spartan surroundings. The furnishings were secondhand but she was proud to have purchased everything she needed without asking her parents for a loan.

She reentered the apartment and looked around for her favorite travel mug that fit snugly into the cup holder of her nearly new Toyota Corolla. The car had been a present to herself when she graduated from the Border Patrol Academy in Charleston, South Carolina. She was one of only three female candidates in the class of forty. The other two hadn't made it to graduation.

Maggie dressed into her winter greens and strapped on her weapon. After another quick check in the mirror, she locked up the apartment, and walked out into the cool night air.

She jumped into her car and eased out of the parking lot. The radio set on KBAR-FM filled the car with the high-energy sounds of Shakira. This was her first night back on the twelve to eight-shift and she wanted to surprise the guys with some midnight cheer. She traveled two blocks out of her normal route and bought two-dozen Krispy Kreme doughnuts.

Maggie sailed into Nogales, Arizona in forty-five minutes and pulled into the official U.S. Border Patrol chain-link fenced parking lot – an hour and fifteen minutes early. At the gate a "rent-a-cop," stopped her to check ID. He was new and she didn't know him. Her windshield was missing a U.S.B.P. parking sticker. Even though she was in uniform, he insisted on calling the command center for a description of Maggie and her car. With approval secured over the phone, and a stern warning from the guard to get a sticker, Maggie was finally past the gate. What a jerk. She should complain to Admin.

Maggie's annoyance eased as she steered toward a spot near the fence, far in the back, away from the other vehicles. Big trucks and SUV's filled most of the spaces and she preferred to park her little Toyota where it was less likely to get dinged.

She entered the main Border Patrol building, which was shared with U.S. Customs.

Marty Fallon was the first to see her. He grabbed at the box of doughnuts. "What's this – a bribe to get a new window sticker?" he asked.

9

"Hands off, Fatso." Maggie held tight to the box and answered in mock annoyance. "How'd you hear about the sticker already? I swear these walls have ears."

"I answered the phone when Diego called. Thought about telling him to look for a birthmark on your right thigh, but then I imagined he just might try that." Marty chuckled. Maggie glared back at him.

Marty lunged for the box again. "Come on Maggie, it's been a tough night. Lighten up. Share the wealth."

Maggie tossed the box at him and he caught it deftly with an appreciative smile. She liked Marty. He was her first partner when she signed-on, four years ago. He had really gone out of his way to show her the ropes and make her first weeks as trouble-free as possible.

Maggie followed Marty into the cafeteria, where most of the previous shift had already gathered for coffee and chatter. The new shift began to drift in one by one. Marty held up the box to show off the Krispy Kreme logo, and a cheer went up.

"Way to go, Marty," someone shouted.

"Don't thank me. Early bird princess bought them," said Marty, nodding over his shoulder toward Maggie. He placed the doughnuts on the nearest table with a sweep of his free hand and an exaggerated bow.

Maggie smiled widely as "her guys" made short work of the doughnuts.

The agents each thanked her as they passed by, either to go on duty or to head home. *"No hay de que, mi muchacho."* Don't mention it, my boy, she told them. No one needed a translation: Spanish was a requirement for the job. It was almost midnight and time to check with the assignment desk. Maggie refilled her coffee cup. She and Marty left the cafeteria together. Maggie remembered his earlier comment, and asked, "What was so tough about tonight?"

"Shooting at Organ Pipe. Park Service rangers contacted us about eight. They spotted unusual activity on Puerto Blanco Drive. When we got there, found one dead, two wounded."

"Let me guess. A *coyote* shot a *mule*,"

Maggie knew all the street names for the bad guys long before she joined the Border Patrol. The term drug mule, or mule,

10

was slang for a human smuggler, carrying a load of drugs on his back across the desert. Coyotes smuggle illegal aliens into the U.S. for a fee.

"Not this time. A family from Guatemala, Mother's dead. Father shot in the stomach, may not make it. A seven-year-old female got dinged in the leg,"

"Dolce Dio en cielo." Dear God in heaven. "What went down?"

"As best we can piece together, eight illegals were being led through Organ Pipe. Bandits attacked them. Shots were exchanged. When we got there the guide and bad guys were gone. The illegals were huddled trying to stay warm. Injured and dead woman, choppered out – rest taken to Customs."

Maggie reached the end of the hall and started to head toward the assignment desk.

"No, this way." Marty grabbed her by the collar. "You're riding shot-gun for me tonight. Already cleared it with Stacy."

"Alright! Where we going?"

"Back to Organ Pipe. I have a theory and you can help me prove it."

* * * * *

The two left the building and walked to the motor pool where they found their assigned four-wheel drive, extended cab Ford 250. Marty drove fifty miles due west of Nogales as fast as the truck could go on the rutted, dirt roads. An hour later, Marty pulled over, stopped and powered the windows down.

"Where are we?" asked Maggie.

Marty shut down the engine and unbuckled his seat belt. He didn't answer right away. He welcomed the silence and waited for his eyes to adjust to the near total darkness. Maggie waited patiently. When he could see again said, "Puerto Blanco Drive, about a hundred yards from where it happened. We're just north of the border. Can you make out the fence over there?" Marty pointed straight ahead.

"My theory, since you didn't ask, is that finding those illegals may have been a set-up. We were supposed to find them here; then after we leave, they use this same spot for a drug crossing. If I'm right we should see some activity before daylight."

"Not a bad theory. So, want ah play strip poker? Brought the cards."

"No wise-ass. I need some rest. Working a double, you know. Take the first watch."

He handed Maggie a pair of night vision goggles. "Here, stick your head out the window; make like an owl. Wake me in a couple of hours." An hour later, Maggie heard the faint sound of a vehicle approaching.

"Marty, wake up!" She shook his shoulder gently. "I think I hear a truck."

Marty was instantly alert.

The noise grew louder. Just across the road, a military Humvee came into view. With her goggles, Maggie could see that the vehicle showed no official markings but she knew it had to be Mexican military. It stopped twenty-five yards in front of their pickup. A spotlight instantly blinded them. They ducked down to avoid the light and whatever might follow.

Still crouching, Marty turned on the engine. He drove straight for the intruders. Just as he reached the front of the Humvee, he turned hard left and headed east along the road they had taken in. Marty stopped after a few hundred yards. The Mexican's followed and stopped fifty yards behind.

With an ear-shattering, explosive clatter a machine gun roared to life, Maggie whispered a brief prayer. "*Madre mio* pray for me now and at the hour *de los mi muerto.*" The mini-explosions, muzzle flashes, and streaming white tracers terrified her. Dirt kicked behind them. A cloud of dust temporally hid them. Maggie had seen a demonstration of machine guns firing on a target range, but this was frightfully different. She had never looked straight into a blazing barrel before.

Marty threw the truck in low and gunned the engine. It kicked up dust and stones in its wake. The Humvee jerked forward in pursuit. It opened up with the machine gun again. Marty could see the tracers "walking" up his rear through the mirrors.

Maggie grabbed for the radio mike to call for help, but fumbled and dropped it. As she reached down to retrieve it, rounds hit the truck bed. The side panels rattled. The sound of metal tearing metal reverberated inside the cab.

12

Traveling too fast on the uneven furrowed dirt road, Marty lost control, swerved and hit a boulder. The left front tire blew and the truck started to roll, but righted. It lurched forward for a few agonizing yards and died in a shallow wash just as rounds reached the cab.

"Get out!" Marty screamed.

Maggie didn't need a second invitation. She bolted, crouched low, ran ten yards and dove onto the ground behind a huge bolder. Marty wrenched open the driver's side door and did likewise. The blinding, brilliant explosion shook the surrounding. The back of the Ford truck rose six feet into the air; then flipped over back-to-front. It returned to earth a fiery jumble of broken glass, melting plastic and twisted metal. Maggie screamed. She watched Marty thrown forward by the blast. She cringed when his head hit a rock. Over the fire's roar she didn't hear the sickening smack.

Chapter 4

Sitting in the battered Jeep Cherokee, Maliq took a long, deep drag on his cigarette. It would be two hours before his next break. By Islamic law, smoking was *al Khabaa'ith*, evil and unlawful but, since he had to adopt many ways of the infidels why not smoke? It was very satisfying, although he didn't care much for the menthol brand that he'd purchased by mistake. The cool aftertaste was displeasing. He preferred English Ovals or a Turkish Fatima. He hadn't smoked during his travel to America four years earlier.

Through the Jeep's mud-streaked window unending rain drum over enormous, rubbery fronds and plop to the jungle floor. It smelled like sweaty socks after a soccer match and he much enjoyed intervals of the masking cigarette smoke. Stepping from the vehicle he threw the butt in a puddle. Then, hunched over trying to stay dry, he dashed into the nearby building.

The dirt road that led up to the building and dead-ended there morphed into a muddy trail. No one dared walk or drive along the lonely stretch from the nearest village five miles away without explicit permission. This area of the Philippines was controlled by *Abu Sayyaf*, the "Bearer of the Sword," a group of Islamic fundamentalists who wanted to create a separate, independent Philippine State. They had ties and received money from al-Qaeda for their struggle.

Two *Abu Sayyaf* men guarded the building. Each had a World War II-era U.S. Army-issue carbine slung over the shoulder of their short-sleeved jungle camouflage fatigues. Colt-Browning

.45's rested on their hips. They stood off to the side under the shelter of the roof smoking and talking. Their occasional glances toward the door suggested that they were discussing the foreigners in their midst. They spoke in *Chabaca*, a mixture of Spanish and a native dialect common in Mindanao.

From the entrance it looked like any small town industrial building, but very much out of place here, some seventy-five miles north of Zamboanga City. Its construction was of bare cinderblock but care had been taken to ensure that it could not be seen from the air. The corrugated tin roof was painted in blended shades of green and the windows were spray-painted black from the inside. A sign over the door explained its function: *Esquala de Kabasalan* – A school.

The interior contained only one large room. A portable blackboard with letters of the Spanish alphabet printed neatly across the top stood near the front beside a small table and folding chair. This morning, nine eager students were seated at standard classroom desks found in most high schools. They listened carefully as the middle-aged, stocky instructor spoke each word clearly, as he wrote across the board:

"*Este ... una ... mapa ... de ... Mexico.* Repeat, please."

The nine English speaking, combat-trained, Saudi al-Qaeda fighters repeated his words in unison.

"Very good." He turned toward the students and looked at those in the first row. "Translation anyone?"

Maliq was the first to raise his hand. He was muscular and trim; his light-gray eyes set off his olive skin and dark brown, wavy hair. But for his mustache he could have passed for a teenager. At twenty-four, he wasn't the oldest, but was most assuredly the leader of the group.

"Put your hand down Maliq, that's too easy for you," said the instructor.

Before Maliq got his hand down, the satellite phone in his pocket vibrated. He excused himself and walked outside to take the call. If the other students were watching they might have noticed the instructor's eyes widen ever so slightly.

A moment later Maliq returned to the classroom. He held an Army .45 in his right hand. All eyes in the room were riveted on the weapon as he walked to within an arm's length of the teacher, who backed away, toppling the blackboard with a thunderous crash.

The teacher tripped, stumbled across the room and slammed against the far wall. He tried to speak, but couldn't catch his breath, let alone make a sound. His back to the wall, he slid down until his ass hit the floor. He flung both hands over his face.

Maliq paused just long enough for the instructor to fully grasp his pending death. He fired the first round into the heaving chest. After a beat, three unnecessary, but extremely satisfying shots followed.

The blasts reverberated painfully around the room. The odor of gunpowder filled the nostrils of the paralyzed onlookers. Then it mixed with the stink of defecation as the instructor's bowels emptied. Bewildered students jumped up, some holding their hands over their ears, others their noses.

Some were seeing death for the first time. Desks flew over. Zubayr and Karim ran to the rear of the room and stumbled outside.

The rest looked on in horror at the huge holes in the instructor's chest that oozed blood across his slumped body. Blood and body fluids formed a crimson pool that spread in a widening arc across the wooden floor.

Questions and profanities bombarded Maliq in Arabic as the room erupted in unintelligible racket.

Abdul screamed above the din. "Maliq, have you gone mad?"

Maliq raised his left hand. The clamor stopped. "Clean up this mess," he ordered softly. "I'll explain later."

He clicked the safety on the weapon and returned it to the stunned guard who stood silent at the doorway. He tossed the phone into a trashcan and, without another word, walked out the door.

Outside, Maliq leaned against the wall out of the rain. His head was raised heavenward, and shook from side to side repeatedly. His unfocused eyes searched for an answer. *How in the name of Allah did the CIA* ... his thought hung incomplete. He brought his hand to his forehead and closed his eyes. He had just killed Manny Falstino, Filipino native and the best *Abu Sayyaf* Spanish teacher on the island. It could take weeks, if not months, to replace him.

It was a stroke of bad luck but it could have been disastrous if that call had come later or not at all. Maliq's caller had told him Manny was an informant. Maliq clenched his fist as he realized that the operation may have been compromised and be aborted. He knew he'd be told fairly quickly if Manny's treason had doomed their plans; but for now, language training would continue with audiotapes.

* * * * *

The Arabs slept on U.S. Army cots, in large tents set over wooden platforms. Maliq commanded a tent all his own; the others lived communal style, four to a tent.

After six weeks in the jungle, Maliq found the closeness and dampness foreboding. He felt uncomfortable living amid the dense vegetation. He thought for a moment about the dry desert climate of his homeland but banished the vision quickly lest it weaken his resolve.

Two days after he executed Manny Falstino, Maliq received orders to report to the headquarters of Lucian Reyes, second-in-command of *Abu Sayyaf.* Standing beside the rear wall of the school, Maliq watched as his escorts' van arrived. Ferdinand Marquez, whose weapon he had borrowed to shoot the Spanish teacher got out of the vehicle and walked over to him. He patted down Maliq thoroughly. It irked Maliq that the *Abu Sayyaf* treated him now as an outsider, like someone who might harm a fellow Muslim. He wouldn't, of course; unless he was a spy like Falstino.

Maliq climbed into the front passenger side of the van while another guard sat directly behind him, cradling an AK-47 on his lap. After a two-hour ride, the guard in the back spoke. "Sorry Maliq – orders." He placed a blindfold over Maliq's eyes.

This ritual angered Maliq even more than the body search. It reminded him of the night his father died. Ten minutes later they arrived at camp. The blindfold was removed.

Maliq had been inside the small barbed wire fenced compound three times before and knew which building they were taking him to. It was the only wooden structure in the compound. The other buildings consisted of six thatched huts each surrounded by sandbags and containing a gun emplacement. The compound was devoid of trees and shrubbery, allowing for clear fields of fire. Overhead camouflage netting covered the wooden building and fortifications. Maliq guessed that the facility was new and seldom used, because the fence posts were not weathered and the barbed wire had not yet rusted. The defensive positions didn't appear to contain permanent gun emplacements, nor was the office equipped with the sophisticated communications hardware normally found in the headquarters of a second-in-command. Maliq wondered if this compound was built just for his infrequent visits. As the van jerked to a stop he heard a familiar deep voice, say in English: "Hurry, we must conclude our business quickly."

The speaker was Lucian Reyes, standing on the top step of his small office headquarters.

Maliq rubbed his eyes in the bright light, and looked up at him. "Praise be to Allah." Reyes gestured for Maliq to follow. "Come inside, out of the sun."

Maliq followed Reyes. He was a big man, well over six feet tall and built like a professional wrestler. He dressed in jungle greens like the rest of his men. His clothing showed no sign of rank, but he carried himself with the self-assurance of command.

The building contained only three rooms. They entered the office. Beyond an interior doorway Maliq saw a young woman playing with a small boy of about five. The woman wore a white blouse with black slacks. Her head was covered with a scarf, but she was not veiled with a *hijab*. She looked up and their eyes met. For the first time Maliq was stirred by the beauty of a Filipino face. The little boy giggled as he hugged a stuffed panda bear that the woman pretended to take away from him. His laugh was infectious. Reyes seemed annoyed that the door was open. He walked over blocking Maliq's view and shut the door hard. He motioned to a chair in front of his desk for Maliq. They both sat.

"My brother, you have done a very, very bad deed," said Reyes.

"But he was an *inform ...* "

"Let me speak." Reyes cut Maliq off in mid-sentence. "Even giving you the benefit of the doubt, that Falstino was an informant, you did not have the authority to kill one of our own. Do you have any idea how we deal with an act of treason?"

18

"I would …" Maliq started to answer, but again Reyes cut him off, this time by holding up both hands.

Maliq now understood that this was not a meeting, but a lecture and by the hardening tone, not one he'd soon forget. This surprised him. He and al-Qaeda intelligence had provided an enormous service to *Abu Sayyaf* by exposing and eliminating a bastard spy in their midst.

Already sweating from the heat and humidity, Maliq experienced a tinge of fear. Not fear for his life, but a fear that he might have doomed the mission. He tugged at his collar and shifted in his chair.

Maliq took a pack of cigarettes out of his shirt pocket and took his time lighting one. He hoped the delay would allow him time to think of an argument that might appease his host.

Reyes regarded him impassively.

"You and your team have been welcome guests and we wholeheartedly support your mission, whatever it might be. But what you have done cannot be condoned or overlooked. Therefore, you will not be getting a new Spanish instructor and you will leave Mindanao as soon we can arrange for your departure."

Maliq lowered his head and closed his eyes in disbelief.

Reyes continued, "Just in case you're wondering, Osama has already been notified. He agrees with this decision. We will inform you when it is time to depart.

Maliq recognized that he was he was being dismissed but felt it was important that he tell Reyes what he had learned. "But Falstino was reporting right to the Americans in Manila, he told them about my team …" Once again, Maliq stopped talking in mid-sentence. He had heard a familiar sound, frightening even for a trained warrior. It was the whistle of incoming mortar fire. The first round landed thirty yards away.

Both men instinctively dropped to the floor as windows shattered. Reyes crawled toward the door where the woman and boy were playing.

The next round exploded just beyond the back of the building, taking most of it down. Pain seared through Maliq's ears, rendering him temporally deaf. Glass shards struck his left hand. He looked at the blood dripping down his arm, but felt no pain.

The wooden structure roared into flames. Reyes and Maliq tried to stand. The building screeched like a wounded bull. The floor tilted toward the rear. When the walls collapsed both men fell, rolling off the disintegrating floorboards into a smoldering pile of debris where the back half of the building had stood just seconds earlier. Maliq recognized the odor of burning flesh.

The only remaining signs of the woman and boy were a bloodstained panda bear that lay beside a singed scarf. A sandal secured to what once was a delicate foot completed the scene. Fortunately, the hazy smoke and dust made it difficult to see beyond a few feet. Maliq covered his mouth and nose. Reyes did likewise. Bleeding from his nose and eyes, he motioned for Maliq to follow him. Maliq was dazed. He couldn't hear. He trailed Reyes instinctively.

Automatic small arms fire erupted all around, as the defenders held off what Reyes suspected by the sound of the firepower was at least a platoon-sized unit of the regular Philippine Army advancing on their position.

He led Maliq to the nearest hut. It was simply furnished with a cot, footlocker, and sideboard. Reyes shoved the footlocker away. It covered a trapdoor. Lifting it up, he started down a rope ladder.

Maliq followed as a hail of bullets riddled the hut. One round knocked the heel off his boot, wrenching his ankle just before he entered the shaft. At the bottom, Reyes grabbed a flashlight that was tied to the ladder and aimed the beam down a long narrow tunnel. It was not quite high enough for a grown man to stand upright but the two were able to bend forward and trot. Maliq hobbled noticeably on his sore ankle and his missing heel. Dirt dropped down from overhead. It covered their hair and fell down the back of their shirts as one mortar round after another exploded above.

The tunnel ended at another rope ladder. Reyes climbed up, lifted the camouflaged cover and looked around. They were fifty yards beyond the compound fence. The firefight was well to his rear; no one appeared to be in the immediate area. Both men climbed out and once again Maliq followed Reyes as he ran toward a well-concealed Dodge truck a few yards distant. Reyes jumped in and started the truck. Maliq pulled himself into the passenger seat and the two made a rapid escape along the narrow jungle path that now substituted for a road.

After an hour of riding through rough jungle terrain in silence, Maliq's hearing returned, although a loud ringing remained. He longed for a cigarette, but he had dropped them during the escape and he knew Reyes didn't smoke.

Finally Maliq summoned the courage to ask the question that they both knew was coming. "The woman and child ... members of your family?"

Reyes took a breath, held it and exhaled fully.

"Yes. She's my daughter, Imelda, and he was my grandson. My son-in-law was the guard you passed at the front gate. He and the rest of those men are most likely dead now." Tears spilled down Reyes' cheeks, turning pink as the moisture mingled with the caked blood that encrusted his sunken eyes.

Maliq looked away quickly out of respect for Reyes' private sorrow. After a long silence, he offered a prayer. "May Allah greet your daughter and grandson in Paradise this day. *Assalamu alaykum.*" Peace be upon you.

Regaining his composure Reyes said, "You and I fight in the name of Allah, as Muslims have for thousands of years – but we fool ourselves if we believe our struggle is about God. It is about land, wealth, and control over the masses. Allah is only the excuse."

Maliq was troubled by Reyes' words but let them pass, reminding himself that they were uttered by a man overcome with grief. Both men were silent again during another hour of bumpy, hazardous travel. As Maliq started to recognize the terrain, Reyes said, "This changes nothing regarding our earlier conversation. I'll notify you when it is time for your team's departure."

"Yes, of course." Maliq hesitated then added, "I am deeply saddened over your loss today."

Reyes acknowledged the comment with a slight nod. He deposited Maliq back at the school and quickly drove off.

Maliq gathered his men and told them about the firefight and Reyes' decision to ship them out. He did not mention the death of a beautiful woman and small child. No need to share his latest experience with the collateral damages of war. The acting medic of the group removed small pieces of glass from Maliq's hand and wrapped it tightly. His ankle hurt more than his hand but he didn't mention it, aware that the throbbing ache would probably go away in a few days.

He wanted to call Afghanistan but knew the situation did not follow the guidelines for initiating contact. Maliq had just been granted his unarticulated wish to leave the Philippine jungle. For this he was happy, but not knowing his next destination made him uneasy.

The next day the *Abu Sayyaf* guards disappeared from their posts. That night the *Esquala de Kabasalan* mysteriously caught fire and burned. No one was injured in the fire, which was quickly contained by a few villagers who just happened to be in the vicinity. However, the message was clear – the foreigners were no longer welcome.

The Arabs now slept next to loaded weapons and posted their own security.

Chapter 5

Tonight, Carlin Ward was filling in for Johnny West, the early evening KBAR FM weeknight disc jockey, who had caught the flu.

Carlin Ward and his wife, Dora, had moved to Tucson from Chevy Chase, Maryland, three years earlier when Carlin took early retirement; but retirement to Carlin meant more than golf, a good book, and a rocking chair. He attended investment seminars, published an entertainment magazine, and returned to one of his first loves, broadcasting. He auditioned and was hired for a weekend DJ shift at KBAR FM, where he felt right at home with the soft rock format and the "rip and read" news duties.

No, Carlin at age 58 was hardly retiring. He kept close tabs on his political contacts in the east and flew back often to stay in the loop, just in case he got the urge to rejoin the madness. He was still a full partner at the highly regarded political consulting firm of Ward, Whitman and Cross LLP.

The studio light flashed red. "On Air" lit up in white above the door. Carlin read:

"Two Border Patrol agents were injured last night while on duty in the Organ Pipe National Monument according to a Border Patrol spokesman who did not release the names or condition of the injured. However, an unidentified source has told KBAR News that a shooting took place with suspected drug runners. The incident happened just a few miles from where agents caught eight illegal border crossers earlier in the evening. Three of the illegal aliens

23

were reported shot during their capture, one, a female, died from wounds and two remain at Tucson Genera. The second adult is listed as critical, and the other in serious condition. The names of the dead and injured have not been disclosed. It is believed that one is a female child. Authorities are not releasing additional details about either incident at this time. This has been a KBAR news update ... right now we'll take a short break for a message from our sponsor, Pueblo Dodge."

Carlin Ward didn't need to signal his engineer to play the taped commercial; it was already blasting in his headset as the studio light turned off.

Holding down the intercom button, Carlin said, "One hell of a night for our guys."

"Scary," came the reply.

"Something has to be done. The criminal element has completely taken control of our border." Carlin's voice sounded exasperated. "Now we've got a wounded youngster and it sounds like her mother's dead and father's on life support. The liberal in me wants to provide security for those poor souls and place water along the trails. The conservative side wants to build the next great wall."

"I hear ya, Carlin, but what to do?"

"I don't know. But personally, I've got to try to do something."

The taped commercial neared the sixty-second mark. "Wanta go right to Cher or back to you?"

"Go to music."

Completing his shift at ten, Carlin left the studio and drove directly to Tucson General. He knew it was crazy to go at this late hour, but he wanted more information on the shooting victims, especially about the young child. This was not investigative reporting; that was not his job. He was driven simply by his own genuine, growing concern about the serious troubles occurring daily on the border.

Carlin parked behind the hospital, close to the Emergency entrance. He entered and surveyed the waiting room. Immediately he caught a whiff of the medicinal odors and disinfectants. An elderly man and woman huddled together as far away from the entrance and service window as possible. The woman looked as though she was in pain and must be the waiting patient. A heavyset Asian-looking woman in a white uniform sat behind the window looking too busy to be bothered. Carlin decided to follow the signs pointing to the main lobby and cafeteria.

With no press credentials or familiarity with the hospital's disclosure policy, he headed for a safe haven – the cafeteria. There he saw two women and a man sitting at a table talking quietly, sipping coffee from paper cups. Carlin decided coffee was a good ruse and headed for the vending machines.

With coffee in hand, he chose a table close, but not obviously too close to the threesome who were the only others in the room. The younger woman, somewhere in her mid-twenties, was in a wheelchair with her leg heavily wrapped. Multiple large bandages plastered her forehead and chin. The older couple looked like worried parents.

As hard as he tried, Carlin could not overhear their conversation but he managed to grab a word here and there as they spoke in English and Spanish.

"Madre muerto ... shooting ... Marty ... hurt ... monument ... coyotes."

He heard just enough to know that he was probably looking at one of the wounded from last night's action in Organ Pipe. *She must be one of the Border Patrol agents.*

Carlin decided on a direct approach. Walking over to their table he asked, "May I get any of you some more coffee?"

They abruptly stopped speaking.

The young lady placed her hand to her head, as if embarrassed by her appearance. Eventually she spoke. "No thanks, we're just leaving."

As the older man and woman started to rise, four people burst into the room.

"There she is!" A short, bald-headed man waved a microphone, pointed in their direction. A woman with a flash camera started taking pictures. Carlin realized that the newshounds had found a quarry and saw his opportunity. With over twenty years experience handling pushy press mobs, he knew just what to do.

He turned toward the four and shouted, "Stop right there! No more pictures. And you – turn off that recorder. Move away from the door and let us pass." Carlin's outburst startled the foursome. They backed away from the doorway as ordered.

"Let's go." Carlin grabbed the wheelchair with both hands and motioned with his head for the older couple to follow him out. Once outside the cafeteria he whispered, "Which way?"

"Left! Elevator's on the right," answered Maggie.

Maggie's mother and father, looking bewildered, followed the man who was pushing their daughter, in great haste, down the hospital hallway. The reporters followed, but hung back at a respectable distance.

Luckily, the elevator doors opened just as they approached. Two nurses strode out and hurried off down the hallway. Once all were inside the elevator, Maggie spoke. "Push three, four and five Dad, and who, in God's name, are you?" she asked straining her neck to look into the green eyes of the handsome, six-foot three Carlin Ward.

He kept his hands on the wheelchair, returned Maggie's look and said, "Show me the way to your room and I'll explain."

When the doors opened on the fifth floor, Maggie said, "Let's go. Turn right, room five-oh-eight, third door on the left." Carlin pushed Maggie toward her room. When they reached the nurses' station, the duty nurse stood up and scowled at the entourage. Maggie's parents hesitated.

"Mom, Dad, I'll be all right. Why don't you go home now? Both of Maggie's parents kissed her on the cheek and quietly left. Carlin quickly pushed Maggie's wheelchair to her private room. She hopped out of the wheelchair and jumped onto the bed. Now alone, Maggie coldly stared straight at Ward. "Start explaining – and this better be good. Make it quick, too, the warden is probably on her way already."

Carlin stood stiffly by the foot of the bed. "My name is Carlin Ward. I just got off the air where I reported the news about your ordeal at Organ Pipe and I wanted to learn more; that's all."

Maggie grimaced and stared at him in disbelief.

"So, you're no different than that group you chased away. Very clever, I'll give you that. Now beat it."

The duty nurse, Lola Diaz, appeared at the door. "Everything okay in here? Bedtime sweetie, say goodnight."

26

"No, it's not okay in here. This guy's a reporter. Get him out of here,"

Maggie said, kicking out with her good leg in Carlin's direction.

Carlin protested, "No, no I'm not. I just want to help. May I visit you some other time?"

Maggie kicked out again grazing Carlin's arm, "Get out, before I call security."

Carlin hunched his shoulders and backed away. He did an about face and reluctantly headed for the door. The nurse glared at him. She was blocking part of the doorway and Carlin had to turn sideways to edge past her.

"Wait – wait," Maggie called abruptly after his retreating back. "Aren't you the weekend DJ on KBAR? The guy who's always bragging about his wife? She's an animal rights advocate and an artist, right?" asked Maggie, cocking her head.

Carlin stopped just outside the door, and stuck his head back. "Guilty as charged."

"I adore you."

"He's a little old for you, honey," interjected Nurse Diaz with a ghost of a smile. "But he has to leave right now even if you do adore him."

Maggie smiled broadly, waved and said, "Come around two tomorrow. I'll put your name on the list, Mr. Ward. You just can't be like those monsters downstairs."

"I'm not, you'll see, thanks, thanks. See you tomorrow. Oh, whom do I ask to see?

"Margarita Smith. I'm undercover, get it?" she pulled the sheet up over her head.

Carlin didn't get it.

Maggie's voice was muffled under the sheet. She whispered, "Real name's Lopez." Then in full voice, "Ask for Maggie Smith."

Carlin got the pun and left. So she was feisty, and a clown. He knew just how to handle her. All those years managing politicians had taught him a little psychology, among other things, he thought. Walking down the hall he was feeling good that he had at least gotten to first base.

He walked past the cafeteria on his way back through Emergency to his car. He was going to stop for a celebratory coffee, but hesitated at the entrance when he saw the four reporters huddled at a far table. He'd celebrate elsewhere.

* * * * *

Early next morning, Carlin rolled over and kissed Dora, his wife, on the neck. Her eyes opened and she smiled at him.

"That was a nice wake-up call. Is room service on the way?" she asked with a yawn.

"No sweetheart, it was just something that I needed to do – a thank you, of sorts, for being a wonderful wife, animal advocate, and an artist."

"Are you feeling okay?"

"Yes, sweetheart, I have to go to the office early and get in touch with some people back east."

He hadn't mentioned his trip to the hospital last evening. He'd just told her that he'd stopped for coffee after his show. He saw no need to explain further since he didn't yet know where the interview with Maggie might lead, if anywhere. He also felt that Maggie still wouldn't trust him unless he could tell her a thing or two that she didn't know.

Carlin rented a small office near the University of Arizona campus. He loved being around eager, ambitious young people. He felt energized by their enthusiasm for life. He also loved college sports, especially basketball. The professional teams were a hundred miles north in Phoenix, but distance wasn't the reason he didn't go to the Suns, Diamondback or Cardinal games; he just preferred sports at the college level. Having been born and raised in Philadelphia, he was weaned on basketball at the Palestra where on any given night you could see Penn, Temple, Villanova, LaSalle, or St. Joseph's play each other for city bragging rights. The excitement was indisputable.

Carlin opened his office, went to his computer and logged on. He dashed off an email to his former Washington office to see if anyone was around. It was eight-thirty in Washington and his partner Robert Whitman answered the message immediately. Carlin picked up the phone and pressed speed-dial three. On the second ring, Whitman answered the phone.

"So – Carlin, to what do we owe this honor?"

28

"Bobby, I need some information and I need it this morning."

Carlin quickly explained all he knew about the shooting incident in the Organ Pipe National Monument two nights before. "Snoop around Bobby and see what more you can find out."

"Give me till three."

* * * * *

At precisely noon Carlin's time, the phone rang.

Whitman's tone was brisk. "Nobody's willing to say much about this one, but I did learn a few things," he told Carlin. "The two injured Border Patrol agents are Margarita Lopez and Martin Fallon. Lopez's got a second-degree burn on her leg. Fallon has a severe concussion and hasn't been conscious since he went down. A heavy caliber weapon shot up their vehicle. The FBI suspects the Mexican military."

Bobby had apparently found the right source for information.

"The two agents were choppered out within minutes of the incident by a Border Patrol Black Hawk, which was patrolling near the area. They saw the truck on fire from the air. The three illegal aliens who were shot earlier that evening were from Guatemala. The woman was dead at the scene. The man with her got hit in the stomach and died last night. A seven-year old girl is still in the hospital with a slight leg wound. They believe that she is the daughter of the two deceased. That enough?"

"Yeah, terrific Bobby. Thanks." Carlin smiled in anticipation of his meeting with Maggie. He hung up and left the office for a quick lunch.

Carlin couldn't wait for his two o'clock meeting with Maggie. He arrived at the hospital thirty minutes early and waited in the car. He read every section of the *Arizona Star*, spending most of his time devouring the sports pages. Somewhere a clock gonged twice, he folded his paper and left it on the passenger seat.

Carlin entered Maggie's room in time to hear a news anchor describing a firefight on the island of Mindanao, where Philippine regular forces had killed fifteen *Abu Sayyaf* Islamic insurgents three weeks before at a jungle camp. Maggie looked up, waved, but kept her attention on the small screen. Carlin watched the end of the film clip depicting a row of uncovered bodies, then turned his attention toward Maggie. She peered up with a huge smile and hit the mute button on the TV control.

"Hey, Sherlock how's the snooping business?"

"You'd be surprised,"

He handed her a bouquet of roses and flopped in the visitor's chair nearest Maggie's bed. He was much more relaxed than he had been the previous night.

"Gee, you didn't have to bring flowers, Mr. Ward."

"Please call me, Carlin, and yes, I did."

"Thanks, Carlin." She caressed a flower petal gently and smelled it. "They're beyond beautiful."

A nurse who was in the room checking Maggie's blood pressure volunteered to find a vase. She took the flowers from Maggie and left.

Carlin and Maggie spent time getting acquainted. After they had exchanged background information about family, friends, schools, and incidental interests, Maggie asked, "So, what are you really after, Mister Ward ... eh, Carlin?"

Carlin shifted forward then leaned toward her, "Just what I said last night. I want to help in some way."

Maggie fluffed up her pillow, sat up straight and looked right into Carlin's face, "Why and how do you propose to help?"

"The why is easy; the how might depend on you."

Carlin explained that he felt saddened and somewhat alarmed about the violence happening on the border. "I'm well connected in Washington and I could possibly expend some political capital in order to assist the Border Patrol."

"Wow," said Maggie, "If you have so much political capital, you should be talking to the head of the INS, not a foot soldier like me."

"No, I want to talk to you – a foot soldier – whose life is on the line every day. I want to know from the bottom up what's needed and learn how I might be able to help. I'd like to go on patrol with you and Martin Fallon."

He paused to let Marty's name sink in, awaiting Maggie's response.

Her smile abruptly left, her mouth turned down and the voice grew harsh. "Okay, so you learned my partner's name. Are you going to scoop the competition and broadcast a KBAR news flash along with my name, as well?"

"Of course not. What can I do to gain your trust? I'm not a reporter. I just read the news on weekends. I'm here as a concerned citizen who just wants to do something about the constant border troubles."

Before Maggie could respond a tall, black man dressed in a dark blue suit barged into the room unannounced. He approached Maggie and showed his credential. "Miss. Lopez, I'm FBI agent Norcross and I'd like a word with you in private. Sir," he added, looking down at Carlin, "you'll have to leave." Carlin frowned but reluctantly left for the solarium at the end of the hall.

An hour later, the FBI agent left. Maggie sent a nurse to inform Carlin that he could return. Upon reentering Maggie's room Carlin took his seat and asked, "Guess you can't tell me what that was all about?"

"Of course not, but I can tell you that he reminded me not to talk to the press about anything and he thinks you represent the press."

"Well, I don't and I'm getting tired of being accused of being a reporter. Maybe I should stop reading the news and just play records."

Maggie shrugged her shoulders. "Carlin, I'm tired right now. Can you come back after dinner? I need a nap." She also wanted more time to think about his motives after he disclosed Marty's name. Maybe he is an investigative journalist despite his denials.

"One last question," said Carlin. "Do you know the status of Martin and the three illegal aliens?"

"No, and if I did, I wouldn't tell you," the response loud, the anger undeniable. "You know, sometimes you do act like a reporter." Maggie pulled her knees up, grabbed the covers tight to her chest, and put her head down.

Ignoring her outburst, Carlin eased up from the chair. He took a step toward Maggie. He continued talking as he reached out to gently touch her arm. She pulled her arm away but Carlin kept his hand on her. "As of this afternoon there has been little change in Martin, I believe that he's still unconscious. The Guatemalan man

31

died last night. It's probable that he was the father of the seven-year-old girl who was only slightly injured. Her mother was DOA."

Looking back up at Carlin, Maggie placed her hand over his. "I'm sorry. I thought you were still fishing for information. I'm sorry." A tear trickled from each eye. Carlin put his other hand on top of hers.

"Let go, Maggie. I know you're hurting behind all that gaiety and bravado."

She withdrew her hand and looked around for a tissue. Carlin handed her the box from the mobile patient caddy.

"Thanks." She took one and wiped the tears away.

Both were quiet for a minute.

"I'll be alright. Is what you're telling me public knowledge?"

"No, and neither is this, Maggie. The FBI is fairly certain that you were attacked by the Mexican military using some heavy caliber firepower."

Maggie's eyes widened and her mouth opened slightly. It was evident that she was surprised by how much he knew. "The FBI agent wouldn't even confirm that to me. How'd you find out? Who's your source?"

"Now who sounds like a reporter?"

Maggie giggled. The mild outburst had produced a runny nose and involuntary tears. She wiped again and blew her nose softly.

Carlin turned for the door. "Get *undercover* again. I'll see you after dinner."

* * * * *

The FBI agent who had chased Carlin from Maggie's room was leaning against the passenger side of Carlin's Toyota Prius as he approached. Carlin noticed him as he hit the automatic door opener from across the lot.

Agent Norcross was bitter about the assignment to baby sit a border patrol agent who merely got involved in an incident with the Mexicans. He though his next assignment was going to be the intelligence supervisor's job in Hawaii. Norcross was bitter. *Heaven help the SOB who crosses me during this shit detail.* The only comforting aspect of the this assignment would be that he'd be able

32

to spend some time with an old pal, Sam Arnold, who left the FBI to become sheriff of Pima County – the desert that surrounded Tucson.

"Mind if we talk for a minute?" said agent Norcross. Without waiting for an answer, Norcross opened the passenger door and got in the car.

Carlin quickened his pace, reached his car, opened the driver's door and slid behind the wheel. "What do you want?"

The agent leaned close while placing Carlin's newspaper under his arm. "I understand you're a reporter, looking for information."

"That's not true!"

"Agent Lopez cannot disclose information regarding an ongoing investigation. So, I suggest you wait for news at the B. P. Office of Public Information, down on Ajo Way.

"Is the FBI threatening all of Maggie's visitors or just me?" Carlin turned toward the agent and lifted his chin.

"We're not threatening anyone; just reminding visitors who ask her too many questions." The agent's voice oozed with sarcasm. "But it has come to my attention that you already posses some classified information and it better remain unpublicized, or you *will* find yourself in a threatening situation. *Comprende, mi amigo?*"

The agent's high school Spanish pronunciation was atrocious, but Carlin understood. He understood that the agent had probably placed a bug in Maggie's room. He looked around the parking lot for the FBI communications van. He didn't see one. He'd have to be more careful; and so would Maggie, if she decided to take him up on his offer of help.

The agent opened the door and got out. His exaggerated smile was a stern warning. Carlin got the message. Carlin backed out of his parking spot and slowly drove off. Agent Norcross removed his cell phone and hit the speed dial. The County sheriff answered immediately. "Sam, target's on the road, pulling out of Tucson General onto LaCholla."

Carlin eased out of the lot and headed toward home. Four blocks from the hospital, a county sheriff's car moved behind him and hit the flashers and siren. Carlin pulled over. Traffic slowed as drivers peered in his direction. Carlin looked through his rear view mirror where he could see the officer looking down, checking his computer screen. After what felt like an eternity to Carlin, the officer got out of his car, put on his headgear and walked over to stand just behind Carlin's rolled down window. Outside of his view, the officer unhooked the holster strap, flicked the safety off his weapon and placed his hand firmly on the grip.

"License, registration, and insurance card."

Carlin reached into the glove box where he always kept his registration and insurance card. The folder wasn't there. He pulled his wallet from his coat pocket, located his license, and handed it to the officer, buying time to find his other documentation. A second search of the glove box proved fruitless.

"Officer, my folder with the registration and insurance card seems to be missing." Carlin scratched his head. He continued to rifle though the glove box spilling most of its contents on the floor.

"Get out of the car."

"What?"

"Out of the car now. Hands on the roof and spread the legs. I won't ask nice again."

Carlin obeyed the order as a second cruiser pulled up behind them. More flashing lights. More stretched necks as traffic crawled by.

The officer ran his hands up and down Carlin's body. It was the first time Carlin had ever been frisked and he didn't like it. The officer made him put his hands behind his back and then cuffed him. He pulled Carlin by the cuffs and guided him to the rear door of his cruiser. Mortified that he might be recognized, Carlin turned his face away from the traffic and put his head down. The officer placed one hand on top of Carlin's head and guided him into the back seat of the vehicle.

Carlin spoke urgently. "Sir, please check the computer. Motor Vehicles will have my name matched with my plate number."

"You don't have a plate, that's why I stopped you."

"You've got to be kidding. Officer, I have the title at home – may I call my wife on my cell?"

"You'll get one call at the station. If you're gonna blab, I'll have to read you your Miranda Rights. If you keep quiet, we can skip the formalities," the officer said. "Look, this car has been reported stolen, there's no tag, and you can't find the registration. I gotta do what the book says. If you cooperate and the car ain't hot, you'll be home for dinner. If you're gonna be difficult, plan on spending the night in the tank with some foul smelling, puking drunks."

Carlin already smelled something rotten – an FBI asshole.

Chapter 6

Carlin Ward's first time in a holding cell was, as the officer had promised, a short stay. Having no ambition to become a long-term resident, he had decided that the quickest way out was to cooperate. One call to his wife, who brought the title for the Prius, followed by a brief appearance in front of a magistrate, and Carlin was a free man.

Dora wanted all the details: Where was his registration? What happened to his license plate? How could he get into such a fix? Carlin was in no mood to explain. Even though his release was comparatively quick, it was already well after 9:30 pm. By the time he retrieved his car from the county pound at a cost of $175 it was too late to return to the hospital for his appointment with Maggie. It was even too late to call.

* * * * *

Maggie was surprised, disappointed and a little angry when Carlin didn't show after dinner. *He should have called. Why didn't he call?* Maggie decided on a stroll around the hospital. She abandoned the wheelchair and walked with a slight limp, favoring her burned right leg. A nurse had substituted two smaller Band-Aids for the large ones that had covered her face the night before. Maggie had also washed and combed her hair for the first time since entering the hospital. These small improvements changed her mood decidedly for the better.

The walk wasn't just for exercise; she was looking for Marty, the Guatemalan child, and information. By now Maggie and nurse Lola Diaz had become quite friendly so she stopped by the nurses' station hoping for information. Nurse Diaz looked up with a smile. Maggie asked, "What floor is Marty Fallon on?"

"Let me see if I can find out for you, honey."

Maggie looked around as nurse Diaz pulled up her patients list on her computer. A two-minute search revealed nothing. "Sorry, he's not here now."

"Okay," said Maggie. She started to walk away, but returned. "Can you tell me the name of a Guatemalan child who arrived the day before me?"

Nurse Diaz smiled apologetically, "I'd like to help you but it's against the rules to provide that kind of information. You understand."

"Yes – yes, of course." Disappointed, Maggie stepped away from the station.

"Then again, I don't see any harm in telling you that I have seen a very small female patient around the corner in 515." Nurse Diaz pointed to the right.

Maggie's wide smile showed her appreciation, "Thanks, you're an absolute angel." She headed in the direction indicated by the nurse's outstretched arm. She found room 515, tiptoed to the doorway and looked around. Both beds appeared empty. Maggie stepped into the room and spoke softly. "Is anybody home?" A small, dark-haired child's head appeared from behind a huge stuffed tiger. Tears ran down her puffy cheeks and she sobbed quietly. Her breathing was ragged. The small, tragic face looked at Maggie uncomprehendingly. Maggie remembered she was Guatemalan and repeated her question in Spanish. *"Esta tu en la casa?"*

"Si, tengo aqui." Yes, I am here, answered a very small, shaky voice.

Continuing in Spanish, Maggie asked, "May I come in?"

"Yes." The child controlled her sobbing and stared up at Maggie. "Do you know my mommy and daddy? They got hurt. Do you know where they are?"

Maggie knew, but clearly this lonely mite hadn't been told the horrible news as yet. She hedged. "No, I don't know them, but perhaps I can help you find out where they are." Maggie walked over, sat on the edge of the bed and changed the subject. "Is this your tiger?"

"Yes, and she has a baby, look."

Maggie petted the tiger and saw the baby tucked between its legs. "Oh my, how cute. What's your name?"

"Margarita, Margarita Domingo."

"Margarita! Wow, that's my name too. Friends call me Maggie."

"Will you be my friend, Maggie? I don't have friends anymore."

"You don't? Sure. I'll be your friend, forever and ever."

"Is forever a long time?"

"Pretty long."

"Okay, I want to be your friend forever too." The child looked past Maggie toward the door and blurted out, "Did you find my mommy and daddy?"

Maggie turned to see a gringo doctor approach the child's bed. It was obvious that he knew enough Spanish to understand. He responded in broken Spanish, "No, I don't know where they are right now."

He turned his attention to Maggie. "Who are you? Where's the agent watching her?"

Walking into the room at that moment, INS Agent Jessica Morales looked surprised to see anybody but the child in the room. She turned to the doctor beside the bed. "Doctor Whittlesey, what's going on in here? Who's she?"

Maggie answered. "I'm a patient."

Morales cast an unfriendly look at Maggie and said flatly,

"Well you'll just have to leave. This room is off limits to everyone but me and her medical staff."

Maggie turned toward the child and reached for the little hand that she extended. *"Hasta luego, mi bella nina."* She leaned over and lovingly kissed the child on the top of her head. She left with a smile and a nod toward the grim-faced Doctor and the INS agent.

"Bye, Maggie. I love you. Come back later." said Margarita.
"I love you, too. I'll be back. Promise."
"Promise, promise?"
"Promise!"

Maggie had achieved her goal; she now knew where the child was and her name. *Imagine, Margarita, just like me; Margarita Domingo.* Maggie walked back to her room feeling elated and yet deeply depressed. Who was going to tell little Miss Domingo about her parents death and when? What was going to happen to her?

* * * * *

Carlin followed Dora into their driveway. Dora guided her Ford Explorer into the garage; Carlin parked out front and took his time going to the front door where his wife already stood with the door open.

"Now – can I get a full, detailed explanation? Dora demanded.

"Let me put on some coffee – full, detailed will take some time."

Dora waited patiently while Carlin made a pot of decaf. He poured a cup for both of them and then he joined her outside on the back patio. Carlin lowered himself onto the thick-cushioned chair beside his wife and leaned back against the soft headrest. He smelled his coffee, took a sip, swallowed the steaming liquid and looked straight into his wife's eyes; dagger eyes that had watched his every movement since he had entered the house.

He told Dora everything from the time he left the KBAR studio last evening, right until she had picked him up from jail three hours ago. He left out nothing, including his feelings that he, personally needed to do something – anything – that might help resolve the chaos on the border. "I don't know what's needed," he concluded forcefully, "but I'm prepared to camp out in Washington if necessary, and beg, or batter some politicians into action."

Dora got up from her seat, leaned over and gave Carlin a peck on the cheek, "I understand now, Carlin. Do what you feel you must; and if I can help, just ask." She smiled down on him, slid the screen-door aside and headed into the house. "I'm going to bed now – you coming?"

"In a little bit."

She paused in the doorway. "Now, don't stay up all night planning how to get back at that FBI agent."

"How'd you know what I was thinking?"

"Carlin, it's been twenty years. I know how devious you can be." Dora walked into the house and closed the sliding door.

Carlin sat on the patio reliving the last twenty-four hours over and over again. When he had figured his next move an hour later, he decided it was time for bed, and turned in. His last thought as he drifted off was – what part of Alaska would FBI agent Norcross dislike the most?

The answer came to him when he awoke next morning – Barrow Bay, the northernmost outpost.

* * * * *

Ted Lane, deputy director, CIA, called Jim Crowley, head of Southeast Asia Counterintelligence as soon as he left a White House briefing. He asked Crowley to meet him at Washington's West Potomac Park. Lane had learned just before the briefing that they had lost a significant "plant" inside *Abu Sayyaf*. The amount of HUMINT, human intelligence, from the Philippines would now be seriously diminished. This was a gut-wrenching loss and Lane needed to know if the problem could be fixed.

Crowley got up from his seat on the park bench as Lane entered the path, and casually walked beside his superior.

Lane spoke. "Jim, have any word from Saint Joseph?"

"Saint Joseph" was Manny Falstino's code-name, assigned because he was born in San José , a town 150 miles north of Manila.

"No, it's been two weeks. They got him," Crowley answered.

"They got him, meaning he's dead?"

"We believe he's dead and they had to know his contact to get to him. We've removed both of our guys in Manila."

"Shit, that'll leave us dumb and blind in Mindanao. We'll have to look for a new back door." Lane stopped walking and lowered his head for an instant. Crowley waited a step ahead.

Lane resumed his walk, "See if Kuala Lumpur can help. I don't want to lose sight of those Arab bastards learning Spanish."

Crowley fell in beside his boss. "Ted, you know it'll be – freaking – impossible to replace the likes of Saint Joe, but I'll see what I can do to pick up their trail."

Ted placed his hand on Jim's shoulder. "This is important, Jim. Pull a rabbit out of a hat, if you have to, but get it done – real sorry about Saint Joe."

They turned and walked back toward the city. Their mood was as gray as the January sky.

Chapter 7

The noon sun beat down on Roger Lacson. He was dressed smartly in his beige tropical slacks, pale yellow shirt, and navy blue sport coat.

Roger was in Kuala Lumpur for the vacation of a lifetime. In his twenty-seven years on planet earth he had never ventured so far or to such an exotic destination. Born and raised in Canton, Ohio, Roger had never left the lower forty-eight except for a vacation in Hawaii with his parents when he was ten. His Filipino parents were married in Honolulu.

He had moved to Tucson, Arizona five years ago and forged his love of sports with his ability to write into the perfect job – sports reporter for the *Tucson Star* in beautiful, sunny, southern Arizona. But when the slot opened up on the city desk that paid better and would advance his career, he had jumped on it.

He now had two weeks off before the news desk assignments, and he had decided to take this crazy trip. His tennis buddy, Steve, had booked the trip but had to back out when his grandfather died. Roger grabbed the trip for half price. He also thought that the break would be a good diversion for him. If he stayed home, he'd just be moping over the loss of his beloved sports job. He just knew that he was going to hate covering local news.

Roger was a bachelor and planned to stay unattached indefinitely. He loved the freedom it provided. Having watched the married world around him including his mom and dad, who after forty-seven years of marriage still held hands, concluded that coupled-life still came with restrictive clauses. That is, most everything had to be done together, or else you had to have a spectacularly good reason for doing something alone – like going to Kuala Lumpur on the spur of the moment. This was just the kind of place his hero, James Bond, would visit for a quick dinner and an even quicker seduction. Maybe he'd get lucky here as well, Roger mused.

Roger had a few significant girlfriends in his past but he never wanted to progress past the dating and occasionally "staying over" stage. He had bailed-out on Susan when she suggested that they live together. He knew where that trail led – marriage – heaven forbid. Roger figured he was doing her a favor, knowing she wouldn't be happy very long living with a nut who always had his nose stuck in *Sports Illustrated* or was at a road game somewhere across the country.

Roger walked along Jatan Pudu, a busy street in Kuala Lumpur's Chinatown section. The aroma from the street vendors' cooking intoxicated him. He smelled squid and chicken frying in deep pans of oil. Chinese men, women and children scurried everywhere. It was hard to tell shoppers from shopkeepers. He peered into the stalls where vegetables, spices, clothing and trinkets rested, ready for inspection. Plastic, wood and cardboard bins lined the sidewalks. Children weaved in and out of the stalls at a dizzying pace. Roger viewed the organized chaos in amazement.

His mind drifted back to Tucson. Only God knew how much he'd miss reporting on Arizona basketball. Now he'd have to pay his way into McKale Sports Center. With his pay increase, he'd be able to afford a season ticket, but he knew the seat wouldn't be down on the floor right beside the coach and assistant coaches.

Abruptly rejoining the present, Roger remembered that he was hungry. He looked for a decent restaurant close to The Merdeka Inn, his luxurious but inexpensive hotel. He had taken an overnight flight from Tokyo with a stopover in Singapore. He had watched the morning sunrise glisten off the calm waters of the Strait of Malacca.

He was euphoric but felt a hint of remorse that Susan wasn't sitting next to him to share the moment. By the time he had cleared Customs and got to his hotel it was well past noon. He was tired, famished and looking for a good American meal. There wasn't a fast food joint in sight. *Where are all the Burger Kings when you need one?*

The cab from the Sultan Aziz Shah Subang International Airport had first taken him to the Merdeka-*Garden Hotel*. When he tried to check in, the desk clerk couldn't find his reservation. Damn.

"Do you have a reservation for Stephen Thomas? The room was originally booked under my friend's name."

"No sir, I'm sorry there's no reservation for Mr. Thomas either," the clerk told him.

After a few tense moments, the hotel manager arrived. He was familiar with the confusion over the two similar hotel names. He had apologized and ordered a cab that would deposit Roger at the Merdeka *Inn*.

The driver, realizing that the short five-block ride wouldn't result in much of a fare, took a route that practically encircled the city.

"Those Towers are the tallest in the world, right, driver?" Roger imagined himself dangling from underneath the famous connecting bridge like Sean Connery did in the movie *Entrapment*.

The driver had pretended not to understand. He wanted to keep Roger's focus off the landmark Petronas Towers. The towers could be seen from just about everywhere in the city. He didn't want Roger to get oriented and eventually realize that he was driving in the opposite direction from his hotel.

They proceeded east and headed south over the Klang River. The cab traveled north for five miles before heading south again, re-crossing the river eventually back onto Jatan Pudu, a short walk from where they had started forty-five minutes earlier. If Roger had any suspicions about the curious route he didn't say anything, but paid the fare.

Dollah Jaffar had been stationed at a sidewalk cafe directly across the street from the Merdeka-Garden Hotel and had watched Roger arrive. Relaxing and sipping iced tea he was caught completely off guard when Roger left the hotel within minutes of his arrival, jumped into a cab, and sped off. Dollah hadn't expected his mark to be leaving the hotel so soon. He rushed to his motorbike and pursued Roger's cab, but by the time he traveled the four blocks to where he last saw the cab, he was too late. The cab was across the river and out of sight.

This was bad, very bad. Now Abderraouf would be very angry with him. Dollah sought to impress Abderraouf, the highest ranking and only Saudi al-Qaeda operative he'd ever talked with or actually met. Dollah hung around the Merdeka-Garden for another hour hoping that Roger might return. When he didn't appear Dollah headed back to the safe house.

Abderraouf Mohammad was waiting when Dollah hurried into the apartment. Hearing Dollah describe his miserable ineptitude was almost more than Abderraouf could bear. He was ready to kill. Dollah had no doubt that he could very well end up dead if he prevented Abderraouf from accomplishing his mission. *As Allah wills it,* was Dollah's only thought.

"How could you lose him, you idiot?" Abderraouf screamed. His face reddened as he cursed in a language Dollah didn't understand. He pounded his fist into his palm after each word, "Are … you … sure … it … was … agent … Estimo … camel … brain?"

"Yes, it was him."

Dollah related how his cousin had followed the agent as soon as he emerged from the gate of Flight Number 102 from Singapore. He had trailed the Filipino man wearing the blue blazer all the way to the taxi station, and then called with the taxi plate number while Dollah waited at the Merdeka-Garden Hotel. "The fare was an American Filipino on Singapore Flight 102. He went right to the Merdeka-Garden Hotel. Everything matched, just like you told me," he assured Abderraouf.

In addition to supplying the agent's itinerary and attire, Abderraouf's Syrian intelligence sources in Tokyo were to have faxed a picture of agent Estimo; unfortunately, it never arrived.

Abderraouf had been told that agent Estimo would only be in Kuala Lumpur for a few hours covering his tracks before leaving for Manila. He could be on his way back to the airport already. His instructions were to see that agent Estimo did not leave Kaula Lumpur alive.

"You go back to the Merdeka-Garden," he said, turning to Dollah. "If Estimo comes back, kill him!"

During the few moments when Dollah had chased Roger's cab on his bike, he failed to see an Airport Coach sedan that pulled up to the curb a block away from the Merdeka-Garden Hotel. From it, another American of Filipino heritage stepped on to the street, a dark blue blazer slung over his shoulder. CIA agent Rogelio Estimo had also deplaned from the first flight from Singapore, and unobtrusively headed for the front desk of the Merkeda-Garden Hotel.

As agent Estimo waited to register, the front desk clerk was placing a call to Roger Lacson's hotel. "Mr. Lacson has forgotten his American Express card. Please tell him that he should return to the Merdeka-Garden Hotel as soon as possible to retrieve it." He replaced the receiver and turned his attention to Estimo.

*****

Not finding an American burger joint, Roger had settled for Rosario's, a moderately priced Italian eatery close by, where a meatball sandwich satisfied his hunger for beef.

When Roger returned to his hotel the desk clerk handed him the phone message from the Merdeka-Garden Hotel. Roger checked his wallet – sure enough his American Express card was missing.

"Would you please call me a cab?" Roger said looking at the note.

"Where would you like to go?" asked the clerk.

"Back to the Merdeka-Garden Hotel."

"It is a short walk from here – see here, on this map." The clerk handed Roger a city map and pointed to the two hotel locations." Roger grimaced. He realized that the cab driver earlier had taken him for a ride physically and financially.

"Thanks," said Roger and walked out of the lobby.

Dollah could not believe his good fortune when he saw Roger Lacson strolling casually once again in front of the Merdeka-Garden Hotel's beautiful rosebush lined walkway. Allah had answered his prayers. He saw Roger enter the hotel and go up to the front desk. He observed the clerk hand Roger an envelope and watched as Roger put it in his coat pocket then walked to the back of the lobby and disappeared into the men's room.

46

Watching from the front door of the hotel, Dollah knew that this was his opportunity. He paused for a moment while a woman with two small children got into the elevator. An elderly man was sitting in a chair reading a newspaper. The clerk was in the small room behind the counter. No one would notice him entering the hotel. It was providence.

With his head down and turned away from the front desk, Dollah nonchalantly crossed the lobby. As he reached the men's room door he unsheathed the Indonesian *kirsa* hidden in his belt. He pushed through the door and saw Roger facing the urinal. No one else was around. It was almost too easy. He was already imagining Abderraouf''s beaming smile as he praised Allah and Dollah in the same sentence. Dollah raised the knife over the unsuspecting man at the urinal. One quick downward thrust and an infidel spy would be dead.

Chapter 8

Dollah's arm reached its apex but refused to obey his command to continue the downward thrust that would kill the man standing at the urinal. A powerful hand had a vice-grip on his wrist. Then an arm reached from behind him and wrapped itself under his chin, cutting off his air. Dollah's feet left the floor. He kicked out furiously, thrashing in the air and crashing against the stall door to his rear. As hard as he tried, he couldn't free himself. With the air in his lungs completely exhausted, he slid into unconsciousness. Just as he passed out, he wondered if Allah would still greet him in Paradise after this greatest of failures.

Startled by the uproar behind him, Roger Lacson pulled up his zipper and turned quickly to see what had happened. His terrified gaze fell on a man leaning over the stall behind him with a stranglehold on another who was kicking spasmodically as the life appeared to drain from his eye-bulging, reddened face. A thin wavy blade fell to the floor as the pinned man reached up with both hands in an attempt to work free. Abruptly, the man went limp. As his dead weight dropped to the floor he buckled at the knees and fell forward. His head bounced once on the tile floor and came to rest on Roger's left foot.

The other man came out of the stall, lifted the knife off the floor with a handkerchief and dropped it into the trashcan.

Roger Lacson exhaled for the first time since he had turned around.

"Help me put him on the hopper," ordered the man, who, Roger noticed for the first time, could have passed for his twin. Roger did what he was told without hesitation.

The man took a hypodermic needle from a case inside his coat pocket, leaned over and administered an injection to Dollah's left leg.

"Will that shot finish him off?" Roger heard himself ask, in a disconnected high-pitched voice. The man ignored him.

Completing the injection, the man stood up, replaced the needle in its case, and turned toward Roger. "Walk in front of me straight out the back door by the pool. Walk quickly, but don't run. Don't make eye contact with anyone. Don't say anything. You won't be harmed and I'll explain once we're outside." The stranger issued these orders far too calmly for Roger's psyche.

Roger followed his instructions explicitly. Once outside, the stranger led him past the pool and out the hotel's wrought-iron back gate. They turned left and walked along the flowered-bordered sidewalk away from the Merdeka-Garden Hotel. Roger silently wished that he never see it again. Once outside the shadow of the hotel, the stranger spoke.

"Your name is Roger Lacson; you're a sports reporter for the *Tucson Star*. You're here on vacation. You flew in from Tokyo this morning on Singapore Flight 102, and a cab brought you to this hotel by mistake. You're booked at the Merdeka Inn around the corner," said his look-alike.

Roger regained some of his composure. In his best sarcastic tone, he said, "Now tell me something I don't know, or I'll yell for help right now."

The man stopped in his tracks, turned and stood nose-to-nose with Roger. "You'd be dead already if I hadn't been in that washroom and if I wanted to kill you, it would have happened already, so don't threaten me."

Roger quickly lost the attitude. He started walking again and waited for more explanation.

"You do know the man behind you in the men's room intended to kill you? The good news is that he thought you were me. The bad news is that he isn't dead and will probably awaken before the cleaning crew discovers him. He'll wake with a severe headache

… and he'll be looking for you, pal. My name is Rogelio Estimo and yes, I am CIA," said Roger's new best friend.

"I figured as much. Can you prove it?"

Estimo flashed a disgusted look. "We need to split up. Walk to your hotel, change, and take a cab to the Kaula Lumpur Visitors' Center. Look for a uniformed driver standing next to a white Mercedes. When you approach him, say, 'Home, James,' and get in."

"Home, James? You're kidding!"

"Shut up and listen. I'll only give these instructions once, and your life depends on getting them right. The driver will take you to the KL Plaza and leave you off on Jalan Tun Razak, that's T-U-N-R-A-Z-A-K. From there it's a three block walk to the U.S. Embassy. Walk directly there, do not stop for anything. Show the guard your passport; request the officer of the day. When she arrives, ask for Ulysses Samuel. Got it?"

"Yes."

"Hope so," said agent Estimo as he turned back towards the Merdeka-Garden Hotel and disappeared down a side street. Roger discovered that he was trembling. He made a conscious effort to control his breathing and nerves. After a few minutes, a feeling of undeniable excitement began to replace his fear. "Sean Connery, eat your heart out – this is for real," Roger said to himself.

* * * * *

The sun felt cooler on his back as it lowered toward the horizon. Roger checked his watch. It was almost six when he approached the Marine private at the gate of the U.S. Embassy and asked for the officer of the day. When Army First Lieutenant Sparks arrived, Roger asked for Ulysses Samuel as instructed. The female officer appeared to be expecting him and led him through the gate into the lobby of the four-story structure. The Lieutenant waited on the other side of the screening device, which looked just like the one at the airport. Roger passed through the without setting off an alarm. She then escorted him to a small conference room on the second floor. She called it a conference room but Roger could tell an interrogation room when he saw one.

50

The room was no bigger than ten by twelve feet. A metal table bolted to the floor took up most of the space. Two four-inch diameter iron rings hung just under the tabletop overhang on each of the long sides. Roger imagined how it might feel to be manacled to a ring. He raised one up with his right hand. It squeaked as he lifted it up fully and clanked loudly against the table when he let it fall. A chair was placed at each end, while a third was positioned to face what was obviously one-way glass, built into the wall. Roger picked up the chair facing the glass; moved it to the other side of the table and sat. At least the observers would only see the back of his head.

A few minutes later agent Estimo burst into the room and offered his hand. "Welcome to the United States of America. How you feel?"

Roger shook his hand, shrugged, and gave him a perplexed look. The door opened again and another man entered. He pulled his chair close to Roger and sat. He did not offer his hand.

"Roger, this is agent Dillon Connelly. You and he should be seeing a great deal of each other over the next week," said Estimo.

"How so?" asked Roger.

"Let's back up for a minute. First off, I need your solemn word that everything you hear, see or become aware of through our contact must remain secret as a matter of national security. Do I have it?"

Roger hesitated. "Can I decide after I hear what you have to say? To give you an update, when I return to Tucson, I'll be covering news, not sports and this has all the earmarks of a front page story. Of course, as a reporter, I'm obligated to protect my sources, just like Woodward and Bernstein."

Agent Connelly tightened his jaw and his neck veins bulged. "Should I just kill him now or wait until he leaves the embassy?"

There was a silence, as all three eyed one another, after Connelly's absurd question. The CIA did not have a license to kill; especially other Americans, especially in the U.S. embassy, thought Roger.

Agent Estimo evidently guessed that their threat had little effect on Roger. He broke the silence. "All joking aside, do I have your word?"

Roger nodded in the affirmative. Agent Connelly just grinned.

"Now, we would like you, for the next few days, to continue to be me, so I can slip out of Kuala Lumpur unnoticed," said Estimo.

Roger leapt up kicking back his chair. "You're kidding, right?" He was shouting.

"No, we're not," answered Estimo.

"Here I figured that you were going to fly me back to America on a cool military jet, pay me for my troubles, and ask me to forget everything."

"Well, you figured wrong," said Connelly. "Now, sit back down."

Roger sat. His dislike for Connelly spiked.

"How much is this favor worth?" asked Roger.

Connelly's reply startled him. "How much is your life is worth?"

"What the in the world do you mean?"

"Well, if you don't help us – and we don't fly you home on a cool, military jet – how long do you think you'll remain alive here?" asked Connelly bluntly.

Roger was on his feet again. "This can't be happening. You can't blackmail an American citizen. You've got to protect me!"

Estimo interrupted. "Please, please. Sit and remain seated, I'm getting whiplash."

Roger sat.

"Now, you're partly right. We have a moral obligation to help you, but legally we don't. You were a target of a terrorist organization on foreign soil. Outside of this embassy we have no responsibility for you. Frankly, it would have been better for the CIA if they had killed you, thinking they got me. However, should you decide not to help us, we will get you back to America safely.

If intimidation wasn't going to work, then agent Estimo had to play his trump card, patriotism. "But you'd be doing the Agency, and the U. S. of A., a monumental favor if you help out and you'll be protected every minute you're here."

"How long do I have to decide?"

"Before you get up from that chair again." Connelly leaned menacingly toward Roger as he spoke.

Roger was faced with responding to the only potentially life-threatening question that he had ever been asked. And he had to decide immediately.

Unfair.

He heard that high-pitched, disembodied voice again. This time it said, "Okay, what exactly do you want me to do?"

Connelly reached over and slapped Roger on the back; harder than necessary, Roger thought.

"Now that I'm on the team, can you please tell me why I – that is, you, were targeted for assassination?"

"Now you may stand," said Estimo, ignoring Roger's question. "Agent Connelly – swear in acting agent Lacson." Connelly stood.

"Roger Lacson, do you solemnly swear to uphold the Constitution of the United States of America, and affirm that all you hear and see regarding your temporary status with the CIA will forever remain secret, so help you God?"

Standing for the third time, Roger raised his right hand and responded, "I do."

The agents knew that the oath was not legally binding, but it would make Roger feel included, and they hoped that it just might make him think twice before ever disclosing details of his "tenure" in the secret service.

"Now, by the numbers, who, what, where, when and how?" said Roger.

"Remember – Roger Lacson the reporter is not in this room," Estimo stated with emphasis.

"I know, I know."

Agent Estimo began with a sanitized explanation. "We're shadowing a group of bad guys thought to be somewhere in Mindanao. I've been assigned to find where they are now. The bad guys here must have monitored my leaving Tokyo yesterday on the same plane you took. It was a coincidence that we look so much alike and that we were both wearing blue blazers. At the Merdeka-Garden Hotel, I overheard the desk clerk call you to come back for your credit card. After changing my clothes, I went to the lobby men's room. It was quite by chance that they moved on you while we were both in the latrine."

"Then, you didn't kill the bad guy, hoping that I'd play along, right?"

"Right."

"Who's the assassin?"

"His name is Dollah Jaffar, a local, but we know he's got an al-Qaeda boss pulling the strings," Connelly said.

"An *al* what?" asked Roger.

Standing abruptly, Estimo moved toward the door. "Connelly will explain the rest, gotta go."

Roger frowned involuntarily when he heard he'd have to rely on Connelly for his safe keeping. Connelly caught the look, as did the camera hidden within the sprinkler nozzle above them, streaming, in real time, the encoded digital video back to an office in Langley, Virginia. Jim Crowley, Southeast Asia Counter Intelligence watched the proceedings with keen interest.

No one was behind the one-way glass.

Chapter 9

One major advantage of "signing on" with the CIA was the luxurious, free accommodations within the United States Embassy. The food wasn't bad either, mused Roger Lacson. The downside was that he wasn't, as yet, permitted outside of his self-imposed jail. It had been two days since he had agreed to help agent Estimo and no one had told him anything yet. The good news/bad news was that he hadn't seen agent Connelly either. But after having read every magazine available and watched the handful of videos in the Embassy library, he was bored. Totally bored.

Roger was thinking about asking for his freedom tomorrow. Might as well go home and get back to the old life as sit here. He had just turned in for the night when the phone rang. It was agent Connelly. "How's things in solitary confinement?"

Naturally, Connelly would try to make Roger feel worse than he did already.

"Just great. If I have to watch Bill Murray in 'Ground Hog's Day' one more time, I just might go out looking for, what's his name, Dollar myself."

"Dollah, his name is Dollah."

"Right, Dollah."

"Well, I don't want you to go stir crazy, so I've got a little excursion planned for us this evening. Up for it?"

Roger hesitated. "Tonight? It's ten o'clock. I'm ready for bed."

"Yeah, tonight, that's an order not a request."

"How soon? Where are we going?"

"I'll be up in a half hour to go over the details or should I send for Lieutenant Sparks to keep you company 'till then?"

"Why would I want Sparks to keep me company?" Roger tried to picture the business-like female Army officer who had escorted him to the conference room upon his arrival.

"Now hold on, before you say yes, let me tell you. She's married to a guy with a black belt in karate, who just happens to be the current Marine Corps South Pacific middleweight boxing champ. And, he just finished ..."

Roger cut him off. "Real funny. You're a regular Jay Leno. See you in thirty."

"Get dressed in that outfit you wore on the flight here." The phone clicked off without a goodbye.

Roger had thought that Connelly's attitude toward him would have softened a little after he had agreed to help, evidently he had figured wrong.

Exactly thirty minutes later, there was a knock at Roger's door. Anxious to get out at last, he hurried over and opened it. His knees almost caved. Lieutenant Sparks stood there, dressed in a see-through, white silk blouse that left little to the imagination. Her long black skirt was slit to her thighs and taut.

Her short platinum-blond hair formed a dazzling halo around the delicate features of her face. She wore an almost white eye shadow above and a near purple below her sparking blue eyes. Her pale, rose-colored lipstick glittered golden flecks. Roger inhaled her. He didn't recognize the perfume, but he'd never forget its bouquet. Roger was afraid to look directly into her eyes. He feared that if he did, his knees might not hold. She smiled shamelessly as she turned a slow three hundred-sixty and asked, "Do you like it?"

"It?" Roger's gaze dropped from her to the floor and he felt himself blushing.

"Yes, it. The outfit. My 'take me out to the disco attire.'"

"Yes, of course, it's – it's very pretty. But who's going to a disco? Where's agent Connelly? Why are you out of uniform?"

"There's been a change in plans. Grab your jacket and let's go."

Roger was more nervous now than when Dollah had dropped his knife and done a header at his feet.

"I don't think so! What's going on here? What if your husband discovers you going to a disco and…and you dressed like that?" Rogers's voice went alto as it cracked on the last word.

"I thought you liked my outfit?" Sparks leaned back, lowered her chin and puckered her lips in an exaggerated pout.

Roger stood motionless with his hands on his hips, like the father of an erring daughter who'd been out past curfew. He waited stern-faced and silent.

"I'm dressed like all the women you'll see tonight … and what husband? I'm not married nor in the Army. I'm CIA. Connelly told me to get you and meet him at The Glitzy Disc on top of the Petronas Towers. Now, let's go." Her tone went from seductive sweet to "drill sergeant" in an instant.

She didn't tell him they were stopping for dinner first.

Roger attempted to regain his composure. Thinking back to his first encounter with Sparks, he was amazed at how efficiently a military uniform could obscure such a magnificent figure.

"Okay, I'm ready already." Roger stepped around a footstool, picked his jacket off the sofa, and then followed Sparks out the door. She pulled a decorative silk shawl around her, which covered her top, adding a necessary touch of modesty to her appearance.

An elevator took them to the basement garage where the white Mercedes with driver awaited them. Roger opened the rear car door. "After you Lieutenant Sparks."

She bent over to enter the car, stopped, rose up to her full height and looked down at Roger. "I told you, I'm not in the Army. My first name's Nicole; call me Nicki. Got that?"

Roger flinched at her command. "Yes sir, Nicki it is." Roger held the door and glanced down as Nicki slid onto the back seat, revealing almost all of her right thigh.

She caught him staring. Roger quickly looked away, put his hand to his mouth and faked a cough. He closed the door, walked around to the other side and climbed in beside her. He was too late to see her lips tighten to suppress a smile.

Nicki was enjoying the tease, but it was time to get serious; this was a dangerous assignment. She clutched her small black leather purse tightly, reassured by the solid feel of the short-barreled Walther TPH 6.35mm, a scaled-down version of its famous cousin the PPK, which nestled inside.

The driver sped up the ramp to street level. They stopped at the rear gate where a guard motioned to the driver to lower the heavily-tinted windows. The guard looked inside. He recognized the driver and agent Sparks and eyed Roger carefully. Satisfied, he nodded and the gate swung outward. The driver raised the windows and accelerated. He drove to the Kuala Lumpur Visitors' Center where Roger and Nicki switched to an awaiting cab.

Roger shook his head and asked, "What's this all about?"

"Don't ask too many questions; enjoy the night."

Roger wondered just how much more enjoyable this night was going to be. Here he was, with a gorgeous woman, going out on the town in a decidedly romantic Oriental paradise. Was it time for the hero to get the woman, he wondered? The only negative, he concluded, was that at some point he was going to end up around, near or with agent Connelly.

Damn.

The cab driver came to a stop at the Merdeka-Garden Hotel. Nicki opened the car door and started out. Roger pulled on her arm. "Wait, wait – what are we doing here?"

"We're having dinner at the Lotus Blossom restaurant. It's only eleven o'clock, too early for the disco." Again she stepped toward the curb.

Roger remained in his seat, "I can't go in there. I had dinner already. Please, anywhere but here," he begged. The fearful look was genuine.

Nicki leaned back into the cab, "Roger, get a grip." She reached over and grabbed his arm firmly and pulled him out of the car. She lowered her voice so only Roger could hear, "We need to be seen here. This is a public place. We'll be safe. Besides, Connelly can't be very far. Now come on."

Reluctantly, Roger escorted Nicki up the steps and into the hotel he had sworn never to see again, let alone enter. The Lotus Blossom restaurant was located off to the right rear of the lobby. The hostess apparently expected them and they were seated immediately. Their table was centered behind a huge plate glass window, overlooking a delightful flower garden. Outside, soft pink-colored lights created a surrealistic view. The hostess held the chair for Nicki. Roger took a deep breath and sat too. He would try to relax and enjoy the spectacular scenery, not to mention his glamorous companion.

An attentive waiter brought them glasses of iced water and warm bread, along with menus and a monstrous wine book that he handed to Roger.

"Do you care for a cocktail?" asked the waiter, looking first at Roger and then toward Nicki.

"No thanks, nothing for me. Roger?"

"Yes, I'd like a beer. Got Bud Light?"

The waiter grunted almost imperceptibly but Roger heard him.

"No, no, make that a martini."

"Gin or vodka – up or rocks – olive, twist, or onion, Sir?"

Roger looked up at the faintly smirking waiter. "No Bud, eh? Skip the cocktail, I'll chose a wine from this directory here." Roger began to page through the oversized tome.

"Very well, I'll be back for your order shortly." Before he left the waiter retrieved the linen napkin from Roger's pewter service plate, snapped it to the side with a flourish and placed it on his lap. Nicki's was already across her shapely legs.

Instead of returning to the kitchen the waiter walked outside. When he reached the pool he removed a cell phone from his jacket. He called an unlisted number and left a simple message on the answering machine. "Lotus Blossom, table for two, ready now."

Dollah heard the message as it was recording. He jumped up from the reclining chair, almost knocking over a coffee table. The table was covered with dirty dishes and teacups that had accumulated over the past two days as he kept his vigil by the phone. Dollah said a silent prayer, grabbed his brand-new stiletto off the kitchen counter, and sped out the door. This time he would succeed or else put an end to his own regrettable existence.

On the way to his motorbike, Dollah retrieved the cell phone Abderraouf had given him and punched-in the number.

Abderraouf answered on the first ring. "Yes, Dollah."

"I just received word that Estimo is in the Merdeka-Garden Hotel restaurant. I will not fail you this time."

Abderraouf answered coldly, "I hope not. Report back when it's done."

The phone went dead. Dollah pocketed it, mounted his bike and steered directly for the Lotus Garden.

Agent Connelly was standing behind a palm tree across from the Merdeka-Garden Hotel. He watched Dollah pull up to the curb on his bike just ten yards from where he stood.

Dollah walked around to the rear of the hotel and entered the pool area. Connelly crossed the street and entered the hotel. He passed the lobby and took a seat just inside the rear door. He grabbed a magazine and pretended to read. Connelly saw a waiter leave the restaurant, walk by him and stop near the pool. The waiter lit a cigarette. A man approached him. Connelly recognized Dollah. The two spoke briefly then the waiter put out his cigarette and went back into the restaurant. Dollah strolled over to the far side of the pool and sat on a chaise lounge. He was a solitary figure as the pool was officially closed for the evening.

Deciding that he was too exposed where he was, Connelly moved back to the lobby. He sat where he could view the rear hotel entrance and the hallway to the restaurant.

Wine, a light dinner and no dessert took over an hour. Roger became talkative after a few glasses of the Fagi Battagha–Verdicchio Classico recommended by the sommelier when he learned that both were ordering a fish entrée.

"I'm not sure I made the right move leaving the sports desk. I truly believe local news will be a big disappointment after covering Arizona in the '97 National Championship, an 84 to 79 win in OT over powerhouse Kentucky."

Nicki listened attentively and politely although she had no interest in sports or Roger's future life. She did little more than nod, smile and offer single word responses. Nicki reminded herself that she was working. Roger felt his heart beat faster and faster – was he falling in love? Nicki would soon forget about the short Filipino-American who crossed her path this night. Roger, however would dream about and talk about this date long after the memory of his near-murder faded into oblivion.

After dinner a much more relaxed Roger led Nicki to the curb where their cab awaited. He looked around to see if anyone was

60

noticing him with his attractive date. "Petronas Towers, driver." Roger delivered the command with slightly inebriated authority. "One or two? asked the driver.

Nicki considered for a moment. "Two," she answered. Roger hadn't noticed agent Connelly sitting in the lobby as they had left the hotel. Nicki had seen him but had made no sign of recognition.

Dollah, alerted when the couple called for their bill and prepared to leave, was already at the curb, on his bike and ready to follow. The waiter had repeated their conversation to him, and he knew that they were probably heading for the Glitzy Disc. He had already determined that it was just too crowded around the hotel to make a move. He would be patient. The right time and place would present itself.

Connelly's black Ford Taurus was illegally parked across the street. Moments later he emerged from the hotel and the three vehicles headed for the Petronas Towers in succession.

The cab arrived at the Tower Two main entrance as ordered. The Glitzy Disc was on the eighty-eighth floor of Tower One, but Nicki wanted to walk across the famous, flexible sky bridge. Except for the entrance guards Tower Two was deserted. The elevator bank was eerily silent. All the offices and shops were closed and the ride took only forty-five seconds to arrive at the 42nd floor. Nicki and Roger left the elevator arm in arm, but when Roger saw that Nicki intended for them to walk across the bridge 550 feet above ground, he stopped her. "The wine has made my stomach a little queasy. Can we do this another time?"

"Sure. I get that way myself sometimes." She smiled sympathetically.

They backtracked and waited for a down elevator. One arrived, and they stepped in just as an up elevator opened. Before their door closed completely Nicki saw Dollah walk in front of it. Nicki guessed that Dollah had seen them, and jerked back quickly placing her hand inside her purse.

Roger noticed the look on her face. "Anything wrong?"

"No, no. Just making sure I have my makeup." She fiddled with her bag and straightened her skirt for effect. Roger bought the act.

At street level, they walked quietly over to Tower One. Nicki looked back over her shoulder more than once. She kept her hand inside the purse out of Roger's view. At the entrance they joined a large crowd going up to the eighty-eighth floor.

The Glitzy Disc was the hottest nightspot in Kuala Lumpur. In order to bypass the long double line that encircled the entire penthouse floor and gain entrance to the VIP door you really needed to know someone. Only celebrities and genuine VIPs made it past the bouncer and tuxedoed gatekeeper. Another Nicole, this one a renowned actress from Australia, had been there last evening with her entourage and was expected to return this evening as well.

Nicki flashed her official ID at the charmer in the tux, and he motioned for the bouncer to remove the rope from a stanchion to let them enter. To Roger's boundless satisfaction fifty pairs of envious eyes watched as the short Oriental with the looker were whisked into the disco.

Dollah saw too, and groaned inwardly. He had just missed a golden opportunity by arriving belatedly on the forty-second floor of Tower Two. Now he'd have to wait for hours.

From the rear of the line, agent Connelly observed Dollah watching Roger and Nicki as they disappeared into the disco. There were too many people around for Dollah to act, he reasoned. He decided to return to the ground floor. He knew that Dollah would never get past the bouncer with any type of weapon and Nicki was already inside with her heat.

The disco, jam-packed elbow-to-rib, hip-to-thigh, and pelvis-to-ass seemed surreal to Roger. It was noisy, and discordantly dark except when a flashing strobe light hit an eyeball. Cigarette smoke blended seamlessly with marijuana and intruded all nostrils, smokers and would be non-smokers alike. The hazy cloud moved and swayed with the sweating throng in the enormous disco overflowing with beautiful women who outnumbered the men three to one. The women's clothing was worthy of a Victoria Secret runway show. Roger never had seen, such a collections of lovely creatures before and surmised that he may never have the opportunity to do so again.

He stood apart from the cool men who were attentive to their own dates and openly gawked at every woman that entered his unobstructed view. His eyes locked onto a white, suede outfit that suddenly appeared three feet away. The bikini bottom with its eight-inch leather strips hanging off the hips did little to conceal the wearer's rear end and long legs. The top was a pair of isosceles triangles draped loosely over her front and back held together by thin shoulder straps. As she leaned toward her date, Roger had an unimpeded view from her neck to her navel. He gulped, looked away toward a yellow form-fitting spandex-clad figure headed his way. Nicki watched him in amusement from the corner of her eye as she scanned each face for a sudden appearance of Dollah. It was too crowded to get near the bar. Nicki gestured toward the floor-lighted dance platform and mouthed, "Let's dance!" Roger followed and soon they were gyrating to the music of a German band that was screaming unintelligible lyrics in broken English.

If it hadn't been for Nicki and all the other beautiful women pressed up close to him, Roger would have bolted for the door already.

They stayed for two hours at Nicki's urging. "Can we leave now?" Roger asked.

"In a little while. Our outing has to appear to be a genuine date."

The object was to keep Dollah waiting, but Nicki didn't want to spell-out to Roger that he was live bait.

At 3:15 Roger looked as though he was about to drop.

Seeing his sorry condition, Nicki relented. "Okay, we can go now."

They left the club and walked to the elevator where five other couples were waiting. Dollah took the next elevator to the first of five below ground level parking floors, and then walked up to the street. He figured Roger and Nicki would hail one of the cabs lined up across the street from the main entrance.

He guessed right.

Dollah was already on his bike, and followed close behind their cab.

"Since we didn't get any drinks at the club let's go to my place for a nightcap," offered Nicki. She turned toward Roger and put her finger up to her lips to prevent him from responding. She then leaned forward and spoke to the driver. "Two hundred Jalan Pultra, Pultra Place Apartments."

Roger was too tired to ask questions; besides, at that moment Nicki laid her head on his shoulder. The scent of her perfume and the warmth of her body sent an instant message to his groin.

"We have to make this look convincing," she whispered.

"Whatever you say," Roger replied, looping his arm around her.

The apartment building was located five miles north of town on the west side of the Klang River, very near to where Roger had been taken for a joy ride on his first day in Kaula Lumpur.

Through the rear view mirror, the cab driver looked at the cozy couple and at the motorbike that had followed them from the Towers. He pulled into the parking lot of the apartment building and looked back for his fare. Nicki paid him then asked, "Can you wait for an hour? My boyfriend will need a ride home. You'll be paid well for the time." The driver agreed. Nicki reached inside her purse and handed the driver twice the fare she had just paid along with a healthy tip. The driver smiled approvingly and watched the couple walk arm in arm to the front door.

Once Roger and Nicki were inside, Dollah drove his bike up to the driver's side of the cab and inquired, "Cousin, how did you get to the front of the line when those two arrived?" He nodded in the direction of the entrance.

"With an enormous bribe which I plan to collect from you later."

"Did you get an apartment number for me?"

"No, but the gentleman is coming back down in an hour. I'm to wait."

"Very good. Here's what I want you do when the man comes back." Dollah explained his cousin's assignment in detail.

The CIA apartment that Nicki escorted Roger into commanded a spectacular view of the city with the Petronas Towers squarely centered. It was furnished in a luxurious South China Sea island decor. Roger could see into the bedroom and eyed the hand-carved teak poster bed placed over a magnificent oriental carpet. The silk bedspread was a work of art embroidered with decorative Chinese figures that Roger remembered once seeing in a museum.

Nicki entered the bedroom and removed the bedspread. "You look exhausted, poor puppy, lie down here."

Roger took off his jacket and eagerly flopped onto the bed as ordered with grand anticipation. He tingled as he lay in bed fully clothed, imagining how it would soon feel when she returned to undress him.

Nicki went back into the living room. She approached the picture window and pulled the sheer curtains closed. She turned her back to the window; then slowly stripped off all her clothes and flung each garment across the room with an exaggerated motion. Dollah and the cab driver stared unwaveringly at the silhouette from the parking lot.

Hidden from the voyeurs, Connelly watched from across the street in his darkened car. He'd seen that act before, but from a lot closer and without diffusion from a sheer curtain. Poor Roger missed the show. He had passed out as soon as his body went horizontal. When Nicki finished her striptease she turned off all the lights, picked up her disco outfit and walked into the bedroom.

Standing naked next to the bed, she looked down at Roger, smiled and removed his shoes. He moaned, put a bear hug on his pillow, and rolled away. Nicki ruffled his hair and went into the walk-in closet. She selected a pair of tan slacks, blue cotton blouse, and a brown vest which had a holster sewn under the left arm. She retrieved clean underwear from a hand-painted Chinese dresser and went into the bathroom to shower and change.

She opened a safe hidden behind a mirror where a medicine cabinet usually hung. From it she retrieved a People's Republic of China 7.65mm, Type 67 silenced pistol. It was specifically designed for clandestine quiet work. She took the Walther from her purse placed it in the safe and closed it. She placed the pistol in the vest holster, which was open at the bottom to receive the long silenced barrel.

An hour later, she woke Roger. "Time to go home, you wild beast."

"Okay," Roger mumbled as he sat up on the strange bed. Too tired to know or care where he was, Roger flung his legs over the bed, put on his shoes, and half stumbled out of the apartment. Nicki guided him to the elevator. "Tell the driver to take you to the U.S. Embassy and remember I paid him already, including a nice tip."

"Umm."

With his eyes half closed Roger walked out of the apartment building. He looked for the cab. It was parked right where they had gotten out an hour earlier. The driver appeared to be asleep. Roger tried the door. It was locked. He knocked on the window. The driver jumped and looked over at him but made no move to unlock the door. Roger made door-opening hand motions and pointed to the locked door. Instead of complying, the driver started the cab and drove into the parking lot. After twenty yards, he made a sharp U-turn and headed straight for Roger. The bright lights from the oncoming vehicle, the roar of its engine and squealing tires startled him wide-awake. The noise also enveloped three quick successive clicks that emanated from behind him. Before he could react, a body flew out of the darkness and shoved him aside. The cab sped by and peeled out the driveway onto the highway.

As Roger got up, a second figure appeared out of the shadow of the building and charged toward him. It was Dollah. The man who had tackled Roger got up faster but received the incomer's blow before he could brace for the attack. Roger recognized Dollah. "No – not you! Not you again!"

Dollah's arm came down hard, aimed at the chest of Roger's rescuer. It was agent Connelly. Connelly grunted as the knife pierced his chest inches from his heart. Roger stood helpless as Connelly grabbed Dollah by the arm to prevent a second thrust, then weakened and slid to the ground. Dollah stared at the trembling Roger. It puzzled him that the man didn't come to the aid of his friend. The individual standing before him looked far too scared to be a trained agent. Dollah charged anyway. The bloodied blade rose in the air. Roger turned and ran. He felt the knife nick his flesh, tear into his jacket, slicing it clear down the middle. Roger stopped and turned to face his attacker. As Dollah's arm rose up again Roger swung a roundhouse punch. He missed, half turning away from Dollah, nearly falling. Then he heard a muffled sound he couldn't identify. He saw the expression on Dollah's face change from rage to incomprehension. Dollah collapsed, once again, right at Roger's feet. This time he would not be getting up.

Roger saw Nicki standing feet wide apart, both arms extended, her pistol now pointed at him. She saw the look on his face and dropped her stance. Nicki ran back to where Connelly lay bleeding and knelt over to feel his neck for a pulse. She sighed deeply, closed her eyes and shook her head. "No, no. Oh God, please no." The last "no" was a drawn-out cry and grew louder and louder.

She laid both her hands over Connelly's chest where the blood gushed with each heartbeat. She heard a wheezing sound and knew that a lung must be punctured. She removed her vest and tore off her blouse. She screamed at Roger who was now standing over her. "Go back into the apartment. Forget the elevator. Take the stairs – go into the kitchen. Grab the plastic wrap under the sink. Hurry!" Roger ran.

Nicki pressed the blouse against Connelly's chest. She wrestled a cell phone from her pants pocket and hit speed dial one. "Emergency – need an ambulance and clean detail at Alpha Two Hundred: One agent down, one civilian dead." She flipped the phone shut and returned her attention to Connelly. Roger arrived breathless with aluminum foil and plastic wrap. Nicki grabbed the plastic, ripped the roll out of the box and yelled. "Lift him up. Help me take off his shirt." Roger pulled at the short-sleeved shirt just under Connelly's collar, ripping the buttons off. He easily pulled Connelly's arms out of the shirt.

"Hold him up more," demanded Nicki. Roger knelt at Connelly's head and gently lifted him under the shoulders. He assisted Nicki as she wound the plastic tightly around the semi-conscious agent's chest. The wheezing stopped. Roger gently laid the agent down. Connelly's eyes popped open. He tried to speak but couldn't. He coughed once. Blood squirted out the sides of his mouth. His eyes closed again and exhaled fully. Nicki spoke softly. "Don't die on me. Don't die on me now." She stroked his forehead and pushed his hair back. She prayed but she wasn't hopeful.

A white ambulance and two black vans approached soundlessly to within inches of them and screeched to a halt. A half dozen men and women dressed in hospital attire jumped out. Two placed Connelly on a stretcher and carried him to the ambulance. Two others maneuvered Dollah into a body bag and took him to the nearest van. The ambulance and the van with Dollah's corpse pulled out. The remaining crew began a thorough cleanup of the bloodstained driveway. The spent cartridge and Dollah's knife were retrieved. The whole operation was carried out with a speed and efficiency that amazed Roger.

As lights appeared in some of the apartments, a female member of the team dressed in a police uniform woke the night manager. She explained that here had been a car accident in the parking lot. He was to tell the wakened residents that no one was seriously hurt and that the accident had been cleared from the lot.

The team's supervisor motioned for Nicki and Roger to leave. Seeing Nicki without her blouse, Roger took off his ripped jacket and placed it over her shoulders. She glanced at him. "Thanks." She put her arms through the sleeves and buttoned the jacket. She picked up her vest and weapon, and led Roger across the street to Connelly's black Ford Taurus. She drove away from the apartment just as the sky began to lighten. Nicki headed the car toward the Embassy. Neither she nor Roger spoke.

Overwhelmed by the events of the past few minutes, Roger felt the tears on his cheeks. He sobbed softly. Nicki couldn't even muster the compassion to console him. She had a much bigger heartache. Not only had she botched backing up a partner – Mrs. Nicole Connelly had also failed the man she loved.

* * * * *

Jim Crowley, head of Southeast Asia Counterintelligence received a dispatch from the U.S. Embassy in Kuala Lumpur, dated 02FEB01, it inexplicably arrived seven days late. He read the dispatch sitting on the soft leather sofa in his Langley office:

URGENT   SECRET   02FEB01
AFTER ACTION REPORT:

During a routine operational stakeout at an al-Qaeda operative, Dollah Jaffar, agent Dillon Connelly was critically wounded when his gun failed to fire and jammed. Agent Nicole Sparks-Connelly subsequently shot and killed Jaffar. (Unbeknownst to Agency, Connelly and Sparks were married in Hawaii 03NOV00 during their last rotation stateside.) Clean team sanitized action site before police were notified. U.S. citizen, Roger Lacson witnessed the killing. Negotiations are under way with Malaysian authorities for return of Jaffar's body and joint resolution of incident. Local political fall-out is not anticipated.

68

Agent Nicole Sparks-Connelly has submitted her resignation, which will be forwarded in next dispatch.
John Williams
AIC Kuala Lumpur, ML

He finished the dispatch and placed it face down on the table in front of him. He was alone in the room but wished he wasn't. He wanted to share the bad news with someone but not his boss, CIA director, Ted Lane. He ran his hands through his thinning hair; furrows in his forehead deepened. When would the news from Southeast Asia improve? In January he had lost Manny Falstino, a deep plant inside *Abu Sayyaf*. Now a seasoned agent whom he personally knew and trusted was critically wounded. Then the capper, Connelly had secretly married an agent assigned to the same station and the same detail. Agent Connelly had shattered all the rules with that deception.

Crowley had never met agent Sparks-Connelly, but that would be rectified tomorrow. Right now she was somewhere over the Pacific flying commercial carrier to D.C. via the quickest, most direct route.

Crowley also wondered if Roger Lacson would be causing him any future problems. After all he'd been through, it would be hard to predict. Crowley knew that KL agent in charge, John Williams, had debriefed Lacson and delivered a stern warning never to talk about anything he saw in KL that pertained to the CIA. Crowley still worried. After all, Lacson was a reporter. Lacson had been transported by MATS on 4FEB01 to San Francisco and flown commercial to Tucson. Maybe the FBI should pay him a visit.

* * * * *

Nicki leaned her head against the 707's window and glanced out at the black horizon, wishing that the last twenty-four hours could be replayed. Her swollen, reddened eyes reflected the sadness that was crushing her. She no longer cared what the future held; as of *that* night, her present would never disconnect from her past.
Hopefully they'll ask me to bite a cyanide capsule.

Chapter 10

Maliq received word that he and his team would be leaving Kabasalan, their camp for the last seven weeks, early the next day. They would be hidden for a few days in Midsayap, a town near Cotabato City. From Cotabato a motor craft would take them offshore where a ship would depart 12 February for Jakarta. Arrangements were still being made for their passage. Maliq was told to have his men packed and ready at 6:00 a.m. for the 150-mile trip. Maliq had been informed that the groups' eventual destination would be Bogotá, Columbia.

Next morning, a beat-up school bus arrived to pick them up an hour late. The nine Arabs, dressed in jeans, short-sleeved shirts and sneakers, boarded the bus. Each carried a duffle bag, which they deposited across the back bench, then took an inside seat as instructed by Maliq. The bus was primarily used to transport farm laborers to the pineapple fields. It would attract very little attention along their route. Ten local men had been hired to travel on the bus and sit in the window seats – a precaution suggested by the local *Abu Sayyaf* leader. The fieldworkers were doubtless happy to get paid just for taking a bus ride.

The bus arrived on the outskirts of Midsayap at midnight. Maliq had noticed that they passed a Catholic Church a few blocks back. He was anxious to see a Mass as part of his ongoing education in the ways of the Mexican culture. The Arabs were greeted by a local Muslim cleric who led them to an empty three-story apartment building. He showed them to the basement, which was divided into

70

four large rooms. Three were for their use and contained four cots each. The cots were stained, smelled sweaty and were without sheets. Nonetheless, the accommodations provided a welcome reprieve from their recent jungle camp. The fourth room was reserved for a maintenance man who had been given a few days off and told to leave town. A shared bathroom was at the top of the stairs on the second floor.

Maliq knew the history of Midsayap before he had arrived. Though predominantly Christian, Midsayap had a large Muslim population. In order to protect themselves the Christians had formed an armed militia to combat the Islamic Moro National Liberation Front. The town was rarely peaceful.

The next morning, Sunday, Maliq was anxious to attend his first Mass. He wanted to take Abdul with him but feared two strangers might arouse suspicion. The cloudless, sunny morning raised Maliq's spirits, as did the urban setting of the small city. Maliq left the apartment at 11:30 for the noon Mass. With a slight limp, he walked the seven blocks to the church at a leisurely pace.

The Holy Trinity was relatively new and modern in appearance. Standing at the entrance, Maliq studied the altar. Beyond it was a stained glass diorama of the risen Christ, arms extended upward. The head of a dark-bearded God-the-Father appeared above the Christ. Radiant gold starbursts shown on a blue sky above the images must have represented the Holy Spirit. It was backlit for dramatic effect. Maliq imagined that even Jesus would be disgusted by the tawdry images.

A balcony above the entrance doors held the eight choir members and a pianist who were rehearsing. Wooden pews down the center provided seating for eighty parishioners. Folding chairs on each side of the altar accommodated additional worshipers. Almost every seat was filled.

Maliq wasn't the only non-Filipino attending Mass today. Ten Spanish nuns who were to begin teaching assignments in nearby schools were among the parishioners. Seated in the first row they were perhaps the reason for the full house. The town's residents focused their attention on the nuns. Maliq took the end seat in the next to last row. He was hardly noticed.

The congregation stood as the priest, Father Mora, and his entourage entered from the rear of the Church. Taken unawares,

71

Maliq was the last to rise, but his slowness went unobserved. The priest reached the altar, turned, and said, *"En el nombre de Padre, y el Hijo y del Espiritu Santo."* Maliq understood the words. Good, the Mass was being conducted in Spanish. The attendees responded, "Ah men," and made the sign of the cross. Maliq mimicked the movements, late again.

This was not going to be easy; he'd have to pay careful attention or his missteps would become noticed. He made it through the confusing process of standing, sitting, and kneeling. He mumbled the verbal responses. When the time came for communion, he noticed that a few parishioners in the rows in front of him did not go forward to receive a wafer and drink from the chalice. When his aisle got up Maliq stayed behind and remained kneeling. However, he observed carefully so he could follow the correct procedures the next time.

All through Mass, Maliq couldn't keep his mind off the Spanish nuns.

When the Mass ended, Maliq moved to the side of the church, away from the parishioners surrounding the priest and the nuns. As the crowd dispersed he watched as the nuns were led to a one-story detached frame house just behind the rectory.

Returning to the apartment Maliq called his men together. "My brothers, I have news. Ten young Spanish nuns have come to Midsayap for our entertainment."

Unrestrained excitement filled the room. Shouts of, "Praise be to Allah," echoed throughout the basement apartment. Khalid did a little dance.

"Please be still," Maliq shouted over the racket while motioning downward with his hands for emphasis. "Listen to me."

Maliq related his experience at the Catholic Mass. "It is not easy to follow the many movements you must make. Stand, sit, kneel, recitals and going forward to receive a wafer and wine."

"We now can drink wine all the time?" questioned Khalid.

"No, only at Mass. You must all attend Mass as soon as we arrive in South America. I want you all to learn the ways of the Mass before we reach Mexico," said Maliq "You will need the experience in order to blend into the Mexican way of life."

The men had been without women for months and loudly voiced their desire to visit the nuns while they slept that evening. Chaos erupted again. Everyone spoke at once.

"No, we cannot risk such a thing as you are thinking. I have a better idea in mind for the holy ladies," said Maliq. "I want two volunteers for a training mission."

Eight hands went up simultaneously. Abdul pushed his way to the front and put his hand in Maliq's face. Karim, way in the back, jumped up on a chair to be seen. Such enthusiasm should be rewarded – Maliq chose Abdul and Karim over the rest.

"Be ready at midnight tonight," he told the two elated men.

At ten, Maliq left the apartment alone. He walked straight to the church along the lightless streets. He went up the stairs to the front door as if to enter. Finding the doors locked he walked toward the rectory and the guesthouse beyond. In the rectory, lights could be seen in the front hall and in an upstairs room, but no one appeared to be awake. He then circled the already darkened guesthouse where the nuns must have turned in for the evening.

Maliq continued walking down the street toward the center of town. He approached a closed gas station where a Toyota pickup and a Chevy Nova were parked. He tried the door to the pickup. It was unlocked. He searched under the floor mats. No key. Above the visor? Again, no key. He checked the ashtray – yes, there it was.

The truck started on the third try. Maliq drove away. He parked within sight of his apartment and waited. At midnight he drove to the front door where Abdul and Karim were eagerly waiting. Maliq motioned for the two volunteers to climb into the back of the truck. "Stay down out of sight and hold on to those gas cans we borrowed." Maliq had taken the four full twenty-liter gas cans from the rear of the school bus. Carrying extra gas cans was a routine precaution for any long distance travel in Mindanao. The pair followed his instructions.

"Got them tight," shouted Karim above the noise of the engine.

Maliq drove to a street directly behind the guesthouse where the nuns lodged. The area was deserted. He pulled over and killed the lights but left the engine running.

"Each take two cans and come here," Maliq instructed in a hushed voice. "Abdul, start at the far left of the building," Maliq

73

whispered. "Karim go to your right until you meet Abdul. Pour the gasoline completely around the building, as close to the foundation as possible. Then walk back to the apartment and take the empty cans with you."

The two volunteers moved along the walls, pouring the gasoline as instructed. Maliq drove the truck over a curb to within ten yards of the guesthouse back door. He got out, weighted the gas pedal down with a small boulder, and then pulled the shift lever into drive. He jumped away as the truck sped forward and slammed into the building.

After the crash there was total silence; then the hot engine ignited the gasoline directly under the truck. In a roaring surge of fire, the gas exploded around the entire building. Maliq watched as flames shot almost to the rooftop. Glass windows shattered. Smoke billowed into and around the wood frame structure. A commercial fire alarm inside the burning building clanged incessantly. Maliq looked on for another moment. No one attempted to leave the building through the flaming doors or windows. He smiled contentedly.

The noise from the alarm, the smell of smoke, and brightness of the fire rapidly aroused the neighborhood. Lights went on everywhere. Maliq walked away unnoticed.

Inside the church the priest and nuns, members of the Holy Eucharist Society, had just concluded a private midnight devotion to the Blessed Sacrament. All rushed to the door to see the guesthouse burning with the fury of Hell. Realizing that the nuns could have perished in the inferno each knelt down and offered a silent prayer of thanks. A fire truck swerved into the church parking lot. As the firemen jumped down and manned the hoses, the fire chief looked over and saw that Father Mora and the nuns were praying on the front lawn of the Holy Trinity, at a decidedly unusual hour. For a split second he wondered irreverently if they were praying that their fire insurance hadn't lapsed.

Safely back in the sanctuary of the basement apartment, Maliq contemplated his team's triumph. He never did learn that adoration of the Blessed Sacrament had thwarted his plan to immolate ten Catholic nuns in their sleep.

74

Chapter 11

Carlin felt nervous. He picked up the phone and dialed the hospital, and asked for Maggie Smith. Maggie answered on the fifth ring.

"Hello."

"Hi, this is the idiot who stood you up last night. Don't say my name – I'll explain when I get there. When's a good time?"

"I don't know if I still want to see you."

"Don't kid right now. I have some important news."

She was intrigued. "Breakfast is over, come anytime."

"Meet me in your solarium in twenty minutes."

Carlin borrowed Dora's car and drove to the hospital, careful not to speed. He looked into his rearview mirror constantly and made sure he didn't run any lights. There was no sign of the fuzz or feds. Carlin reached the hospital in fifteen minutes.

Maggie was waiting on the fifth floor solarium when Carlin rushed in.

"Where's my flowers?"

"Did yesterday's die already?"

"No, but you can't blame a girl for trying."

Carlin had to laugh, even though he was still steaming from his ordeal with the FBI and wanted to get into the business of his visit. Maggie was sitting with her legs curled up on a white wicker loveseat. Carlin approached and leaned over to whisper in her ear. "Listen: I know we can't talk in your room and I'm not sure about

75

here. Can you go down to the cafeteria with me? I didn't see any press on my way up."

"Sure, let's go."

He glanced around. "Where's the wheelchair?"

"I traded it for a powdered Krispy Kreme." Maggie rarely missed an opportunity for a zinger. "The leg's fine, let's go."

As they started down the hallway FBI agent Norcross appeared, striding toward Maggie's room.

Maggie led Carlin in the opposite direction. "Follow me," she whispered. "We'll take the back stairs."

Stopping on the third floor landing Carlin said, "Let's talk here."

Maggie dropped abruptly onto the step. Carlin joined her.

"What in the world's going on?" Maggie asked.

Carlin gave her the short but complete version of his troubles since he had left her last evening. "Our friend agent Norcross set me up big time. My bet is that he's got your room bugged – that's why I suggested we take this little hike."

"I don't know why the FBI would bug my room, but you could be right."

Carlin quickly brought her up to date on the news he had gleaned from his sources. Marty had revived shortly after the medivac chopper took off from Tucson General. The nurse onboard had gotten Marty to count his fingers. This was fantastic news. Maggie knew that the longer a brain injury patient was unconscious, the worse the prognosis. "Where is he now?" she wanted to know.

"He's been moved to a brain injury trauma center in Phoenix."

"Is he alert? Will there be permanent damage?"

"The prognosis is for a full recovery, but don't take that to the bank."

Anxious to share her own news Maggie said, "I found the Guatemalan child – she's in room 515. Her name is Maggie … uh … Margarita Domingo."

"That matches my info," said Carlin.

"What's next for you?"

"I'm making a trip to Washington. You're looking fit. Any word on when they'll let you go home?"

"No, but I'll bet that by the time you get back here, I'll be out. Got a pen and paper?" Carlin pulled out his pocket pal and said, "Shoot."

Maggie gave him her address and phone numbers.

"I'll contact you as soon as I get back." Carlin promised. "If you need me, call my Tucson office, Carlin Ward, Consultant. I'm in the business-to-business phone book. I check my voice mail every hour. I have to go now."

As Carlin prepared to lever himself up from the step, Maggie reached around his neck and gave him a gentle hug. Carlin smiled and held both her arms in response. She broke off the stilted embrace, stood, and started up the steps. He watched her leave. Maggie stopped and called back, *"Muchisimas gracias."* Many thanks.

Carlin paused to translate his response from English and offered, *"El gusto es mio."* The pleasure is mine.

Maggie countered, *"No, el gusto es mio."* She continued up the stairs and he started down. Each heard the sound of the other's footsteps as they made their way through the hollow stairwell.

Washington, DC

Ward, Whitman and Cross maintained an apartment in Chevy Chase View ten minutes north of Carlin Ward's previous Washington area home. He arrived in Washington's Reagan Airport around ten in the evening. He took a cab to the apartment, showered and retired immediately.

Carlin was in his office by eight the next morning. His old corner office was not his anymore, but the small, comfortable space the company provided was ample for his needs. His first task was to arrange lunch with his old college buddy, Jack Adams. Jack was a reporter for the *Washington Times*, the lesser-known Washington daily. Washington insiders who hated the *Washington Post* and the *New York Times* often rewarded Jack with information they wanted leaked. No source ever feared exposure from him.

Jack answered from his private unlisted home phone. "Hello, my good amigo." Jack's caller-ID told him who was on the line and

77

that the call came from Ward, Whitman and Cross. "This must be important to get you out of the desert in February."

"It is. Time for lunch today?"

"For you, yes. The Capitol Café, at noon?"

"No, the Boardroom at eleven."

"It's noisy and the food's terrible."

"Perfect, the Boardroom at eleven.

The Boardroom was once one of Washington's "in-places" when Go-Go girls and booze were the preferred luncheon fare. In the nineties, when even wine with lunch would bring disapproving looks from fellow luncheon guests, the Boardroom fell out of favor. Carlin liked it because the music was loud and most of Washington's elite wouldn't want to been seen there during work hours.

Carlin arrived before Jack and took a booth far from the bar and stage. The place was dark and stunk from decades of smoke and spilled booze. A half dozen mid-level businessmen sat at the bar drinking shots and beer. An underfed, buxom redhead bobbed half-heartedly to the music around a pole.

A waitress came over to take Carlin's order. "Johnny Walker Black, on the rocks, tall glass of water."

She handed him a ketchup-smeared menu and left.

Minutes later, Jack came into the room, squinted, looked around, saw Carlin and walked over to his table. Carlin got up and smiled broadly. Jack reached him and they hugged, as only WASP's do; gingerly, but nonetheless affectionately.

The waitress returned with Carlin's drink and water. She looked questioningly at Jack.

"Just water for me, thanks."

The waitress smirked and left mumbling to herself.

"I'll make this quick – you look uncomfortable," said Carlin.

"No, I'm okay. My editor knows I go sleazy places to meet sleazy people."

Carlin had just taken a sip of his drink and had to stifle a laugh or he would have blasted scotch in Jack's direction. He swallowed hard. "Guess you've got me pegged." He said with a chuckle. "How about we do a leisurely dinner later this week to catch up?"

78

"Fine."

Carlin lowered his voice, although no one but Jack could possibly have heard a word he spoke. The smile left his face and he leaned across the table. "I need you to set up a private meeting at a very private place for me with Senator McGuire."

"You can't do this yourself? You would have gotten him elected President, if the S&L loan scandal hadn't surfaced just before the last debate."

"No, I can't. Besides, I'm going to need you to run interference for me for the next few months. Now, there may not be a payoff in this for you. I'm asking as a friend and a patriot."

"Friend is good enough for me."

"Make the meeting as soon as possible at his convenience, anytime, anywhere."

"Sounds urgent. I'll get on it right away." Jack took a sip of Carlin's water and made a face. "City water, ugh."

"Don't mention me by name when you call."

"I got the picture. There're clandestine meetings and 'meetings that never happen' – this is intended to be the latter."

Jack departed before the waitress returned with his water and menu. Carlin didn't order lunch either. He dropped twenty dollars on the table, strolled past the men's room and found the "Emergency Exit Only" back door open. At the curb, a Budweiser delivery driver was loading a dolly with cases of Bud Light. One case already held the door open. Carlin drifted out the exit and past the driver without being seen.

* * * * *

Jack Adams wasted little time: he called Jim Flynn, the #1 gatekeeper for Senator McGuire as soon as he got into his car. Flynn's voice mail said he was busy and to leave a number, he'd call back. Jack left his number and hung up. He had a very good relationship with Flynn and knew he'd call back at the first possible chance. That chance didn't happen until 8:30 that evening.

"Jack Adams."

"Sorry for taking so long, it's been a bear of a day ... night, whatever."

"No problem, Jim. Need a big, big favor."

"How big?"

Jack paused. "Mount Rushmore size, I guess."

"I'm listening."

"I need to speak personally with the Senator and tonight wouldn't be too soon either."

"I'm sure you'd tell me what this is about if you could so, I won't ask. Right now is a good time. Here's a number, use it just this once and lose it."

"You have my word."

Flynn gave Jack a private number that only the Senator answered. Jack dialed it.

"George McGuire."

Jack hesitated to collect his thoughts. He recognized the Senator's husky voice. "Senator, this is Jack Adams, *Washington Times.*"

"Why hello Jack, nice to hear from you."

The senior Senator from New Jersey and the Chairman of the Senate Intelligence Committee was always the polite politician. Jack guessed that he was really thinking, "how in God's name did that smart ass get this number?"

"Just fine, sir. Senator, I have an urgent request from a close mutual, personal friend. Can't mention his name, but he skipped town a few years ago, now rides a camel out west somewhere. Know who I mean?"

"I'm not too good on riddles, but I think this man would have known my secret service codename during my presidential bid. Right?"

"Yes sir, you would be correct."

"So what does he want that he can't call me himself?"

"He didn't tell me. He's in Washington right now and he'd like to meet with you without anyone – and he stressed *anyone* – knowing."

"I'll call you later tonight." The Senator hung up without a goodbye.

Jack waited. Two hours later the Senator called back. "Jack, tell the camel rider that he should come to my New Jersey home at ten tomorrow evening. Tell him to drive to the back portico and park. No one will be home but me. No aides, no domestics, no wife, she's in LA. Got it?"

"Yes, sir." They both hung up. Jack called Carlin, gave him the senator's instructions, and finally turned in for the night.

The next afternoon, Carlin drove north on Interstate 95. He arrived at eight thirty in Cherry Hill and knew just where he wanted to have dinner before his meeting – Ponzio's Diner.

New Jersey is famous for its diners and Ponzio's was a long-standing south Jersey landmark. Carlin loved eggs for dinner, and breakfast was served round the clock at most diners. After a superb Spanish omelet, home fries, a slice of ham, and a great cup of java, he was now ready for anything. He had no clue how he'd be received this evening.

He stood on the steps of the diner and inhaled the fresh, cool-crisp air and watched as snow began to fall. The tall maple, oak, and cherry trees collected the flakes first. There was a light coating on the grassy areas. The roads so far just looked wet. The sky gave off an eerie glow from the reflection of the falling snow against the backdrop of amber streetlights. A light breeze swirled the snow right into his face. It felt refreshing. He walked to his car with a tight smile, enjoying the winter vista for the first time in a long while.

He pulled out of the parking lot onto Kings Highway and drove toward the town of Haddonfield. Senator George McGuire's postal address was Haddonfield, but the Senator actually resided in the tiny borough of Tavistock, a community of seventeen homes on the edge of an 18-hole golf course. His home was the last one situated on Lane of Acres Road, a secluded and very private dead end street.

Carlin made the first tire tracks on the Senator's snow-coated driveway. As instructed, he drove around the side of the house. The driveway sloped below the road and it continued beyond a detached two-car garage behind the house. It ended under a portico. Carlin's car clock showed 10:01. He stopped.

A light turned on above the sliding glass doors. It opened partially.

An arm reached out holding a tall glass. The arm belonged to Senator McGuire and the glass, he surmised, held Johnny Walker Black.

No warmer welcome could have been extended.

Carlin eased out of the car, walked over, took the glass from the Senator and offered their private toast, "Through cheers or jeers, friends forever."

"Friends forever," responded Senator George McGuire.

Carlin savored the drink, but relished the camaraderie even more.

Chapter 12

Agent Estimo landed in Cotabato City an hour and thirty-five minutes after leaving Manila. The CIA leased an apartment seven miles north of the city. He needed to refresh from the trying week in Manila and to absorb what he had learned. It was another twenty-four miles to his destination today, Midsayap. He didn't want to waste another minute.

As yet, he hadn't fully digested the news from Kuala Lumpur. Agent Sparks' earlier call had jolted him. Their plan to use the American Filipino, Roger Lacson as bait had turned into a disaster. Agent Connelly was critically wounded. She expressed little hope that he'd make it. The news shocked Estimo and offered a prayer. Sparks had resigned because of a botched operation and/or for violating the Agency principle: "Thou shall not marry thy partner." Dollah Jaffar, the al-Qaeda surrogate, was dead, which meant that they would now find it more difficult to locate his handler.

Things were not much better in the Philippines. Estimo had learned that the CIA's deep-plant inside *Abu Sayyaf,* Manny Falstino, had indeed been executed. Then the two most qualified CIA agents in Manila had been shipped out because they were Manny's contacts.

What a sorry mess.

Estimo now made it his personal mission to put a stop to the failures and make valuable use of his time in Mindanao. As soon as he arrived at the apartment, he placed a call. "Fire Chief Marco, please."

83

"Speaking. Who's this?"

"Chief Marco, my name is Rogelio Estimo. You don't know me but Federal Inspector Escaba said he would call ahead – he asked that you relate information you have regarding a suspicious fire last night."

"Yes, the inspector called. Where are you calling from?

"Sultan Kudarat."

"Can you meet me at the Holy Trinity Church at two o' clock?

"Yes, I can be there."

"Good, I'll give you the whole story then. Know where it is?"

"I'll find it, thanks."

Estimo arrived in Midsayap early and found the church. He looked over at the near-completely burned building next to the parish house. He stepped out of the car, walked toward the building, stopped, and crouched under the yellow police tape to get a closer look.

"You can't go in there!"

Estimo looked around for the speaker.

He heard the voice again. "You can't go in there, it may be a crime site."

Estimo looked up and saw a nearly bald head sticking out of an upstairs room in the parish house. "Wait right there!" said the authoritative voice.

Father Mora strode across the distance from the parish house in thirty big steps. "Who are you? What do you want?"

"My name is Rogelio Estimo and I'm meeting Chief Marco." Estimo looked over Father Mora's shoulder. "Here he comes now."

Chief Marco got out of his official fire department car and headed for the priest and Estimo.

"Sorry I had to challenge you," said Father Marco. "We had some strangers here last weekend, and this fire is suspicious."

"I understand."

"Are you a fire investigator?"

"No. But I'm looking into a few unusual events that have taken place in Mindanao over the past couple of weeks, and this fire may be tied to them."

84

Fire Chief Marco joined the conversation. "Hi, Father. Hello, you're Estimo?"

"Yes, chief. Thanks for seeing me on such short notice."

"Well, I'll be leaving." The priest turned to go.

"Wait, Father. Did you say some strangers were here?"

"Yes, I personally didn't see them, but a few of my parishioners said that they saw a group of men arrive late one evening last week. They stayed at an apartment a few blocks from here on Marquez Boulevard. One was even seen attending Mass Sunday."

"Thank you Father, you've been most helpful."

"So you want to know about the fire? said Chief Marco.

"Yes, if you don't mind."

"Follow me." The fire chief ducked under the tape and led the way around the perimeter of the building. Estimo trailed him closely.

Marco kept up a commentary as they walked. "No doubt about it. The fire was deliberately set. A group of visiting nuns would have been asleep inside if it had not been for a midnight service of some kind. Gasoline or kerosene was poured along all four sides of the foundation." The chief stopped at a spot near the street behind the building. "At this curb they ran a stolen truck right into the building." He swung his arm to a spot where a doorway had once stood. "The fire started here, and engulfed the building within minutes. By the time we arrived, it was too far gone to save."

"Thanks, Chief. You and Father Mora have been a big help."

"Guess you can't tell me what your investigation is all about?"

"Right now, I can't – but I promise you if this leads to what I'm after I'll come back, buy you lunch and tell you everything that isn't classified."

"Fair enough. Good luck."

"Thank you." Both got in their cars and drove away.

Estimo headed for the apartment on Marquez Boulevard. He had no trouble finding the building. It was the only non-single family home for blocks. He rang the doorbell marked "Custodio." It was answered by a short, thin Filipino. He appeared to be about seventy years-old. Estimo looked down, shifted his feet in an attempt to appear embarrassed. He spoke hesitantly. "Pardon me,

85

but a few of my friends stayed here last weekend. One of them left a small backpack. Did you come across it by any chance?"

"Let me think." The old man paused. "No, but I did find a green jacket."

"Oh? Oh, that belonged to Juan. May I have it? He'll be happy I got it back for him."

The caretaker smiled, "Of course. Wait here. I'll go get it."

The man returned with the jacket and handed it to Estimo.

"Thanks. Thanks a lot. Do you know who owns this building?

"No, I don't."

"Okay, thanks again for the jacket." Estimo nodded and walked away. He looked above the door and jotted down the number. He dashed quickly to his rental and drove off. After a block he pulled over, impatient to look in the jacket's pockets. He felt outside the pockets first. Something solid appeared to be in each. He reached behind his seat for his briefcase and grabbed a pair of rubber gloves. From the left pocket he pulled out a cigarette lighter. It was an old Zippo. It had an inscription. Although he couldn't read it, he grinned widely. The inscription was in Arabic.

The other pocket contained a small Koran. Folded inside it was a piece of yellow ruled paper. On it, a note was written in Spanish. On the backside were groups of names and strangely Estimo was extremely familiar with nine names and corresponding locations.

Maliq	Miguel	Bonnie Baker	Aspen, Colorado
Abdul	José	Magabucks McDonald	Las Vegas, Nevada
Amir	Alberto	Sen. George McGuire	Haddonfield, New Jersey
Karim	Kruz	Thomas Brooks	Augusta, Montana
Zubayr	Zacarias	Janice Jones	Miami, Florida
Yazid	Huberto	Dan Rose	Scottsdale, Arizona
Shakir	Salvador	Doris Dean	Malibu, California
Naji	Naido	Steven Trent	Carmel, California
Tariq	Tiago	Bart Nancy	Gains Pointe, Maryland

Estimo couldn't contain himself any longer. "Yahoo ... YAHOO!"

He quickly looked around, hoping no one was within earshot. To his relief he saw nobody. Estimo lifted an imaginary drink in the air. "This one's for you my friend. Get well, Agent Dillon Connelly." He put his hands to his lips and tipped his head back. "Ahhh."

* * * * *

Agent Estimo returned to his Kudarat apartment elated. He needed to get back to Manila so that his cache, consisting of the lighter, and the pocket Koran with note, which needed to be shipped off to Washington for analysis. He was certain that he had tracked the Arabs who were in Mindanao learning Spanish. However, they had left Midsayap two days ago. *Where were they now?* He'd love to track them down before he reported to Washington.

His cell phone rang just as he flopped on the sofa to contemplate dinner. "Hello."

"Hello, Estimo?"

"Yes."

"This is Inspector Escaba. Heard that you met with fire chief Marco and he cooperated."

Estimo stood and paced the room as he talked. "Yes, and I thank you."

"Well, you're welcome. I didn't just call for your gratitude. I'm calling because you asked me to contact you if I learn of anything out of the ordinary; and I think this qualifies."

"I'm listening."

"The head of security at Port Cotabato called a few minutes ago and told me about an incident. His name is Felipe Alejandro. He has a surveillance tape that you should see and a night watchman you should talk to."

Estimo listened intently as Escaba went on. Some unidentified men had been observed on the pier whose actions seemed out of the ordinary. Estimo hung up and called the number Escaba had given him. He made an appointment for midnight, when

87

Alejandro would arrange for him to talk with the watchman who had reported the activity.

* * * * *

"Cotabato is a shallow port used for re-supply and offloading of cruise ships and ferries." said Felipe Alejandro. The security chief of Port Cotabato was in an expansive mood. He had talked today to a Philippine Federal Inspector and now he was being courted by, he presumed, a United States CIA agent.

Alejandro was short and overweight by plenty. His double chin and puffy cheeks gave him a cherubic appearance, but his twisted smile suggested a more sinister side, thought Estimo.

Estimo listened intently as they walked along the pier toward the office building. "Yes, I'm familiar with most of the main shipping ports in the Philippines. So, what exactly happened here Tuesday night?

Escaba steered the agent to a doorway at the far end of the building. "Well, let's find Ricky Carlos so you can hear it right from the source. Then we'll go to my office and I'll show you the tape."

Ricky Carlos looked to be about eighteen. He was waiting in the security guards' cafeteria, sipping soda from a can and munching on cheese crackers out of a box. He was a skinny kid dressed in a baggy, blue security uniform far too large for him. He was not armed.

Alejandro pulled out a seat and sat down at Ricky's table. Estimo did the same. "Ricky, this is Mr. Estimo. I want you to tell him word for word what you saw the other night and don't leave anything out."

Ricky took the last sip from his soda and tossed the can four feet into an open trash receptacle. His wide smile showed his satisfaction with the 'basket.' Catching Escaba's glare he lost the smile and turned his attention on Estimo. "It was 'bout two when I heard a motor craft com'n toward me. I thought it was head'n to one of our piers but it moved off and docked at the abandoned warehouse on the other side of our fence." He droned on in an expressionless, soft monotone. "Two men got out and went into a building. Then a whole bunch of guys came out with bags or something and got…"

"I told you not to leave anything out. How many did you count?" interrupted Alejandro.

"Yes, Mr. Alejandro, there was at least eight, maybe ten, I saw."

Alejandro nodded. "Continue, Ricky," he ordered.

"Like I said, they put their stuff in the launch, then half of them jumped in and the launch headed back out. It came back. It had to make two trips to get all the men."

"Did you see where the launch went?" Estimo questioned.

"Yes sir. It went out to a pleasure cruiser, unloaded the men and their stuff. After the second trip the launch came back to the warehouse pier, a man tied it up, got in a car and drove off."

"Could you make out the name on the cruiser? asked Estimo.

"No sir, I told you everything I know sir."

"Thank you, Ricky, said Estimo. "That was most helpful."

"Alright, alright, trash the snacks and get out to your post," Alejandro ordered abruptly. "Now, if you'll be kind enough to come up to my office, Mr. Estimo. I'll show you what the dumb, shit-head missed." He said this in earshot of Ricky.

Alejandro led the way out of the cafeteria and up a flight of outside metal stairs that led to an office built on top of the one story building. The security headquarters was an obvious afterthought added after completion of the administration building.

A technician was fiddling with a short wave radio as Estimo and Alejandro entered. She looked up and asked, "Want to view the tape now?

"Yes we would, honey, said Alejandro. "Lea, this is Mr. Estimo."

Lea and Estimo acknowledged each another with a nod. Escaba sat in an oversized swivel chair. Estimo remained standing. There were eight monitors near the ceiling on metal racks. Each one displayed a different area of the port. On monitor one, Estimo saw Ricky outside walking his post.

"Stop recording on eight and show it there." Alejandro pointed.

"Okay." The woman went over to a bank of tape decks, ejected one tape and replaced it with the one Alejandro handed to her.

The picture was black and white and very fuzzy. It was obvious that the tape had been used over and over again. The image showed a motor launch come into the picture, cross diagonally from top to bottom and then go out of the frame. The features of the helmsman were out of focus and too far away to be recognizable. After a long pause, the launch came back into view. This time, as it made a reverse diagonal movement across the screen one could see that it was crammed with men, although the image was too grainy to count them. This image repeated for a second time. The tape wouldn't be of any use. Estimo thought, it merely collaborated the guard's story. He was ready to offer his thanks and leave. Alejandro looked over at Estimo and motioned for him to stay put. "Don't you want to see the end?"

"Is it worth the wait?"

"I think so. Fast forward to 2:48, honey."

The female technician looked at Estimo, closed her eyes tightly for a second. A bookcase shielded her from Alejandro's view. She responded, "Yes sir!" The "sir" was overemphasized.

When the tape slowed to normal speed once more it showed a car heading toward the camera. The car stopped, backed into the port's driveway and then it drove off in the opposite direction.

"That was taken by camera three positioned out front; I had Lea, splice it onto the end of the launch captured on camera one. If I'm thinking right, that's the launch driver in that car. He got disoriented and started off in the wrong direction. Stopped, turned around and showed us his ass-end, then took off. We can see that the car has a tag; but, of course, we can't make it out. Now, I'm willing to bet, Mr. Estimo, that your people have some equipment that just might clear up the image enough to make out that tag number."

Estimo smiled. "Yes, I might find some folks who could do that for me. Are you offering me the tape?"

"I am. But I would like a favor."

"And what might that be?"

"Lea sweetheart, give me the tape and be a good darling and leave us alone for a moment."

Lea flipped the tape to Alejandro. She walked out the door and shut it behind her.

Alejandro waited until he heard Lea's steps reach the bottom of the stairs. "I'd like Federal Inspector Escaba to know how helpful I've been to your investigation, but you must not let my company find out that I talked with you or gave you this tape."

"I can do that."

Alejandro tossed the tape to Estimo and saluted.

Estimo bobbled but caught the tape. He acknowledged the salute. "Thanks, I appreciate this." He turned and hastened out the door. Escaba leaned back in his chair and smiled broadly. He was quite pleased with his performance.

Lea was at the bottom of the stairs smoking a cigarette. "A sweetheart of a condescending, fat prick, wouldn't you say?"

Startled by Lea's frankness, Estimo measured his response. "I might if I was a female and worked for him."

"That's the correct answer, agent." From behind her back she produced another tape and handed it to Estimo. She became serious. In hushed tones she added, "Here's a movie you'll really enjoy. But before I hand it over, know that I'm literally risking, not just my job, but my life giving you this. Seriously, you must never, ever tell anyone where you got it. Understand?"

Estimo's eyebrows hiked, his lips tightened and he cocked his head slightly. "Absolutely." He took the tape and thanked her. I have a feeling that you've done something extraordinary for your country. Be assured, I'll never disclose where I got this."

Lea's facial muscles relaxed and she smiled. Her Cheshire-cat grin told Estimo that a disgruntled employee probably had just gotten some well-deserved, sweet revenge.

Chapter 13

"Now come in here, out of the cold, please." All of Senator McGuire's requests could sound like an order.

Carlin Ward stepped inside the huge sitting room that overlooked the ninth fairway. He had spent many a day and night in this room, but he had never seen it this devoid of humanity. During the presidential campaign of '92 the room had been packed with aides, volunteers, public relations practitioners, family members, and political groupies. In addition, the door was always open to the numerous local, state, and national Republican officeholders who wanted to be seen with, or offer advice to, the candidate. The various groups had swarmed all over the room. They mingled freely. They had one aim – get their host elected President of the United States. In addition, the assigned secret service detail had been ever-present and everywhere.

It had been a heady time in this small corner of the world.

Carlin moved his drink from his right to his left hand to receive the big paw extended toward him. It was a large hand, belonging to a big man; physically as well as politically. His weight was a respectable two-twenty for a man his size. Carlin was well-over six feet and the senator could still look over his head. The most striking facial features were his light blue eyes and bushy eyebrows. They were eyes that expressed his normally good-natured disposition, but could change in an instant to show displeasure.

Senator McGuire retired early so Carlin was not surprised to find him wearing his pajamas, robe and slippers at this time of the night.

The room was elegantly furnished with oversized leather chairs and sofas organized into semi-intimate conversation pits. One group of seats faced an enormous wood-burning fireplace that gave off a soft glow along with the welcome heat. This was the Senator McGuire's trophy room. Many of his awards and pictures with famous and not so famous people hung on every wall. His biographer need only spend a few days here and his life's story could be written without an interview.

Senator McGuire chose a seat on a sofa looking out at the Christmas-card scene framed by the sliding doors. Carlin sat in a chair to the senator's left and rested his drink on top of the coffee table in front of them. The senator spoke. "Now, Carlin, are you here to see the senator, head of U.S. Senate Intelligence, or an old friend?"

"All three, George."

The senator raised his eyebrows and frowned. "I think not, based on the clandestine nature of your contact and the 'be alone' request."

Carlin smiled. "Well, if I had to rank them, then I must admit, the head of U.S. Senate Intelligence would be way up there."

Senator McGuire shot Carlin a piercing glance. "Okay, what has got you so all fired-up that you'd leave the warmth of Arizona and your lovely wife to visit an old crony like me during the dead of winter? Have you totally lost it?" How is Dora, by the way?"

The two exchanged personal updates; then it was time for Carlin to explain the reason for the secrecy and the purpose of his visit. He told the senator everything that had happened from the time he read the news report on the air about the shootings in Organ Pipe National Monument right up to his encounter with the FBI.

Senator McGuire listened intently. He waited to make sure Carlin was finished, he then asked, "So what can I do to assist you with your endeavor, Carlin?

Carlin reached over for his Scotch and took a healthy drink. He breathed deeply then leaned toward the senator with a serious expression. "For starters, you might look into the Mexican military's activity on the Arizona border. It appears that they may actually be providing armed cover for drug runners. Next, I ask the question:

don't we need changes in our immigration policy regarding Mexican nationals who enter illegally? Or shouldn't the Federal Government assist with enforcing those policies now in effect? The Border Patrol can't do the job alone. Arizona doesn't deploy the National Guard on the border for political reasons and financial concerns as well."

Senator McGuire got up from his seat and strolled over to the fireplace. He warmed his hands and was silent for some time. With his back to Carlin he spoke. "Have you posed these questions to Arizona's leaders? You've got a couple of outstanding men and women in Congress and a superb governor."

Carlin leaned over the side of his chair to address the senator's back. He knew better than to approach the man who was now in serious thought mode. "No, I haven't. First off, this is a national problem, not just a local one. Secondly, I know of no other politician with your access to information, or the ability to spark action should you conclude it necessary. Will you give the problems some thought?"

After another lengthy pause the politician turned around and looked straight into Carlin's pleading eyes. "Yes, I promise to look into the situation regarding the Mexican military. I have seen reports already that support your theory. And yes again, I'll ponder the immigration issues, but they are fraught with political minefields, and the biggest one is located in Mexico City."

"Thanks. I was hoping you'd see fit to help." Carlin stood with a satisfied grin and faced the senator, who walked back to stand beside him.

"For now, let's keep this effort secret. I take it you trust Jack Adams?"

"Completely."

"Good, let's continue to use him. Give him this private cell number 856 ... wait, that son-of-gun already has it. How'd he do that?"

"I don't know. Jack is exceptionally resourceful."

"I'd say so. Carlin, I hate to rush you, but I catch an early plane out tomorrow and I need my rest." He placed a friendly arm across Carlin's shoulder.

"Of course. Thank you, George. You have been most generous with your time this evening. Thanks for seeing me so quickly."

"Goodnight, Carlin."

"Goodnight, Sir."

Carlin left, feeling that he had achieved his mission.

The snow picked up in intensity as he drove south back to Washington. By the time he entered the Baltimore Harbor tunnel it had become downright treacherous. Given the late hour and road conditions, he decided to head into Baltimore and look for a place to spend the night.

Carlin peered through the rapid back and forth of the windshield wipers. It became more difficult to see as ice began to build up under them. The defroster was inadequate for the conditions. Carlin took an exit ramp and the car slid perceptibly. He gently held his foot on the brake and watched the odometer drop to fifteen miles per hour before he applied gas again. He reached over and pressed the button that engaged his flasher lights.

The bright neon signs up ahead blended into a fuzzy, unreadable collage. He didn't need an Omni or a Hilton, but he did have his preferences. Carlin slowed even more to get a better view of the signs.

Out of the corner of his eye he caught the image of a yellow light blinking in his rearview mirror. It had to be a city cinder-spreading truck. It was moving up his rear at a fairly rapid clip for the road conditions. He could hear the truck's engine now as it approached closer.

Can't he see my rear lights? He's approaching too fast. Carlin made an instant decision and turned abruptly into a gas station on his right. Just as he reached the edge of the driveway, he heard a loud crunching sound from the right rear end. Uncontrolled fear shot though his body. On the slippery surface his car slid ten yards into the first row of pumps. The airbags went off. Carlin's head hit the headrest hard and bounced into the driver's side window. The window shattered and small glass missiles imbedded into the side of his face. Gasoline fumes filled his lungs and replaced the oxygen.

Lightheaded, Carlin reached for his door release. It wouldn't budge. He stretched across to the passenger side but couldn't find the handle. Pain shot through his arm. His arm started to bleed. He felt blackness set in.

The explosion rocked the station's convenience store like an earthquake. The huge windows collapsed inward. Everything fell off the shelves. The fire at the pump streaked twenty feet skyward.

The snow got out of its way.

Chapter 14

Carlin's eyes fought the glowing embers above his head. If he tried real hard he could focus on them, but it hurt. He heard a faint rhythmic noise. He concentrated on moving a digit. The little finger of his right hand – it moved. Next he'd go for something big – his entire left leg. It moved, too. Now for the sound. He recognized the cadence. Where had he heard it before … beep-beep … beep-beep … beep-beep? Yes, he knew what it was. It was a machine tracking a heartbeat, but whose? The glowing embers; if he could just focus on them, then the puzzle would come together.

"Welcome back, Mr. Ward. How do you feel?" The words came from a black woman, in all white, who stood at the foot of the bed scrutinizing a clipboard. "They tell me you are one lucky, lucky man."

"Who's the p-r-o-v-e-r-b-i-a-l 't-h-a-a-y?" Carlin's mouth was either filled with cotton or persimmons he couldn't discern which. He was so thirsty.

"The 'they' are the municipal workers who pulled you out of your car before Hell surfaced on Waterview Avenue."

He thought he heard what she said, but the words didn't make any sense. *Before Hell surfaced on water?* He'd sleep on it. Closing the eyes was a lot easier.

Tucson, Arizona

Released from the hospital just before noon, Maggie greeted her parents in the lobby. She was sitting in her wheelchair by the candy stripers' desk near the front door. Nurse, "Angel" Diaz hovered just behind her with a firm grip on her chair. Maggie got up and hugged her mom and dad.

As nurse Diaz reluctantly released her charge Maggie surprised her with a hug and a peck on the cheek. "Thanks for everything," she offered with genuine gratitude. Maggie departed the hospital arm in arm with her parents and they quietly drove her to her apartment. Her mom and dad desperately wanted her to come to their house for a few days, but Maggie insisted that she'd rather stay in her apartment.

Home sweet home. How good it felt to be out of the hospital and back in her sanctuary. She had to straighten up, and clean the coffee pot; it was still half filled with the coffee she had made seven days ago. *Was that all it was – a week? Wow, it seemed like months.*

First thing she needed was to call Nogales. She wanted to know what the supervisors had heard about Marty. When she got through the news seemed reassuring. The Nogales staff told her unofficially that Marty was doing well but that she'd have to call the Department of Information for specifics. She did, but they offered none and they wouldn't even tell her the name of the hospital. *Maybe Carlin could find out?*

After two days of hanging around the apartment, Maggie was tired of reading, watching TV, and catching up with classmates on the Internet. Her parents had brought dinner over every night. That was getting tiring too. But she couldn't ask them to stop and risk hurting their feelings.

Her wounds were healing nicely. The facial abrasions were fading. Her leg burn still required a wrap, but it didn't inhibit her in any way; although she was not in condition to run a marathon or play tennis at the moment. Deep in thought, she was startled when the phone rang.

"Hello."

"Hi. Did you break out or, did they throw you out?"

"Carlin! It's so good to hear from you. Where are you?

"At the moment I'm in Baltimore, St. Francis Hospital to be exact."

"Visiting a friend?"

"No. I'm a patient."

"What? What happened? You okay?"

"I'm fine – a minor auto accident."

Maggie frowned. "If it was minor, why are you in the hospital?"

I'll give you the whole story when I see you. I don't want to talk now. Be back in a couple of days. Hold your questions till then, alright?"

"Okay."

"Good, take care, I'll call soon."

"Bye."

Maggie had a lot of questions, but Carlin left her no choice. She would have to wait. She'd never even got to ask if he could get information on Marty. Maggie wanted to go back to work. She also wanted to find out about Margaret, the Guatemalan child.

The phone rang again.

"Hello."

"Hello, Margarita Lopez?

"Yes."

"Hi, my name's Roger Lacson. I'm with the *Star*."

"Yes?"

"I'm doing a story on the shooting at Organ Pipe and…"

She cut him off quickly. "Sorry, I can't tell you anything. Call Public Information, they're on Ajo Way."

"I know. I went to see them yesterday. They gave me a week-old news release. I would like to talk with you."

"I can't talk about an ongoing investigation. Now, if you'll excuse me."

"Wait; don't hang up, please. What if we don't talk about that night? May we meet and talk about the border problems in general?"

"No, that's not my job. Take that 'no' or I'll call the FBI. They want me to tell them if anyone from the press bothers me."

"Not necessary, lady. Goodbye."

She was irritated to learn that the press had her home number but she was pleased with how she'd handled him.

99

The phone rang yet again.

"What's going on here?" she said out loud as she picked up the receiver.

"Hello, Maggie's Pizza; may, I take your order?"

"So you have a side business. Is that allowed by the Border Patrol? I'm not so sure. This is agent Norcross checking to see how you are."

"Doesn't the FBI have better things for you to do than call on a banged-up Border Patrol agent?"

"At the moment you're part of my job. Everything, okay? Is that Ward fellow bothering you?"

"No, he's not, thanks for asking and good night Mr. Norcross."

"Good bye, Miss Lopez."

Maggie hung up. The only bother at the moment was Agent Norcross. Maybe she should have mentioned Roger Lacson. It might have kept him busy for a while. Too late and she wasn't about to call him back.

After she hung up she stared off into the distance. *Did that S.O.B. bug my phone?* Maggie decided to thoroughly clean the apartment. That would take her mind off M and M – Marty and little Margaret.

Chapter 15

Agent Estimo awoke famished. He'd had two successful days in Mindanao and was anxious to get his information and evidence back to Washington. But first he wanted to review the tape Lea had given him, just in case it led him further along in tracking the Arabs. He felt certain that it was the Arabs shown on the tape leaving Port Cotabato, but they could still be headed somewhere in Mindanao. Or they could have left the Philippines entirely. Estimo wanted to know their destination.

Breakfast was as close as his refrigerator. He had stocked up with supplies yesterday and there were a number of choices for breakfast. He decided on waffles. He made coffee and waited for the waffle iron to get hot. It was eight o'clock already. He had slept late after his midnight appointment last evening.

As Estimo finished the last bite of a buttery, syrupy waffle his cell phone rang.

"Estimo here."

"Sorry to bother you, this is Inspector Escaba again."

Estimo rinsed his fingers off. With the phone stuck between his head and shoulder he answered, "You're no bother, I guarantee you. What can I do for you?"

"Well, I have to admit I was curious as to how things went with Alejandro, and I wanted to ask you to please stop by if you plan to leave from Manila."

"I am deeply indebted to you," Estimo assured him, "and I will definitely stop by before I leave. Things went extremely well. I met the guard who made the report and I was given a copy of the tape. I also want you to know how helpful Alejandro was to my investigation."

Escaba hesitated before responding. "Did he ask you to say that?"

"Why do you ask? Regardless, it's true."

"He's been hinting he'd like to work for my office and I've had my eye on him, should I need someone in Mindanao; but I don't particularly like self promoters."

"Then in fairness to you, yes he did ask that I inform you of his worthy contribution to my investigation. But I would have told you anyway, most likely."

"Thanks for the honest answer. See you before you leave. Bye"

"Goodbye, Inspector."

Estimo had purposely not mentioned the second tape that Lea had given him. Both tapes were standard VHS long play formats. He needed to buy a player and a monitor. These items were not included with the apartment. The agency didn't expect its employees to have time to stay home and watch movies.

Estimo placed the breakfast dishes in the sink and headed for the nearest consumer electronics store. He bought a tape player and a 17-inch television. Back at the apartment, he fumbled with the cables, clumsy in his haste to set up the unit to play Lea's tape.

The first few seconds were almost totally black. Then an image appeared at a distance. It was of a man; a heavy-set man talking to another person behind a car. Unlike the previous scenes from the first tape, in which the camera was at a constant distance from the action, this one zoomed in on the subjects. This meant that someone had been watching the action and manually operating the camera. Now Estimo could see the features of the men. The heavy one was definitely Alejandro. He was removing the license plate on a car that looked similar to the vehicle shown at the end of the first tape. Then Alejandro replaced the tag and gestured to the other man, evidently telling him to get in the car and to drive it up the street, back up and drive out the other way.

The man did as he was instructed. The scenario that followed was almost exactly as recorded on the first tape only; the angle was slightly different. Estimo watched as Alejandro replaced the license plate with the original and then tossed the plate captured by the security camera into a nearby trash bin. The camera panned to show the car's nameplate. It was a Buick Regal.

As Estimo watched the film, his mind raced. He was working on a plan. By the time the tape ended he knew what he wanted to do.

"Thank you, Lea." He blew a kiss toward the fading image on the screen.

He placed a call to Inspector Escaba and told him about the second tape and what he had seen. "I was just wondering, could you arrange for Alejandro to come to Manila for a 'job interview' tomorrow?"

"I'm certain that could be arranged simply enough." said Escaba.

"Great, I'll see you tomorrow. How's ten sound?"

"That works for me. Bye." Escaba clicked off.

Estimo ejected the tape, placed it with the other in his briefcase and prepared to leave the apartment.

On the way out of town he headed back to Port Cotabato. He drove along the road in front of the port entrance and found what he was looking for, the trash bin shown in the video. He stopped the car, got out, walked over to the bin, lifted the lid and peered inside. It had been recently emptied. There was absolutely nothing in it. Disappointed, he headed back to his car. As he opened the door, a young girl, about eleven years-old ran up to him. She held a large brown envelope in her hands and offered it to Estimo.

"My mother asked me to give you this."

"Well, thank you. Where's your mommy?"

"She's at work in the building across the street. She sent me over to give you this."

"And what's your mommy's name?"

"Lea. Lea Algunes."

"Please thank her for me and here's a little present for you." Estimo handed the little girl twenty pesos.

"Thank you, Mister." She carefully looked both ways then ran back across the street and disappeared behind the port administration building.

Estimo felt the envelope. It was hard, and just about the right shape for a license plate. He remembered the number, it was camera three, on the corner of the building. He looked for it, found it, smiled and waved in its direction.

He imagined that Lea just might be in the wrong line of work. Agent Algunes had a nice ring to it.

* * * * *

Agent Estimo checked into the Traders Hotel overlooking the bay. The next morning it was a short walk to Inspector Escaba's office located in the heart of Manila's business district. Estimo arrived at Escaba's at ten o'clock, two hours before Alejandro was expected. The two men met in a private screening room. Estimo showed both tapes.

"Well, if that's Alejandro changing the tag – and it appears that it is – and those men are being transported by *Abu Sayyaf,* then Mr. Alejandro is an enemy of the Philippines," said Escaba.

"How much evidence do you need to charge and hold him?"

"Those tapes and the license plate will do for the time being."

"Inspector, he can never know that I supplied the second tape and the plate. If he ever found out, I believe a life would be in danger."

"For one, you haven't told me how you obtained those items; and secondly, it is my belief that Alejandro will confess to any crimes that he may have committed before nightfall. The tapes and plate would only be used should a trial become necessary and I really don't think it will."

"Can you pick up the trail of those men who left in the yacht?"

"I believe Alejandro can and will help us with that question."

Estimo stood to leave. "I'm staying at the Traders Hotel just down the street. Call me there or on my cell. You have the number. Please make copies of the tapes. I'll need the originals to take back to Washington."

"I will. Now follow me, there's a back stairs out of here."

At the bottom of the stairway, Estimo found the door that opened onto the rear of the building. He looked carefully in every direction before leaving. It was imperative that he not be seen, by

104

the soon to be *ex*-Port Cotabato Security Chief, Mr. Felipe Alejandro.

Back in hotel room he ordered room service and waited for the phone to ring. It was noon: time for the Escaba-Alejandro meeting. Oh, to be the proverbial fly on the wall, thought Estimo.

It was almost midnight when the hotel room phone rang. Estimo was in a deep sleep.

"Hello Estimo?"

Estimo recognized Escaba's voice. "Hello."

"He was a good deal less cooperative than I expected, but as of fifteen minutes ago he confessed to helping *Abu Sayyaf* last Tuesday, as well involvement in some other misdeeds. As far as tracking the group transported onto the pleasure craft, I should have that information for you by early tomorrow. Good enough?"

"Good enough, that's terrific. Great work. Can I buy you a drink or something?"

"A stiff drink would go good right now, but I'll take a rain check. Think I'll go home *early* for a change and shock my wife."

"You do that. Thanks again, good buddy."

Estimo hung up, went to the self-service bar, broke the seal, opened it and took out a cold pony bottle of Korbel. He popped the cork and took a big swig. *This one's for you, Inspector Escaba.*

It tasted a great deal better than the imaginary drink he lifted in his car for agent Connelly's health.

* * * * *

Estimo awoke at seven o'clock with a slight hangover. Champagne did that to him. Coffee would fix the head.

The phone rang as he sipped his coffee. "Estimo, here."

"Good morning and good news." said Inspector Escaba.

"You've got my attention, Inspector."

Can you come over? I'd feel better doing this face to face, rather on the phone."

"You bet. Be over in thirty-minutes."

"No hurry, I'm here all morning."

Both men disconnected at the same time. Estimo felt better already. Good news had done the trick. He reached for the clothes and dressed.

Forty-five minutes later Estimo was seated in front of Escaba smiling in anticipation of what he was about to hear.

"First, the good news."

"Does that mean there's bad news too?" Estimo asked. He lost the grin and leaned forward in his chair.

"As for my concern with this issue, no, but you may look at it from a different perspective."

Estimo shifted his weight and cleared his throat. "Okay, enlighten me, please."

"Alejandro confessed that he received a substantial sum for arranging transportation of a group of nine Arabs to an oil tanker anchored just off Port Cotabato. He hired a helmsman, who rented the yacht that you saw in the video. The night watchman, Rickie Carlos, made a report of what he saw before Alejandro could intercept it. So Alejandro staged the fake license plate video to throw us off. The plate had been stolen from a small time drug dealer's car in Zamboanga City over a year ago. It would have led us to a dead end.

"Does Alejandro have suspicions that we already knew about the fake tag?"

"No, he confessed to that without us needing the tape."

"That's a relief." said Estimo as he pretended to wipe his brow.

"The Arabs left from the small town of Kabasalan on Ten Feb. It was there, a week earlier that an *Abu Sayyaf* member, Manny Falstino, was executed. We don't know why or by whom but we have our suspicions. The Arabs arrived in Midsayap two nights before the house fire next to the church. They could have burned down that's still under investigation. My guess is that they did it."

Estimo nodded, "I agree."

"The tanker, the Panamanian registered, "Lilith" left immediately for Jakarta. Now for the bad news: It'll be in port this evening."

"I guess there's no way we can get a lead on them there?"

Escaba raised his shoulders and turned his palms up. "We don't have assets there. How about your people?"

"I'm not sure, but I'll find out quick enough."

Escaba got up from his desk and extended his arm. The two shook hands vigorously and Estimo headed for the door, stopped and turned back. "Is there any way we can return the favor?"

Escaba smiled. "Not now, but someday. I've got your number and you owe me big time."

"Call me anytime. Thanks."

Estimo was now ready to head back to Washington. He felt good. No, he felt great.

There remained one more task before he boarded his plane. He placed a call to Port Cotabato security and asked for Lea Algunes.

"Hello, Lea Algunes."

"Hi, this is Estimo. Just wanted to tell you before you see it on the news."

"Oh! What?"

"A certain perpetual, condescending fat prick won't be in work today or any day soon."

Lea's voice sounded apprehensive but upbeat. "Oh, Really? How come?"

"Because he's in the slammer and for a long, long time. Most importantly he has no idea how we uncovered his clandestine ways. Rest easy. You took a big risk and I thank you."

"You're welcome, but I'm not sure I agree with your opening statement."

"How's that?"

"Well, with quite a lengthy jail stay, he could learn to be somewhat less condescending."

"I suppose."

"And he could slim down some."

"Yes."

"But."

In unison they said, "But … he'll … always … be … a … prick." Both laughed heartily and hung up after a promise to stay in touch.

Estimo's next call was to Langley. He asked about assets in Jakarta.

Chapter 16

The pounding from the engine room reverberated from the starboard to port bulkheads and back. The vibration passed through Maliq's body as he lay in his hammock. The throbbing was felt as much as it was heard. Maliq's head constantly ached. He squeezed his eyes shut and pulled a cover over his head. His stomach swayed with the rolling ship, keeping him in a constant state of nausea. His stomach was empty, so he knew puking would be a bad idea. He fought the urge. For three days and nights Maliq and his men had endured the torture of the rocking sea..

A few of the men suffered less but most were worse. Their accommodations aboard the Panamanian-registered Greek tanker "Lilith" was not what Maliq had expected, but there was no recourse. Only Captain Dimetri, his first mate, and one crewmember, Petros, knew that the Arabs were on board. The captain had visited only once since they left port. He had told them to stay in their quarters at all times. At midnight they were allowed to exercise on the deck for one hour. Petros, who only spoke Greek, dropped off their food and water and left without conversation.

Maliq stared at the illuminated face of his watch from under his covers. When the digits showed 11:59 he rolled out of his hammock, stood uneasily and staggered toward the ladder leading up to the deck. His team followed him one by one. All were silent. The brisk breeze carried the fresh salt spray into their faces. Maliq breathed deeply and sighed aloud. The sea was rolling, but the sky was clear. Maliq looked to the heavens where it seemed that every star in the universe was visible. He remembered his father taking him for a ride on just such a clear moonless night.

With much difficulty, he lit a cigarette with matches. He wondered again, *where did I leave my lighter?* He inhaled and held the smoke longer than usual, then exhaled, coughing softly. The air and cigarette revived him. He walked over to Amir who had just finished heaving over the fantail. "Worse than a first camel ride, Amir?"

"Wouldn't know, never been on one," he said as he wiped his chin.

Maliq laughed, "I'm ashamed to admit it, but neither have I. This part of the trip will be over soon enough. I promise we'll fly, drive or walk the rest of the way. No more ships." He patted Amir on the back. There was no formal chain of command after Abdul, who was second. But if anything happened to both of them, Maliq had no doubt that Amir would take over. "Did I ever tell you how I first met Osama?"

"No." Amir steadied himself against the rail then sank to his haunches.

Maliq sat on the deck beside him. "It was January 17 of ninety-one. It was the day the Americans started to bomb Baghdad. I was fourteen. My father and I drove south from Riyadh around eleven that night. We were on our way to Sulamaniyah to visit his mother who was ill. The road was practically deserted at that hour. Twenty miles out there was a roadblock. It was a little unusual so close to Riyadh, but since the Americans were ready to cross into Iraq, my father didn't think much of it. It was manned by the military, not the local police. Two guards asked to see his identification. Then they asked him to get out of the vehicle. They took his ID and instructed him to follow them to a command trailer. I was told to wait in the car."

Maliq stood, stretched and sat back down. "After they took my father into the trailer another guard got in the car with me. He taped my mouth shut, tied my hands behind me and placed a hood over my head." Maliq imitated placing a hood over his head. That is why I hated it so much when Reyes' men blindfolded me."

Amir looked over at Maliq and shook his head understandingly.

Maliq continued. "Next I heard a guard in the trailer shout, 'You're lying! Tell me where he is or we'll kill your son.' My father must have said something back but I couldn't hear him. Then the guard yelled, 'Tell me where you are to pick up Osama, or else.'"

The ship shuddered as a huge wave passed and the props broke the surface for a moment. Maliq stopped talking until the *Lilith* steadied.

"I had never heard Osama's name before that. Then there was a commotion beside me. A stranger took off the hood. He untied me, motioned for me to remain silent and removed the tape from my mouth. I was scared and feared I was about to meet Allah.

"You scared? I don't believe it," said Amir.

Maliq ignored the compliment. "The guard who bound me was face down on the side of the road. His head lay in a pool of blood that had spilled from his neck. I heard a gunshot from inside the trailer. The man who untied me, and two of his companions, ran to the trailer just as the two guards came out. My rescuers shot and killed them both. The tall one who appeared to be the leader went in the trailer, came out, walked over to me and told me that my father had been killed. He informed me it would be best if I didn't look, but he said that I could if I must. He said that it was dangerous for me to remain in Riyadh and that I should go with him. I looked in the trailer. My father was dead." Maliq sighed deeply.

"With no family left in Riyadh, I went with the stranger. Three months later I was in Afghanistan where Osama invited me to join his family. I have never left his side until this mission."

His story finished, Maliq got up and joined the rest of the men walking about the deck for exercise.

Amir had many questions but sensed that this was not the time to ask them. Later he might find out whether or not Maliq's father had been on his way to pick up Osama.

Right now he had to throw up again.

Chapter 17
Tucson, Arizona

Roger was having a bad day, a really bad day. It had started when his electric toothbrush failed to oscillate and it went downhill from there. A mild stomach virus developed into a fairly severe case of diarrhea. At the office he was assigned a new cubicle. Located smack in the middle of the newsroom next to the copy machine, it was the space given the lowest ranking member of the department, usually a student trainee. In addition, his mentor and department head, Len Stein, who had convinced Roger to transfer from sports to main news had resigned. John Burns, Stein's replacement was universally detested by most who had ever worked for him. In less than five hours Roger would add his name to that list. The rumor mill alleged that Burns had ordered Roger's desk to be moved.

Roger had reported back to work at the *Arizona Star* four days earlier on Monday. He had returned to the States the previous week and spent the days since getting acclimated to the nine-hour time differential. He also made a serious attempt to recover from the trauma that had usurped his dream vacation in Kuala Lumpur.

His first assignment was to investigate the recent shootings in Organ Pipe National Monument. He was getting nowhere. The Border Patrol Information Office was not answering questions and the agent, Margarita Lopez, who was injured during the action had hung up on him when he called. This was brand-new territory, and he didn't know where to turn next. During his sports reporting days the coaches and players lined up after each game, anxious for an interview. If on occasion they went into hiding after a loss, the U of Arizona's sports information officer would track down the missing coach or jock. Roger almost always produced a piece with an unanticipated angle filled with insider quotes.

Just when he thought things couldn't get any worse, his phone rang. "Roger Lacson, sports – ah, news desk."

"Mr. Lacson, this is FBI agent Norcross. I need to talk with you today. Can you meet me for lunch?"

"Maybe. What's this about?"

"Mr. Lacson, you don't ask me questions, I ask you questions. Understand?"

"Yeah, I do. Sure you're not CIA?

Norcross ignored Roger's rhetorical question. "Be at the Lite Bite, corner of River and First at noon, or I'll arrange for an evening's diversion you won't forget in a hurry. *Comprende?*

Roger shook his head in disbelief. "You're really not going to tell me what this is about?"

"Mr. Lacson!"

"Don't get angry if I show up with my lawyer." Roger's tone was light-hearted.

"Too late, I'm already angry. Show up alone or else don't bother; and don't tell anyone about this meeting." Norcross stressed the word "anyone." The line went dead.

After what Roger had been through in Kuala Lumpur, an interview with an FBI agent was nothing to get worked up about. It just added to the day's frustrations. He wondered if Border Patrol agent Lopez informed the FBI that had he called. If so, he'd make a mental note that she didn't play by the rules, as he had already promised not to bother her again. Roger glanced at his U of A license plate clock. It showed 11:25. Since it was, he figured, about a twenty-minute ride from his office to the Lite Bite, he decided to leave immediately.

Roger's new boss saw him as he walked by his office and motioned for him to come in and be seated. "Hey, Roger Dodger, how's the Organ Pipe story coming?" I'd like it for next Sunday's edition. That means on my desk Thursday, noon." said Burns.

Roger ignored the gestured invitation to enter Burns' office. He stood just outside the doorway. He grimaced and ran his hand through his hair. "It's tough getting people to talk. All they say is: 'It's an on-going investigation' and 'no comment.'" He talked in a low gravelly voice, imitating a recalcitrant information officer.

"Hey, if you can't hack it, I'll give the assignment to Laura."

"I'm not ready to give up yet."

"Okay, good buddy, but don't let me down. I'd hate for you to miss your first deadline. Wouldn't look good on your quarterly performance review."

"I hear ya, gotta go."

"Where you headed?"

"Got a luncheon with a source."

Burns grinned sarcastic and spoke loud enough for those outside his office to hear, "A 'source,' wow. The kid knows the jargon, now if only he can write. Good hunting, Wildcat." Burns cackled at his own play on words as he knew Roger had been the beat writer for the Arizona Wildcats basketball team for the past four years.

Roger hurried out of the building and became mildly apprehensive about the time. He walked at a brisk pace to the parking garage eight blocks away.

The parking lot attendant greeted him. "Hi, Mr. Lacson, got any extra tickets for the Southern Cal game?" Roger slowed, but kept moving.

"No, Bobby, and I won't be getting extra tickets anymore."

"Darn, how come, Mr. Lacson?"

"Bobby, I'm late, gotta run. I'll explain later," Roger replied over his shoulder. He took the stairs two at a time instead of waiting for the elevator. It reminded him of his frightful trip up the stairs to the CIA apartment in Kuala Lumpur. Roger pushed away the anxiety the memory brought. He charged up past the fourth level and had to walk down the ramp to his car on 3A. Slightly out of breath, he stopped behind his white Ford Ranger, placed his hand in his right coat pocket and froze.

He'd forgotten his keys.

He closed his eyes tightly and produced a vivid mental picture of them dangling on the miniature basketball hoop right on top of his desk.

Roger turned and raced down the ramp. He saw the puzzled look on the attendant's face as he sped by the exit gate like a four-minute miler. He only slowed when he hit the intersections where six of the eight lights turned red and he had to stop and wait. Once back in his office building he had to make a time-consuming but necessary stop in the men's room. He reached his desk and grabbed his keys just in time to see the big hand completely cover the little one on his desk clock.

He turned to speed out again and bumped hard into his boss. The run had produced a sweaty brow and easily overcame his deodorant.

"Pardon me!" said Roger.

"Where's the fire? asked Burns. "You smell and look like shit." He pretended to hold his nose.

"Excuse me John. I'm late for an appointment." Roger attempted to walk around his boss.

Burns physically held Roger back. "Well then you'll just have to be late. Come into my office. I want an update on Organ Pipe right now."

Burns had dropped his hold but nevertheless, Roger brushed off the places where he had been touched for effect. "No can do. This is a very important interview."

"Sorry Roger, I come first. My office, let's go!" Burns' voice exploded across the room and his face became flushed.

"John, I can't." Roger saw that nearly the entire newsroom was now standing to watch the showdown. He leaned toward his boss, gently touched his shoulder and offered softly, just above a whisper, "I'm late for a meeting with the FBI."

Burns now played to the audience he had attracted. He swung around and roared, "'F' the FBI – in my office, now!"

The blood drained from Roger's face and he followed his boss across the room. The reporters blocking their path parted like a chorus line making way for the star hoofer as Burns passed. Roger saw sympathy and fear on their faces. Burns waited by his office door for Roger, who trailed behind with his head down. Once inside the office, Burns slammed the door shut. It bounced back open. He slammed it again, harder still. It stayed shut.

* * * * *

At one-thirty there was a gentle knock on Burns' door. Not waiting for a reply, Emily, his administrative assistant, opened it and stuck her head inside. "Mr. Burns, excuse me, but there's a gentleman here to see Mr. Lacson. He says it's urgent."

Roger stiffened in his chair.

"Show him in," said Burns.

A behemoth deputy sheriff stepped from behind Emily. "Roger Lacson?"

"Yes." Roger stood. He had to look up at the speaker, whose high-pitched voice belied his size. Roger knew this was going to end badly.

"I have a warrant for your arrest. You have the right to remain silent and, ..." the officer delivered the Miranda Rights in a steady monotone.

A crowd gathered around John Burns' office doorway.

"Place your hands behind your back, please." The deputy was being overly polite. He must have known that this was a nuisance arrest but he had to follow orders. Roger did as instructed. He was cuffed.

John Burns stood up behind his desk with his mouth ajar. For the first time in many a year he was silenced. Roger was led out of the office, and the crowded dispersed. The room fell quiet as the reporters went back to their desks. Only the ringing phones interrupted the silence.

Burns broke the morbid atmosphere. "Need a volunteer to cover the story on the arrest of 'Roger, the *ex*-Reporter.'" A few chuckled but most looked away. Those who knew Roger were shocked and concerned for him. Barely audibly, Burns said, "Chicken shits," closed his door and placed a call to the managing editor.

Roger was taken to an awaiting sheriff's car parked right in front of *The Star's* main entrance. The deputy opened the rear car door and helped Roger slide inside the caged compartment. The huge man somehow squeezed behind the wheel and drove Roger to the Pima County jail. It was a short ten minutes trip.

Roger asked the same questions over and over to everyone who was involved with his processing. "What's the charge? Why was I arrested? When can I call my attorney?"

Nobody answered him. He was placed in a holding cell. It was big enough for ten people. Roger was the lone occupant so it seemed immense. It was just a little too early for company but they would come in droves in a little while. It was Friday. When twenty shit-faced drunks arrived the place would shrink perceptibly; which it did before midnight.

Roger recalled how upset he had been this morning over a broken toothbrush. He couldn't wait for midnight, so that this day would finally, finally come to a close. At the moment, this was without a doubt the third most miserable day in his young life. The first two both took place in Kuala Lumpur, another place, like this cell, that he planned never to visit ever again.

Roger looked bad, and felt miserable. His face was dirty, sweaty and showed a one-day growth of his dark beard. His hair stood straight up where he had run his hand nervously through it all night. His shirttail hung out in back and his suit coat looked as though he had slept in it; which, of course he hadn't, because he didn't sleep. Sitting up all night in the county jail he appeared the essence of a homeless vagabond. Actually, he hadn't sat all night. He'd stood part of it, as far away from his cellmates as possible. At seven in the morning a guard approached the cell and yelled for Lacson.

"Here," Roger said weakly, and raised his hand.

The guard noisily unlocked the door and pulled it open. Roger stepped over one body sleeping right in front of the doorway and hopped out. Most of those who had awoken looked annoyed at the disturbance.

The guard took him to a communal bathroom where he was allowed to shower unsupervised. He wanted to brush his teeth and change clothes but he couldn't do either. At least he felt a little better after the shower. When he finished he had to go looking for the guard to ask him where to go next. The guard was drinking coffee at a desk just beyond a second locked hall door.

"This way, Lacson." The guard opened the door and steered him to a windowless office. *Oh no,* he thought, *not another interrogation room.* This one didn't have a one-way mirror, but it made him think of Kuala Lumpur again. That uneasy feeling resurfaced.

After a thirty-minute wait on a hard chair, the door opened. The FBI agent stood in the doorway and introduced himself, "Morning, I'm agent Norcross. Hope you slept well." said Norcross. A tight smile told Roger that agent Norcross enjoyed this kind of mental torment, so he decided to be sarcastic but not stupid. Roger was now painfully aware that agent Norcross could have someone thrown in the clinker without much cause.

"My pillow was a little hard, but I slept okay."

"Funny, you look as though you haven't been to bed in weeks." Norcross eased into the chair across from Roger. There was no way Roger was going to act cordial. He slumped in his chair and looked away from the agent.

"I was joking about bringing my lawyer to the meeting yesterday but I want to see him now, before we even begin to have a substantive conversation."

"Not even if I get you out of here, take you home to change and buy you breakfast somewhere?"

Roger turned his attention back to Norcross and stood. "Let's go." The agent had offered just the right incentive.

Norcross led Roger out of the jail and handed him a paper bag with his personal effects. He drove Roger straight home as promised. Neither said a word during the ride. Roger didn't bother to suggest the quickest directions to his place. Not surprisingly, agent Norcross drove nearly the shortest, most direct route to his two-story condo located on the Tucson National Golf Course.

Agent Norcross waited in the car while Roger went inside his apartment. There he brushed his teeth with the still-broken electric brush, took another shower, and changed his clothes. At the moment all he wanted to do was to hit the sack, but a deal was a deal. He returned to the waiting agent.

"Where's a good nearby place for breakfast? asked Norcross.

"The club house; but I'm not hungry, just tired. Can't we talk right here?

"Sure, I was just keeping my end of the bargain."

Roger and agent Norcross strolled across the edge of a nearby fairway and sat far apart on a metal bench.

117

"Mr. Lacson, you have pissed me off like no other of recent memory. Number one, you deliberately missed our lunch date, and two, you told the entire Tucson press corps about our meeting after I emphasized that you keep it quiet. In addition, it has come to my attention that you tried to contact Margarita Lopez about the Organ Pipe shootings. And lastly, I needed to talk to you about your Kuala Lumpur escapades. I was to report back to D.C. on that matter yesterday."

"Let me explain."

Ignoring Rogers' plea, Norcross continued. "So you see, a night in jail was mild compared to what I have planned for you should you piss me off again, just one more fucking time. Understand?"

"Yes, and I see why you might be a little upset; but I can explain."

"Let's hear it, Lacson."

Roger had been listening to agent Norcross with his head down, supported by both arms, and he tried his best not to close his eyes or appear uninterested. Now he straightened up, shifted his position so that he faced the agent and related everything that had happened since the call from Norcross yesterday. He told him about forgetting his keys, the attack of diarrhea, and his demanding new boss who insisted on an impromptu meeting. He had called Ms. Lopez only once, he told Norcross wearily, and he'd promised not to call again after she informed him that she could not, nor would not discuss an ongoing investigation. As far as Kuala Lumpur was concerned, he had spoken to no one, not even his parents or his best friend about his "adventures" there. He shot Norcross a measuring glance. "And, unless someone at CIA directs otherwise, I won't be discussing KL with you either," Roger ended, more defiantly than he felt.

Norcross already knew everything that Roger had to tell him, but testing him was part of the process. Satisfied, agent Norcross stood effectively terminating the meeting. Roger got up as well. He concluded with an oath. "Everything I told you is the absolute truth. So help me God."

Appeased for the moment, Norcross stared down on Roger. "I'll be watching you, so keep your ass out of trouble and your mouth shut about Kuala Lumpur, or else. You only got a glimpse how much pain I can inflict when needed. *Comprende?"*

"I understand perfectly and I have no intention of causing you any more concern."

Norcross walked away without offering his hand or a verbal farewell. Roger's eyes followed the agent until his car disappeared around the bend. He tiredly staggered back to his condo, flopped fully clothed onto the sofa, and immediately became blissfully comatose. He dreamed about Nicki. He could see her angelic face vividly. He could smell her perfume. He could feel the warmth of her magnificent body next to his. It was a good sleep, a very good sleep.

Roger didn't care if he ever woke again.

Chapter 18

At the same time that CIA agent Rogelio Estimo was winging his way over the Pacific from Manila toward North America, Maliq and his men were flying in the opposite direction. The Arabs traveled to South America in groups of three on three consecutive days, on different airlines. One member from each group ostensibly traveled alone. The others flew as a party of two. The Saudi nationals carried forged Syrian, Moroccan and Egyptian passports. The pairs always had matching passports, while the third traveled on a passport from a different country.

Freshly minted Mexican passports were hidden in their carry-on luggage. Their air travel was convoluted, but it avoided a stopover in the United States. The Arabs had to fly from Jakarta to Paris via a quick stopover in Singapore, then flew nonstop direct to Paris. Maliq was in the last group, but spent an extra day in Paris. There he met with an al-Qaeda operative before proceeding on to Bogotá, Colombia, where the others had already arrived.

Tucson, Arizona

Carlin arrived in Tucson at exactly 4:30 Tuesday afternoon. He took an awaiting limo service home from Phoenix. Dora was waiting at the front door when the limo pulled up. He grabbed his bags out of the trunk, tipped the driver and walked over to his wife.

She opened the door for him and kissed him on the cheek as he entered the house.

"Good to be home." Carlin dropped his bags and asked, "How about a hug for the poor sweet baby?"

"Absolutely." This was a household ritual when either one was feeing low. Dora hugged Carlin with a pat on the back and repeated, "Poor sweet baby," three times as required. She broke the embrace. "Now how'd you like a nice home cooked meal, poolside?"

"Sounds delightful."

Carlin freshened up and joined his wife out back where she was mixing a salad. Dora already knew the details of the accident that a Chevy pickup truck with a drunk driver at the wheel had pulled in front of the Baltimore cinder truck and slammed into the rear of Carlin's car and sent him careening into the gas station. The resultant fire and Carlin's rescue by the city workers had become front-page news in the *Baltimore Sun.* A three-column picture had shown two city employees wearing "Baltimore Hero" metals around their necks, beaming as they stood alongside mayor Tibias Brown at Carlin's hospital bedside. The photo also caught a portion of Carlin's college buddy Jack Adams in the background.

"Turn your head. Let me see, scar face."

Showing his wounded side Carlin replied. "It's fine."

Carlin's face was almost healed, although numerous tiny soft-red blotches covered his left cheek. It looked like a case of chicken pox winding down. The cut on his arm was minor.

"My neck and back feel worse than my face but the doctor said that there'll shouldn't be lingering problems. I just need a little more time to get past the pain stage."

Before she took the first bite of the fresh grilled salmon that she had prepared for Carlin's homecoming meal, Dora lifted her wine glass and tilted it toward her husband. "Welcome home, double-o-seven, glad you've returned in one, albeit broken piece. Now, tell me about the meeting with George."

"He asked for you and sends his best."

"Thank him and return my regards. Is there anything at all that you can tell me? I still remember the rules: no 'not for publication' information."

"Well then, there really isn't much to report." Carlin took a sip of his cabernet. He put his glass down and glanced over at Dora. "I asked him to look into the border incident that involved Maggie, and I asked him to review our current immigration policies. I told him we either had to have help in Arizona to enforce these policies or he might consider new legislation that could be enforced."

"What did he say?"

"He said he would do all that I asked and agreed that we should keep everything real, real quiet. We're using Jack Adams as a go-between."

Dora's head bobbed. "I thought that was Jack in the newspaper photo."

"It was. We were both happy that only part of him was visible."

"I guess you want to see Maggie tonight." Dora continued eating.

"No. Not tonight. I'm tired. I'll catch up with her tomorrow."

After dinner Carlin cleared the dishes and cleaned up the patio while Dora finished up in the kitchen. The phone rang while Carlin was in the shower.

"Carlin, phone's for you." Dora hollered through the bathroom door. "It's Maggie."

"Tell her I'll call and see her tomorrow."

"She says it urgent."

The water stopped running in the shower. Dora stood by the door and handed the phone to Carlin when it opened. Dripping wet and standing with just a towel around his waist, he thanked her and grabbed the phone with a soapy hand.

"I don't know if I like the idea of my husband talking to another woman dressed only in a towel," said Dora. Carlin held his hand over the mic end of the phone. Dora's voice was playful and her smile big, which told Carlin that she was joking. He was reassured. The last thing he wanted was for Dora to become jealous of Maggie, as he planned to be in Maggie's company a good deal over the next few months. He sincerely wanted for them to get acquainted. He felt certain that they would become good friends. For one thing, they both shared a pretty good sense of humor.

"Hi," said Carlin.

"Carlin, sorry to disturb you. I'm in a jam. Didn't know who to call. Dad's too old. He'd never find me. Can't call another BP'er 'cause I'd get him in trouble." Maggie was talking at warp speed.

"Slow down, please." Carlin's voice was calm, although his concern was evident. "Give me the nature of the jam in a sentence so I can breathe."

"I'm stuck in the desert. My Toyota is hub deep in sand."

"Thanks. That doesn't sound so critical."

"Well it is. I'm supposed to be home on medical leave and I'm out in the boonies where the bad guys wander most nights. I gotta get out of here before I'm discovered by the Border Patrol or the bad guys."

"Okay, tell me where you are and how to get there."

Maggie explained rapidly. She was back in Organ Pipe near the spot where she and Marty had been attacked by the Mexican military. She went into great detail on how to locate her position. Carlin told Dora what had happened, advised her not to wait up, and took her four-wheel drive Explorer for the trip. Maggie had said that it would take him over two hours to reach her. Some of the dirt roads were pretty bad once one left the Interstate.

Maggie wasn't kidding. The road became a rutted, boulder-strewn trail. Carlin wondered how Maggie got as far as she did in her little Toyota. He stopped as soon as he saw a car up ahead. He flicked his lights off and on three times as they had arranged. Maggie appeared from behind her car and waved. Carlin got out to take a closer look at her situation.

"Sir Galahad, glad you could stop by on such short notice."

Carlin stretched his sore limbs. "Not feeling exactly knightly at the moment."

"Well, thanks for coming. How are you? How do you feel?"

"I'm okay. Let's see what we've got here." Carlin was not in the best of moods and went right to the task at hand. He walked to the rear of Maggie's car, to view the most serious problem. He pointed his flashlight at the left rear tire. It was buried almost to the axle. "Half buried," he mumbled to himself.

"Pardon?" said Maggie.

"Nothing. I can't get behind your car to push you out but I have a chain to pull you. First, though, I want to shovel some of the sand away in front of both left tires."

Twenty minutes later, with the shoveling finished, Carlin backed his car to a spot where he could turn around. He then backed up to Maggie's car, attached the chain under the Toyota's front axle and hooked it around his tow bar.

He called to Maggie. "Put it in neutral, release the brake if it's on, and try to push from the rear as I go forward. Stay away from the front of your car in case the chain breaks. Ready?"

Maggie went behind her car and yelled, "Go."

Carlin put the Explorer in low-low and inched forward. Maggie's Toyota rocked forward but it wouldn't clear the hole she had dug trying to get out under her own power.

Both were looking at the stuck car when they heard another engine and saw headlights. Carlin thought about turning off his lights, but there was only one way for the new arrival to go and he or she would have to stop behind Maggie's car, as there was no way pass on either side. "Let's hope it's the good guys," said Carlin.

Maggie held her breath and stared into the oncoming headlights. A truck stopped just behind her car. It was a white Ford Ranger. Out jumped a short man dressed in desert camouflage fatigues and combat boots.

He wore an Arizona Wildcat baseball cap.

Chapter 19

The short "warrior," strode over to Maggie and Carlin. "Any clue how to get back to civilization? I've been bumping around these rocky trails for over an hour now."

Maggie released the air she had been holding with an audible blow. "You bet, if you help me get unstuck." She pointed to the rear of her immobilized vehicle.

The man looked first at the stuck Toyota and then at Carlin leaning against his Explorer. He followed Maggie as she led him to the rear of her car. Carlin trailed behind and aimed his flashlight on the problem. Together they stared at the half-buried rear wheel in silence. The stranger nodded and stuck his hand out. "Evening folks, I'm Roger Lacson."

"Hi, I'm Maggie Lopez and this is Carlin, Carlin Ward."

Roger wondered if could he could ever be so lucky after all the negative crap that had been passing his way recently. He'd recognized her name immediately though he didn't think that his own name caught-on with her. Carlin reached over and offered his hand. "Welcome. Glad you happened along. We could use a little more muscle."

Roger curled both arms up in a mock bodybuilder pose.

With Carlin in his Explorer pulling, Maggie behind the wheel and Roger's truck pushing from behind, Maggie's Toyota easily broke free from the desert's grip.

Roger's four-wheel drive truck effortlessly plowed through the deep rut left by Maggie's car and Carlin's digging. With all three cars safely back on firm ground, Roger and Carlin stopped their vehicles and walked over to Maggie. She opened her door and stepped out to join them. Maggie smiled at both men gratefully. "I can't thank you guys enough. It might not seem like fair payment, but I'd love to buy you two a drink somewhere. Where do you live, Roger?"

"I live in Tucson," he told her. "I have a condo at the Tucson National."

"Wonderful. I live two blocks away, Old Adobe Apartments, and Carlin's just a few miles north." Maggie looked at them inquiringly. "How about stopping at the Rusty Horseshoe, Ina and Thornydale for a quick one? Know it?"

Both of her rescuers knew the place and accepted the invitation.

"Carlin, can you find your way out of here, or do you want me to lead? Maggie asked.

"I think I'll be alright. Honk if I miss a turn."

It was near midnight as the three pulled into the bar. The place was almost empty and the wait-help looked as though they wanted to close early. They chose a booth and quickly ordered drinks. Roger and Carlin ordered a beer. Maggie passed on an alcoholic beverage and asked for tonic water with a wedge of lime.

Maggie raised her glass as soon as the drinks arrived. "Well again, thank you guys, I was in a fix." Roger and Carlin acknowledged her toast and all three imbibed.

"May I ask what you were doing out there, this late at night?" Roger wanted to know.

Carlin nodded. "I'd like to know too."

Maggie frowned. "Carlin, you and I can talk later. Roger, I'm with the Border Patrol. I'm on medical leave and I shouldn't have been out there tonight." She paused. "I'd like to leave it at that."

Roger thought it best to tell her now rather than later. "Maggie, you're welcome for the assistance tonight, and thank you for the drink, but there is something I ought to tell you. I'm the reporter from the *Star* who called you a few days ago. So I don't want you to say anything that you may not want to see in the paper."

Maggie recoiled. She stared hard at Roger for a long time. Then she relaxed her posture and shook her head slightly. "Well, I'm at a loss for words, but thanks for telling me. Now, I think I'd better go."

Roger reached out to detain her. He looked straight into her eyes. "If I was a slimy investigative reporter, I would have kept my mouth shut and worked you for a blockbuster story."

Carlin intervened. "He's right Maggie, don't go. He could have kept quiet and played on your gratitude for confidential information. At least finish your drink."

"Yeah, Maggie, finish your drink. And there is one question that you must answer me before you go. I spent a night in jail because of you."

"What? That's crazy." Maggie was startled.

"I told you that I wouldn't call you again, so there was no need to rat on me to the FBI." Roger shivered at the memory. "That dirt bag, agent Norcross threw me in the slammer for the night. Why'd you turn me in?" Roger's expression revealed genuine hurt.

"I didn't call him!" Maggie was vehement. "I thought about it, but I swear I didn't call and tell him."

"Roger—did you say agent Norcross?" Carlin looked puzzled.

"Yeah, FBI agent Norcross, tall, good-looking, black dude."

"Son of a bitch. That piece-of-shit threw me in the pokey too, just for talking to Maggie," Carlin told him.

"You're kidding?" Roger's eyes widened and he shook his head in disbelief. "Somebody should throw him in a slammer for a night and see how he likes it."

"I'm working on it." said Carlin.

Maggie's voice softened. "Roger, I'm sorry. But believe me, I had nothing to do with your arrest or Carlin's." Carlin thinks he's bugged my phones. I wasn't sure before but now I think he's right."

Carlin lifted his left index finger in a gesture of certainty. "I know I'm right, Maggie."

Maggie turned to Roger. "Look, Roger, I apologize for being so abrupt, but I'm under a lot of stress. I can't talk about the Organ Pipe shooting, but you asked if we could talk about border problems

127

in general. I think I can help you out there, if you protect me as a source, no matter what, so help you God." Maggie stood and offered her hand to Roger.

Roger stood, took her hand and shook it firmly. "I promise, so help me God." His mind wandered back to a small "conference room" in Kuala Lumpur where he had offered another oath, just a few weeks ago.

Maggie pushed in her chair. "Good night, gentleman. Thanks again. Roger, don't call my house. I'll call you tomorrow at the paper from a pay phone. I'm afraid to even use my cell now. Carlin, when will I hear from you?"

Carlin rested a finger against his temple and thought for a moment. "Let's meet right here for lunch tomorrow."

"Noon tomorrow, here. Good idea. No phone calls. This place serves a mean veggie burger."

Carlin frowned. Maggie flashed a smile, waved to both, and stepped away from the table. She walked unhurriedly toward the door, stopped to exchange words with a couple sitting at the bar, then left the room.

Roger sat back down. He and Carlin watched Maggie go, they looked at each other. Roger's face relaxed into a wide grin. Carlin's smile was nearly as big. Roger looked as though he was about to burst with suppressed amusement. They pointed at each other. Carlin spoke. "Norcross put you in the County jail?" Roger laughed–a big full-body shaking laugh. Carlin put his head back and roared.

"You ... you ... too!" Roger managed to say, almost choking on the words.

It took them a good while to stop laughing.

"Waiter, another round for us jailbirds," yelled Carlin across the room when he could finally talk. Roger had tears in his eyes. He hadn't felt this jovial since the day before he landed in Kuala Lumpur.

Carlin liked Roger and he could tell that the feeling was mutual.

The two men finished their second drinks and stood up to leave. They promised to get together again soon. "Say, do you like college basketball? I think I can still get some tickets to the Wildcats." said Roger.

"Are you kidding? I was born in Philly. Need I say more? I'd love to catch a game. You know Arizona and Temple could meet in the Finals this year."

"I think you're right about that."

"Just name the day."

"I'll work on it." Give me your number." Roger jotted Carlin's number on his notepad.

Carlin thought about their common interests, both loved basketball, both had a score to settle with FBI agent Norcross, and both were pursuing Maggie, albeit for different purposes.

Chapter 20

Maggie and Carlin both pulled into the Rusty Horseshoe parking lot at noon and headed for the same vacant spot. Carlin conceded the space. Maggie rolled down her window and yelled. "Thank you, Sir Galahad." Carlin smiled, nodded and looked for another place to park. After a good night's sleep he was feeling much better than he had last evening. Maggie waited for him on the top step of the restaurant. When Carlin reached her, she stood on her toes and gave him a kiss on both cheeks. "Carlin, you really are my knight in shining armor. Thanks for everything."

Surprised by the reception, he touched his cheek where she'd planted one of the kisses. "Sorry, I was a bit grouchy last night."

"I didn't notice." She slipped her arm through his as they walked.

The "Shoe," as it was called by the locals looked completely different in daylight. Room dividers separated the bar from the rest of the restaurant. The combination of the wide-open blinds and the overhead lights turned up full, created a bright and inviting, family-friendly eatery. A hostess greeted the "father-daughter" couple and sat them at a window booth. Maggie couldn't hold back any longer. "What do you know about Marty? Is the Guatemalan child okay? Where is she? What did your senator friend have to say? Tell me about your car accident."

"Whoa, slow down. Hold on a country minute here."

"I can't. I couldn't sleep last night thinking about you and everything." The waitress arrived, in time to overhear Maggie's last remark. Judging from her expression, she concluded something other than a father-daughter luncheon. The waitress cleared her throat louder than necessary. "May I get you something to drink?" Reading the waitress' thoughts, Carlin teased, "I'd like a cup of coffee, but don't serve my mistress anything that contains caffeine." Maggie missed the joke and asked for coffee. The waitress sneered, and left. "Mistress?" asked Maggie with her eyebrows raised.

"Forget it."

Light dawned. "Oh, the waitress heard me say I couldn't sleep last night thinking about you…"

Carlin cut her off, "Forget it, bad joke."

The waitress returned with the drinks and took their order.

Carlin sat up and looked straight at Maggie. "About Marty, I have good news and some bad. The good bad news is that he is mending well physically. The bad news is that he has lost his sense of smell and needs speech therapy. He might not ever be able to talk completely normally again."

"Oh no!" Maggie swelled up but managed to hold back her emotions.

The food arrived. Both stopped talking. The waitress evidently noticing that Maggie was holding back tears, scowled at Carlin, and flung his burger down in front of him. He glanced up at the server with a questioning look but focused his attention on Maggie's distress. The waitress left.

"Maggie, look at the bright side. It could have been a lot worse. He could still be in a coma or dead." Carlin took a bite of his charbroiled burger and leaned back. "This is very good."

Maggie ignored his compliment on the food. "I know, but." She stopped, took a deep breath and exhaled. "Will he be able to return to work?"

"That'll be up to the doctors and the Border Patrol. Maggie, I wouldn't get my hopes up too high."

"When can I see him?"

"Be patient. I'll let you know. The FBI wants him first and they've been told to wait."

Maggie pushed her veggie burger around the plate, but had yet to take a bite. "Okay."

Carlin told her what he knew about the Guatemalan child, Margarita Domingo. She had been released from the hospital. Her leg wound completely healed and she was now in the custody of Arizona's Child Protection Services here in Tucson. "I'm trying to clear the way for you to be able to visit her." Carlin said. This news cheered Maggie somewhat. "The child has been told that her parents are both dead. She hadn't talked to anyone since, the last I heard."

Hearing this, Maggie's tears overflowed. She wiped her eyes with her napkin, sniffled, and blew her nose. "Excuse me."

"I'm sorry to have to tell you that, Maggie."

Just then the waitress returned with the check. "Will there be anything else?" she asked. Her tone was not the least pleasant. She eyed the tearful Maggie and threw the check if front of Carlin without waiting for an answer. "You alright, honey? You haven't touched your food." The waitress had recognized her as a regular.

Maggie looked up. "Yes, thanks. I'm alright, allergies."

The waitress glared down at Carlin, shook her head and left. Maggie looked puzzled at the back of the retreating waitress. She was aware of the waitress' belligerent tone but was so deep in thought about Margarita that it didn't register why.

"Margarita's legal status must be determined by May 6th which will be ninety days since her entrance into the U.S.," Carlin continued. "I'd like to see her too. She's the real reason I went to go to the hospital the night I met you." Carlin had to rein in his own emotions as he imagined the loneliness and misery that the child must be feeling.

Maggie recovered a little. She smiled at Carlin. "And what did Senator what's-his-name, have to say?"

Carlin lowered his voice. "Senator 'Mac' said very little, but he's prepared to take action and I'm sure he'll help when the time comes. His staff provided the update I just gave you. Which, promise me, you'll never divulge our sources to another soul?"

"I promise. And your accident?"

"Some drunk hit me during a snow storm. I'm okay. Here's a newspaper story." Carlin handed Maggie a folded, beat-up page from the *Baltimore Sun*. She started to unfold it, but Carlin patted her hand. "Read it later, please. Now it's my turn. What were you doing out in the boonies last night?"

132

Maggie tucked the newspaper article into her pocket. "I was looking for a Mexican military barracks near where Marty and I got bushwhacked."

"Did you find it?"

"Yes. It's five miles west of where you dug me out and two miles south of the border."

"Are you planning a commando raid on the place? If so, I don't want to know."

"I don't have a plan right at the moment, but I'm working on one. What'd you and Roger talk about after I left – jail?"

Carlin nodded, grinning. "Exactly. I like him. Don't be too tough on him; he didn't have to reveal that he was a reporter last night."

"I know, but I'm kind of leery of the press after meeting you, and your cohorts at the hospital."

"Very funny. Did you call him yet?"

"Yeah, we're having dinner tonight. I'll try real hard to be cordial."

Carlin smiled. "Be careful. If Norcross sees you beware. These FBI types like to throw people in jail." He picked up the tab and they walked toward the cashier. Carlin put his arm around Maggie's shoulders and gave her a strong squeeze. She smiled, put both arms around his middle and returned the hug. The hostess-cashier beamed as they approached. She admired a dad who could display such affection toward his daughter in public. Her father wouldn't do that, she thought.

Back in his car Carlin pulled the cell phone off his belt before he started the engine. From past experience he had learned that sometimes it was easier to go from the bottom up than from the top down. He speed dialed information and an eager voice found him the number for the Tucson office of the Arizona Child Protective Services. The happy voice placed the call and wished him a good afternoon.

"CPS, Gloria speaking," answered an even more cheerful speaker. "How may I direct you call?"

"Gloria, my name's Carlin Ward and I don't know who I need to talk with. Can you help me?

"Hold please."

Carlin held.

After a few seconds the receptionists came back on the line. "Sir, Mr. Ward, here's Mrs. Santiago, she'll help you."

"What can I do for you, Mr. Ward?" said a businesslike voice with a slight Spanish accent.

"Mrs. Santiago, please don't ask how I know, but I understand that Margarita Domingo, a seven year-old Guatemalan child is in your care."

Her voice was steady and carefully neutral. "What makes you think so, Mr. Ward?

"I really can't say." Carlin tried to sound regretful.

Sounding just as regretful, Mrs. Santiago told him. "Then I can't help you; good bye."

"Wait, please." Carlin wasn't faking sincerity. "This is important, important for Margarita, not me."

"I'm listening."

"I don't know you, but I've got to take a chance that you'll keep a confidence for the child's sake. First, please tell me your position and whether you'd be able to clear the way for a visit with the child, if and only if, you decide that it may be in the child's best interest."

"I'm a case worker, and I could possibly influence the supervisor to agree to such a request, *if* the child is here, and if I believe that it would be in the child's best interest."

Carlin relaxed a little, slid forward in his seat, placed his free hand behind him on the headrest, and leaned back. "Fair enough. I learned of Margarita's location through an FBI source. I also learned that the child has not spoken since she was told of her parents' death. I would like permission for Maggie Lopez, a Border Patrol agent who saw Margarita in the hospital to visit with her"

She interrupted him. "Hold on Mr. Ward. Nobody was allowed to see Margarita in the hospital."

"So, Margarita *is* in your care."

Mrs. Santiago went quiet.

Having established that Margarita was there, Carlin went on to explain, that Maggie did see Margarita in the hospital, even though an INS agent gave her a hard time. "Maggie's genuinely concerned for the child, as am I, a friend of Maggie's. I have no official capacity but I felt compelled to see if I could help. I know

Maggie would not be so bold as to call you. There you have the whole story." Carlin concluded with a mildly exasperated sigh.

"You're very convincing Mr. Ward. Let me talk with my supervisor. Give me your number. I'll call with an answer within the hour."

He felt satisfied with his effort. If this attempt failed, his Washington contacts would eventually cut through the red tape. He just wanted to speed up the process.

He clamped his seat belt, started the car and began to back out of the parking spot. Through his rear view mirror he spotted Norcross, leaning against a car directly behind him. Carlin could almost smell the holding cell. He wondered if he'd need his lawyer this time. He pulled back into the parking spot and got out of the car as agent Norcross approached. Norcross was smiling, but he looked more playful than sinister today. Carlin hoped against hope that he hadn't been listening to his phone conversation. "Shit! Shit, shit, shit," he mumbled under his breath.

"Afternoon Mr. Ward. Another nice day in paradise! Isn't that how you native Tucsonans greet one another?" Norcross was even smiling more broadly now.

"We do tend to say that a lot here. Yes sir, we do." Carlin smiled back just as widely to indicate that he could be just as sarcastic.

Norcross extended his hand as he approached closer. Carlin moved to the rear of his car and bent over in a feigned search for his license plate before he took the FBI agent's hand. The agent withdrew his hand and waited for Carlin to finish his mock search. Satisfied the plate was there Carlin extended his hand. The agent took it. His expression changed to one of mild disappointment. "You think that I removed your plate that day?" asked Norcross.

"Didn't you? And didn't you remove my registration and insurance card from my glove box before I got into my car? I recall you had a newspaper in your hand. Were my documents stuffed inside?"

Norcross shrugged his shoulders and raised his eyebrows. "I'd love to answer those questions truthfully, but due to a national security issue, I can't. I would like you to believe that."

Carlin frowned, put his hand to his chin, and looked pensively at the agent. Surprisingly, he detected sincerity.

"You just had lunch with Maggie. Now, you two are of legal age but you were warned not to talk about her work related accident."

Carlin thought that it was a strange way to describe what really happened to Marty and Maggie. "Yes."

"Well, as long as you don't talk about her work, then there's no reason for the FBI should interfere with your affair."

"What?"

"I watched from the time you entered the parking lot, Mr. Ward. She kissed you going in and you hugged her coming out. I also spoke with the waitress who served you. She told me Maggie was in tears and overheard her say that she couldn't sleep thinking about you." Lord, I can't figure people sometimes. She's so young and pretty and you're old enough ..." Norcross didn't finish the sentence. He collected himself and looked straight into Carlin's eyes. "Maybe she's just after a sugar daddy, Mr. Ward. Ever think of that?"

Carlin was angry, flattered, and bewildered. He decided to respond as flattered and chuckled. "Mr. Norcross, you can't be serious? Maggie and I have become friends. I really think of her as – you almost said – as my daughter. I knew that waitress had the wrong idea. I even jokingly referred to Maggie as my mistress. I swear, Mr. Norcross, we're just new friends getting to know one another. We have some mutual interests."

"I really don't care. Just remember, don't talk about border business. But, for the record, I believe you. Have a nice day, Mr. Ward." Norcross turned and walked toward his car.

"You too." Carlin said over his shoulder as he reopened his car door and got in. He felt as though he had just dodged a bullet – a very large bullet. He had warned Maggie to look out for Norcross tonight but had neglected to do so himself.

Dumb.

* * * * *

Maggie and Roger had decided to meet at a little Italian restaurant in Oracle, five miles north of Tucson. Maggie had doubts that she could help Roger with his story. She suspected that he really wanted to know about the Organ Pipe shooting.

The "My Way" restaurant was located in a strip mall. Roger arrived early for their 6:30 reservation. He drove around the parking lot three times looking for signs of the FBI. Satisfied at last that they were not present, he pulled into a parking spot far away from the restaurant entrance. He sat at a table away from the window to wait for Maggie. She arrived right on time. "Hi there," she greeted him. "Didn't see your truck outside. Thought I beat you here."

"I'm parked down a way. He smiled and told her how lovely she looked. Roger stood and they touched hands briefly.

"Thanks." Maggie was dressed in a white blouse and black pants. Her outfit was accented with a brightly colored bolero. Roger wore his standard work and play attire, khaki pants with blue long-sleeved shirt, open at the neck. He sat and took a sip of beer as Maggie settled in. The waitress, noticing a new arrival, hurried over and asked Maggie what she would like to drink. She ordered a Bud Light.

"My drink of choice, too," said Roger.

"Beer goes good with pasta but I don't do this often." Taking off her bolero she remarked. "This has been a strange day. I went to my mom's for breakfast, had lunch with Carlin and now dinner with you. I'll be headed for a fat farm if I keep up this routine."

Roger mocked disappointment. "Hope you saved room. The food is fabulous here."

Maggie focused on her date. "Roger, I'm really sorry for last night and the way I talked to you on the phone the other day. I'm not usually that short-tempered."

Roger waved a hand understandingly. "Tell you what, let's wipe the slate clean and start fresh tonight." Maggie agreed, she raised her glass and offered a toast. "To a new beginning."

By the end of dinner Maggie and Roger had covered the highlights of their young lives. Maggie did not mention Organ Pipe and Roger avoided the tragic and confidential parts of his Kuala Lumpur vacation when he told her about his recent trip.

As dessert arrived for Roger, Maggie asked, "What can I tell you that might help you with your border story?"

Roger shifted his weight and looked down at his pie a la mode. "Maggie, I was taken off the Organ Pipe story right after we talked this morning. As of now, I'm looking into the plight of the *Glaucidium Ferruginous*."

"The what?"

"The Mexican Pygmy Owl. It's on the endangered list. The Arizona homebuilders say the environmentalists are nuts. I'm to find out who's right."

"Sounds...interesting." Maggie hoped that she mouthed the word with some conviction.

"Yeah, it's a hot topic in Tucson right now. And Maggie, look out for a *Star* reporter, Laura Jones. She's on the Organ Pipe story now. She's very, very aggressive. She won't scare easily."

"Remember, I have my FBI backup."

"Good. I hope agent Norcross won't go easy on her because she's a female."

Maggie looked pensive. "Roger, if you're off the Organ Pipe story, why didn't you just call off dinner?"

Roger blushed. "I, I felt that I should buy you dinner for the trouble I've caused you."

"No, I should buy you dinner for helping last night."

"Come on, let me treat."

"How about we do Dutch?"

"Please, Maggie. "I'll get it. We can go Dutch next time."

Maggie smiled. She realized that Roger had just asked for a second date.

"Okay, Dutch next time. Do you like McDonalds?"

They both laughed. "Actually, I prefer Burger King," said Roger.

"Burger King is it then."

She had accepted his offer. He was pleased, very pleased. Roger paid the bill and they walked out together. Maggie smiled at Roger. "Thanks, Roger. I really enjoyed it." They shook hands, a little firmer this time, and held on longer than necessary. As Maggie walked to her car she unconsciously hummed "You're the one, I know" from Shakira's new CD. Roger whistled "Moonglow" from the romantic movie "Picnic, starring sexy Kim Novak that he had watched on TV two nights before.

A pygmy owl landed next to its mate in an ironwood tree right above Roger's truck. He didn't even notice.

* * * * *

Maggie's phone was ringing as she entered the apartment. She reached it just in time. "Hello."

Without a greeting the voice on the other end began, "Lunch with a radio reporter, then dinner with a newspaper reporter ... don't you have any friends outside of the news business?"

Maggie recognized the voice immediately. "Good evening Agent Norcross. Nice to hear from you." Maggie was buying time to think.

"That's not the truth, Maggie."

Maggie cleared her throat. "Carlin's not a reporter and I didn't discuss border business with either. Please don't arrest them. I made the appointments."

"I know what was discussed. No more arrests. Just promise to keep quiet about matters concerning national security."

"That's covered by my allegiance to the Border Patrol. Don't worry."

"That's all I ask. Night, Maggie, pleasant dreams."

"Good night."

She hung up and mused, "Pleasant dreams to you too, know it all." She was irritated, but relieved that the threat of jail for Carlin and Roger was off the table. But she worried anyway. If he knew everything that was discussed at lunch, Carlin would probably be behind bars right now. For an instant she thought about calling Carlin to see if he was home but decided against it. She'd know by morning if there were bad news. Right now she was in the mood for a warm bubble bath and the pleasant dreams agent Norcross wished for her.

Chapter 21

Carlin answered his cell phone on the first ring. "Hello."

"Mr. Ward, this is Mrs. Santiago, Arizona Child Protective Services." It had been twenty hours since they last spoke.

"Is this the same, 'I'll be back to you in an hour,' Mrs. Santiago?"

"Sarcasm will get you dial tone real fast, Mr. Ward."

"I'm sorry. It's just that I've been so anxious to hear from you. I apologize." Carlin's tone registered contrition.

"Accepted, it took longer because I had to work on the boss."

"Forgive me, please."

"I did. Let's move on." She sounded briskly professional but not unfriendly. "I'm doing this for Margarita. Can you bring agent Lopez here about four?"

"Yes, of course. I'll call back if she can't make it."

"See you at four, Mr. Ward."

"Thank you. Thanks so much." Carlin was talking to a dead line.

He hit Maggie's speed dial number.

When Maggie heard that the visit with Margarita had been set for that afternoon, her squeal made Carlin move the phone away from his ear. He listened as Maggie apparently jumped up and down. He heard her shout.

"Shit, I knocked over my coffee cup." The phone abruptly disconnected, and Carlin deduced that she must have dropped it. He couldn't have felt more satisfied.

They were both quiet during the drive to Child Protective Services. The office, located on the east side of town, was a forty-minute drive. Secretly, Carlin hoped that he too would be able to visit with the child, but he wouldn't do anything that might jeopardize Maggie's visit. Mrs. Santiago and her supervisor Mrs. Angelina Boca greeted Carlin and Maggie in the building's lobby. Maggie followed Boca's well-tailored form to a private office where Maggie received explicate instructions as to how to conduct herself during the visit. Mrs. Santiago led Carlin to a public waiting room.

After the orientation, Mrs. Boca took Maggie to a communal playroom on the second floor where seven little girls of various ages played games in the center of the room. Margarita sat alone on the floor against a far wall, her eyes fixed solidly on the floor. Boca walked Maggie over to the child and addressed the bent head. "Margarita, someone is here to see you," she said in Spanish. "Do you remember Miss Maggie from the hospital? Margarita slowly looked up. Maggie was startled when she saw the pale, sullen little face that peered up at her. The child's red-rimmed eyes showed unfathomable grief. She had lost weight since her hospital stay. A curious look crossed the small sad face. Her eyes locked onto Maggie's.

Maggie spoke softly. "Hi. I'm Maggie. Remember me? Friends forever?" The child did not move. Tears slowly filled her eyes and dripped down her thin cheeks. Maggie's eyes filled with answering tears.

Maggie stooped down toward the child, but without warning Margarita jumped up and flung herself at her. Maggie staggered backward, but managed to keep her feet. She opened her arms and scooped up the child. Maggie straightened up. Neither spoke. After several minutes, Maggie bent over to set the child down whose weight had started to tax her strength. The grip on Maggie's neck tightened. She slid down to the floor and held the child on her lap.

"Hold me, please. Oh, please, please, please."

Maggie looked up at Angelina Boca. Neither spoke the thoughts that hung in the air between them. These were the first words Margarita had uttered since being told of her parents' death.

Quietly, Mrs. Boca turned away and left the room, allowing Margarita and Maggie to become reacquainted. Boca had believed herself impervious to emotional reunions, but that scene had cracked her normally hardened veneer. Her face relaxed into a muted smile. She felt quite satisfied for bending the rules and taking a chance on Carlin Ward's request. She'd go downstairs and thank him after she regained her composure. Returning to her office, Boca read a newly arrived email message from the CPS state director in Phoenix.

Angelina,

You will be receiving a call from a Mr. Carlin Ward. He will request visits with the Guatemalan child, Margarita Domingo. Mr. Ward may be accompanied by border patrol agent, Margarita Lopez. You are to allow them both unlimited visitation rights *by order of the governor*. Any questions, please call.

E. Barnes

Angelina Boca stared at the message. She leaned forward in her chair, her nose almost touching the computer monitor, and read it again. Who were these people? *By order of the governor*? She had never seen such a request before. Boca called for Mrs. Santiago and shared the message with her. "Have you ever?" said Boca.

"No."

"Go get Mr. Ward and take him to Margarita, please."

Mrs. Santiago left Boca's office and found Carlin where she had left him in the lobby. She smiled at him and beckoned. "You may follow me and join agent Lopez upstairs with Margarita." Carlin wondered at the dramatic change in the caseworker's attitude. Her air of gracious patronage had vanished, replaced by a sudden desire to please. She led Carlin upstairs to join Maggie and Margarita. "You can stay as long as you like and return anytime, Mr. Ward. Of course, agent Lopez can as well." Mrs. Santiago left Carlin at the entrance to the playroom where Maggie and the child were still sitting on the floor. Margarita had released her grip on Maggie's neck and now rested her head on Maggie's breast. Maggie cradled and rocked the seven year-old as she might an infant.

142

Santiago turned back toward her office. "Let me know if you need anything, Mr. Ward," she whispered.

Carlin nodded in her direction but stood motionless in the doorway of the playroom. He watched, not wanting to break the spell. At that moment, time evaporated. The tough, feisty border patrol agent had temporarily vanished. A table lamp missing its shade cast a shadow of Maggie and Margarita on the far wall. The image of Michelangelo's *Virgin and Child* flashed through Carlin's mind. His introduction to Margarita could wait. He backed out of the doorway and returned downstairs.

Chapter 22

Estimo got off the plane at Washington National. He arrived exhausted but mildly upbeat. His boss, Jim Crowley, had suggested that he bring the cigarette lighter, Koran, and list that he had found with him rather than send it ahead by diplomatic courier. Estimo couldn't have planned it better. He'd hand over all of the material and deliver a face-to-face report at CIA Headquarters. He anticipated that the Director himself might even be present, as well as scores of minions.

He took a cab straight to Central Intelligence even though he really wanted to go to one of the many Washington area CIA apartments to take a shower and change. Upon arrival at the CIA Langley complex he was shown straight to Crowley's top floor office. Estimo didn't know his boss all that well.

The head of Southeast Asia Counterintelligence's greeting was businesslike but friendly. Crowley had come around from his desk to greet him. "Let's sit here." Crowley led Estimo to a pair of curved sofas set in front of a low round table. He sat on one and pointed for Estimo to take a seat across from him. "Congratulations, Rogelio. From earlier reports it seems you've had a productive trip to Mindanao."

"Yes sir, thank you."

"We were shocked to learn of Connelly's death. How are you holding up? You two worked together for a good while."

"I'm okay now. It was a hard blow though. May I ask if you have seen Nicki?"

"Yes, she reported two days ago. We've put her on six months administrative leave ... enough time to think over her resignation. Naturally, she blames herself for his death. The after-action report indicated that Connelly's weapon misfired and he had to step in front of Dollah Jaffar in order to save the civilian, Roger Lacson"

"I didn't know that. That makes a big difference."

"Yes, but Nicki doesn't want to see it that way." I've asked her to stay in Washington for a few days in case we need a second interview. Before she heads home why don't you visit her? I'm sure she'd like to see you."

"Of course."

"One last thing before we move on to Mindanao. Did you know that Nicki and Connelly were married?"

"No sir." Everyone at the Embassy knew they were an item ... ah ... together a lot, but I, for one, never suspected that they had married."

"Sorry, I had to ask – for the record – you understand?"

"Yes, sir."

"Okay, now let's head down to the DD's office. He wants to hear this report directly from you."

Estimo made a detailed report of his activities and successes in Mindanao.

Deputy Director Lane joined Estimo at the podium when he had finished. He thanked Estimo and asked everyone to remain seated. He wanted to delegate a few assignments. He turned to Estimo. "I believe Jim wants you back in his office."

"Yes, I do. Please wait for me there, Rogelio."

As Estimo left the room he overheard Lane say, "We lost the Arabs in Jakarta in mid-February, the seventeenth, I believe. Since we still don't have assets there, does anyone have any ideas how we might pick up their trail? And did we learn anything from Jaffar's cell phone?"

Estimo felt that his performance rated five stars for both the fieldwork and his presentation, but the loss of Connelly greatly troubled him and he felt little exhilaration. He thought about Nicki on his way back to Crowley's office. He dreaded the visit with her. After all, it had been his idea to use Roger Lacson as a decoy.

He also wondered why he had been excused from the meeting. He assumed that it was because of the usual departmental bullshit ... Separation of Church and State ... Fieldwork and Analysis.

Stone age rules.

Chapter 23

The fishing village of Las Lisas, Guatemala was as far south and west as it could get without the inhabitants actually residing in El Salvador. Its few hundred residents barely survived on the fish they caught just off the Pacific coast in old, rickety skiffs and with vegetables grown in their communal gardens. Once a month the international organization, Food for the Hungry provided milled cornmeal for tortillas. There was no industry in Las Lisas and more than fifty percent of the male population had departed over the last decade to seek a living elsewhere.

Manuel Sanchez had heard the stories. The stories of how easy it was to travel north to the United States and the good life that awaited anyone adventurous enough to go. He was also in the habit of repeating the stories to anyone who would listen. His best friend, Juan Perez was weary of hearing Manuel's tall tales. "Manuel, why don't you just leave? Go! Go to the United States and stop talking about it." The two men were sitting on overturned fruit baskets outside the *Mercado de Carne*. Like most things in Las Lisas, as Manuel would have been quick to point out, the market belonged to the past. No one remembered how it came by its name, and Manuel couldn't recall a time when one could buy meat there.

"Juan, I want to go but I want you to come with me."

Juan only shook his head. "It's your move."

Juan and Manuel were playing checkers on the red and white oilcloth that covered a small sidewalk table. Its two-inch alternating red and white squares formed a perfect game board. They played here every day but Sunday at five o'clock sharp.

Juan looked at his friend. He studied the board. "Manuel, I'm not going. I know your sister and brother-in-law have gone. Why don't you follow them?"

"I will." Manuel stood up and flailed his arms excitedly. "I will. By God in Heaven, I will sell everything and take the bus to Mexico City where they give you food, money and take you to the border. I have heard the stories."

Juan glanced up. "Did you get a letter from your sister yet?"

"No, I guess they are still not settled." Manuel sat back down, made a triple jump over Juan's pieces, and relaxed his face in a toothy grin.

Manuel had no way of knowing that his sister, Dolores Domingo had died ten days earlier in the Arizona desert of a gunshot wound from a *coyote*. His brother-in-law had lasted another day before he too, succumbed in a Tucson hospital – a victim of the same shootout. Twenty-one hundred miles from Las Lisas his orphaned niece, scared and alone, had been consigned to a temporary foster shelter in Tucson. At this very moment, INS authorities were looking for any one of little Margarita's relatives, an uncle like Manuel Sanchez would do fine.

Mexico City

Manuel Sanchez sat in the back of a flatbed truck. He'd had to pay four hundred pesos or about thirty-five US dollars for the ride from Mexico City to the border near Nogales, Mexico. The bus would have cost more, stopped often and delivered him to one of the major border towns. These towns were to be avoided at all costs, so the stories said. The truck driver delivered plywood from Nogales, Arizona, the twin city across the border from Nogales, Mexico, to a lumberyard in Mexico City. For this task he received no pay, but he was permitted to keep all the money that he collected to take passengers north. He wasn't allowed to take the immigrants any farther than the Mexican border. He was not a smuggler.

There were always more than the twenty the driver could transport waiting around the *Terminal Central de Autobus* station located a few blocks from his lumber delivery stop. The twenty travelers were chosen by a lottery. Manuel had been one of the lucky ones. His wait for transportation north was only two days. Some waited weeks. Others got discouraged and returned home before their number was ever picked.

Manuel was disappointed that the stories about the free transportation from *Cuidad de Mexico* to the U.S. border had proven to be untrue; but a thin elderly man sitting beside him in the bouncing truck had told him that travel from the border all the way to Phoenix would not cost anything. This news eased his anxiety

* * * * *

After the tiring twelve-day and eleven-night trip, Manuel's backside ached more than he would ever had imagined possible. He stood up from the hard truck bed where his seat was softened only by a thin blanket folded into a twelve-inch square. He watched for the first hint of light from the east, and shivered in the cool dawn air as the wind pushed against his upper body. He wrapped the blanket over his head and around his shoulders. The others still slept. He stared at a notch in the far ridgeline where the sun's first beam would soon appear. If he concentrated hard enough on the sunrise the pain might ease. The driver had told the travelers three hours earlier when they had stopped for gas that he expected to arrive at the final destination about sunrise.

That destination was *la ladrillera*, the brickyard. The place wasn't a brickyard anymore but an assembly area two miles south of the tiny Mexican town of El Sasabe. The town was some fifty-miles west of Nogales. *La ladrillera* had only three other resident-travelers when Manuel and his nineteen companions arrived.

The truck driver hit the brakes hard. A huge plume of dust settled onto the back of the truck as it came to an abrupt stop. The riders were thrown forward and then jerked back. Those sleeping were now wide-awake. A fit of coughing broke the morning silence. The driver hustled everyone out including the lucky passenger who

149

had ridden in the front. Manuel was the only passenger who had not rotated into the cab during the course of the journey.

Three rusted car shells, an old bus that hadn't seen the open road in twenty years, and *el Capitan's* shack provided evidence of human activity amid the vast desert expanse. Manuel was struck by the bizarre presence of plastic shopping bags blowing around in the wind. Hundreds of them hung haphazardly from cactus arms, scrub brush and ironwood trees. Piles of trash surrounded the perimeter, clearly marking the boundary of *la ladrillera.* This stopover would be Manuel's last temporary home before travel to the United States, now just a few miles away.

Manuel was nervous as he stepped down from the truck. Each phase of the trip seemed more difficult than the last. He worried about what would happen next. At this moment he was an outcast among outcasts. He was the only non-Mexican. He knew this was the reason that he had not been invited to sit next to the driver during the entire trip from Mexico City. Manuel's Spanish pronunciation was quite different from his fellow travelers. Becoming self-conscious he had not talked much during the journey and had not acquired a single friend. God, how he wished Juan had come along.

Manuel didn't know it but the Mexicans were just as nervous. They stood huddled together near the shack. Like Manuel, they were cold, tired, hungry and thirsty. As the camp organizer, Senor Torres stuck his head out the shack door to greet the new arrivals, a late model, shiny, black Buick Park Avenue pulled alongside the empty lumber truck. More dust swirled around the camp. The driver remained in the car, while a casually but expensively dressed stocky Mexican emerged from the passenger side. He walked over to where the truck driver and Torres were conversing. A few moments later all three men turned and approached Manuel, who was sitting alone on the ground by one of rusted cars. He stood up as they neared. "Manuel, I have wonderful news for you," announced the truck driver. Manuel dusted off his behind and eyed the three men, but said nothing.

"Manuel, this gentleman is Javier," continued the truck driver, patting the man from the Buick on the shoulder, "and he has a job for you."

Javier extended his hand as he reached Manuel. Surprised, Manuel hesitantly extended his arm. Javier clasped Manuel's hand with both of his in a firm, reassuring grip. They were soft and warm to the touch. Javier smiled into Manuel's bewildered face. "This definitely is your lucky day, Manuel. These gentlemen have suggested that I offer you this opportunity out of all the men who will assemble here today. I have a job near here in Nogales that will last for months – a job that will pay you fifteen hundred dollars U.S. That same amount you need for a guide to America, so you'll arrive with plenty of extra cash," said the man from the Buick.

Manuel's jaw dropped. His head jerked involuntarily. The shock was twofold. Firstly, the story *was not true,* the trip from here to America with a guide was not free after all? And secondly, he was apparently now being offered a chance to earn the fee right here in Mexico.

Javier pressed Manuel's hand once more. "The job is manual labor but you're being paid well over the going rate. What do you say?"

Manuel shaken and unsure how to answer the stranger, stared at him dumbly. The truck driver, seeing his perplexity put his arm around Manuel and steered him toward the Buick. He spoke confidentially. "Manuel, this is an unusual and wonderful opportunity for you to earn honest money here in Mexico before you head north. Don't ask questions just take the job, my friend."

Manuel wondered if he could trust the judgment of a man who had never once asked him to sit up front and who, to this point, had barely even spoken to him. He allowed himself to be led over to the Buick, and Javier opened the rear door for him to enter. The smell of the new leather and the gentle flow of warm air from hidden vents overwhelmed his better judgment. He slid onto the seat with encouragement from Javier. Senor Torres handed Manuel his blanket and knapsack. The door shut.

The Buick driver turned and briefly greeted Manuel, who still hadn't found his voice. Javier waved goodbye to the truck driver and Torres and walked around to the other side of the car. He opened the door and flopped his bulk beside Manuel. "*Vamonos por favor, José,*" he said to the man behind the wheel. The Buick was placed in gear and its powerful engine hummed quietly as it eased out of *la ladrillera*. Manuel's fate, it seemed, had been decided for him. He wondered why he had been chosen.

The only other new, black car he had seen before was one la bad omen.

Strange, thought Manuel, *a luxurious car ride had never been mentioned in the stories.* Then again, the stories never had foretold a fifteen hundred dollar fee. Manuel was confused. He wished that he could just go home and play checkers with Juan in the afternoon sun.

If only ... I'd let him win every game.

Chapter 24
Bogotá, Columbia

Maliq sat alone on the balcony of the private penthouse apartment. He looked east where the Cordillera Oriental mountain range rose above the city. Clouds covered the peaks that he knew would not be snowcapped like the mountains above Kabul. He wondered if he'd ever see Kabul again.

He was a guest of Antonio Coba, a young cousin of Pablo Escobar, the ruthless, deceased head of the Medellin drug cartel. By 1995 the Medellin and Cali cartels had been decimated by the Colombian government, but some remnants survived and a few men like Coba lived in grand style from the drug profits of past decades. Maliq surmised that Antonio hoped an association with him might lead to a source of Afghanistan heroin. A profitable deal would gain Antonio a new product that would enhance his small, almost insignificant marijuana business.

Maliq relaxed in deep thought. He was planning his team's next hurdle: the jump from Colombia to Chiapas, Mexico. He took a big gulp of lemonade, then stood, threw his arms over his head and stretched. Afterward he resumed his comfortable position, easing back down onto the heavily padded, chaise lounge. A knock on the front door startled him. Maliq sat upright. A maid called, "Housekeeping. Housekeeping."

"No gracias. Limpia muchas tarde, senora," Maliq shouted, practicing his Spanish, while he returned to his peaceful repose. He

had told the maid that she should clean much later. He was pleased with his growing command of Spanish. Since the Arabs arrival in Bogotá they had used Spanish almost exclusively. In public they spoke only Spanish or whispered in Arabic. A word in English would have gotten them shot here in the heart of this drug lord controlled section of the city where they were housed.

Maliq was contemplating three different choices – fly commercially to Mexico City with a connecting flight to Cristobal de las Casas or fly with a load of drugs to a jungle runway in Guatemala near the southern Mexican border. The third choice was a high-speed boat trip from Cartagena, across the Caribbean to Puerto Barrios on the southern coast of Guatemala that would still leave a long overland trip. They couldn't fly commercially with their Mexican passports for the first time from Colombia to Mexico, and he didn't want to use the Syrian, Moroccan, or Egyptian passports for a second time in-bound. Additionally, Maliq had promised his men that they would not travel by boat again, and he needed to keep that promise.

Maliq heard another, stronger knock on the door. *"El Tigre,* it's Antonio. Open the door." Antonio Cobo never used Maliq's real name; he called him "Tiger" or "boss in Spanish."

"Un momento, Antonio."

Maliq took his time getting up and going to the door. Before his hands reached for the deadbolt he had made a decision. He and his men would fly with the drugs to Guatemala. His mind raced to the negotiation process. He wondered how much Antonio would try to extract from al-Qaeda.

"Buenos dias, Antonio." Maliq held the door wide for his host to enter. "Join me on the patio," he invited. "I never tire of the view."

"But of course."

Maliq returned to his lounge. Antonio pulled up a chair beside Maliq and sat down. "Have you decided how you want to travel to Guatemala?"

"Yes, we'd like to fly with the cargo."

Antonio nodded his approval. "Good choice. It is safe and fast. The cost to you will be *nada,* nothing. What I need to know is how much SWA *chatarra* I can expect on a monthly schedule, and at what price?" SWA *chatarra* was Southwest Asian heroin, in this instance, Afghanistan produced. Want some *chiba chiba*?" asked Antonio, lighting up the high-potency Colombian marijuana in a pipe.

"No, gracias." Maliq did not use drugs and disliked being around them. He found it distasteful to have to deal with Antonio and his kind. But he needed Antonio's help. "I have been authorized to offer you twenty-five percent off the current price of fifteen thousand U.S. dollars a kilo, for six months, and the market price thereafter. The deal is for one year and you will be our only customer in Colombia."

Antonio had just taken a deep drag on his pipe when Maliq disclosed the prices. The smoke went down his throat. He coughed uncontrollably and dropped the pipe. The street value, after cutting, would range from $125,000 to $135,000 per kilo. Antonio was already scheming how he could extend the time frame beyond the year's commitment. When he could finally speak he said, "Fair enough. How much can they deliver and when can I expect the first shipment?"

"When we are safely in Guatemala, I'll give you the name of a contact in Paris. Those details can be better discussed with him."

Antonio seemed satisfied. "How soon would you like to go?"

"The sooner the better for both of us. You tell me."

"We plan a run the day after tomorrow. Can you be ready?"

"We're ready now. Make the arrangements."

Antonio got up, leaned over and offered his hand. Maliq rose and received Antonio's firm grip and an exaggerated handshake. Antonio smiled broadly, put his other hand on Maliq's shoulder and then pulled him forward. The embraced was more in the Latin tradition. Maliq wondered if he was going to touch cheeks as Arabs did. When the awkward hug ended Maliq watched his jubilant host head toward the door. Maliq concluded that the quoted price was too low, but it was of little concern to him after all.

"Adios mi amigo. Adios," said Antonio, almost singing the farewell.

"Adios, Senior Cobo." Maliq reclaimed his seat, sipped his drink and returned his gaze toward the mountains. He wondered how the stupid Americans would feel if they knew that their filthy

drug habit was financing his travel and the message from Allah that was soon to be delivered. He smirked and reached for his cigarettes.

Maliq was very much surprised to see a single engine plane when he exited the minibus that transported his team to a small jungle airstrip. It was almost dark and a thick, heavy fog was beginning to settle here on the mountain plateau thirty-five miles southwest of Bogotá. Maliq grabbed his duffle bag and was first off the bus. He headed straight for the plane. It's engine screaming at full throttle. He had to lean forward slightly to remain steady. The pilot eased the engine back to idle. The noise and wind dropped significantly. Antonio saw Maliq and hurried to meet him. "May I help with your luggage?" asked Antonio loud enough to be heard over the engine noise.

"No, gracias." Maliq hollered back. He threw the bag over his left shoulder and offered his right hand.

Antonio shook Maliq's hand and rightly interpreted the worried look on his face. "El Tigre, you are looking at the latest and finest addition to my air cargo service company. It is a Pilatus, PC12 turboprop. It's Swiss made and flies like a jewel." Antonio chuckled at his own clever analogy. The two walked slowly toward the plane.

"I didn't question your choice of planes, Antonio."

"No, but you had a curious look on your face when you saw it."

Maliq hesitated. "Well, I did expect a twin-engine job for such a long flight."

"It has a range of over 4,000 kilometers. It cruises at 30,000 feet, although my pilots prefer thirty feet over water."

"Say no more; where do you want us?" Maliq's team was stretched single file from the bus almost to the plane.

"Right up here." Antonio led Maliq to the folding-step door. "You will sit in the copilot's seat. There are four other seats and the rest will have to sit on the 'bales of hay' already loaded in the main cabin. And remember this is a non-smoking flight – don't light up my hay." Antonio laughed again; he was in very good spirits.

Maliq and his men took their places and the plane taxied down the runway as soon as the door was closed. It was heavily loaded and only barely cleared the treetops. Even over the roar of the full-throttled engine, Maliq heard branches slapping against the undercarriage. His view out of the flight deck window was too good. The plane banked hard left on a forty-five degree angle, avoiding the now menacing, black, mountaintop that Maliq had so admired from the apartment. His harness straps dug deep into his shoulders.

A loud bang sounded in the back. Cargo and, or one of his men, must have slammed against the bulkhead. The pilot leveled the plane but stayed low just above the foliage. He shot a glance at Maliq and hid a thin smile. Maliq realized that he had been holding his breath and exhaled loudly. He was nervous and decided to switch seats with someone in the cabin before landing. He offered a silent prayer to Allah. The plane banked hard again and Maliq's stomach knew it before he did. He had better change his seat soon before he threw up on the controls. Maliq wondered whether he had made the right transportation choice.

The plane nosed down, the sky cleared and Maliq could make out the reflection of a river. The Magdalena River flowed north between the Cordillera's Occidental and Oriental Mountain ranges. Twenty minutes later, Maliq watched the Magdalena merge with another river. He could make out the Occidental range spread like five fingers as it disappeared into jungle. It would be safe now, at an altitude of two hundred feet, to turn due west toward the Caribbean. The pilot executed the maneuver with only a slight bank. There was a scheduled refueling stop in Sapzurro, a tiny town just inside Colombia on the Panamanian border. The following stop would be Puerto Barrios, Guatemala.

Maliq indicated to the pilot by pantomime that he wanted to go back into the cabin. With a nod, Maliq was given permission. He removed his harness, extricated himself from the seat and squeezed into the main cabin.

He would not return to the flight deck for the remainder of the trip. He had seen enough mountains and treetops a mere ten feet below a plane's belly to last a lifetime.

Chapter 25
Senora, Mexico

The morning chill gave way to milder air about eleven. Manuel Sanchez sat alone in the backseat of the Buick that had brought him from the brickyard toward Nogales, sipping from a twelve-ounce bottle of water. The driver was doing likewise behind the wheel. The mariachi music of Vicente Fernandez, Mexico's impresario extraordinaire bounced off the rolled-up windows, the volume turned up near the level to cause pain. Manuel liked music but preferred it much softer. It wouldn't be turned down until Javier Ortega returned to the car.

At the moment, Javier was inside the biggest house that Manuel had ever seen. He wondered if this was what might be called a mansion or was it a castle? He had never seen either and he didn't want to show his ignorance by asking the driver; not that José could have heard him over the music. Javier had been in the house for over two hours.

The car was parked in the shade of a juniper tree on a brick driveway that encircled the fountain in front of the house. A seven-foot adobe wall enclosed the compound, which included at least two additional structures that Manuel could see from his location. An iron fence had magically opened when they approached and automatically closed behind them when the car drove through. Manuel wondered if this was some sort of a prison.

When the last song ended, José ejected the CD, and before he slid in another he turned to Manuel. "Do you know who lives here?"

It was a rhetorical question. José knew Manuel wouldn't have a clue, even after he told him. "Pepe Brogadas. Pepe Brogadas lives here, the richest man in all of Mexico. You can tell your children and grandchildren someday that you saw the mansion of Pepe Brogadas." José didn't bother to explain that Pepe made all his money in the drug and prostitution trade.

"So this is what a mansion looks like," said Manuel.

Instead of replying, José placed another CD in the player. As the trumpets and Fernandez's strong voice assaulted Manuel's eardrums once again, José spotted Javier coming out the front door. It was held open by a bull of a man, still wearing his pajamas despite the late hour. José immediately lowered the volume of the CD to an almost inaudible level. "That's Pepe," said José in a reverent voice, nodding toward the door.

He jumped out and opened the rear passenger side door for his boss. Javier took his seat, and then ordered the driver to go to Apache Cave. "Time for a good meal. José, Manuel, how are you?" Not waiting for an answer, Javier continued speaking. "They say that Cochise hid a lot of gold in Apache Cave. You heard of Cochise, Manuel?"

"No senor." said José.

"Well, he was the most fierce Apache warrior to ever live in these parts. He killed a lot of people, white settlers, soldiers, Mexicans and even other Indians. He taught the U.S. Calvary some lessons too."

"I have not heard of this man."

"No matter. Apache Cave is now the finest restaurant in Nogales. Hungry?"

"Yes, sir. Very hungry."

"Good."

Fifty minutes later José guided the car through the busy border town of Nogales, Mexico. Just before he reached the U.S. port of entry, where the traffic came to a complete stop, he turned right, crossed the railroad tracks, and entered a less traveled section of the city. After another two blocks, José stopped right in front of the restaurant. A bouncer-type, standing in front of the place, frowned at the parked car until he saw who was about to get out. Manuel had expected to see a real cave, but the restaurant looked just like any other storefront business.

"Sit still, José. I can open the door. Wait here with Manuel. I won't be long," said Javier.

Hours went by, and Manuel watched the sun set beyond the western hills of Nogales. José slept. Manuel was happier than he had been during the wait at the big shot wearing pajamas' house; at least the music was not blasting. Javier's "not long" was three hours. Manuel needed to go to the bathroom and was by now extremely hungry. He tried to open the door but it was locked and he could not unlock it. Before he attempted to wake José he saw Javier finally emerge from the restaurant. "Wake up, you lazy boy. Open the door, my hands are full." Javier kicked the side of the car to awaken his driver. José jumped up, got out of his seat and quickly opened the door. "Sorry, boss."

Javier flopped in the back seat next to Manuel. He handed him a big Styrofoam container and plastic utensils. He tossed José an identical meal.

"Eat up boys. This is the best food you'll get in Nogales." Manuel opened the lid and peered down at a brown rice, string beef and refried beans. Two hot corn tortillas wrapped in thin wax paper completed the meal. The steamy aroma intensified his hunger. He snatched the fork from its plastic wrap and dug in. Javier was partly right; it was the best meal that Manuel had ever eaten anywhere. Javier sat back and watched, in mild amusement, as Manuel devoured his dinner. Manuel finished before José and asked where he might go to relieve himself. Javier called to the driver. "José, are you finished? Manuel needs a bathroom. Let's hurry to the Ortega house." José hastened to finish his food and started the engine. Mariachi music shattered the quiet. José quickly shut off the CD player. He turned to look back over the driver's seat at Javier, who was frowning. "Sorry again, boss." José put the car in gear and drove away.

It was only a five minute drive from the restaurant to the Ortega house. It was completely dark when they arrived. No lights were on in the house. It wasn't what Manuel had expected after the luxury he witnessed earlier. It was a single-family brick house. The houses on each side were torn down rubble. Remnants of a tin roof, wooden floors and piles of brick lay in what must have been shallow cellars.

No one appeared to be about the house, or the entire neighborhood for that matter. The three men left the car and walked to the front door. Javier produced a key, opened the door, and stepped into the front room. Manuel followed and José trailed behind. "The bathroom is in the back," said Javier. He waited until Manuel had left the room and turned to José. "Where's your muscle?"

"He'll be here in a few minutes, we're early."

The house was completely dark, but Manuel found the bathroom in the very rear of the house. When he came out his eyes had adjusted to the darkness and he looked at his surroundings. The back door was boarded shut, as was the rear window. The house was sparsely furnished. The kitchen contained a table and two chairs. There was no furniture in the middle room. The front room contained a very well worn cloth sofa and a wooden folding chair. Javier and José were standing just outside the front door talking to a third man.

Manuel approached and opened the door. He started to walk outside but José put his hand on Manuel's chest and stopped him on the top step. Manuel's growing sense of unease turned to apprehension. He began to perspire but felt increasingly colder. He shivered. Javier looked back at Manuel. He said nothing, turned away, walked leisurely over to the car and got in.

José spoke. "Manuel, this is Paco." Manuel eyed the new man. He was tall, wide and apparently very strong. The stranger's chest stretched a tee shirt to its limit and his bare arms displayed the muscles of a bodybuilder. He massaged a rubber ball in his right hand continually that had the desired effect of enlarging his bicep with each firm squeeze. "You and Paco will be staying here for a while. Work starts soon so get some sleep."

José touched the top of his head in a sloppy salute, and he too turned and walked over to the car. He jumped into the driver's seat and drove off with Javier.

Manuel watched the Buick travel down the street and turn at the end of the block. He felt lost and disconnected. The chain had been broken. The truck ride to the *la ladrillera* followed by the

Buick ride to the mansion, the restaurant and the wonderful meal. That was history. This was now. A ripple of fear flashed through his body. It started at the base of his neck and traveled down his spine like an electric current. He shivered again noticeably.

Paco pointed for him to reenter the house. Manuel did and Paco followed. Once inside, he offered Manuel a bottle of water and told him his bed was upstairs. He also gave him a flashlight. "Here, use this to find your way. There are no lights in this house. If you come down during the night to use the bathroom, call me before you hit the bottom step." He took a pistol from behind his back and waved it at Manuel. "I wouldn't want to shoot you by mistake. Javier would get mad at me." Paco went to the front door. He placed an iron bar across it and padlocked the bar to a latch bolted on the frame. "The key is around my neck and I will shoot you if you try to get it. If this happens Javier will not be quite so angry with me for killing you."

Manuel felt more than disconnected. Fear gripped his gut and pulsated through his slender body. He turned on his flashlight. His hand shook violently. The swaying beam found the stairs. He wobbled up to look for the bedroom. He had to fight just to keep his legs under him. He didn't say a word to Paco. As he climbed the stairs, he whispered a prayer. "Dear Mother of God, protect me and take me from this place. Guide me back home and I will shout your praise each and every day till I die. And I will tell all of Las Lisas the *true* story about travel to America. Please, Mother Mary. I beg you."

Manuel found the bedroom and collapsed onto a thin mattress that lay on the floor. Although scared and tense he was mentally and physically exhausted. Sleep came easily. He dreamed of playing checkers with Juan in the afternoon sun. Then it started to rain and the rain became a heavy downpour. Lighting flashed and thunder filled his skull. Juan disappeared and the thunder became the voice of God. "Wake up, wake up, Manuel. Time for work."

The voice of God was Paco yelling close to his ear; the lightning, a flashlight beam aimed right in his eyes. Manuel lifted up. The top of his mattress was soaked where Paco had poured a half bottle of water over his head. Manuel looked up for the face of his tormentor beyond the light. He ran his hand across his eyes, squinted and asked, "Who is it? What time is it?"

"It's me, Paco. Midnight, time for work."

Manuel staggered to his feet and followed the beam of light through the hall and down the stairs. It finally stopped in the kitchen, which was now completely packed with burlap bags half-filled with dirt.

"Carry these bags to the front door. Hurry, the truck will be here soon."

Manuel was trying to wake up and process what was happening. He was alert enough now to be sure that this was not part of the dream. It wasn't.

Manuel's nightmare had just begun.

Chapter 26

Manuel grabbed the nearest bag and attempted to lift it. He tried three times to hike the bag off the floor. At 145 pounds he was too small and weak to lift the bag over his shoulder, so he dragged it toward the living room. Still half asleep and in the dark he caught the bag on a slightly raised floorboard where the middle room met the living room.

It tore. Fifty pounds of dirt began to seep out. Paco saw that Manuel's progress had stopped, and he approached with his flashlight. He aimed the light at the hole in the bag. The beam then left the hole. It traveled up Manuel's leg, up his torso, chest, neck, and stopped right between his eyes, blinding him.

He heard the crack before he felt the pain … excruciating pain on the left side of his face. Paco's weapon was a leather strap fastened to a wooden shovel handle. Four beer bottle caps with the serrated edges out had been stapled to the strap's end. Blood trickled down Manuel's cheek. He screamed. The next whack caught him on the shoulder. "The louder you yell the harder I hit," said Paco. "And I keep hitting until you stop." Manuel only grunted with the last strike, and Paco kept the strap by his side. "Push that bag against the wall and get the next one. Pick it up this time. The bags are only half full."

Manuel wiped the blood off his face with his shirtsleeve and did as he was told. He lifted the bag in front of him, barely a foot off the floor and inched it toward the living room. He had to pause every few steps. This awkward position caused him to stop, lower the burden and rub the pain set deep inside the middle of his back. Manuel knew that he couldn't transport all of the bags piled up in the kitchen in this manner.

Despair took hold. By the time he moved five bags to the front room he heard a truck arrive. Paco unlatched the front door and opened it. A Ford Econoline panel truck backed right up to the top step. With the back doors opened outward no one from the street could see what was about to be loaded.

Paco went outside and greeted the driver. As he did so a police car pulled alongside the curb next to the truck. Manuel seized his chance. He pushed the truck panel door closed and ran toward the police car. Paco caught sight of Manuel out of the corner of his eye as he ran toward them. He thrust out a leg and Manuel went sprawling. Before Manuel could yell out Paco grabbed him by the hair and dragged him back into the house. He handcuffed Manuel to the front door latch. Paco brought a six-inch blade up to Manuel's face. Even in the darkened room he could make out the shine of steel edge. "One sound before I come back and you'll be buried with this knife still in your chest."

Manuel watched Paco stroll back outside at a leisurely pace. He walked over to the officer who was now leaning out of his car, conversing with the truck driver. Paco reached into his pocket and handed the officer something. "You are extra generous tonight," said the officer. "Me and my men are most appreciative … and thank you for picking the garbage off the sidewalk just now." He laughed, rolled up his window and slowly drove off. Manuel overheard the exchange.

Repeating his earlier prayer, he resigned himself to his torturous situation and resolved to give Mother Mary more time to prepare a miracle. Paco returned to the house and unshackled the silent prisoner. He had the knife in one hand and the strap in the other. "I believe you'd prefer the strap than the knife, no?" Manuel didn't move. "Answer me!"

"Yes, Paco."

"Yes, what?"

"Yes, I prefer the strap."

Paco then delivered ten hard strikes. Manuel crouching on the floor, covered up. He took most of the blows on his arms and top of his head. He didn't dare whimper. The beating finally ended.

"Now get on with the loading. Take the bags all the way into the truck."

Manuel felt dizzy and spent a minute on the floor to recover before getting up. Welts formed on his arms and head. Surprisingly, he didn't feel much pain. He guessed that he would probably hurt a lot more later on tonight. He rose, stumbled toward where he had left the last bag, and picked it up. He tripped over something as he carried the bag toward the front of the truck. It was metal and about four feet long. He had fallen over a hand truck. Deliverance. *Was this a minor miracle – a sign?* No matter, it brightened him somewhat. He grabbed the hand truck and moved all the bags from the kitchen into the truck in less than an hour. When he couldn't fit any more bags into the vehicle he hid the hand truck under the kitchen table and called Paco who was resting on the sofa. "I can't get any more bags in the truck."

Paco went outside and awakened the driver who was asleep in the cab. The driver started the engine and drove off. Paco relocked the front door and said, "Go back upstairs and get some sleep." Manuel found his room, flopped on the mattress, took a drink from his water bottle and drifted off while repeating his personal prayer.

Two hours later Paco was once again pouring water on Manuel's head. "Let's go, second shift."

"Okay, okay, I'm awake," said Manuel. He ached all over. His back, legs, arms, everything hurt. He discovered a gash on his knee where he had fallen on the sidewalk. His face and head stung from the earlier beating. He didn't know how much more he could take this night.

He crawled down the hall and raised himself up by holding onto the railing at the top of the stairs. He leaned on it heavily as he limped down. As soon as he reached the bottom step, the truck driver marched over and stuck his fist up to Manuel's face. "Paco, this prick stole my hand truck. I had to carry the bags off the truck and into the wash without it." Manuel trembled. Would they execute him for taking the hand truck?

Paco roared. He laughed so loud Manuel thought that he might wake up the whole neighborhood. "I thought the little shit finished fast. Here's fifty bucks buy another one. He reached into his

166

pocket, pulled out some bills, and handed them to the truck driver. "It's okay Manuel, stop shaking, you did a good thing. We need to work faster. Now we can fill the bags all the way. They will weigh one hundred pounds, but with the hand truck you will be able to move them."

Manuel loaded all the bags the truck could hold, informed Paco and headed off to bed without being told. The room began to lighten as the sun's first rays peeked over the border town and snaked through the cracks of the boarded-up windows. A rooster crowed as Manuel dozed off. It reminded him of Las Lisas and the rooster that called him to breakfast every morning.

"Mother Mary, please take me home."

"Mother Mary, please take me ..."

"Mother Mary, please ..."

"Mother Mary ..."

"Mother ...."

A medicinal sleep came to him.

No dreams. No nightmares. No pain.

Chapter 27

The flight in the single engine turboprop was, as Antonio Cobo had suggested, the best choice for Maliq and his men. It was safe, fast, and deposited the Arabs just a mile south of the Mexican border near the tiny Guatemalan town of La Mesilla.

The spot was perfect, located as it was, a short distance from Mexican Route 190, a principal highway that shot directly to their next destination, San Cristobal de las Casas in the Mexican State of Chiapas.

Cobo had arranged for two Jeeps with drivers to take Maliq and his crew across the border into Mexico, a few miles west of the nearest checkpoint. The road their guides chose was not much more than a wide footpath. It reminded Maliq of the escape route Reyes' had taken, sans jungle, after the raid on the *Abu Sayyaf* encampment. The hilly, rocky terrain made for a difficult crossing, especially with five men crammed in one Jeep and six in the other. No one fell out. No one complained.

Once across the Mexican border the vehicles steered into Cuauhtemoc on a genuine, though narrow, dirt road. The Arabs were dropped off at a small hotel where the owner was delighted to receive nine unexpected guests.

Maliq was exhausted after nearly three days of almost sleepless travel. The flight had been uneventful but the tension of every landing and takeoff from Bogotá, Sapzurro, Puerto Barrios and La Mesilla on short dirt landing strips, at night had unnerved him. In addition, there was the added stress of avoiding drug enforcement officials from the United States and Central American countries. Maliq had been on edge every minute of the trip.

Although only nine-thirty in the evening, he ordered the men to their hotel rooms for needed rest. He would do the same.

Twelve hours later, he was awakened from a deep sleep by a cacophony of truck, bus, motorcycle, and car traffic. The north side of the hotel had no sidewalk and the main artery into and out of Mexico. The road passed within inches of its wall. The sun streaked through vertical blind slats and formed alternating light and dark bars on the gray wall just beyond the foot of his bed. For an instant he thought that he might be in prison. He could smell coffee and hear Spanish chatter over the traffic noise below his open window. He guessed the time to be around ten. He couldn't remember the last time he had slept for so long.

Maliq dressed and drifted down from his second story room to a small courtyard in back of the hotel where half of his men sat drinking coffee and conversing in Spanish about nothing in particular. *"Buenas tardes, El Tigre,"* said Amir. All the men had taken to calling Maliq, "Tiger," since Antonio Cobo had given him that name in Bogotá. Amir had also emphasized the word "afternoon" in his greeting.

"Buenas tardes, los hombres." said Maliq.

"Coffee?" Amir had the pot in the air and started to pour before Maliq answered. He said something else but his words were drowned by the strident sound of a horn from a big diesel truck. The horn blew again and again. Maliq made a face held and his hands to his ears, before he grabbed the filled coffee cup and took an empty seat. "Thanks, Amir. Let's pack up and get out of here. It's so noisy. Don't know how I slept so well. Where are the rest?"

"They are walking around the town. They'll be back soon. Great breakfast. Let me find a server for you." Amir quickly raced into the hotel.

Maliq, talking to Yazid and Shakir as he sipped his coffee, paid little heed to the six men who meandered into the breakfast patio area. The newcomers pulled two tables together, a short distance from where Maliq and the others sat. Four sat down with their backs to Maliq. The other two, whom Maliq could only partially see, sat at each end of the table. He thought that they looked vaguely familiar.

Amir returned with a waiter in tow, but instead of joining Maliq's table he walked over to the new group of six, grinning broadly. "Well, don't you gentleman look magnificent?" The entire table burst into laughter. Maliq was baffled. Still laughing, the four men turned around in their chairs and pointed to Maliq. "Don't you recognize us, *el Tigre*? asked Tariq.

Maliq got up and moved closer. After two steps he stopped, squinted and began to laugh along with them. It was the rest of his team. They had purchased new clothes and hats, completely changing their appearance so that Maliq had mistaken them for locals. He continued walking toward the table and stood beside it. "Great job. I salute you. You fooled me."

"Remember Alberto and Hernando our drivers from last night?" said Amir. They have a proposal for you."

"One moment, José, Maliq used Abdul's new Spanish name. "Stand up, all of you, let me see the complete outfits."

The four stood and took a mock bow, holding their hats over their hearts. Until now, all nine Arabs had worn dark blue jeans, various tee shirts or short-sleeved shirts, and popular American brand sneakers.

The foursome had been very clever; no two looked alike. One wore white baggy pants, rope belt, white shirt and straw hat of an Indian peasant farmer. Another could have passed for a ranch foreman, in jeans, cowboy belt, plaid shirt and black Stetson. The third was dressed as a Mariachi. He had black-studded pants and matching jacket, white shirt with ruffles, red vest, low boots and the biggest sombrero south of the Rio Grande. The fourth wore gray slacks, tan dress shirt, open at the neck, and a sport coat with leather trim on the collar and pockets, had the look of a sophisticated casually dressed Mexican businessman.

Maliq shook his head in amazement at their ingenuity. "Well done, well done. What kind of outfit did you get for me?"

"The second-hand bazaar is just across the street. Go look at the general rank military uniform. We saved it for you."

Maliq grinned. "Sounds nice but I think I'll wear something that just might attract a little less attention. Naido, get your guitar, and let's hear a song." Maliq aimed his remark toward their newly transformed mariachi companion.

Maliq saluted the four men and turned his attention to the two drivers from last evening. They had remained seated at the ends of the table. "Okay, José," Maliq liked the rhyme, and used it often. What kind of proposal do our friends have in mind?"

At a signal from Amir, Alberto spoke. "*El Tigre*, I'm sure you feel confident that you and your men could handle any problems that might arise on your way to San Cristobal. But there are some very bad men in these parts. They prey on the immigrants going north. And I'm not talking about local bandits. No, I'm talking about the *Mara Salvatrucha.*"

"What's that?"

"It's a gang of trouble makers, left-over freedom fighters from the jungles of El Salvador. They have no homeland, no purpose, so they make war here against travelers. Sir, they are cold blooded killers."

Maliq considered rapidly. His reply was curt and businesslike. "Go on. What is your proposal?"

"We will drive you to San Cristobal in a small bus, for a small fee."

Maliq made a quick decision, he had no wish for any trouble along the way. He nodded agreement to Alberto's proposal and the two men quickly negotiated an acceptable price. Next stop San Cristobal de la Casas … home of a new Islamic settlement. Maliq wanted to visit the Arabs that he had learned lived in the area. He hoped that they might provide a staging area for future missions to America. He was also aware that it was a part of Mexico in turmoil. A group that called itself *Zapataristas* still fought a hundred-year-old land reform revolt.

Viva Zapata!

Chapter 28

Estimo had the feeling that he was being blown-off the search for the Spanish-speaking Arabs. His suspicions hardened into certainty when his boss, Jim Crowley sent him to Tucson to check up on his look-alike, Roger Lacson. He recalled the short, nervous sports reporter with some affection. After all, he had volunteered to serve as live al-Qaeda bait and enabled Estimo to leave Kuala Lumpur unnoticed. In addition, Estimo felt partially responsible for the frightful night that Roger had experienced out there in front of the CIA apartment.

Lacson must have been scared shitless during the second attack on him by Dollah Jaffar. Then he had to witness Jaffar's and Connelly's deaths ... what a sorry way for a civilian to end a vacation. But checking up on Lacson was the FBI's job, and Crowley mentioned that FBI agent Robert Norcross had already met with Lacson.

Before Estimo caught the plane to Tucson he tried three times to get through to Nicki Connelly without success. Privately he was relieved that he didn't have to visit with her. He didn't know how well he'd handle the situation. He wasn't sure how he'd convey that he was distraught that they had both lost a wonderful partner and oh, by the way, exactly where the hell were you when Connelly was stabbed to death?

He arrived at 3:15 in the afternoon and checked into a cheap motel within sight of the Tucson airport, hopeful that he'd get orders to leave quickly. He called Roger Lacson at the *Arizona Star* to find out when and where it might be convenient to meet. Roger sounded astonished to hear from him, but agreed to have dinner that night. Roger had suggested that they dine at the Arizona Inn, halfway between his office and the airport. "The food's outstanding," Roger had assured him. I assume you're, that is, the federal government will pick up the check."

"But, of course, it's the least we can do for the extraordinary service you provided the Company." Roger set the time at 7:30. But as he hung up with Estimo, Roger shivered at the thought of reliving the tragic end of his trip once again.

* * * * *

The dinner conversation surprised Roger; Estimo didn't ask one question about the action that had resulted in the death of agent Connelly. The only official business discussed at all was about Roger's meeting with FBI agent Norcross.

Roger gladly told Estimo how he had been mistreated and sent to jail, as was his friend, Carlin Ward, for just speaking with Maggie Lopez, a border patrol agent who was involved in a shooting incident that was rumored to involve the Mexican military. This information perked Estimo's interest. He was familiar with reports of the Mexican military crossing the border. Since he had nothing better to do while on the shelf, here in Tucson, he told Roger that he'd like to meet border patrol agent Lopez.

Roger tightened his lips and shrugged his shoulders ever so noticeably. "I'll ask her but I can't promise that she'll agree to see you. She's very secretive about the incident on the border." In his best official manner, Estimo hinted that, like the FBI, the CIA didn't have to *request* meetings when people had information that might concern national security.

As Roger finished his crepe desert he looked around the room's warm, comfortable décor. Estimo followed Roger's gaze. "Great choice, Roger. The meal was excellent and this place makes me feel like I'm in my grandmother's dining room, not a public restaurant."

"This place is almost seventy-five years old. It's definitely has an atmosphere that'll mellow you out."

"I agree. Thanks for suggesting it."

As Roger had correctly guessed, Estimo grabbed the check before he could even pretend to reach for it.

Under the clear cloudless-night sky Estimo bid Roger farewell on the steps of the Arizona Inn and then lingered there. As soon as Roger was out of sight, Estimo phoned FBI agent Norcross to compare notes. Their findings matched perfectly. Estimo looked up at the star-filled canopy and smiled at the sparkling universe above. He thought of Connelly and his mind drifted to Bobby Kennedy's memorial to his slain brother at the 1964 Democratic Convention with the lines from Shakespeare's *Romeo and Juliet* that Bobby had recited from memory:

> *When he shall die*
> *Take him and cut him out into stars*
> *And he shall make the face of heaven so fine*
> *That all the world will be in love with night,*
> *And pay no worship to the garish sun.*

Estimo tasted a salty moisture and wiped his face.

The air felt warm on his skin after the mid-March damp, cold and windy climate that he had endured this morning in Washington. Estimo, even in his sorrowful moment, found himself strangely relaxed for the first time in months. He turned and went back into the inn, found the desk clerk, took a room and then headed for the bar for a nightcap or two or three. This old western-world place fitted him tonight like well-worn college sweats. He luxuriated in the feeling. He'd go back to the airport motel for his clothes in the morning. Tonight the CIA was going to make amends for the mistake that it had made by banishing him to Tucson.

He drank to the dearly departed: Martin, John, Bobby, and his partner, Dillon Connelly.

Chapter 29

Maliq slept in the front seat of the minibus as it pulled into the late afternoon shade cast by the Templo de Santo Domingo. The 16th century church was located seven blocks from the city's central park, the *Plaza 31 de Marzo* smack in the middle of *San Christobal de las Casas*. He awoke when the bus came to a complete stop and he jerked forward. He heard the driver pull up the emergency brake. Maliq looked out his front row window seat. A long line of colorful awnings sparkled against an off-white church wall.

Beneath the coverings indigenous natives were selling locally produced wares, along with fresh mangos, figs, plums, green beans and chilies. The driver looked over at Maliq and answered his unasked question. "They're Tzotzil Mayans from the villages of Zinacantan and San Juan Chamula. They come here every day to sell hand-made dolls, woodcarvings, candles and tablecloths to the few tourists who come here during the winter. The locals buy the fruit and vegetables."

"We're staying near Chamula. How far is it from here?" asked Maliq.

"Just a few kilometers north."

"Our guide should be here at sunset. Is this the church of Santo Domingo?"

"Yes."

Maliq nodded in the direction of the driver, then slid back down into his resting position and closed his eyes once again. Most of his team was also resting. A few talked quietly.

The driver opened the front door to let fresh air into the bus. Three children rushed over and pleaded with the passengers to visit their family's stall to buy religious candles. The driver chased them away. Suddenly, the crowd noise grew noticeably louder. Everyone in view rushed forward and lined the street. A roar went up, and people waved wildly as an open Jeep drove past the church. A man wearing combat fatigues stood up in the mud-crusted vehicle and waved back to the crowd that swelled to six and seven deep at the curb. The man wore a ski mask and held an automatic weapon over his head. Seconds later, the Jeep was gone and the assembly dispersed. Maliq leaned over the driver's shoulder straining to see. "Who was that?"

"The subcomandante."

"The what?"

"The subcomandante. He's the leader of the *Zapatistas*. Eighty years ago a man named Emiliano Zapata from Morelos led a land reform war. The battle still goes on, but today the stakes have been raised. This group now wants independence for the entire state of Chiapas. The man in the mask, he is called Marcos."

Maliq's eyes followed the path of the Jeep until it had disappeared. "Does he live here in the city? Why does he wear a mask?"

"So the authorities won't arrest him when he doesn't wear it. Can't catch a man you can't identify. He struggles and fights for all the oppressed in Mexico. Like Zorro in the movies he wears a mask. I am told that he lives in the mountains near where you are going."

"Interesting. I'd like to meet this man."

The driver's glance was a warning. "Do as you wish, but I suggest that you stay clear of him and his gang."

The driver's remarks only made Maliq more anxious to meet the subcomandante as he shook his head as if in agreement.

The bus passengers returned to their seats and rested once again. The shadows from the church wall crept across the road as the sun lowered. Out of the darken sidewalk, a man dressed in Indian clothes suddenly appeared at the open bus door. He startled everyone; then asked for Miguel *el Tigre*. The entire bus roared to life. The men laughed aloud at hearing an outsider call Maliq by his nickname.

"I am Miguel," said Maliq as he stood, stretched and yawned. "Who are you?"

I'm Roberto and I have transportation around the corner. Please come with me."

Maliq roused his men, thanked the driver, grabbed his gear and walked alongside their new guide. "Your accent is different from the others. Where are you from?" Maliq asked.

The guide ignored his question. "Follow me, please."

Maliq repeated his question. The guide frowned but answered. "I'm a Spaniard."

"How long have you lived here? Did you come here alone?

The guide stopped and looked directly into Maliq's eyes before he spoke. "I came here five years ago with twenty fellow brothers of Islam. Now please hold your questions for the *Imam*. He waits for you at the *Markaz al Islami*. It serves as our Mosque and school."

* * * * *

The group climbed into a parked open stake-body truck. They drove out of the town and headed toward higher altitude. The truck belched blue smoke as it chugged begrudgingly up the steep mountain road toward Chamula. They passed many Indians walking and on horseback, who led burros packed high with leather sacks filled with unsold goods. The driver used the horn more than the brakes as he swayed past them at high speed on the twisting mountain road. The bouncing truck swung wide around curves where Maliq looked down and saw rusted wrecks from previous mishaps. He threw away an unlighted cigarette and unwrapped a fresh pack of Tums. He popped four into his mouth.

177

Chapter 30

Maggie woke up feeling as giddy as a teenager. It was Sunday and she planned to take her mom to Mass, go home with her for brunch and then play tennis with Roger. He had called her yesterday and invited her over to his complex where he said that the tennis courts were always available on Sunday. He didn't play very well he had informed her, but would give it a go. Maggie had told him tennis was one of her great loves.

She showered, slipped into a white dress for church then packed her tennis clothes, racket, and sneakers into her Nike sports bag. She looked up as she left her apartment. The sky was overcast but didn't look like rain. She called Roger to confirm their date. "Hi, Roger, we still on for two?"

"You bet."

"Now, I haven't played since my *accident*. So I'm pretty rusty," she warned.

"Don't con me. I'm sure a state champ can shed rust in a hurry."

"I'm serious. Don't be too disappointed if I'm off my game today."

"I'll try not to gloat if I manage to win a point. See ya at two."

They both clicked off.

Maggie hummed as she got into the car. Her bright mood was a departure from the gloominess that she normally felt on a gray day. She smiled. It must be Roger's invitation, she decided. After Mass, Maggie changed clothes in her mother's bathroom and ran out the door before anyone could remark about her skimpy tennis outfit.

* * * * *

She was rusty, but way above Roger's game. She tried to take it easy on him without being obvious. She hit powder-puff returns instead of her trademark demon slams. Her serves were aimed three feet in front of him instead of the out-of-reach rockets that she was capable launching. After the first set, they took a break and sat on a bench to quench their thirst. As she drank some water, she glanced sideways at Roger. She was aware that he had been covertly admiring her body since she got out of her car. She knew she looked good and she didn't mind if Roger noticed. Actually she *wanted* him to notice.

"Maggie, I had dinner with an old friend last night, and ..." Roger stopped talking, searching for the right words. He looked serious. Maggie's heart skipped and she thought, *My God, an old girlfriend has surfaced ... just my damn luck.*

"... and he wants to meet you."

He? Relief brought a dazzling smile to her face. "Okay, but why?"

Roger looked slightly perplexed then added. "Well, before you agree so fast. He's ..." Roger stopped talking again, looked around, leaned toward Maggie and almost whispered, "CIA."

"You have a CIA friend and he wants to meet me because ...?" Maggie was curious.

"Because I mentioned the Organ Pipe incident and he just said that he'd like to talk with you. So if you don't mind ..."

Maggie cut him off. She stood up and looked down on him. She wrinkled her nose, narrowed her eyes, and jutted her chin forward. Her look frightened him. "Roger, why did you even mention Organ Pipe to him?"

"I, ... I don't know. It just came out in conversation."

"Roger, isn't the FBI enough to deal with? I don't need the CIA on my case too." She was almost hysterical now.

Roger looked around again. "He's an old friend," was all he could think to say.

179

"I'm sorry. I have to go." Maggie threw her gear into her sports bag and stormed over to her car.

Roger stood up and called after her. "Maggie, please. Maggie, I didn't mean to cause you any more grief. I'll tell him no. Maggie, don't go."

She ignored his plea, got into her car and drove off too fast leaving a patch of rubber on the lot.

Roger stood frozen by the bench. His heart sank. He cursed softly. "Damn you, Estimo. Damn you, don't screw me again."

Maggie's fury settled into a dull feeling of disappointment the more she thought about Roger's poor judgment. She wondered why Roger had talked about Organ Pipe at all. Had he been bragging, ignorant, or acting stupid? She knew he wasn't stupid. She felt betrayed. Her face flushed as she recalled how ready she had been to jump into his arms. "And the skin I displayed this morning, bare midriff and thigh-slit shorts. What was I thinking? Why'd I wear a two-piece outfit the first time we played? Ooow! Foolish! Foolish girl!" Maggie was almost screaming. She pounded on the steering wheel. She drove out of his development and straight toward home.

Roger called Estimo as soon as his hand stopped shaking. "Estimo, you've done it again! You've ruined my life again."

"What? Hold on, Roger. Explain, please."

Roger recounted the scene that had just taken place during his tennis date with Maggie. "Unless she thinks of something worse to call me, she'll never speak to me again," he said.

Estimo offered to fix the problem. "Give me her number and just wait there until I call you back."

Maggie's cell-phone chimed. She looked at it on the seat and let it ring. It was probably Roger. It stopped, rang again. The caller ID showed "restricted." She couldn't let a phone ring. She reined-in her emotions and answered as calmly as possible. "Hello." She expected to hear a contrite Roger, but an unfamiliar, upbeat voice answered back.

"Hi Maggie, my name is Rogelio. I'm a friend of Roger's.

After a long silence she asked, "Is your last name Estimo?"

"Will you stay on the line if I answer honestly?"

"Maybe."

"I need a commitment here, Maggie, no waffling," he said lightheartedly.

Maggie suppressed a smile.

"Okay. I'll commit to *one* minute. The clock is running."

"Yes, I'm Estimo, and I can explain but we need to meet. Cell phones won't do. *Please.* I can clear Roger's good name."

She interrupted. "I doubt it!"

"I can unequivocally vouch for him."

"You're asking me to take the word of a complete stranger. Would you in my position?"

"Probably not."

Maggie didn't respond.

"Are you still there?" said Estimo.

"I'm thinking. Your truthfulness has given me pause."

"Not to pause, my time's almost up. Please! Please, say yes."

She took a deep breath and exhaled. "Are you sure you're not a lawyer?"

Estimo chuckled. "Hurl your insults. Go on, I can take it for Roger's sake."

Maggie couldn't stifle a laugh. "When and where?" she conceded.

"As soon as possible. You name the place."

"I'm just headed home to shower and change," Maggie said. "Meet me in about an hour in the parking lot of the Rusty Horseshoe at Ina and Thorndale. If you need directions, I recommend that you ask your friend to show you the way."

She hoped that Estimo didn't miss the not-too-subtle hint to bring Roger along. Maggie thought that she detected a smile in his voice as he said goodbye.

Point. Game. Set. Match Estimo.

Chapter 31

When Maggie saw the two men standing beside Roger's truck, she did a double take. Roger had never mentioned a twin, or even a brother for that matter, and she definitely remembered his saying the CIA agent was just a friend.

As soon as she found a parking spot, both men rushed to her door. They dropped to one knee as she got out. Each carried a bouquet of deep red and pink roses mixed with wild orchids. Each thrust the bouquet toward Maggie. This movement effectively hemmed Maggie next to her car. Both kept their heads down and awaited her response. Maggie was amused. Roger looked up and pointed at Estimo. "He can explain everything. He's a good explainer."

"I know that much about him already. Thank you for the gorgeous bouquets." Maggie took the flowers and laid them on the front seat of her car.

"On your feet guys. Let's go inside for a drink."

Over beers for Estimo and Roger and a Sprite for Maggie, Estimo explained how he had met Roger in Kuala Lumpur. He told Maggie that Roger had performed an extraordinary service to his country by assisting the CIA. He also had been in contact with FBI agent Norcross, he said, and he knew more about the trouble on the border with the Mexican military than he was free to discuss.

"I mentioned to Roger that I was here to look into border incidents and he said that you had been involved in one," Estimo said. "So I told Roger that I'd like to hear what happened. He said he'd ask but hinted you'd be reluctant to talk. That's the whole story."

"So you're not *old* friends?" Maggie was still cautious.

"No, we just met three months ago. But we've been through a lot together. "This guy here," Estimo placed his hand on Roger's shoulder for emphasis, "literally put his life on the line; right, Roger?"

"Well, I didn't feel that I ...."

Estimo stopped him. "Modesty aside, Maggie he did. He's one brave patriot."

"Really, Roger?"

Estimo answered, "Yes, Maggie, It's the honest to God truth. But please don't ask about it or we'll have to ... ah, well, you know."

Maggie leaned back and put her hands up in mock surrender. "I can do that." Thank you Rogelio, you *are* a good explainer. Roger, I'm sorry I lost my temper this morning. I acted like a juvenile."

"No need for an apology," said Roger. Feeling the tightness in his chest easing.

Estimo said, "Forgiveness all around."

Roger raised his glass. "I'll drink to that."

They all drank.

Estimo set down his drink after the toast and said, "Maggie, do you feel comfortable telling me what happened that night on the border?"

"Show me your credential." She turned to Roger. "Roger, please excuse us."

Roger took a walk outside while Maggie told Estimo everything that had happened since that January night at Organ Pipe. She told him about little orphaned Margarita and Carlin and Roger's trip to jail. She left out Carlin's trip east and his meeting with a high-ranking U.S. senator.

Estimo nodded and paused, assessing Maggie's information and formulating his next step. "Maggie, I have a question for you."

"What's that?"

"If you saw an Arab, do you think you could visually distinguish him from a Mexican national?" Maggie wrinkled her brow and thought hard before answering.

"Well, I don't think I ever met an Arab, so I'm not sure I could on sight. But as soon as he opened his mouth, I'd know."

"Ah, that leads to my second question. I imagine you're second or third generation, right?"

"Third."

"Did you speak Spanish growing up?"

"Yes, my father's bilingual but my mother's English was just so, so. I spoke Spanish as a child and learned English starting in first grade."

"Okay. Do you think you could discern a difference in accent between say, a Spanish-speaking gringo and a Spanish-speaking Arab?"

"Perhaps, but I've never heard an Arab speak Spanish either."

"Would you participate in an experiment if I could arrange one?" said Estimo.

"I suppose. Does this have anything to do with whatever Roger did for you?"

"I can't say right now. I'm kind of flying solo and I've got to play things close to the vest for a while. If I learn to trust you as much as I do Roger, I'll tell you more." Estimo straighten up in his chair. "Thanks for all your help already."

Maggie stood up and extended her hand. "I look forward to your trust and working with you, agent Estimo."

Estimo took her hand and instead of shaking, he kissed it. Maggie smiled. Satisfied with their talk, Estimo paid the bill, and they went outside to find Roger. Estimo excused himself. He knew Maggie and Roger still had to iron out their morning spat. He watched as they walked to Maggie's car and stopped to converse. After a minute, Maggie kissed Roger. The kiss was brief, but right on the lips. It was followed by a tight bear hug. Maggie then slid behind the wheel and drove off. Roger turned to Estimo with two thumbs up.

Mission Maggie accomplished.

Chapter 32
Chiapas, Mexico

Maliq looked straight ahead as the truck bounced along the rutted, boulder-strewn road. He could only see what the headlights illuminated. The side window reflected his blurred image, created by the dull lights from the dash. Beyond the window, the darkness increased with distance.

The vehicle entered a village with little notice. It was early evening, but only a few people appeared on the sidewalks. The truck traveled through the town, turned off a side street, then stopped.

Maliq leaned toward the driver. "Where are we?"

"We're just beyond Chamula," said Roberto. "We'll stay here this evening."

"Where's Imam Nafia?"

"He's at the settlement about a hundred kilometers from here." The driver opened his door.

Maliq grabbed his arm. "Let's go on. I want to see the Imam tonight."

Roberto pulled his arm away. His eyes widened. "I will not drive any farther. It is too dangerous. We sleep here tonight."

Maliq didn't like taking orders from strangers. He stepped out of the truck and glared back. It was too dark for the driver to see Maliq's face. Roberto walked into the building and lit a candle. Maliq went to the rear of the truck and called his men down.

Khalid overheard the exchange and was close enough to see Maliq's anger. "What do you want to do, *el Tigre*?"

"We'll stay here tonight but tomorrow we look for weapons. No one will make decisions for us again."

"I have a knife."

Maliq paused. "Wait until we all get weapons." The men followed Maliq and Khalid into the building then settled down for the evening. The driver had left already by a back door.

* * * * *

The group departed Chamula before dawn.   At mid-afternoon the truck approached a plateau with a grand overlook and lurched to a stop. Twenty Tzotzil Indians knelt on the side of the road looking out toward three hills beyond the far side of a thirty-mile wide valley.

"What are they looking at? asked Maliq.

"The most sacred valley of San Lorenzo Zinacantan. The dip between the first and second hill is called the 'Navel of the World.' To the Mayan this is the center of the universe," answered Roberto.

Everyone got out of the truck to stretch and watch the Indians in their reverie.

"Look, they pay homage to the belly-button of the world." Maliq yelled to his men. All laughed. The Indians paid no attention to the strangers.

"We are headed for that spot and you may not joke about it after you see it up close," said the driver.

The sun hung just over the horizon. The clouds glowed an angry orange-maroon. As the road spiraled downward the surroundings turned from a pine and oak forest to near tropical. Maliq shivered. He remembered the closed-in feeling that had troubled him in Mindanao.

Roberto pulled off to where a trail dipped completely below road level. He stopped under an overhanging boulder, which completely hid the truck from the road. "Everyone out," he called. "Help me cover the truck." He began to lift a pile of recently cut branches that lay by the trail. The Arabs looked to Maliq for approval. He nodded, and they moved to help the driver arrange the heavy branches until they completely hid the truck.

186

"Follow me, Roberto said. "We have a couple of miles walk before dark."

He set a fast-paced march back across the road and down a natural trail toward a small mountain. After a few miles Roberto pointed to what looked like a tiny opening to a cave and hiked toward it.

"Your new home," Roberto chuckled, "This way through the Navel of the Universe." Then he climbed up a few feet and squeezed into a narrow opening. Maliq had not expected a cave in a jungle. He hesitated but followed.

"Vamonos muchachos," he called his men.

Once inside the darkened cave the men walked for fifteen minutes then turned a corner. The dim light from the cave opening at their rear had disappeared but blazing lights ahead startled them.

"My God, what is this?" Maliq covered his eyes with a hand. The appearance of a natural cave gave way to a stone stairway lit by many torches reaching higher than the tallest building in Afghanistan.

The men bunched up as they all turned the corner; stopped and gasped at the sight that had jolted Maliq. After a moment they recovered and climbed in silence. Fifteen minutes later they reached a mammoth chamber that extended fifty yards in all directions. At the opposite end they saw another tunnel. A cool breeze brushed over Maliq, indicating an exit. The air and a natural glow of dying daylight brought a brief smile of relief to his lips. Roberto kept plodding on; Maliq staggered as he looked up.

The chamber was rimmed with shoulder-high torches, but it was so vast that he could not see the ceiling. Stylized drawings of animal-like shapes adorned the walls in all directions as far as he could see. Their footsteps, which had reverberated up the steps, fell silent as they moved into the chamber and walked toward the light. The sound returned when they reached the short tunnel that led to the outside. The men relaxed and began to talk among themselves as they neared the exit.

Maliq, close on Roberto's heels, was the first of the Arabs to reach the opening. He stopped. He spread out his arms and shouted:

"Allahu Akabar, Allahu Akabar.
Ashahadu an la ilaha ill Allah ..."

187

Maliq's men could not believe the words echoing through the chamber. Their leader was speaking in Arabic for the first time since they had left Afghanistan. He was calling them to prayer.

Shocked, the men rushed forward. Abdul, in the rear, pushed past a few men already standing transfixed in front. When he reached the landing outside of the chamber and looked out over the horizon he saw why Maliq had called them to prayer. Maliq had dropped to his knees. Abdul did likewise.

Then all the men, including Roberto, assumed the position of Islamic worshipers in a Mosque. Roberto positioned himself slightly to the right of the setting sun. Everyone adjusted to the same angle – as an arrow would fly – straight to Mecca.

They had indeed passed through the belly button of the universe and come out on the other side. No one was laughing now just as Roberto had predicted.

Maliq prayed and wondered. *Was this a dream? Was this how Allah had gone from Mecca to Jerusalem in one night, through a magic portal?*

Allahu Akabar. Allah is greater.

After prayers they all got up and crowded near the edge a landing sixty feet above ground and looked out upon the nearly completed excavation of a well-preserved Mayan archaeological site. The landing stood atop the highest pyramid in the complex.

Maliq peered out over the five hundred yards of expanse beneath him. He scanned ten additional pyramids and temples unlike any that he had seen in Saudi Arabia or Afghanistan. Most were only half the height or lower than the one on which they stood upon but each was a marvel of architectural perfection.

A line of stone-carved, lion-like animals formed two rows of sentries on either side of a golden-tiled road that led through the center to another pyramid at the far end. Most of the lions had fallen off their pedestals. When Maliq looked down he saw a labyrinth of complex courtyards and corridors leading to rooms in a small palace missing its roof off to his right.

"Maliq, is this what Paradise will look like?" Amir said breaking the silence.

Maliq looked deep into Amir's questioning eyes, gave an almost imperceptible shrug of his shoulders and remained mute.

188

Chapter 33

Lance corporal Arnold Reynolds, special ops, U.S. Marine Corps removed the field glasses from its hard leather-case. He wiped the lens with a soft chamois cloth. He pressed the eyecups to the sockets of this tired eyes. He focused on a Jeep that had pulled alongside a newly excavated building nearest the great pyramid. Two men get out. Reynolds recognized one as subcomandante Marcos by his ever-present pipe, ski mask, and three-starred-general baseball cap.

Marcos and his companion stayed in the shadows and aimed their own binoculars on activity near the top of the pyramid. Reynolds turned his glasses toward the pyramid as well. His mouth opened in surprised as he saw ten men bow down, Middle Eastern fashion. It was obvious that they were Muslims at evening prayer. Reynolds knew that there was a Wahhabi school somewhere in the area but he had never seen Muslims praying here at the ruins of Palenque. Reynolds had not moved from his "hole" for the last twelve hours so he knew that the Muslims must have gotten to the top from one the unexcavated sides of the pyramid. Palenque was not open to the public yet and the archaeologists had left two weeks ago. They would not return until April.

*　*　*　*　*

Maliq now had a new respect for the Mayans. He had thought that all Indians lived in teepees. What he saw now baffled

189

him completely. Maliq's academic schooling had stopped at age fifteen. From then on he had trained for combat and learned little else. He knew that he was in the western hemisphere, specifically just above Central America. Even entering the magical Mayan belly button of the universe, he knew that there was no way that he and his companions could have traversed through the earth to the Middle East. He also knew that Egypt, like his homeland, Saudi Arabia, didn't have a climate capable of producing so much vegetation. Deep in the recesses of his mind, he speculated that ancient Babylon might have looked like this.

"Well, *el Tigre,* how do you like Palenque?" said Roberto.

Maliq could not see through the fog stationed in his head and merely stared at his guide. "Where in the name of Allah are we?" he asked, clearing his throat.

"Palenque," Robert answered. "It is an ancient Mayan capital. It flourished from about six hundred to eight hundred and then was abandoned. You are standing on the largest temple and there are four other major temples in the complex. There is much that you cannot see from here."

The men standing behind Maliq remained silent, afraid that it would be sacrilegious to speak in what was plainly a very sacred place.

Maliq looked in every direction. "I want to know more. Tell me about the Mayan."

"Later. For now, let's go and see Imam Nafia."

* * * * *

Lance Corporal Reynolds watched Maliq and his entourage walk down the two hundred steps to the base of the pyramid, then head toward a path to the smaller but also spectacular Temple of the Jaguar. He shifted the glasses back to Marcos and his aide. They got back into their Jeep and drove off into the jungle.

Moving his glasses back to the Arabs, Reynolds' observed the last of the men cautiously descend the front, steep steps of the pyramid. They all walked toward the Temple of the Jaguar. The group left Reynolds' line of sight behind the smallest pyramid in the complex.

* * * * *

To gain his attention, Amir tapped Maliq on the shoulder. "Did the Egyptians come here and build these pyramids?"

"No, Amir. Roberto told me the ancestors of those Indians we saw on the road built them about the time Mohammad walked among us."

"Could that be?"

"It may be so. Who can tell?"

The group followed Roberto around its side of the Jaguar pyramid where they found a tent community. The military tents with their jungle camouflaged stood out against the solid sepia shades of the pyramid. Five smaller tents housed six to eight people and surrounded a square tent big enough for fifty standing adults. Inside the big tent a prayer service was clearly under way, and Roberto held his hand up for Maliq and his men to stay back. Thirty pairs of shoes were lined up in front of the tent's open flaps. Maliq and his men crept silently past and settled themselves on a crumbling stone altar. They waited for the service to end.

Fifteen minutes later they heard the shuffling of bare-footed men leaving the mosque, talking quietly amongst themselves as they retrieved their shoes. A few looked over toward the Arabs but went on their way. Others recognized Roberto and nodded in his direction. The last man to leave the tent was the Imam. He smiled broadly and walked toward the Arabs, who scrambled to their feet so that they could properly greet him. Roberto hugged him and turned to Maliq. "Miguel, this is Emir Nafia our leader in Mexico. He came all the way from Granada Spain."

"May Allah bless your mission." said Maliq, bowing formally.

"He already has. Let's talk tomorrow; I have business with my council this evening."

"But of course," said Maliq bowing again.

Nafia was the man Maliq had wanted to meet, the Imam who had led the twenty Muslims to Chiapas five years earlier from Spain.

Roberto caught Maliq's attention and showed the Arabs the tent reserved for them. The driver asked if they needed anything. Maliq shook his head no and Roberto went on his way.

191

* * * * *

Outside the tent Maliq faced his men. "It is time to get some weapons," he said.

They entered the tent; and Maliq looked from one face to another. "Yazid and Tariq, go outside and stand guard." He didn't want anyone to overhear his conversation.

"Where can we get weapons out here, *el Tigre*?" asked Abdul.

"I'm not sure we can. The only guns I saw were in the hands of the military, the police and that subcomandante. We can't steal from the police or military but maybe we can buy from Subcomandante Marcos." Amir added, "I'm certain we can buy guns as soon as we get out of these mountains."

The Arabs went back outside and prepared a sumptuous meal over the fire that their hosts had readied for them. They roasted lamb, slightly burnt the corn-on-the-cob, and warmed their tortillas. Fresh coffee completed the meal. Maliq ate slowly, enjoying every mouthful. It was the best supper that he had eaten since leaving Mindanao.

Finishing his coffee, he stood and walked over to retrieve one of the bedrolls lying just outside the tent. He pushed aside the tent flap, spread his bedroll near the front and stuck his head outside, "Let's get some sleep. I'll take the second watch."

The men hurriedly finished their meals, picked up their bedrolls and followed Maliq inside the crowded tent to find a spot to call their own for the night.

Maliq was restless and slept very little until midnight when the first guard, Yazid shook him awake. Maliq crawled out of his warm sack. He went outside and called quietly to Tariq. "Don't wake anyone else. One guard should be sufficient for this small area. I just wanted our host to notice that we were security minded."

"Very well," Tariq tiptoed silently into the tent.

* * * * *

The special ops Marine, jubilant that he had been granted permission to leave his hole after twelve hours, watched Maliq close up. Not only had he observed him, he had also filmed it. His special-issued sniper rifle came equipped with a zoom night-vision Zeiss telescope. A lead from the scope was attached to a micro digital recorder positioned in a cavity drilled into the weapon's deep stock.

He would soon report via satellite phone, and by 0600 hours the Pentagon would have the film to puzzle over, along with Lance Corporal Reynolds' abbreviated narration. His earlier phone transmission relating the Muslim prayer session on the pyramid probably had generated fake yawns and a few wisecracks from his superior. Maybe the film would wake them up that something very unusual was going on here.

Chapter 34
Nogales, Mexico

The gunshot startled Manuel. He bolted up from his mattress, rushed to the top of the stairs, and peered into the darkness below.

He heard Paco scream, "You stupid son-of-a-bitch! How far did you think you'd get?" He knew it was Paco's gruff voice.

Manuel listened for an answer to the question. None came.

"Manuel." Paco waited but Manuel didn't respond and he called again much louder. "Manuel, get down here. Hurry!"

Manuel tiptoed back to his room and pretended to sound sleepy, not fully awake. "Yes, Paco, I be there quick." Manuel answered in a shaky voice. He put on his shoes, grabbed his water bottle and flashlight then hurried down the stairs.

Paco's heavy breathing gave away his location in the blackened room. Manuel knew better than to turn his light right at Paco; he aimed at the floor, just below where he heard him breathing. It illuminated what Manuel expected, but dreaded to see – a body, lying face down on the blood-soaked floor.

"Eduardo will be here with the van soon. We wait." said Paco, standing over the body. Manuel heard footsteps coming from the direction of the kitchen. They continued through the middle room and stopped alongside the heavy breathing. Manuel slowly panned his beam onto a pair of muddy boots.

Paco turned on his own light and focused it on the man standing next to him. "Manuel, this is Pepe. Now hold the light on your face." Manuel obeyed. "Pepe that is your new partner." Manuel heard the familiar sound of the Ford van approaching. It stopped in front and backed up to the door. Paco stepped around the body to the front door. He unbolted the latch, opened it and stood aside.

Eduardo got out of the driver's seat, climbed over it, and opened the panel doors outward in order to enter the house directly from the van. He stopped when he saw the flashlight beams on the body. "What in God's name?" he said.

"He tried to escape. End of questions. Now get the bastard's body in the van and dump it. No, wait. Pepe take his boots," said Paco. After Pepe removed the boots the driver reached for the head, lifting it slightly. The head slipped out of his bloody hands and banged back onto the floor. "Jesus Christ."

He wiped his hands on his pants, grabbed the body again, this time under the shoulders. Pepe reached for the feet, but only snatched air as Eduardo pulled the body forward onto the van. Manuel stood firmly on the bottom of the stairs. He kept his light on the body as they dragged it away. He started breathing again when Eduardo shut the van's doors and started the engine. Paco moved to re-bolt the front door. "Pepe, throw the boots to Manuel then take him with you and show him how to use a shovel. Manuel, put on the boots."

Manuel sat on the steps, removed his shoes and put on the boots. They were too big but it bothered him more that they had just come off a dead man.

"Hurry, we're falling behind schedule," said Paco.

Manuel followed Pepe to the trapdoor in the kitchen. They descended a wooden ladder to the tunnel's damp dirt base six feet down. A rope pulley swayed alongside the ladder, ready to raise the full bags of excavated dirt. The tunnel sloped downward, reaching thirteen feet below street level. Pepe and Manuel walked fifty yards eastward before heading due north for another two hundred yards before stopping. Pepe flicked on four battery lamps. Manuel eyed two shovels and a pick that leaned against the spot where the shaft abruptly ended. Twenty burlap bags and a hand truck lay next to the shovels.

"Felipe was stupid," Pepe said.

195

"Who?"

"The man Paco shot."

"Why?"

"Because no one can escape by the front door with Paco on guard."

"Why'd he try to escape? The pay is good and when we're finished we'll have enough money to go to America."

Pepe looked at Manuel like he was the dumbest mule on the planet. "Manuel, the day the tunnel is finished is the day we're suppose to die. They are not going to let us live knowing where the tunnel starts and ends."

Manuel's mestizo features blanched as the blood drained from his face. His mouth opened but no words escaped.

Pepe leaned down so that he was eye-to-eye with Manuel. He placed his right index finger an inch from Manuel's nose.

"Don't worry. I have a plan. Just do as I say and you'll get out of this tunnel alive."

Manuel nodded.

"Now my friend, start with the pick," Pepe said. His tone was friendly.

"Yes, boss."

Manuel grabbed the pick. It was heavy. Because there was not enough overhead room, he had to swing from the side making the work even harder. It was hot in the tunnel and his shirt felt clammy with sweat. This was going to be much harder than moving the bags on a hand truck from the kitchen to the van. Pepe sat on his shovel and watched Manuel struggle.

After five minutes, Pepe stood up. "Stand back. Give me the pick. You bag, or we'll never finish our quota before dawn."

Ten minutes later there was enough dirt to fill a hundred pound bag. Pepe held the bag open; Manuel shoveled. The bag filled. Manuel dragged it over to the hand truck and began the long walk back toward the house. He heard the pick thud into the rock and earth. Manuel wondered who would load the truck.

"Dear Mary, Mother of God, thank you for Saint Pepe," Manuel repeated the mantra over and over as he rolled the heavy loaded hand truck over the rutted tunnel dirt floor.

196

Chapter 35
Nogales, Arizona

Maggie hurriedly walked to her post at the Dennis DeConcini point of entry checkpoint, ten minutes early. She was happy to finally be back at work although her supervisor didn't put her back on the road. Instead she was loaned out to Customs. She stood behind Alan Robertson, whom she would relieve at eight, and watched the action. Most agents hated this assignment: observing day workers and tourists pass back and forth between the border towns with the same name, Nogales, for eight tedious hours. She was too excited to sit in the cafeteria, so she drank coffee and looked over Alan's shoulder for any irregularities.

He stopped a young Mexican-American woman. She looked about nineteen, dressed in a miniskirt, pullover long-sleeve sweater and a waist-length knit poncho. When Alan asked for her ID, she shuffled her feet and looked down.

"Want a closer look at her before I leave?" asked Alan, turning to Maggie. Extra clothes on a warm morning usually signaled a red flag.

Maggie nodded. "Come with me, Miss" she said, leading the woman to a small anteroom just off the walkway and asking her to take off the poncho. She performed a pat-down and stood back.

"Do you want to declare anything before a strip search?"

The young girl's eyes filled with tears. She reached down inside her bra and pulled out two plastic bags. Each bag contained seventy-five Ritalin tablets. Maggie led the woman back outside and handed the evidence to Alan, who would escort her and the drugs to the hearing room at Customs. She would be fined $312; the pills confiscated.

Maggie perched up on a stool after the switchover while Alan Robertson leaned over the counter and announced, "Let's go, keep the line moving." The day's shift flashed by; Maggie was surprised by the late hour when her relief arrived.

By 4:15 Maggie was back in the cafeteria filling her travel mug with fresh coffee for the ride home. She felt a tap on her shoulder and turned. CIA agent Estimo was standing behind her. Maggie narrowed her eyes suspiciously. "Something I can do for you Mr. Estimo?

"Actually there is. Estimo said sporting a big grin.

Maggie took a sip of coffee. "What's up?"

"Is there someplace private that we can talk?"

Maggie pointed to a table for two away from the small group of agents who hovered close to the doorway.

"That table looks fine." said Estimo.

When they were seated, he pulled out a pocket tape recorder and plugged a lead from a headset into it.

"Put these on and tell me what you think."

Estimo pushed the play button and Maggie listened intently. When the sound ended she took off the head set and handed it to him.

"Okay, what do you want me to tell you?"

Estimo stopped the tape and looked up. "Could you tell a difference between the three speakers?"

Maggie pursed her lips and nodded in the affirmative. "Yes, definitely."

Estimo explained further. "They all were speaking Spanish as a second language. The first was a French diplomat."

"Oh, really?"

"Yes, now, could you identify the second and third?

"The second was a typical American college student, right? I don't have a clue about the third."

"Yes, the second was a friend's son, second year at Southern Cal. And the third was an Arab interpreter for the UN."

198

"They all spoke quite differently."

"Do you think you could tell an Arab speaking Spanish if you heard one a next time?"

"I think so." She reached for the headset. "Let me hear the tape again."

Estimo rewound the tape and replayed it. Maggie shook her head as she listened for a second time.

"Oh yeah, I can tell the difference big time." Still wearing the headset, her voice rang out. A few agents in the lounge looked over at her having raised her voice, and looked away as Maggie took off the headphones with a shrug and grinned.

Estimo pocketed the tape recorder. "Very good, Maggie."

He paused for a moment, "Now I'm going to tell you about Roger's experience in Kuala Lumpur and what I was doing in Mindanao and how it may all tie together."

Maggie pulled her chair closer to the table and leaned toward Estimo. She was dying to hear some clandestine CIA business. "I'm listening."

After a strong warning against her ever talking about a national security issue, Estimo explained that Roger had been nearly been assassinated because of the resemblance between the two of them. Estimo relayed that Roger volunteered to become a decoy so he could leave KL while thought to remain there. "The decoy succeeded, but it ended in tragedy. My partner was killed along with an assassin."

He waited for Maggie to make eye contact: "Roger witnessed both killings."

Maggie was genuinely shocked. "Jesus, I had no idea."

"I had tracked some Arabs who were learning Spanish in Mindanao," Estimo continued.

"Wait a minute," said Maggie, interrupting. "I remember seeing a news clip about the Philippine army killing a bunch of terrorists in Mindanao. Carlin and I watched it when I was in the hospital. Were you there?"

Estimo nodded. "That happened two weeks before I got there, but the ambush took place just a few miles from where I was." He asked, "Who's Carlin?"

Maggie looked down, "Just a friend. He came to see me in the hospital when I got hurt."

"A friend? Or a good friend, like in competition for Roger?" Maggie's eyes returned to Estimo, her lips forming a smile. "No, Carlin's just a friend."

"That's a big toothy smile for *just a friend.*"

"Come on, Mr. Inquisitive, he's just somebody who has helped me a great deal since my *accident.* He and Roger have become close friends too. They have this mutual *thing* about college basketball."

"You make it sound like a terminal disease. It just happens to be my 'thing' as well. It's the middle of March Madness."

"I know, Arizona won Saturday."

"They're in the Sweet Sixteen and so is my Georgetown."

"Carlin is having a party Friday night for the Mississippi game. I'll see if I can get you on the guest list, if you'd like.

"I'd like that. What's Carlin's last name?"

"Why? You going to do a background check?"

"Of course not, I'd just like to know my host's full name."

"Ward."

Maggie stood. "Shall we go?"

They left the cafeteria together and headed for the parking lot. He opened the door for Maggie. "I'll get word to Roger so you two can make arrangements to go to Carlin's together." Maggie got into her car and roared off.

As Estimo slipped behind the wheel of his rental, he reached for his cell phone. He called FBI agent Norcross and asked for just one thing. How soon he could obtain a background check on one, Carlin Ward, 1000 Cactus Lane, Tucson, Arizona.

Norcross told Estimo that he already had a "BG" on Ward and asked if he'd like a copy before the Arizona-Mississippi game.

Estimo couldn't help but wonder if he FBI was checking up on him.

Chapter 36

The encampment stirred as the first rays reflected an orange hue off the top of the big pyramid. Maliq stuck his head into the Arabs' tent.

"Good morning, men. Abdul, Amir; join me outside as soon as you're dressed."

Both men looked over at him and nodded.

Maliq was finishing his second cigarette of the day when the two men joined him. He put the cigarette to his lips and took a long drag, his eyes on their expectant faces. Then he threw down the butt and ground it out with his boot.

"Let's take a walk." They headed for a flat stone area that they had learned was called a ball court. Maliq stopped walking and gazed at the ancient sunken court. He tried to visualize the deadly game that had been played on it.

Maliq stopped at one of the center rings that were located on each side of the ball court, halfway down the fifty-yard-long arena. The ring had a hole one foot in diameter about five feet above the playing area. Maliq sat down on the stone court and lit another cigarette. His men joined him on the hard ground and waited.

"Roberto told me that the Mayans played a sort of football on this court," Maliq said. He smoked in silence for a moment.

"They used a big rubber ball about the size of a human head.

Amir jumped up. "Like a soccer ball, ah?"

"About that size but it was very hard.

"This is a small court. How many were on each team?" asked Abdul.

"Each team played with seven men."

"Did they just kick it like we do?" Amir demonstrated by kicking an imaginary ball.

"No, they kept the ball in the air and moved it forward with their knees, hips, elbows, and any part of the body but the hands. The object was to put the ball into that hole above me." Maliq pointed above his head.

"Sounds more difficult than soccer, said Amir.

"Roberto also told me that the team that lost." Maliq paused for a long time. Abdul and Amir leaned toward him. Maliq waited longer still and finally continued, "The team that lost … all seven were beheaded. And the leader's head was placed in that hole."

Abdul went over and peered into the hole as though it still might contain a head, or at the least some ancient blood. He placed his hand in the reservoir, feeling the smooth surface. Amir shook his head in disbelief.

"I'd like to see the head of Roberto here when we depart but we need him to drive us. I've decided we'll go tomorrow morning if it can be arranged." said Maliq.

Amir placed his hand on the knife handle under his shirt. "I would like the honor, *el Tigre.*"

"It is yours, if we return here someday." Maliq said without hesitating. Following breakfast and morning prayers, Maliq's eyes searched for Emir Naïf, leader of the Mexican Muslims. He finally spotted him, the last to leave the prayer tent.

"Emir, may we speak now?" asked Maliq.

"But, of course," said the Imam. "Follow me."

Maliq bowed his head slightly and trailed behind Emir who led him down a trail to a secluded clearing behind the Pyramid of the Jaguar.

Their talk was brief. Maliq explained that he and his group would not like living in Mexico and had already decided to move on. "Emir, thank you for your hospitality, I wish you well. Can Roberto drive us back to San Christobal in the morning?"

Emir took the news calmly that he had expected. "But of course, *el Tigre.* I will arrange transportation for you and your men."

* * * * *

Before nightfall Subcomandante Marcos was seen riding through San Christobal. This time he even stopped outside the hotel Diego de Marariezegos. As soon as the Jeep came to a halt, a crowd surrounded him. He stood up in the topless vehicle, smiled, and waved to the throng. A cheer went up. Marcos called for the children. The adults backed away and guided their sons and daughters to the front. Marcos had bags of candy and began handing them out. A shirtless, shoeless seven-year-old boy inched forward. Before he put his hand out for the candy, he saluted. Marcos started to give the boy a treat but stopped. He returned the salute, then grabbed him in his arms and held him up for the crowd to see. "This young boy salutes me, but it is he that inspires us to fight on. The spirit of Zapata lives in his soul. *Viva Zapata!*"

The crowd took of the chant. *"Viva Zapata! Viva Zapata! Viva Zapata!"*

Marcos put the boy down and gave him the rest of the candy. He told him to share it with the other children. He sat down and instructed his driver to ease the vehicle through the crowd and out of the city. This moment would not soon be forgotten by the faithful.

* * * * *

It was still dark when Roberto led Maliq and his men back up the front of the great pyramid and down through its interior to the base of the Navel of the Universe. The parked truck remained concealed on the side of the road where they had left it three days earlier. Roberto was only too happy to drive the outsiders back to San Christobal. He did not care for any of them, especially their arrogant leader Miguel. Miguel, the tiger.

Chapter 37

Carlin answered his cell phone on the first ring. It was Jack Adams his old college buddy from Washington. "I think we should meet for a drink; say at the Peabody." The Peabody, a famous landmark hotel in Memphis, Tennessee is located as close to midpoint between D.C. and Tucson as one could get without utilizing GPS.

"When?" asked Carlin.

"Tomorrow's good for me. How about buying me that dinner you promised in January?"

"You're on, six at the Peabody. I'll make reservations for dinner and two rooms."

* * * * *

Jack was sitting at the bar when Carlin arrived, an hour late. "Sorry," Carlin apologized. Over dinner, Jack laid out all that he had learned from Senator McGuire who had called him over to his Watergate apartment the night before. After coffee and a couple of brandy nightcaps the two friends retired to their rooms.

Carlin rolled over for the tenth time. He squinted at the clock. It was 3:35 a.m. only five minutes since the last time he checked. The many pieces of a complex puzzle wove in and out, through and around his brain. He was concerned about telling Maggie classified information but he knew that he had to confide in her. The rapidly firing synapses wouldn't rest. Sleep was out of the question.

His right leg inched to the side of the bed and over the edge. Gravity did the rest. His foot flopped onto the floor. He pushed his left leg parallel and sprung up into a sitting position, eyes still firmly closed. He walked over to the television and retrieved the remote. Instantly the action on the screen grabbed his attention. He'd watch "Dances with Wolves" for the twenty-fifth time rather than lie sleepless in Memphis. He wished that he could magically teleport himself to Tucson. He couldn't wait to tell Maggie what he had learned from Washington.

Carlin and Jack shared a cab to the airport. They said a brief farewell and walked to their respective gates. Each had booked the earliest flight out. Carlin would be back in Arizona before lunch. He made a quick call to Maggie. "Can you call-in sick and pick me up in Phoenix?" She sounded surprised by the request but agreed. Yes, she'd be there at eleven.

* * * * *

Maggie met Carlin curbside then maneuvered her way out of the maze known as the Phoenix Sky Harbor International Airport. She found her way onto Interstate 10 and waited impatiently as Carlin settled into his seat. Carlin's call had seemed urgent but he was taking his good time before reporting on his mysterious trip to Memphis.

Carlin turned toward Maggie, his tone holding a seriousness that she had not heard before. "Let's start with some facts," he said. "According to a recent government report, a major Nogales drug lord named Brogadas pays the Mexican military to run interference for his weekly runs. You and Marty Fallon had the misfortune to get in their path."

"Our government *knows* this," Maggie said. "What do they plan to do about it?" Her question came out louder than she had intended.

"Maggie, I used the term 'government' loosely. I can assure you that less than a dozen know about this. Which reminds me ..." He glanced sideways at her. "I could be shot for what I'm telling you."

"Carlin! You don't have to remind me." Maggie's voice exploded inside the small car's cramped interior. Her face flushed.

205

Carlin flinched. He hadn't meant to insult her. "This is new to me, Maggie. I've never shared classified information with anyone who wasn't cleared before. I'm sorry."

Both were quiet for a moment. "I'm sorry, too," Maggie said in a controlled voice. She relaxed her grip on the steering wheel.

Carlin took a breath. "New topic: CIA agent Estimo tracked nine Arabs from the Philippines to Jakarta. They apparently were taking Spanish classes in Mindanao before they were abruptly asked to leave. Their teacher was an American undercover agent. The Arab's found out and killed him."

"So, why's Estimo in Tucson?"

"Essentially to keep an eye on Roger, seems he got caught up in some CIA business in Kuala Lumpur."

"I thought that was the FBI's job?"

"It is but Estimo was there with Roger, so both agencies are making sure that Roger keeps quiet about whatever it was that he saw over there."

"Estimo told me Roger's life was at risk."

"Oh?" Carlin's eyes widened. "Anything else?"

"No, not really." Maggie held back with her knowledge, for now. She braked gently and pulled into a gas station and got out of the car to fill up. Carlin followed her and stretched.

"Want me to drive for a while?"

"Sure, if you'd like."

Back on the road, Carlin continued his report. "The Arabs, they believe the same nine from the Philippines, were tracked to Paris where they flew on to South America."

Maggie nodded thoughtfully. "Makes sense, if they were learning Spanish that they'd travel to South America. Any clues as to what they're up to? And why do we care about them?"

"The CIA thinks that they are members of al-Qaeda."

"What's that?" Maggie lowered her head and peered at him over the top of her sunglasses.

"It's a radical Islamic fundamentalist group. They helped defeat the Russians in Afghanistan, and now want to export their beliefs throughout the world; by force, if necessary."

Maggie faced Carlin. She closed her eyes for a moment. "Like that group we saw on TV when you were in my hospital

206

room? Remember, the Philippine army killed a bunch of Islamic terrorists?"

Carlin looked back at her. "Yes, that was *Abu Sayyaf,* al-Qaeda financially supports them."

Carlin drove out of the gas station and quickly took them up to seventy-five. He gave a sigh glanced at Maggie and continued his commentary. "A military recon team reported seeing a group of nine Islamic worshipers at a Mayan archeological site in Chiapas."

"When?"

"About a week ago."

"Do your sources think it's the same group that went to South America?"

Carlin shook his head and tightened his lips. "They don't know."

He pushed her little Toyota up to eighty and passed five big rigs before easing back into the right lane. "I have a hunch it's the same group."

Maggie frowned. "Obviously, you think there's more on their agenda then fun in the sun."

"That's a given; but I can't help but wonder if agent Estimo could offer some insight. Do you think Roger knows him well enough to ask?"

"Now it's my turn." Maggie's excitable tone caused Carlin to stiffen. "Carlin you can't mention this to anyone – ever." She paused abruptly, and leaned forward to check an upcoming road sign.

"Let's stop at the Picacho Peak rest area. We can talk there. I'd like some ice cream."

Carlin hit the brakes harder than he preferred to avoid missing the approaching exit. The banked turn caused Maggie to shift hard against him. A sixteen wheeler roared by, air horn blasting. "A little more notice, next time, please."

She lowered her eyes meekly. "Yes sir, Mr. Ward. Sorry."

A gray Chevy van had an even harder job making the Picacho exit. Its driver was in the passing lane when Carlin unexpectedly hit the ramp. The driver had to pull onto the roadside service lane and back up a half-mile.

Chapter 38

A huge woman, far too large for her pink pedal pushers dragged an oversized Pullman right into Maliq as he cleared terminal B at *Bonito Juarez* airport, Mexico City. He staggered back and grimaced, swallowing an Arabic curse. He didn't know a Spanish profanity. He made a mental note to acquire a few.

To reach their next stop, one hundred and fifty miles south of the U.S. border, Maliq decided to split his group into four pairs again. He would travel alone. Six bought tickets for the last afternoon flight to Hermosillo. Abdul, Khalid and Maliq would spend the night in Mexico City and board the first flight in the morning.

* * * * *

A late model black Buick parked directly under the *PROHIBIDO REBASAR* sign closest to the *Mexicana de Aviacion* "arrivals" curb. Abdul spotted it first, grabbed Maliq's arm and pointed to it. Javier watched them cross the airport road and median that separated them. He opened the rear door and stood by nearly standing at attention.

"Bienvenidos a Hermosillo Senor Tsighis." Javier didn't know which one of the three approaching men was Maliq. He searched each face for a reaction. He guessed the leader was the one

in the middle. Javier was driving because he'd have three guests and he didn't fully trust José with such precious cargo.

"Gracias. Mucho gusto en conocerte. Maliq reached for the beefy hand extended in his direction. Javier was pleased. He had correctly picked Maliq from the trio. "I am Javier. "The rest of your men are in Nogales. We'll be there in a couple of hours."

Maliq got into the rear as directed along with Khalid. Abdul jumped into the front seat.

"Thank you for the ride." Not wanting to make small talk with a stranger, Maliq peered out his window. They sped onto a highway that skirted the northern edge of the grungy city. The dusty streets resembled Kabul, he thought. It was hot and windy. Maliq was glad the car's windows were up and cool air blasted throughout the luxurious interior.

Antonio Cobo had arranged for his Mexican customer, Pepe Brogadas, to house Maliq and his men. Al-Qaeda's first shipment of heroin had reached Brogadas the week before. The quality and price had excited the drug lord and he was only too happy to host the man who could assure a continued supply.

The trip to Nogales took longer than anticipated as Javier had to detour around a Mexican military checkpoint that had been set up that morning. Brogadas paid well not to be harassed by the military around Nogales, but Javier knew better than to chance a stop without knowing the name of the shift commander; especially with a car full of foreign undocumented travelers. If the cargo had just been drugs, a deal could easily have been cut for safe passage.

* * * * *

Maliq hadn't expected the opulence he viewed from the second story window of his suite, which overlooked the grand courtyard of the *Hacienda de Oro*. This place must be over the top even for a drug lord. Every inch of wrought iron was trimmed with gold highlights: railings, fountains, sconces, lawn chairs and tables, and even a decorative old wagon wheel. Although Maliq shook his head in disgust at the show of excess; he would use Brogadas' influence and resources that he needed to complete his mission.

Workers below him hung lights in preparation for a welcome fiesta, planned for sunset. He saw a few of his men relaxing poolside, where near naked girls walked around with trays of fresh fruit and cold drinks. Some of the men wore bathing suits and were engaged in animated conversations with a group of finely toned teenagers wearing string bikinis that covered only a fraction of their seductive figures. Maliq frowned. He must get his men out of here as quickly as possible.

Maliq spotted a tall redhead. She looked Anglo. Tomorrow, he murmured. Tomorrow will be soon enough to get my men out of this decadence. Tonight I will close my eyes to this evil. Tonight I will be a gracious guest. After the party, when my men have retired I will sleep with *la muchacha roja.*" He took a cigarette out of his top pocket and lit it, inhaling deeply, tasting the smoke. His eyes searched for the redhead. She had moved beside an enormous man wearing a golden robe who stood out of the sun under an archway across from Maliq's view. He looked up at Maliq. "My daughter. Isn't she beautiful?" He stroked her shoulder length hair with fatherly affection.

Maliq threw Brogadas a look that he hoped from a distance passed for a smile. He dropped his cigarette onto the tile floor and stomped on it harder than necessary. He unraveled a fresh roll of Tums and popped one into his mouth. Turning away from the window, he wished now, more than ever, that he had learned at least one curse in Spanish.

English would have to do. His lament was muted. "My host's daughter, shit. Damn it. Son hov-a-beech!"

Chapter 39

Carlin spied the gray van as it pulled into the rest stop and cruised under the single palm tree that offered the only shade from the noon-high sun. He had noticed a similar van that had hovered three and four car lengths behind them ever since they cleared the airport. He had already stopped in front of the store, but instead of turning off the ignition he backed up and steered over to the gas pumps.

"We can't need gas already," said Maggie.

"No, but I want to top it off for you. Go get your ice cream. None for me, thanks." Carlin patted his midsection for emphasis. Maggie walked toward the seven-foot tall Frosty Freddy mascot and entered the store.

"Christ, Smitty," said Norcross. "Can't we get anything right? The damn bug isn't broadcasting ten feet away. Can you install another mike when they go inside?"

"Moot point – he's minding the car – they don't need gas already." Jim Smyth was the driver as well as the electronic surveillance technician. Inside the van, Norcross removed the headset he was wearing and climbed over into the passenger's seat. He looked out the windshield to confirm Smyth's observation.

Carlin set the pump on automatic and strolled over to the van. He noticed that the driver's window was tinted. It was opaque, which violated state law. He knocked on the window. The window remained up and the driver silent. He banged hard on the door. From the inside he heard soft voices, the window rolled down a crack.

"Yo, watch you don't dent my door. What the hell do you want? I'm trying to catch a few winks," said the driver.

Carlin tried to look into the van but the window wasn't low enough. "Sorry. I was just wondering if agent Bobby Norcross wanted some ice cream, my treat."

The driver wrinkled his brow. "No one here but me. Get lost fella, or I'll dial nine-one-one." The window rolled up.

Carlin slowly walked back to Maggie's car. As he neared the vehicle he heard a familiar voice. "Bet you can't get more than a buck and a quarter into that tank." He recognized the baritone voice as belonging to FBI agent Robert Norcross.

Carlin looked to see where the pump had stopped and squeezed the handle until another fifteen cents registered. He replaced the nozzle in the pump. "Buck thirty five. You lost the bet." Carlin tried to sound glib but his legs buckled slightly and he had to fight to keep his hand steady. He screwed on the gas cap and turned to face Norcross. He put both hands in his pockets. If the agent had a listening device in Maggie's car, Carlin knew he could be going away for a long, long time. Leaning heavily against the car, he threw Norcross a tight-lipped grin.

Maggie rapidly took in the situation as she returned to the car. Could Norcross have bugged her car and overheard what Carlin and she had been talking about? She remembered Carlin's warning and wondered if she was in trouble. She tried to recall if she had said anything incriminating, realizing with shock that she had been about to relate her conversation with CIA agent Estimo. Thank God they had stopped for ice cream.

"Maggie, move your car over by the van and join us inside," agent Norcross yelled. He motioned for Carlin to follow him. Norcross reached the van and opened the rear doors for Carlin to enter. He waited for Maggie. When she stepped into the van Norcross climbed inside and shut both doors. It was dark and cool. Carlin was right, it contained very sophisticated-looking electronics. His head dropped and he closed his eyes. He hoped Norcross couldn't hear his heart pounding.

Norcross stood over Carlin and Maggie who sat on the only two available swivel seats in the rear working area. The agent ran his hand through his hair and sighed. "Okay, you caught me. I was trying to find out what you were up to with a Washington reporter in Memphis, Mr. Ward, but our electronics fizzled. So may I ask for your cooperation here, or do I need to escort you to jail again?"

Carlin closed his eyes and contemplated the extremely large caliber bullet that he had just dodged. "Of course I'll cooperate," he said. But I can't talk in front of Maggie and your driver." Jim Smyth hadn't taken his eyes off Carlin since he had entered the van. Smyth shrugged "Listen to that bull crap, will ya?" he said.

Norcross ordered Maggie and Smyth out of the van.

He turned to Carlin. "We're alone now. What was so important for you to rush off to Memphis, Mr. Ward?"

"We back to *mister* and *agent* again, Bob?" Carlin's tone was curt. He was beginning to regain his composure after being scared shitless.

"This is serious business. We can be formal or informal; but I want straight answers, Carlin Ward."

Carlin leaned back in his seat, trying to stall for time. He wondered if he should play his trump card.

"I'm waiting, Carlin my boy."

Carlin heard Maggie and Smyth talking outside. He nodded his head in the direction of the sounds. "This vehicle isn't soundproof, Bob Norcross."

Norcross yelled loud enough to be heard outside the truck. "Smitty, you and Lopez walk over toward the store and keep other ears away from here."

Smyth rapped twice on the side panel. "Okay, boss,"

Norcross waited until Smyth and Maggie's voices faded away. "Now, Carlin, please." Norcross relaxed and leaned against a metal rack supporting his malfunctioning receiver.

Carlin hesitated. "Okay. I went to Memphis to pay a dinner debt I owed an old college buddy. We like to do crazy things once in a while."

Norcross leaned close to Carlin's face, his voice rising. "Don't tell me what I already know. You paid for dinner and the rooms but you didn't go there just to repay a debt. What'd you talk about?"

Carlin stood and placed both hands in front of him, an invitation to be handcuffed. "Bob, I just can't tell you that. So do what you have to do."

"Sit down," Norcross ordered. Carlin sat and pulled his hands back. Norcross slumped on his seat and stretched out his long legs as far as he could. He shook his head gently from side to side and smiled. "Okay. Tell me what you can and I'll go elsewhere to fill-in the blanks."

Carlin relaxed. Like Norcross, he leaned back and extended his legs. "Alright. I met with a government official a few months back. I asked her to look into the border incident where Maggie got hurt." Carlin guessed that Norcross had already figured that he was referring to Senator George McGuire even though he had used a female pronoun. Carlin saw no reason to name names unless he was threatened. "Jack Adams my college buddy, passed along some confidential, but assuredly unclassified, information to me."

"And ..."

"And – I won't disclose what he told me."

'Carlin, I pretty much know what happened to Maggie at Organ Pipe and I think you do too."

"Well then we don't have to go there."

Norcross frowned. "If I had a tape of you and patrol agent Lopez talking in the car earlier you both would certainly be swimming in a lot of hot–make that boiling–water right now." Norcross made a hissing sound and raised a waving hand in the air. "But since I don't have a tape – the fucking thing wouldn't even record from here to your car – and you won't cooperate, I think that we should call this meeting to an end."

Carlin started to rise. Norcross pressed him gently back into his seat. "I want you to know that I strongly believe that you, Maggie and Roger Lacson are all involved with issues that concern national security – that's my job. So I want you to figure out a way to let me know what's going on. Then I can make a judgment as to whether or not the FBI needs to take action. Can you think of a third party who can't or won't disclose a source for any reason?"

"Like who?" Carlin tilted his head slightly.

"Like a priest ... a lawyer?" Norcross paused and tilted his own head in response. "Or a reporter?"

214

Carlin straightened up and pressed a finger to his chin. "Yes, I happen to know a couple of each."

"So it looks like we understand one another," Norcross said. All I'm after is what I think you three are pursuing – border matters – that might concern national security. I don't care who supplies the info or how it's obtained. I just don't want to be left out of the loop. Understand?"

"Yes, I do. And I'll discuss it with my," Carlin paused searching for the right word, 'associates'."

They shook hands.

"Meeting adjourned," said Norcross.

Neither Carlin nor Maggie uttered a word during the ride home.

Each was visualizing twenty-years in a ten by twelve, concrete enclosure equipped with a bunk, two stainless steel fixtures, and a grouchy roomie.

Carlin eased the car into his driveway. They both got out and walked away from the house and car to a spot where they felt certain that their conversation couldn't be overheard. "What were you going to tell me before we stopped for ice cream? Carlin asked.

Even out in the open, Maggie looked all around before answering. "Estimo had me listen to a tape of three Spanish speakers. It was a second language for each. He asked me if I could tell the difference between them."

"And, could you?"

"He told me one was an American college student, one was a French diplomat and the third, an Arab United Nations interpreter."

"Well?"

"I could tell the student right away and the diplomat sounded more Castilian but the Arab had a very different accent and cadence. I told Estimo that I thought I could tell that speech pattern if I heard it again."

"Spanish speaking Arabs?" Carlin looked at Maggie. "Do you think that we can trust Estimo?"

Maggie smiled. "He trusts me."

"Then we need to let him know what I've learned. Norcross suggested I might confide in a priest, lawyer, or reporter, any third party who wouldn't or couldn't divulge their source. He wants any

215

person who would then pass information from me to him." Carlin paused. "Do you think we should involve Roger?"

Maggie shrugged. "Why not? He was part of this CIA business before we were. I'll ask him if you want."

"I'd feel a lot better if we had Norcross on our side."

"Amen. Should we do this? It's illegal for the FBI, CIA and Senate Intelligence to share info!"

"I know. We have to be cautious. Norcross opened the door a crack for us to clue him in, but we need to bust it down. Talk to Roger, at a secure location, and get his thoughts. We should meet again as soon as possible."

"Settled," said Maggie.

They walked back towards her car. Carlin held the door open and Maggie slid inside. "Thanks for the lift."

She smiled and rolled down her window, "Anytime and thank you for the mid-day excitement."

"Sure." Carlin watched Maggie drive away. He remembered his suitcase was still in her trunk. He frowned and walked into the house.

* * * * *

Roger agreed to cooperate. The following day he passed along to Estimo all that Maggie had told him.

A conspiracy had been born.

216

Chapter 40

He didn't keep his word. Maliq stayed on as a guest of Brogadas for more than the one day he had promised himself. His host had too much to offer, and he didn't want to offend him.

In the meantime, Brogadas had explained that he wanted quadruple the supply of Afghanistan heroin. He also asked if Maliq and his men would join a raid that he planned on his competitor, Raynaldo Tellez. A hit on Tellez would be good for Maliq's organization, Brogadas explained, because he could then charge higher prices, which he pointed out jovially, would increase Maliq's profits. Maliq's only interest in drug trafficking profits was in what they could buy – safe passage to the United States. He didn't want to risk involvement in the raid, but it seemed unavoidable. He agreed to participate.

* * * * *

Maliq and his eight men formed up with twelve of Brogadas' soldiers. They were transported by three brand new Rhino Raptor MK IV model Humvees configured for troop transport. Located forty miles west of Nogales, Tellez's compound was a slightly less opulent version of Brogadas' headquarters. What did surprise Maliq was the support from a squad of Mexican military that lobbed mortar shells over the fifteen-foot walls. He heard the distinct 'thump' after each 81mm shell was dropped down the tube and fired. The rounds whistled overhead and the explosions shook the ground. Small arms fire pockmarked the walls and set fire to the wooden front gate. The attack lasted only ten minutes. No one shot back as Tellez and his men were driven under cover by the mortar fire. Brogadas smiled, although no one was hurt or killed on either side, a message had been sent. Tellez would move his operation out of Sonora, knowing that the military supported Brogadas and that they desired to do business with only one local drug lord.

Brogadas had offered many options for Maliq and his men to enter undetected into the U.S. The first, travel with an escort of the Mexican military; second walk with a coyote leading a group of illegals. The third offer was passage through a tunnel that now neared completion. The tunnel interested Maliq most; but it would be fool-hearty for the whole band to use the same route and risk getting caught. He decided to split up his group and take advantage of all three options.

Maliq had been completely won over by Brogadas and his generous hospitality. The Mexicans acted more like Arabs than he would have thought possible. He discovered that the redheaded woman was not Brogadas' daughter, but just one of the most beautiful in his plentiful harem; and he was only too happy to share.

* * * * *

Under the Arizona/Mexico Border

The dirt fell into his eyes, nose, and down the back of his shirt, but Manuel didn't care. He was digging upward, toward freedom and a new life in America. Pepe urged him on.

"Dig faster. Hurry, Paco and Javier will be back in a few hours to check on us again. Go. Go. Go!"

Pepe had done all of the digging since Manuel had become his partner, but Pepe was too tall to position himself on the bags near the ceiling, so he had handed the shovel to Manuel who climbed up onto the bags.

Manuel knelt on the night's full sacks of dirt, piled one on top of the other forming a four-foot tower. He jabbed upward hard

218

with a short handled spade. The tough brown earth was packed tight. A spark flashed onto his face as he struck a boulder. He scraped along its bottom, searching for its edge. The spade inched upward along the edge of the boulder.

As Manuel pushed, the spade suddenly sank into the earth up to its handle. He twisted it with all his strength and pulled down. Small rocks and earth gave way. A hole the size of a bucket opened and exposed a star-filled, moonless night sky.

"Yes!" Manuel yelled. "Yes, we are through."

A voice came from below him. "Hey! What the fuck are you doing up there?"

It wasn't the voice of Pepe.

Chapter 41

Manuel paid no attention to the voices and the commotion below him. He continued to dig upward. His arms ached but adrenalin surged through his body, giving him the strength to dig harder. More earth gave way, completely engulfing him in a dense, suffocating shower. Now the hole was wide enough for him to squeeze through. Someone grabbed his foot. He kicked back violently. His oversized dead-man's boot came off easily. He heard his attacker fall to the floor of the tunnel. Reaching through the hole with both arms, he braced one elbow firmly against the boulder and heaved himself above ground.

A shot exploded below him. He pulled his legs through the hole. Manuel crawled behind the huge boulder next to where he had emerged. He heard two more shots. He must block up the hole somehow. He had to move fast. A rock slightly larger than the hole lay a few feet away. He reached for it and with difficulty lifted it and staggered under its weight back toward the hole.

A hand reached up, followed by the top of someone's head. The head was bald. It wasn't Pepe. Manuel dropped the boulder. It smacked against the head, and then filled the hole. He heard a muffled scream. The hand hung on to its grip momentarily atop the ground. It then slowly slid beneath the rock and disappeared.

Manuel was soaked. He felt his undershirt and shorts clinging to his body like sea-soaked fishnets. Dirt covered his arms, short-sleeved shirt and jeans. He looked more like a clay sculpture than a man. He felt a sudden chill, and his body began shaking. He felt his arms cramping. Dazed, he sat abruptly on the ground. Tears and mucus turned the dirt in his mustache to a muddy paste. His chest heaved, and his lips trembled. He knew he had to move. But as he started to stand, he saw the ground rise and fall, and he fell, once again, onto his hands and knees. He lunged forward and threw up.

He wiped his mouth with the back of a dirty hand. "Dear God, why?" His voice quivered. "Why didn't Pepe make it out?" God didn't respond, but a coyote's howl jolted him into action.

Slowly Manuel rose and staggered around the big boulder. His eyes darted in every direction. He smelled the sharp tang of freshly cut wood. A newly constructed outhouse stood ten yards away. He walked over and peered inside. It was dark, but he could see that the seats had yet to be installed.

Manuel turned and hurried away. He steered clear of the darkened house nearby where he believed the users of the new outhouse must live. A man exploded from the house. Manuel dove behind a saguaro cactus. The man looked around and ran toward the big boulder where Manuel had just made his escape.

Manuel had seen enough. He jogged through the darkness and was surprised to find a dirt road running along the wall separating Mexico and the U.S. He followed it, and found that he was able to run faster in the rutted tire tracks.

He had run for only ten minutes when a car's headlights appeared. The vehicle approached too fast for him to jump aside and hide. He slowed to a walk, still following the road. Having discarded his other boot, he was now walking barefoot. The car stopped ten feet ahead. The driver's door opened. Manuel stood still, eyes blinded. Like a jackrabbit prepared to leap in any direction, he awaited the driver's next move. "Pray for me Mary, Mother of God, now and at the hour…"

"Drop to the ground, face down. Hands behind your back." The command was in Spanish and sounded like a woman.

Manuel went to his knees just as the first of four shots blasted in his direction. Maggie watched the dirt kick up near the man on the ground. Then she heard a fifth shot. A bullet whooshed over her head. A sixth blasted out her truck's front windshield.

"Damn, another vehicle damaged report," she couldn't help whisper sarcastically. She hit the ground and aimed her service

221

weapon where she had seen flashes. Maggie reached inside the car for the radio mike and called for backup. At the top of a rise in the dirt road, she watched a crouched figure run to a parked car. The vehicle had been parked there with its lights off which came on as the car backed up beyond her line of sight. She took aim but it was too late to get a clear shot.

Maggie stayed on the ground. "You alright, over there?"

Manuel raised his head and started to get up. "Yes, I'm not hurt."

Maggie shouted, "Stay down. Don't move!"

Manuel flattened against the ground once again. He saw the flashing blue lights before he heard the sirens. Three Border Patrol trucks pulled up behind Maggie. Six patrolmen hurled themselves from their vehicles. Four hit the ground, weapons drawn, and aimed in four different directions. Two bent over toward Maggie.

Manuel leaned on his elbows and watched the driver of the first truck speak to the female officer. Manuel knew that he was temporarily safe from Javier and his killers; but he was about to be arrested for entering the U.S illegally. *Will they put me in prison or will they send me back to Javier? Dear Mary, let it be jail, please.* The Guatemalan refugee was mumbling when Maggie, accompanied by two men in uniform approached. They stood over him for a moment, then reached down and lifted him off the ground, handcuffed him, and walked him over to the closest truck.

"This is the dirtiest one I've ever collared. What'd you do, crawl *under* the wall?" said Border Patrolman Kelly to no one in particular. He spoke in English hence Manuel's explanation remained unspoken.

Chapter 42

Maggie glanced at her watch. It was twenty minutes after midnight. She stood, stifled a yawn, stretched, picked up the paperwork and placed it in an envelope marked "interdepartmental." She used a felt marker to check the "ACCIDENT REPORT" box. She walked down the hall and slipped it into the "out" bin. Along the way she passed the interrogation room.

She peered through the wire-mesh window. The illegal she had stopped was alone in the room. He was on his knees praying. Maggie quietly opened the door and entered. The man was shackled to a metal bench bolted to the floor. Manuel squinted at Maggie, raised himself up and then sat down on the bench in silence. Maggie assumed that in the dark earlier the detainee had not seen her clearly enough to now be certain that she had been the agent who had caught him.

Under the bright room lights she noticed the man wasn't just dirty like most illegals that haven't bathed in days or weeks. This guy had globs of dirt in his hair and across his back. Dirt overflowed from his belt. It was caked on his arms. He wasn't wearing shoes. Maggie remembered agent Kelly's question to him when he was cuffed: *"What'd you do, crawl under the wall?"*

"How are you?" Her voice was soft and friendly. "I am agent Lopez, the agent who stopped you." Maggie moved toward the man and leaned her left arm on the edge of the table that separated them.

He looked like he was going to cry. "I'm okay, but very afraid."

223

"What's your name? Where are you from?"

"Manuel Sanchez. I live in Las Lisas."

"Do you know who was shooting at you?"

"I told the other agent. I couldn't see."

"How did you get so much dirt on you?"

"From the tunnel when I broke through."

A customs officer whom Maggie knew charged into the room with a tall, blond man whom she didn't know. She turned to face them, turning on her sweetest smile to ease the tension of their disapproving looks.

"Lopez, what are you doing here? You're not authorized to speak to him." Officer Dilks' upper lip tightened as he spoke. He held the look, waiting for Maggie's reply. The second man just stood stiffly, his arms folded, slowly shaking his head. He glared coldly at Maggie.

"I nabbed him; and I was curious about his story."

"I know you were involved in his detention and the shoot-out. But you don't interrogate anyone in my charge." Dilks' anger was not only genuine, but overdone for the benefit of his guest.

"Sorry, didn't mean to break the rules." Maggie dropped the smile and tried to appear contrite. Since there seemed to be no introductions, Maggie stuck her hand out. "Good evening, I'm agent Maggie Lopez." She paused and waited for a response.

The man unfolded his arms and grudgingly received her hand. "I'm John Williams." He relaxed his stance, but offered no title with the name.

"Please excuse us, Lopez," said Dilks

"Surely. Sorry again." Maggie looked back at Manuel, and out of sight of the other two, winked and mouthed the word, *tarde*. She hoped Manuel understood that she wanted to see him later. She left making sure to ease the door completely closed but ever so softly.

* * * * *

Maggie couldn't risk going home without learning where they might deposit Manuel Sanchez. Normally the illegal alien would be taken to the holding pen, but she was suspicious because

224

of the unidentified interrogator. She couldn't just stand out in the hallway. She needed help and once more she thought fleetingly of Marty. She walked outside and wandered over to the VIP parking lot. A gray van similar to the one that FBI agent Norcross drove sat at the far end of the lot. Maggie walked to it and tried the doors. They were locked. Looking over toward the building she slipped her hand onto the back door latch and turned it. It swung out and opened. She stepped inside.

Just like agent Norcross' van, it was filled with sophisticated electronics. She knelt near the rear door and watched the building's entrance until her eyes blurred. She rubbed them and when she looked again officer Dilks and his guest, 'no-title Williams' were walking down the steps. Her chest tightened and she breathed hurriedly. They stopped by one car, talked for a while and then continued toward the van. Maggie stopped breathing completely as the two reached the van. The horn honked as a keyless entry device was triggered. Maggie jumped, letting out a grunt. Fortunately, Williams was talking too loudly to hear her.

Williams opened the driver's door. "You know what I think? I think he skipped out on a fee then ran away. The coyote found him and tried to kill him, send a message to others."

Dilks held the door open as Williams slipped behind the wheel. "Yeah, I agree," Dilks said. "And as far as having family here, they all say that. Besides most Guatemalans go through Texas where it's a much shorter route."

Maggie cocked her head and closed her eyes. She blocked out the voices and concentrated. *Manuel was Guatemalan ... his last name was Sanchez ... could it be possible?* The van's engine started. Maggie snapped back from her reverie, realizing she was trapped. Williams rolled down the window. "Well, thanks for the call. You never know. At first glance, I thought he looked like a mule too. Find me a *loaded* mule and the DEA will buy us both a nice dinner."

The van backed out of the parking space. Maggie hugged the floor. She shivered and felt cold sweat under her arms. The vehicle bounced onto the now quiet streets of Nogales and picked up speed as it entered Interstate 19 going north toward Tucson. Williams turned on the radio and sang along with Elvis.

Ten miles later he slowed pulled off the highway into a gas station in Rio Rico. He parked, got out and went inside the all-night store. The station was well lit, but stood alongside a wash where the darkness closed in fast. Maggie had to risk flight. She hadn't heard Williams lock the doors, but she still prayed silently that the alarm wouldn't go off as she flung open the rear door. It didn't. She pushed the doors partly closed and scrambled into the wash as another car's lights approached.

Williams came out of the store with a donut and a cola. He got in the van and backed up. When he stopped, the back doors flew open. Maggie heard the new arrival shout, "Hey, fella your back doors are open."

Williams stepped out of the van, stuck his head into the back and closed the doors. He looked all around as he walked back to the driver's side. He brought a finger to his head in a salute to the stranger. "Thanks."

Maggie was relieved to see the taillights of the van turn for the ramp to the Interstate and head north. She waited twenty minutes, then climbed out of the wash and walked into the store. The store clerk looked up from a magazine as she entered. He searched the parking lot for a car.

"Flat, few miles back," said Maggie answering the unasked question. It was 2:45 in the morning. "Got change for a dollar?" Quarters in hand, Maggie returned outside to the pay phone to call the only person she knew who'd help at this ungodly hour.

She dialed the number she now had memorized.

* * * * *

His caller ID displayed an unknown number, but Carlin knew who was on the other end of the line. He answered anyway. "Maggie, can't you get into trouble during normal working hours. I'm an aging senior who needs his rest?"

Nora sat up and looked over at her husband silhouetted against the dim nightlight. She raised both hands in the air in a display of surrender, flopped back down, rolled over and pulled the covers hard.

226

Chapter 43

At exactly 4:00 a.m. Carlin pulled into the gas station in Rio Rico. He spotted the lone figure sitting at a table outside the store, sipping from a paper cup. He parked near the table, got out of the car, covered his mouth and faked a loud yawn.

"Coffee?" Maggie held up a second paper cup. "It cures that 'overslept' feeling." She smiled and nodded for him to come over.

Carlin wanted to imbue misery, but Maggie once again managed to disarm him. He took a seat across from her, grabbed the coffee and smiled back with a hint of sarcasm. "You know, my wife thinks I'm nuts and I'm beginning to agree with her."

"I'm sorry, Carlin"

Carlin dropped the smirk. "Now, what's so urgent this time?"

Maggie explained the previous night's action, ending with her recent predicament. Carlin shook his head in disbelief. "Maggie, you could have been fired for climbing in that van."

"Believe me, I thought of that. Plus I imagined a probable criminal trespassing charge thrown in for good measure."

"What's next, Houdini?"

"I want to go to my office and check the records for the Organ Pipe action of six-Feb." Soon they were on Interstate 19 heading back toward Nogales.

"So, you think this Manuel Sanchez might be related to Margarita?"

"It's a long shot, but Las Lisas must be a small town. I didn't connect the two until Dilks said Manuel was Guatemalan and that he

227

claimed to have family in the U.S. Manuel told me he was from Las Lisas, but I didn't think Guatemala."

"Where's Manuel now?"

"I don't know. That's another reason why I need to go back right now."

Maggie was on a caffeine-high. Carlin yawned again. This time it was for real. He rubbed his eyes then focused on the highway.

As they neared the border patrol complex, Maggie said, "Pull into the Burger King lot." She pointed out the entrance. "When it opens at five, refill your coffee. They'll give you a receipt for parking. Put it on your dash then find me over there." Maggie nodded toward the tall white customs building across the street. As soon as Carlin came to a stop she jumped out of the car and ran out across the lot.

As Maggie neared the building, she stopped abruptly. Dilks was walking out the door with Manuel Sanchez in tow. They approached a parked prisoner transport van.

A driver and guard climbed out of the vehicle and walked over to Dilks and Sanchez. Maggie ducked behind a park car and watched as Dilks grabbed Manuel by the collar and shoved him forward. Dilks placed both hands on the driver's shoulders then put his nose right in the man's face. "Henry is your car parked at the rest stop?" said Dilks loud enough for Maggie to hear.

The driver leaned his head back as far as he could still in Dilks grasp. "Yeah."

"Then take him to Douglas, in your car, like we discussed. Wait in front of the Gadsden Hotel. A black Buick will pull behind you. A guy named Javier Mendez will show you his Mexican driver's license. Release the illegal to him and return here."

The guard escorted Manual to the rear of the vehicle, shoved him inside, jumped up, and slammed both doors shut. Dilks released the driver from his grasp. The driver walked to the vehicle checked that the back doors were lock then headed for the cab.

Dilks shouted, "Hurry, the Buick will be there right after the border opens." The transport pulled away. Dilks turned, trotted up the steps and walked back into the building.

228

Maggie overheard everything. The van pulled away turned toward Douglas. She also had noticed that the driver and guard were not in uniform.

She froze in place. *Think. Think. Do I go back for Carlin? Run to my car? Call a supervisor?*

She chose option one.

* * * * *

Until now life in U.S. custody hadn't been bad. Manuel had been allowed to clean up, been fed and someone had even found a pair of shoes that fit better than his lost boots. That all changed when he heard three words: *black, Buick,* and *Javier.* His heart pounded. He closed his eyes and prayed. He knew that if his body entered the black Buick only his soul would exit. He opened his eyes and looked down at his jeans darken around the crotch. The urine felt warm running down his leg, then turned cold. Manuel tasted bile. His stomach retched and suddenly with no regard for his fellow passenger, he heaved the contents of his half-digested dinner in the direction of the guard seated directly across from him.

The guard jumped up. "Jesus! Jesus Christ! Roger, stop the fucking van. Stop."

"I can't stop. We'll be late. You heard Dilks. We have to be in Douglas before the border opens."

"Please. I have to get out and get this shit-head's puke off me. And he pissed himself too. God damn."

* * * * *

Maggie ran back to the Burger King parking lot. Carlin's head leaned peacefully against his car window. She banged on the windshield. "Carlin, wake up. Unlock the door!"

Carlin bolted up. He shook his head and looked around for the freight train that must be headed his way. As his head cleared, the emergency crystallized into one panicky agent, Maggie Lopez. The fear on her face said it all. He hit the door lock release. "What's happened?"

Maggie jerked the driver's door open. "Move over. I'll drive. I know the way."

"The way to where? Slow down." Carlin hopped over the armrest and Maggie slipped into the driver's seat.

She gasped for air and coughed, then tore out of the parking lot. Carlin's Prius had a lot more spunk than her old Toyota Corolla.

Carlin watched Maggie's facial contortions as she drove erratically. "Tell me what's going on?" He was stern.

Maggie glanced over at him. "Alright. Give me a minute. I'm calculating the fastest route right now."

Carlin took a deep breath, exhaled and sat in resigned indignation.

"In this car the fastest route is the smoothest roadways, although the longest in miles," said Maggie.

"The fastest route to where?"

"Douglas."

"Okay, we're on our way to Douglas at four something in the morning. How about a reason?"

"Something's not right."

Carlin smiled mockingly. "You can say that again."

Maggie ignored him. She waited a moment.

"They're shipping Manuel to Douglas right now."

"Why? What's there?"

"Nothing. There's no logical explanation for taking him there. Dilks mentioned the Gadsden Hotel and something about a black Buick. That's why we need to get there before the border opens."

Once on the highway, Maggie pushed the needle to eighty-five.

* * * * *

The transport driver tried to calm his cursing, puke-splattered guard.

"Jerry, I can't stop now. Wait ten minutes and we'll be at the rest stop where I left my car last night. We gotta do the prisoner exchange from my car in Douglas.

Chapter 44

Maggie flew past the transport as it slowed to enter a rest stop. She took her foot off the gas but didn't hit the brakes. She didn't want the driver to see that she was about to pull a double "U" and follow him into the rest area. She caught a glimpse of Carlin closing his eyes and holding on to the top of his head as she pulled the wheel hard to the left. His little car went airborne for a few feet and then scraped over a boulder.

She was blinded momentarily by an oncoming motor home, seeing there were no other vehicles headed her way, she completed her U-turn. She repeated the maneuver just past the rest stop, this time clipping the tailpipe as she left the median. The car crossed the two lanes and shot up the exit ramp. She eased into the rest area and drove to the rear lot designated for trucks. Coming to a stop between two Wal-Mart double tandems, she put the car in park and kept the engine running.

"Now what? asked Carlin.

"I don't know. Maybe one of them had to go to the men's room." Maggie shrugged.

"Carlin, please be a darling and go check things out."

"Why me?"

"Because I'm still in uniform," she was beginning to loose her patients. "Go see what they're up to." Her voice was firm.

What Carlin heard was a command not a request. He opened the door and slowly slid out, mumbling under his breath. "I see another jail cell in my future." Carlin closed the car door. He walked across the lot and through the open area between two buildings. On his right were the rest rooms; on the left a visitors' information center which was closed. Only four cars and the prisoner transport vehicle were parked on the lot designated for cars. Carlin stood behind a soda machine and looked around. He saw the driver of the van walk to the back and open its doors. A man jumped out and jogged to the men's room. The driver pulled the short prisoner out of the van and walked him over to a Chevy Malibu. Five minutes later, Carlin saw the other man come out of the washroom. He dried his face and hands with paper towels. His hair soaked with water ran in streams off his head and down his shirt. He crumpled the paper towels and dropped them in a trash receptacle. Combing his wet hair, he strolled over to the Chevy where the driver stood waiting. "Hurry," Carlin heard the driver yell.

The man walked faster, reached the car and jumped into the back seat. Then the driver escorted his prisoner toward the restrooms. Carlin reached into his pocket, retrieved a few coins and pretended to buy a soda. With a firm grip on Manuel's arm, the driver moved past Carlin and walked into the men's room. Carlin followed them. As he approached the men's room, the door flew open: Manuel burst past him and ran out toward the back parking lot. The driver rushed after him but smacked head-on into Carlin. Both went down. Carlin lifted himself to his knees and then deliberately fell back across the sprawled man struggling to stand up. The man finally shoved Carlin aside. The man jumped to his feet, and ran toward the front, yelling for the guard in the car.

Outside, Manuel ran past a big truck, he heard a low voice call, "Manuel. Over here."

He stopped. A lady in a border patrol agent uniform was standing next to an odd-looking car, holding the rear door open. He recognized Maggie, but didn't move. He shook his head. In the distance, he heard the prison van driver yell for the guard.

Maggie waved her hand. "Over here. Quickly."

Manuel stood frozen.

"I'll take you to Margarita."

232

Manuel's eyes widened. He dashed toward Maggie and dove into the car, Maggie slammed the rear door shut behind him. "Down on the floor. Stay down!"

Maggie jumped behind the wheel and drove out cautiously between the trucks. The transport driver appeared in the causeway between the public washrooms and the visitors' center. He threw a fast glance in every direction. A second man joined him. It wasn't Carlin. They watch as she drove away. In her mirror, she saw them running over to the two trucks.

Maggie drove east toward Douglas. She didn't want to alert Manuel's jailers by crossing the median again. Five miles farther east, she exited Interstate 10 at the Pantano Road overpass and headed west toward Tucson. "Manuel don't you dare get up."

"Yes, ma'am. Where we going?"

"I wish I knew. I only wish to Hell, that I knew where we're going. And knew what it is that I'm doing."

* * * * *

Watching from his vantage point beside the soda machine, Carlin knew he had to get out of sight by the time the men returned. He tried the door to the visitor's center, but it was locked. He walked around to the front of the building, found no place to hide, and retraced his steps. He decided on the ladies room. He went in, picked out the center stall, then locked the door and sat.

Almost as soon as he had hit the latch, a hand rattled the door to his stall. He held his breath.

"Sorry," said a female voice. The door to the next stall opened.

Carlin heaved a sigh of relief. He lifted his feet so that his size eleven loafers didn't show under the stall. He rested them against the stall door.

He heard the toilet flush and the woman leave the stall, followed by water running at the sink.

The woman screamed.

Carlin jerked back involuntary. The hairs on the back of his neck stiffened.

He heard the woman at the sink yell. "My husband's right outside!"

233

"Sorry, madam. Sorry. My mistake," It was a male voice, high-pitched with obvious embarrassment. Carlin heard the ladies room intruder's steps recede and the door squeak closed.

Then Carlin listened as the woman walk out and silence returned. It was quiet enough to hear a fly buzzing overhead, continually banging against the skylight that announced daylight had arrived. He felt pain on his right elbow and looked at the scrape he had earned while rolling on the concrete earlier. He felt a small lump on the back of his head. His hair was matted, presumably with his own blood.

Carlin's thoughts wandered to his wife. *God, how can I tell Nora that thanks to Maggie Lopez, I spent the night hiding in a women's restroom?* Some things just defied explanation and this was one of them. Carlin heard the toilets flush eight more times before he considered it safe to leave his hideout.

Chapter 45

Cinco de Mayo was a full week away. The Mexican fifth of May celebration commemorated the day in 1862 when a few thousand Mexicans beat a contingent of Europe's elite military–*la Frances*. It was also the date on which Maliq planned to take his men into the United States.

Maliq gathered them for a meeting. They assembled in the principal guesthouse of Senor Brogadas' former competitor Vincente Aguilar, who had vacated the compound under extreme duress a few weeks earlier.

All nine gathered beside a magnificent old dining table that would easily have accommodated twenty. Maliq remained standing. He took a pack of cigarettes from his shirt pocket, shook out one, tamped it against the table, and lit up. He inhaled deeply and blew the smoke toward the ceiling. He paused. His men sat in silence, waiting.

Maliq looked slowly around the table. The time was near when they would enter the United States. They would do so in three groups. Each group would be unaware of the others' means of crossing. They would each have instructions and a specified timetable. Maliq took another drag on the cigarette and threw it on the floor. "I will review with each of your individual assignments and travel plans. Once we cross, you will be on your own. There will be no further contact until we are reunited in Afghanistan. This will also be the last time that I address you by your Arab names. Amir, remain here. The rest of you – go outside until I call."

Amir watched as the others filed outside in groups of two and three.

"Sit here, my friend Alberto." Maliq patted the chair on the end position, then sat beside the man with the new name. "Alberto, who is your target and where does he live?" Maliq didn't smile and his voice sounded an octave lower than normal. He popped two Tums into his mouth and leaned back. He studied his most eager and lethal team member.

He could visualize Amir slicing the head off the Spanish Muslim truck driver and placing the bloody cranium in the Mayan ball court reservoir.

"He is Senator McGuire. He lives in Haddonfield, New Jersey." Alberto continued with the detailed travel plans that had been communicated months ago. His voice was solemn, matching Maliq's tone. "I will travel by bus from Tucson to Phoenix and fly from there to Newark, New Jersey. Then I take another bus to Philadelphia. There I will buy a used car and drive to the Haddon Hills apartments in Westmont, New Jersey. This is where my contact, Faizah Ghailani, lives." Faizah was a Domestic Services International employee who had been hired by Senator McGuire. She had worked for him over the past nine months.

Satisfied that Alberto knew his assignment and how to accomplish it, Maliq stood. "You'll be in my group when we cross. You don't need to know any more about that part of the mission." Maliq lit another cigarette then told him to leave and send in Abdul.

Abdul sat in the chair vacated by Alberto. "A cigarette, please."

"Abdul," Maliq forgot his recent rule and called him by his Arab name, "you don't smoke."

"No, but José does."

Maliq laughed. Abdul had broken the tension. Maliq extended the pack towards him. Abdul took a cigarette. "Light, please." He waited as Maliq dutifully lighted the cigarette extended from his pursed lips. Abdul then took a drag, swallowed a cough, and forced a smile. He took another puff without coughing and leaned across the table. "My target is Magabucks McDonald. I buy a used car when I get to Phoenix and drive to the Sunset Motel in Las Vegas. There I wait for my contact, Ghada Siddiqui." Abdul's usual soft monotone had become brisk and businesslike.

"Very good, José." It must be Spanish names only from now on, Maliq reminded himself. "One other thing. You will lead the group who will walk across with some Mexicans. Your guide will be the best *coyote* on the border. He has never failed to get his charges safely to their drop-off. I will give you more details later. Send in Karim; and remember to buy your own cigarettes from now on."

Abdul chuckled.

Maliq heard him calling for Kruz before the door closed. Karim came in. "Good day, Miguel. Kruz Gonzales at your service."

"Very good, Kruz." Maliq complimented Karim for using his and Maliq's Spanish names and for using a common Mexican idiom.

"My target is news anchor Thomas Brooks. He will be vacationing in Augusta, Montana," said Karim.

Maliq reviewed every detail with each man. After the last man left the room, Maliq stood. He smiled and brought his hand down hard on the table. He shouted. Come in here, all of you!" Clearly wondering what could be wrong, the men pushed their way back into the room. Expectantly, they stood and looked at Maliq, who was still smiling.

"Excellent. Excellent. Men when we're finished America and the world will remember what we do on September eleventh." Now, let's go back to Brogadas and celebrate."

A roar went up from the assassins.

Chapter 46

Carlin listened for one more flush, the ninth, before he came out of the stall, pushed the ladies' restroom door open a crack and peeked out in both directions. No one was in sight. He brushed through the door and hurried directly into the men's room. Standing at the sink, he addressed the mirror.

"Well, Mr. Ward, I'd say you do look the worse for wear."

A traveler with a toddler entered the room. Carlin cleared his throat and splashed water onto his unshaven face. He turned his head in an attempt to view the lump he felt, but it was too far behind. He wet his comb and gingerly combed the hair over the bruise. The comb resisted the spot where blood had clotted. A second look in the mirror reflected little improvement.

He walked outside into the sunlight and rubbed his yes. He slipped his sunglasses on and leaned forward against the wall to stretch. His pre-marathon pose didn't even begin to relieve the cramps he had acquired from his long night's vigil sitting on a hopper.

He walked to the curb and looked around. It was a much busier stop at seven than it had been at four-thirty that morning. Cars, trucks, campers, minivans, and motorcycles lined up in orderly fashion on both sides of the mammoth complex. Truckers, bikers, and vacationers formed a continuous procession to and from the restrooms. He didn't expect to see Maggie and Manuel among the

238

crowd and he had no clue how he was going to get home without calling his wife. Nora had to be the last resort.

"Hey, Carlin. Need a ride?"

The familiar voice came from behind. Carlin turned to see Roger Lacson dropping coins in the soda machine. Carlin lowered his shoulders. He didn't realized how tense he had been until he heard the familiar voice and smiled. Roger retrieved a Coke and aimed it at Carlin. "Want one? The powdered coffee sucks."

"Yeah."

Roger tossed the can and dropped more coins in the machine.

Carlin popped it open, avoided the spray, and took a healthy swig.

"Thanks, that rattled my eyeballs some."

Roger grinned. "Ready?"

"You bet."

As they walked to Roger's truck, Carlin asked, "Where's my car?"

"Don't know."

"Where's Maggie?"

"Don't know."

"Where's Manuel?"

"Don't know a Manuel. But I suspect that Maggie and your car are at the same locale."

"A remarkable reporter you are." Carlin rolled his eyes in half-feigned exasperation.

"It's very hard to be a worthy reporter when the interviewee deflects every question. Maggie said to come to this rest stop, see if you're here, and if you were, take you to my place. So, since I found you, we're headed to my place. Okay?"

"Yes, right after we stop by the Gadsden Hotel in Douglas." Carlin walked ten paces away from Roger, unclipped the cell phone from his belt, flipped it open, and called his wife with a sanitized update of his past evening. Her questions were as plentiful and pointed as his answers were short and evasive.

* * * * *

Traffic was exceptionally light approaching Douglas. When the hotel came into view, Roger followed Carlin's instructions to

239

park a block beyond it and across the street. Carlin looked at the five-story, square, twin towers. It looked too modern, he thought, for this old western border town. He walked cautiously toward the hotel. A black Buick was parked in front, a man sitting behind the wheel with the windows down. As he neared the car, Carlin heard mariachi music. He looked around for the man he had wrestled but didn't see him. He crossed the street well beyond the Buick and entered the hotel.

In contrast to its stark curbside appearance, the spectacular lobby gave credence to its reputation as "one of the last of the grand hotels." Once inside the view was dominated by a brilliant-white Italian marble staircase. Atop the steps, a forty-foot Tiffany stained glass mural rivaled the beauty of the Grecian marble work. It was rumored that the ghost of Pancho Villa made its home here.

Among the twenty gringo guests who wandered about the room, one man, obviously a Mexican, caught Carlin's attention. The man appeared agitated. He paced back and forth at the top of the landing. He fired rapid Spanish into his cell phone. Carlin inched closer. He heard the man say, *"Senor Dilks, Donde es Manuel?"* Carlin's Spanish was scanty, but good enough. This was the man waiting for Manuel. Taking a cue from his newly found FBI and CIA friends, Carlin snapped a mental picture of him, and replayed the Buick's tag number in his head. The man finished his conversation, pocketed his phone and turned toward the front doors.

Carlin noticed how flush-faced the man had become. He then followed him across the lobby toward the exit. He was careful to keep a tourist couple, wearing matching outfits, between him and his 'mark' as they also headed out the front. At least the male tourist had the good sense to wear a New York Yankees baseball cap, instead of a cute little beret like the one that his travel-mate wore.

Outside, the Mexican put his head down and bolted for the Buick. He opened the rear door and flopped onto the seat. The music lowered significantly and the driver asked, *"Donde va, Javier?"*

"Hacienda de Brogadas. Y pronto!" said the man. Carlin overheard, although he had stopped at the front door and pretended to admire the jewelry display in the hotel window. He now knew the man's name. He repeated it silently. Javier. He also softly repeated his destination, "Brogadas." The Buick pulled out and sped down

the street as Carlin checked the tag number once again: Sonora 168-SNN-8.

Carlin waved at Roger sitting behind the wheel of his truck a block away. Roger drove to meet him. Carlin crossed the street and climbed into the passenger's seat. Fearing that Roger's truck might be bugged, he leaned over and whispered in Roger's ear. "Let's go to your place, as ordered by that car-thieving, human-traffic-smuggling, stunt-driving woman of yours."

Carlin took out a pen and one of his business cards. He wrote down the names and tag number, feeling upbeat about his clever detective work. He frowned though. Serious charges could now be brought against Maggie and all of her accomplices, present company included.

They remained silent all the way to Tucson both thinking that Roger's car might be bugged.

Carlin closed his eyes. His head dipped slowly until his chin rested on his chest. Fatigue overcame the fading adrenalin surge, and he dozed off twenty miles before they reached Tucson.

Chapter 47

Maggie gripped the wheel tight to keep her hands from shaking. A dozen thoughts flashed through her head. Concentrating on only one thing seemed beyond her. She had to focus. In a minute she would arrive with her illegal human cargo at the junction where Interstate 10 forked. Texas or Tucson?

She realized she was in the far left lane. Because of the heavy traffic, she couldn't exit east if she had wanted to, one less decision. Tucson and points north and west became her only options. She moved over to the center lane. Now at least she'd have choices in the event that she could decide on a route. Manuel had not moved or uttered a sound since Maggie last yelled at him.

"Think. God, help me! You get paid to think under pressure. Now do it." Maggie spoke her petition aloud, and immediately it seemed that the Almighty heard her. A clear picture of Marty Fallon's mountain retreat formed in her head. The cabin was located near the village of Overgaard in the White Mountains, a hundred miles east of Phoenix. Maggie guessed the fastest route was probably through Phoenix, but she took the longer and less traveled road through Salt River Canyon.

Marty, her severely injured partner, had insisted she use his primitive bachelor cabin in the mountains whenever she wanted. She even remembered that the key was hidden under the second of three potted plants on the back step. She had only gone there with him once before. It would take near total recall to find it again but it was the best hideout she could have chosen.

"May I sit up now?" a soft voice asked in Spanish from behind her.

Maggie considered. It should be okay for him to sit up front, she decided. Actually it might look more suspicious for him to remain in back. She pulled over to the side of the road and motioned for him to sit beside her. The faint odor of urine and vomit became stronger when he jumped into the passenger seat. Maggie withheld, for the moment, the questions she wanted to ask, and drove on.

She had traveled only a few miles when she heard a siren blast and saw flashing lights behind her. A shiver went through her and her stomach muscles tightened. "Manuel, don't say a word. Not a sound, understand?"

"Si. Yo comprendo."

She pulled over, rolled down the window and waited.

"Registration, insurance and license ma'am." The deputy sheriff asked politely. She knew he must have noticed her uniform and had to be wondering about Manuel beside her.

She looked up and shrugged. "What's the problem, deputy?"

"Registration, insurance and license, please." He was a little less pleasant. Maggie closed her eyes and drew a deep breath.

She reached into the glove box and prayed that Carlin had left the documents there. She grabbed a folder and opened it. She breathed easier when she saw the registration and insurance card inside. She took the license from her wallet and handed all three items to the deputy. In the mirror she watched him return to his vehicle and perform the requisite computer check. She recalled the penalty for harboring an illegal entrant. *Five years max, plus two hundred and fifty thousand dollars.* After a few minutes the deputy returned beside Maggie's window.

"You were doing fifty in a thirty-five. This car was reported stolen but apparently had been returned to the owner. Are you driving Mr. Ward's car with his permission, Agent Lopez?"

Maggie forced a smile as she slightly bent the truth. "Yes, of course."

The deputy handed Maggie the documents. "No citation; professional courtesy. But I bet you wouldn't let me bring anything illegal from Mexico, like the man beside you, would you?"

Maggie looked away, returning Carlin's documents to the glove box. She felt the blood leave her face. *How could he have known? Is he going to arrest us?* She straightened up and smiled weakly as she looked at the deputy.

"Well, I might allow you an extra bottle of José Cuervo, but never a 'José' like my gardener here." She tapped Manuel on the shoulder. Manuel trembled at her touch and dropped his head. He didn't understand the words but he knew they were talking about him.

"Okay. Drive slower or my buddy ten miles up the road may not be as forgiving."

"Thanks for the favor, deputy. And I'll watch my speed." She quickly closed the window before the deputy could get a whiff of Manuel's vomit and urine-splattered jeans.

* * * * *

Maps show Arizona State Highway 77 with a dotted line, indicating a scenic highway through the Salt River Canyon. Most travelers heading north along the route, watching the sun bounce off the golden cliffs, as Maggie did this morning, would likely vote for double dots. Maggie ignored the view. She tried to remember the landmarks to Marty's place. About thirty miles past the canyon she recalled that they had made a left at the first traffic light in Show Low, the town named after a gambler's card draw. The next turn was exactly two miles past a restaurant called the Red Onion. Maggie found the eatery and pulled into its lot. "Hungry?" she asked Manuel, who had not uttered a word since before the traffic stop.

"*Si.*"

She got out of the car, leaned over and spoke softly. "Stay put. I'll be right back." She automatically hit the remote, locking all the doors. Manuel looked at her when the doors clicked.

Twenty minutes later she returned, carrying a large brown bag. She placed it on Manuel's lap, strapped herself in and drove off. His tired, sagging eyes brightened when he smelled and felt the warm food on his legs.

* * * * *

244

Javier Mendez's thoughts turned back to his younger life as his driver headed back to Mexico from Douglas. He had come off the streets of Tijuana. His first job at age twelve had been running errands for his dad. His dad was a street merchant by day and a smalltime drug dealer by night. Life for Javier had not been so bad. His problems began when his father used too much of his own junk. After he overdosed, his older sister had turned to prostitution. Javier learned how to pimp.

The Buick sped toward the Brogadas compound. Javier had intended to return with Manuel, the Guatemalan tunnel digger who had gotten away from Paco. Javier wasn't personally responsible for the escape, but he had hired Paco, and his boss' retribution would surely touch him in some manner. The photo of Paco's body dominated the front page of today's *La Prensa de Nogales.* The caption alluded to a rival drug gang payback.

To run from Brogadas was not an option. Mexico was not big enough. Javier wondered if he'd end up on the front page of tomorrow's newspaper.

* * * * *

Carlin collapsed on Roger's sofa. He felt like he had died, been embalmed and dumped there by a team of morticians. "You're welcome to the spare bedroom," said Roger.

"This is fine."

Roger took a pillow from his Easy Boy and flipped it to Carlin. "Guess we wait for Maggie's call?"

"Uh huh."

Roger walked into the kitchen and made a peanut butter and grape jelly sandwich. He heard Carlin's wispy snore before he had poured an accompanying glass of milk.

* * * * *

Sitting by his pool sipping orange juice on ice, Brogadas rested alone. His Arab guests were forty miles away planning their clandestine entrance into the United States. He slouched in his chair

245

and wondered. *Should I tell Maliq about the security breach or just let him use the tunnel as planned?*

He remained undecided.

Chapter 48

Maggie found the key and unlocked the back door. The warped door opened partly and then stuck. She put her shoulder to it and pushed. The door sprang open, and she half stumbled into the kitchen. Manuel followed carrying the food. He placed the bag of food on the table.

Exploring each of the five rooms, Maggie found dust in the cabin that could be measured in inches. She cleaned off the kitchen table and set a place for Manuel to eat. She handed him a burger, French fries, and a fountain soda. Then she walked outside to make calls. Her cell phone showed no service but she dialed anyway. There was no signal. The phone was useless. She went back inside. She grabbed the car keys and told Manuel she'd be back in ten minutes.

"Si." he said with a mouth full of fries.

She drove along the heavily-wooded trail road until she reached the macadam highway. She placed the phone on her lap and looked down for signal strength bars. Ten miles from the dirt trail where she had entered the highway, she got one bar. Two miles farther she saw five, which indicated full strength.

The first call was to Roger. While she waited for an answer, she noticed her battery registered low power. "Damn. What next?" Her charger lay on the kitchen counter back in Tucson. Roger answered. "Hi sweetie. Where are you?"

"My battery's running low, so just listen. Grab your cell phone and charger, get Carlin and come to Overgaard pronto. It's a hundred miles east of Phoenix. Meet me at the Red Onion; it's a restaurant right on route Sixty." Suddenly she became aware that there was no response. She checked her phone.

It was dead.

When had it died? She drove all the way back to the Red Onion and called Roger's condo from a pay phone. No answer. She didn't remember his cell number or Carlin's.

Next, Maggie called her supervisor. "Hello, Stacy, this is Lopez. Won't be in tonight."

"What's the problem?"

"I'm in the Phoenix area. Car trouble."

"Thought I saw your car in the lot when I arrived?"

Maggie had to think fast. "Oh yeah. I got a ride home last night. I'm having trouble with that old VW convertible I sport around in."

"Didn't know you had another car. Listen, I can send somebody up for you."

"No thanks. Need to get this junker fixed once and for all."

"Okay … But listen to this. That Guatemalan illegal you caught last night."

Maggie stopped breathing. "Yeah?"

"Got away from Dilks. The chief's been raking him over the coals but good."

"No fooling. Ouch!"

"Get that car fixed. See you tomorrow. Take care."

"Bye, Stacy."

When Maggie returned to the cabin, she found Manuel still sitting at the kitchen table, apparently waiting to be told what to do next. She figured it would take Roger about three hours to reach Overgaard, providing he even had heard her instructions. She led Manuel to the shower, and found some of Marty's clothes. Size-wise, they would swallow him, but at least they were clean. Then she collapsed on the sofa for a quick nap. She slept holding her service weapon in her hand under a pillow. She had checked the safety twice before settling down.

* * * * *

Maggie felt a tap on the shoulder. She jumped to a sitting position, fanning her weapon around the room. It was Manuel. He backed away, tripped on a throw rug and fell to the floor. He sat up and waved his arms wildly.

"Don' shooo! Don' shooo!"

"Sorry," she said in Spanish. "You frightened me." When she stood up to help Manuel to his feet, she noticed that it was almost dark. She asked him want he wanted.

"I need paper for the toilet."

She found toilet paper in a kitchen pantry. When he came out of the bathroom she beckoned him to the door. "Come with me."

On the way back to the Red Onion, Maggie finally interrogated him. By the time they reached the restaurant Maggie knew Manuel's life story and the details of his month and a half in captivity. She knew he was the brother of the dead Guatemalans and Margarita's uncle. She'd wait some before telling him that his sister and brother-in-law were dead and his niece was in child protective custody.

Maggie spotted Roger's truck in the parking lot of the Red Onion. "Yes!" she yelled. Manuel jumped. She put a hand on his arm to reassure him. Her "rangers" had arrived. She had made up her mind to appear *in control* when she met up with Carlin and Roger, but inside she was a volcano of raw emotion, ready to blow.

Roger was standing just inside the restaurant entrance and looked out through a small plate glass window. When he saw Carlin's car pull into the lot, he jumped up. It was too dark to identify the driver but it had to be Maggie. He hurried back to the table where Carlin was finishing a hot roast beef sandwich. "She's here!" He spoke at the top of his voice. Four diners looked in his direction.

Carlin held up his right hand. "Be there in a minute."

Roger didn't hear him. He had rushed back to the front door and burst through it. He jogged toward the sleek-looking hybrid. It had stopped and the driver's door opened. Maggie hopped out. Her open arms locked onto Roger. She dropped her head to his shoulder.

He tried to push her back to look at her, but her grip was too tight. "Maggie, you alright?"

The question released all the emotions she'd been holding in check. She managed to emit a muffled no. Roger felt warm tears on his neck and listened to her gasping sobs.

"Oh Roger ... I wasn't sure ... you got my whole message ... before the battery went dead ... Thank God ... you did." Maggie spat out the words between sobs.

Roger held her tighter until the crying weakened. He stroked her back. "Sweetie, it'll be okay. Have no fear, Roger's here."

Neither paid attention to Manuel in the oversized clothes, who had climbed into the driver's seat and now watched them through the open car door.

Carlin had been watching all three from the front steps of the restaurant. He waited for Roger and Maggie to release their embrace then walked over to them.

She turned as Carlin arrived and repeated her welcome, although the sobbing had lessened and her hug wasn't so intense. Carlin managed to create space between them and looked down at her.

Maggie took a couple of deep breaths, and wiped the tears away with the back of her hand. She smiled weakly and looked toward the car. "This is Manuel." *Manuel, mis amigos Carlin y Roger."*

Carlin and Roger nodded in Manuel's direction. He smiled cautiously in return.

Carlin dropped his smile. "I suggest we get out of here." They took his advice and moved to their vehicles. Carlin rode with Roger while Maggie led the way to the cabin with Manuel beside her.

* * * * *

Carlin, Roger and Maggie sat at the kitchen table sipping bottles of warm water. Roger said, "The meeting of the *Tucson Three* will now come to order." His attempt to lighten the atmosphere, which had grown heavy during the ride back to Marty's

250

cabin, did not amuse Maggie. She wasn't in the mood for his allusion to nefarious trial monikers.

"That's not funny, Roger!"

Roger sighed. "Well, if we don't do something dramatic, and soon, we'll go on trial even if we don't have a good group name."

"Okay." Carlin looked at his companions. "We need to agree on a course of action. Maggie you look like you want to say something."

Maggie stood. "I say the only thing to do is for you two to turn me in, and clear yourselves. Here, Carlin, take my weapon." She pulled it from her holster, checked the safety, grabbed the barrel, and extended her arm toward him.

"Put that away." Carlin pushed the weapon aside. "Roger and I are in too deep to get out now. Maggie, sit! Let's go over everything that we've learned to date. Roger, start by telling us about Kuala Lumpur.

"But I swore an oath."

"Roger, we need to put everything on the table here. Besides, I have a top-secret clearance," said Carlin

Maggie spoke up. "And Estimo already told me most of what happened, so …

Roger cut her off. "He did?"

"Yes, Roger. I'm so proud of you. And now's the time to tell you how sorry I am that you had to witness the death of that assassin and Estimo's partner." She leaned over the table and took both of Roger's hands in hers.

Carlin jumped in. "Now hold on. You're both ahead of me. Roger, from the top. Please."

Roger recalled his Kuala Lumpur adventure from the time he had landed until he departed. He didn't mention CIA agent Nicki's see-though-blouse and his infatuation with her, but he told them everything else in minute detail.

Maggie winced as Roger described how he had to hold up Connelly while Nicki tried to stop the bleeding and seal his lethal lung wound with plastic wrap.

When he finished, Roger closed his eyes. All three remained quiet for a moment.

Carlin broke the silence. "Okay, Maggie. You're up."

Maggie blinked, sat up straight. "Where should I start?"

"Organ Pipe. Roger's been after that story since the night we met him."

Maggie glared at Carlin then relaxed her expression. She began, as suggested, with the Organ Pipe shoot-out. She finished by recounting the police stop with Manuel in the car and her arrival at the Red Onion parking lot. Carlin could see that she was near tears again. He made a fist and tapped her on the chin. "Speeding with an illegal in the car – not too smart, girl."

Maggie smiled, as Carlin had hoped. She put her hand over her eyes for a moment. "I know. Thank God you left the paperwork in the glove box."

"They're always there except when a sneaky FBI agent removes them." They laughed.

"Okay, my turn." Carlin took a big swig of warm water, made a face, and spoke. He started with his first trip east and his meeting with Senator McGuire where he had asked him to look into Maggie's run-in with what he suspected was the Mexican military. He skipped the auto accident and hospital stay.

Next he relayed what he had been told by Jack Adams during his overnight stay in Memphis last month. Senator McGuire had confirmed that the Mexican military supported drug runs. He relayed that Estimo had tracked nine Arabs who were learning Spanish in Mindanao. He believed that the same Arabs then traveled to South America and later on to Mexico.

Carlin stood up to emphasize the importance of his next remarks. "Now, Norcross desperately wants to learn what I know and I'm prepared to tell him, but only if he will protect the three of us from snagging an illegal. And only if he obtains immunity for me, for disclosing classified information. Norcross and the FBI are the key to a deal for the *Tucson Three.*" He looked at Maggie after using Roger's name for them. She closed her eyes and tightened her lips.

Carlin ended his story with his trip with Roger to the Gadsden Hotel. He reviewed every detail. He mentioned the name of the man who was to pick up Manuel: Javier. He reported the Buick tag number from his notes and the name, Brogadas, where

Javier was headed as he had sped out of Douglas. Brogadas was the name of the drug lord that Senator McGuire told him received cooperation from the Mexican military. The puzzle was nearly complete.

Manuel pretended to sleep on the sofa in the front room while the meeting dragged on into the night. He rose up once when he caught Javier's name amid the unintelligible English babble.

It was decided that Carlin and Roger would return to Tucson in Carlin's car. They'd leave Roger's truck for Maggie. Manuel would stay put with Maggie. Roger's job was to approach Estimo and insist that he get Norcross involved. The FBI's participation was paramount if they were to avoid jail without initiating Carlin's "last resort" plan. If everything worked as designed, Norcross and/or Estimo would visit Maggie tomorrow. Roger would only come back if Norcross wanted him along. Carlin would lie low. If the FBI wouldn't play ball, then Carlin would take appropriate action. He pleaded with Roger and Maggie not to ask for details now, but hold them. He told them no to worry. He had promised a backdoor for each of them. No jail time.

Maggie wasn't convinced, but as of this moment, she had no way out on her own.

Roger wondered if one could be awarded a Pulitzer Prize while residing in a Federal penitentiary.

Chapter 49

Soon after Carlin and Roger drove away from the cabin, Maggie placed Roger's cell phone in its charger for the night. She checked its clock. It was almost midnight. Manuel had fallen asleep. She shook him. He jumped off the sofa and yelled: "Yes, Paco. Yes, Paco. Ready to dig, Paco."

Maggie gave him room to hop around looking for his shoes. When his eyes focused on Maggie he sat back down on the sofa. "Excuse, please." he said.

"It's okay, Manuel. You're out of the tunnel now. Calm down."

Manuel took a deep breath and leaned back on the sofa.

"Manuel, you can take your shower now and go to bed upstairs."

"But I washed all over yesterday, Senora."

"I know, but we wash all over every day here."

He scrunched his face.

"*Señorita*, before, let us talk. Earlier I overheard Javier's name. Are you going to send me to him? Please no. He will kill me."

"No, Manuel." She placed a hand on his shoulder. "My friends are going to see that you remain here in America or return home to Las Lisas. Don't worry about that. We are all risking jail in order to keep you safe."

Manuel sat up straight and asked the question Maggie had been dreading but knew would come eventually. "Can I see my sister soon?" Manuel leaned forward eagerly.

Maggie bit her lip. She hesitated. Was this the time to tell him? Or should she wait until others were around? She had no idea how he'd react. Manuel was staring at her, waiting for the answer. She knelt down even with his head, took his hands in hers and looked into his expectant, dark eyes. "Manuel, I have some very bad news."

Maggie's preamble alone was enough. Manuel jumped up, accidentally knocking her back. She fell.

He screamed. "No! Don't tell me bad news. Tell me good news." He was looking down at Maggie sprawled on the floor. Maggie felt uneasy with him standing over her. She quickly got to her feet and prepared for a further outburst.

"I'm so sorry." She paused.

He held his breath. His facial muscles twitched; his eyes bulge. Redness rose up from his neck and surfaced on his face.

"Manuel, I'm sorry, but your sister died crossing the border." He fell to his knees, pitched forward and rolled onto the floor.

"Manuel, your brother-in-law died too."

Manuel didn't hear Maggie's last words. His sorrowful wail had drowned them out. During a lull in his crying she blurted out again, louder, "Your brother-in law died too."

Manuel stopped crying and rocked on the floor.

"Dear Mary, Mother of God, pray for us sinners now and at the hour of our death." It started softly but quickly grew louder until he was almost screaming. He repeated the mantra faster and faster.

Maggie grabbed his arms and pulled him up. "Manuel, stop. Stop!" He didn't stop but he reduced his chant to a whisper. He tore away from Maggie's grip and clasped his hands over his face.

"Manuel, stop. Listen to me." Maggie pulled his hands down. His face had become a soggy, wrinkled mass of flesh.

"Listen. Margarita needs you more than ever. You must get hold of yourself. You must be strong for her. She has lost her mother and father. You must be here for her."

A glimmer of understanding appeared in the eyes peering back at her. He tried to speak, but no words came. A new flood of tears rolled down his cheeks and onto the floor. Maggie reached out her arms. She pulled the little man toward her. His aching, spent body comforted her even as her own warmth seemed to calm him. They sobbed together.

They cried for Margarita's loss, for Nicki and Estimo's loss, and for their own sorry, shitty circumstances.

When Maggie regained control, she stood back and kissed him on the forehead. "Go to bed, Manuel. You can shower in the morning. Try to sleep. We'll need all our strength tomorrow."

Manuel looked up at Maggie. When he saw her red eyes and the pain that registered in her face, his fear gently dissipated –not the heartache–just, at last, the fear. The fear that had gripped him since the day he had departed Las Lisas. He opened his mouth but again no words came.

He walked upstairs as in a trance.

Maggie lay down on the sofa. She couldn't sleep. She worried how to tell him the details of his family being shot to death. How they were needlessly murdered by brutal drug runners, supported by the Mexican military. The very same bastards that shot at her and forever ruined Marty's life. She wondered, does the CIA have license to kill?

Just before dawn she dozed off.

* * * * *

The referee pushes the challenger away and begins the count: One ... two ... three ...four ... five ... six ... seven ... eight ... nine, the bell rings.

The bell rang and rang and rang–agent Norcross finality reached for the phone. "Hello."

"Bob. Wake up. Estimo here."

"I was one count from being champ. One lousy second."

"What?"

Norcross clung to sleep. "I had him. I finally had him."

Estimo ignored the semiconscious babble. "Bob, get dressed. We need to talk."

Norcross rolled over and scowled at the clock. "Estimo, it's five-oh-five. Get lost."

256

"Can't. I'm already in your lobby."

Norcross sat up at this. Estimo had finally awakened him.

"Seriously, Bob, I have very important information that requires immediate FBI attention."

Norcross looked across the room at yesterday's wrinkled pants slung over a chair. "Okay. Be right down." He fumbled the phone back onto its cradle.

Norcross stalked across the huge, comfortable lobby of the Westward Look Resort. It was deserted except for the CIA agent who seemed relieved to see him. The two huddled by a low-burning fire that cast a warm reflection off each face.

"Bob, how do I say this?" Estimo paused for a long time. "I have information from someone who I insist–no, demand–must remain anonymous."

Norcross stared. "Are you evoking a national security issue?" he asked, punching each word.

Estimo leaned in closer. "I am, because it is."

Norcross narrowed his eyes and sat back in his chair. "Then I can live with that for the time being."

"Okay, now here's *a request*. I'm going to lead you to an illegal alien who escaped from a border patrol agent."

Norcross interrupted. "Do I know this agent?"

"Ah … no. My request is that I want you to place the illegal in Federal custody."

Norcross got up and helped himself to coffee from an urn across the lobby.

Norcross returned to his seat. He took a sip of coffee and looked at Estimo and shook his head. Did the alien cross into Arizona–and is he still here?

Estimo closed his eyes in thought. "Yes and yes."

"Then I can't honor your request." He paused, tilting his head. "Can't do that–*unless*. Unless the alien crosses state lines."

"If he does, then you can take custody?"

"Yes, if you can prove it."

Estimo smiled broadly. He proceeded to brief Norcross, directing him to the village of Overgaard in east central Arizona. "You should leave right away, this morning."

257

He handed Estimo an Arizona map with the fastest route marked on a street map and a hand-drawn map that would lead him directly to the cabin after he turned off the highway. Norcross stood up. As Estimo rose he added casually, "The illegal alien is being held by Agent Maggie Lopez."

Norcross sank back into his chair. "I thought you said Lopez wasn't involved in the escape."

"She was and she wasn't. But Maggie definitely was involved with his capture both times."

"*Both* times. Tell me more."

"Hold your questions until you talk to Maggie."

Norcross got up again and the two men walked to the parking lot. Norcross slipped behind the wheel of his rental with a complaint. "I haven't had breakfast yet."

"On the way you'll pass some half-dozen IHOPs. You'll have time to stop. Matter of fact, I want you to stop for at least thirty minutes."

"Why?"

"You'll find out." Estimo knocked on the car's hood. "Drive carefully."

Norcross shook his head and backed out of the lot. He drove slowly down the long driveway, then took the road leading out of Tucson, and headed north.

Estimo whipped the cell phone from his belt and dialed Roger's cell number. Maggie answered on the third ring. "Norcross is on his way. Roger and Carlin are staying here for now. It's probably best if they remain on the sidelines." He then gave her an early morning assignment that he knew would cause an explosion.

"You're crazy! Why?"

"Just do it and call me when you get back to the cabin." Estimo hung up before she could protest further. Maggie should get back to the cabin before Norcross gets there, Estimo thought, providing he stops for pancakes.

Chapter 50

Estimo's maps were precise and easy to follow. Even with a stop for breakfast Norcross arrived at Marty's cabin by 10:00 a.m. As he pulled in between two trees where others had previously parked, he saw Maggie accompanied by a short Hispanic, about to step inside the cabin.

Maggie looked over her shoulder at Norcross and held the front door open. He waved. Maggie tossed him a casual salute. She stood by the door and waited. Norcross hurried over.

"Been out to the store already?" Norcross asked.

"No, actually we just got back from a photo op." Maggie continued to hold the door. Norcross had to duck to get inside.

"A photo op?"

Maggie shut the door. "I'll show you later. Agent Norcross, meet Manuel Sanchez."

"Manuel, es Senor Norcross de los Federales."

Norcross extended his hand. Manuel barely touched it.

Maggie walked into the kitchen. "Come in here, guys. I'll warm up the coffee." Norcross followed her. She repeated the offer in Spanish and Manuel joined them. She heated the left over morning coffee and served it.

Norcross nodded toward Manuel, "How's his English?"

"Four words."

"They are?"

"Toilet paper ... don ... shoot." said Maggie.

Norcross almost spit out his mouthful of coffee laughing. He cleared his throat. "I must admit, he's got all the essentials down for a happy life here."

Maggie smiled "I'd have to agree."

Manuel knew that they were talking about him and looked to Maggie for a translation. She gestured toward an inner door and addressed the fugitive, *"Manuel, necessario hablo a Señor Norcross. Va a otra cuarto, por favor."*

Manuel took his coffee and returned to the living room as instructed.

Norcross, still smiling over Manuel's working English vocabulary, removed a micro-cassette tape recorder from his pocket and placed it on the table. "Okay Maggie, how does this begin? 'Once upon a time down on the border,'…"

Maggie settled herself across the table from him.

"Actually, it does. But first some ground rules: No recording. Second, my sources remain undisclosed. And third; Manuel is to be placed under federal custody."

Norcross tucked the tape recorder in the pocket of his trousers, hitting the record button as he did so. "Okay, no recording. Estimo and I have agreed that due to national security issues, I will not require sources. At least for now. However …" he looked to her. "I cannot place Manuel under federal custody unless he has traveled outside of Arizona."

Maggie slipped a five by seven inch photo across the table. She paused and sipped her coffee with an air of suppressed triumph, while Norcross examined the photograph.

"Ah, this morning's photo op." The picture showed Manuel facing the camera with his right arm over his head, pointing to a sign painted on a stone cliff that read:

You are leaving
NEW MEXICO
Land of Enchantment

"You may need reading glasses," said Maggie, "but the small road sign to the left says: 'Welcome to Arizona.' The location is a trading post on Interstate Forty, exactly one hour and thirty-five minutes from here."

"Guess that covers everything." Norcross, held up the photograph. "May I keep this?"

"Of course." Maggie smiled and held his eyes with hers. "May I hold on to the recorder until we finish? Sometimes they turn on 'accidentally' in one's pocket."

Norcross coughed as he fished the recorder from his trousers. Maggie heard the faint click as he turned it off and placed it on the table. She decided not to mention his sleight-of-hand.

Maggie leaned back in her chair and took a deep breath. "Okay, once upon a time on the border," she began.

Norcross produced a Pocket Pal from his coat and struck a writing pose. "You mind if I take notes?" he said with a hint of sarcasm.

"Not at all." Maggie began her tale. "Okay my partner, Marty Fallon, and I, by the way, this is Marty's cabin, were on a stake-out in Organ Pipe. As you may know, he had chosen the spot because there had been a shootout earlier that day between drug runners and some illegals."

She lowered her voice to a whisper, even though she knew Manuel wouldn't understand. "Manuel's sister and brother-in-law were killed in that shooting. His niece survived. She's now in an Arizona Child Protection Services home in Tucson."

Maggie continued in her normal speaking voice. "After Marty and I got shot up by the Mexican military, which, by the way, you wouldn't confirm …"

Norcross shrugged in mock helplessness.

"… and I was convalescing in the hospital, I saw a news clip about the Philippine government's raid on *Abu Sayyaf* in Mindanao. Later I found out that the group had been harboring nine Arabs who were learning Spanish there.

"The nine Arabs left Mindanao in a hurry after their Spanish teacher was murdered. The teacher received a U.S. salary, if you know what I mean."

Norcross nodded. "What time frame we talking about?"

"The first week in February. It seems that this group had an interest in traveling throughout the U.S."

Norcross frowned. "How do you know that?"

"According to my source they left some documents behind in Mindanao that listed nine specific locations."

Norcross rubbed his chin. It was obvious that he wanted to ask questions, but he didn't.

"The next possible sightings were Paris and Bogotá. From there they may have traveled next to Chiapas, Mexico. It seems that nine followers of Islam met with a settlement of Islamic fundamentalists that have lived in that area since '95."

"Go on."

"Last week I was asked to listen to a tape of people speaking Spanish as a second language. I was asked if I could tell the difference between an American student, a French diplomat, and a UN Arab translator."

"And could you?"

"Yes. I have a copy of the tape. Want to hear it?"

"Definitely."

Maggie took a cassette from her purse and slipped it into Norcross' micro-cassette player. When the tape finished playing, Manuel stuck his head into the room. *"Disculpeme, por favor."*

"Not now, Manuel." Maggie told him in Spanish.

"Es muy importante, señorita." he said.

"Que es? Maggie's tone was harsh as she asked Manuel what was so important that it couldn't wait.

Manuel spoke excitedly.

When he finished Maggie furrowed her brow. "Is that true?"

"What did he say?" Norcross wanted to know.

Maggie translated. "He said he heard Spanish spoken differently too, like on the tape"

Norcross stood up. He reached out a hand for Manuel's arm and gently drew him into the kitchen. He looked at Manuel but directed a question to Maggie. "Ask him which of the three speakers it sounded like."

She asked Manuel the question then translated for Norcross. "He said the last one, the Arab speaker."

"Ask where he heard them."

"Donde oyes?"

262

Outside the tunnel house, Manuel told her. Maggie relayed the information to Norcross.

Norcross asked, "What tunnel?"

Maggie sent Manuel back to the living room before replying.

"Manuel told me that he had been held for the past six weeks by a drug lord and forced to dig a tunnel from Nogales, Mexico to Nogales, Arizona,"

"Where is this tunnel?"

"We don't know exactly. We need Manuel to show us."

Norcross pushed his chair back and stood up. "Let's go."

"Wait a minute. There's more you need to know. Sit down, please."

Norcross shrugged his shoulders and tightened his lips. "We're wasting time. We need to locate that tunnel, right now."

"I agree. But listen."

Reluctantly, Norcross sat down.

"We need to look for the tunnel at night without being seen. And, here's a big *and*—we need to keep Manuel out of sight."

"Why?"

"Right after I relinquished Manuel to Customs, he was about to be driven to Douglas and turned over to a Mexican national, named Javier. The guy was going to take Manuel back to Mexico and kill him. Manuel knows the beginning and end of the tunnel. They want him dead."

Norcross whistled. "Now I understand why you guys wanted him placed into protective custody."

Maggie inclined her head. "Well, thank you, Agent Norcross! This Javier left Douglas for a drug lord's place, a man who's known to DEA as the 'King of Pot' in northern Mexico. His name is Brogadas."

Norcross wrote fast. He looked up when Maggie paused.

"We also know that this man has the full cooperation and support of the Mexican military on the border. I wouldn't be surprised to learn that it was his drug run that almost got Marty and me killed."

They looked up. Manuel had reentered the kitchen. Maggie guessed it was because he had heard Javier and Brogadas' names mentioned. Maggie assured him that he was going to be safe but that they needed him to help find the tunnel entrance and exit.

Manuel closed his eyes for a moment and lowered his head. Maggie sensed his fear.

Abruptly, Norcross took charge. First, he instructed Maggie to close up the cabin. Then he said he wanted her and Manuel to ride with him to Tucson. Maggie insisted on driving Roger's truck back.

Norcross agreed. "But Manuel has to ride with me," he said. Manuel was nervous about the arrangement but Maggie promised to stay right behind them. In minutes they were out of Marty's cabin. As Maggie held the front door open, Norcross ducked but not low enough. He banged his head and spat out a curse. Maggie locked up, replacing the key under the flowerpot, then jumped in Roger's truck. She was dying to call Estimo and Roger but Norcross had warned her not to call anyone, especially on her cell phone. She decided to take his cautious advice.

With her heart beating as fast as the truck's engine, she followed Norcross's car down the highway and raced toward a scary, unknown future.

Chapter 51

Norcross rolled down the driver's window and shouted over to Maggie as she pulled alongside. "I've got to stop at the FBI building in Phoenix. You can follow me or meet me in Tucson."

"I promised Manuel I'd follow."

"If we get separated the building's in the 200 block of Indianola Avenue."

"I won't lose you."

Maggie didn't lose him. When his car turned into the employee garage under the orange edifice, she followed, and Norcross arranged for her to park next to him. Norcross got out of his car and walked over to Maggie. "I've had second thoughts about taking Manuel upstairs with me. I won't be long. The car doors are locked; keep an eye on him." He handed her the keys.

"This mean you trust me now?"

"Maggie, I've always trusted you. It's the company you keep that has me worried." Maggie started to say something. Norcross put his hand to his mouth and made a zipper motion. He walked away toward the basement-level elevator.

Maggie smiled then waved across at Manuel. He raised his hand but his face remained solemn.

* * * * *

Maggie noticed a change in Norcross as soon as the elevator door opened. He walked slower and had lost the bounce he had shown forty minutes earlier. His lips had tightened; his cheeks were drawn and his brow knotted. When he saw Maggie looking at him, he smiled. Maggie slid over to the truck's passenger's side and rolled down the window. "Everything all right?" she said, handing him back his keys.

He stopped before his opened his car door. "Yes. Everything's fine."

Maggie felt he wasn't telling the truth. "Where next?" she asked. Up close, she noticed perspiration above his upper lip.

He stopped and wiped his face with a tissue. He leaned against the truck's cab.

"Maggie, do you know a place where we might keep Manuel under cover after we locate the tunnel tonight? I might not be able to arrange for federal custody in Tucson."

"I think we have two options," said Maggie.

When she questioned him, he admitted that he had not received the cooperation of his superiors regarding Manuel's custody.

Norcross straightened up. "We need to hook-up with Estimo. Where would be a good place to meet?"

"May I use my cell phone?"

"No."

Maggie shrugged. "Then we can either surprise Roger or go straight to my apartment."

"Which do you recommend?"

"Roger's place, definitely. It's a public facility on a golf course and we'll attract less suspicion."

"Then we surprise Roger and hope he's home. We'll call Estimo when we get to Tucson. I'll follow you."

"If you lose us," said Maggie, "go to the Omni Resort and I'll look for you in the lobby."

He tapped his fingers on her window as she started to raise it and she lowered it again.. "I went to Roger's once before, in case you didn't know. Let's *var-mo-los.*"

Maggie ignored his horrendous mispronunciation. "Right, let's get going."

266

Norcross slipped behind his wheel. The two-car caravan left the FBI garage and headed for Tucson.

* * * * *

Maggie rang the bell to Roger's apartment while Norcross and Manuel waited in their car. Roger opened the door. She stepped inside and kissed him hard on the lips. She closed the door with her foot and hugged him tight. "Oh, I needed that," she said. She broke off the hug and looked around. "Where's Carlin?"

"He went home a few hours ago."

"Norcross is outside with Manuel. Is it okay to bring them in?"

Roger shrugged. "Yes, by all means."

"Manuel will need a place to stay tonight. It'll have to be here or my place."

Roger didn't hesitate. "He can stay with me."

"Are you sure? You'll be harboring an illegal who's now a fugitive as well."

"Yes, of course. Besides, I don't want a strange guy sleeping at my girlfriend's apartment before I do."

Maggie winked. "So when are *you* coming over for the night?"

She turned before Roger could answer and reopened the door. She waved to Norcross and flashed him an "OK" sign.

Roger pushed the door partway closed then grabbed Maggie around the waist. He pulled her tight against him and kissed her on the neck.

She giggled. "Stop that." She pried his hands away and bumped him back with her rear end before Norcross and Manuel reached the doorway. "We have company."

Norcross allowed Manuel to enter first, then followed him into the house and put his hand out to Roger. Roger shook it firmly. "Come in, come in."

"Thanks for the invite. Glad you were home," said Norcross.

Maggie stood beside Manuel. Roger came over and patted him on the shoulder.

"Welcome to my home, Manuel. Can I get you anything?" Maggie translated for Manuel and then reported back.

267

"He said he doesn't want anything and he's very thankful for your hospitality."

Norcross looked around. The bachelor condo was furnished comfortably enough: leather sofa, lean-back chair, large plasma television hanging on one wall, and an expensive-looking stereo with all the obligatory accessories sitting on a brass and glass rack.

"Take a seat, Bob." He watched Norcross's expression to gauge whether or not it was okay to use his first name again.

Norcross didn't react. "We need to call Estimo on a land line."

"Sure." Roger went into the kitchen and returned with his 'walk-around' phone. He handed it to Norcross, who dialed Estimo's number.

"Estimo? Norcross here, I'm about to return your early morning favor. You woke me at five this morning, now I promise you that you'll be up until five tomorrow morning."

Maggie and Roger listened intently. Manuel leaned against the wall waiting for Maggie to tell him where to go.

Norcross arranged for Estimo to join them in half an hour at Roger's. He handed the phone back to Roger.

Maggie looked to Norcross. "Bob, I've been in the same outfit for two days. I'd like to go home and change. Can I have forty-five minutes?"

"Of course, Maggie. Put on some dark jeans and a dark top, okay?"

"Sure, but ..."

"No questions now, please. Details when Estimo gets here."

Maggie shrugged. "Roger, can I borrow your truck?"

Roger smiled and raised his eyebrows. "Want me to drive you?"

"No thanks." She said almost before Roger stopped speaking, guessing that he had something more amorous in mind. Reluctantly, Roger handed her the keys. She turned and hurried out the door.

* * * * *

When Maggie returned, Estimo was sitting in Roger's recliner faking sleep. Roger was in the kitchen with Manuel. Norcross stood as she entered and pointed to Estimo. "Your tax dollars at work," she laughed.

Estimo jumped up, grinned, and grabbed Maggie's hands. "Good to see you again. Are you up for a long night with the FBI leading the charge?"

"I feel better after a hot shower and change of clothes." She turned to Norcross. "How do I look, Bob?"

Maggie pivoted around to model her black jeans and dark denim top. "Very good," said Norcross, "Near-ninja, as required."

Estimo, wearing beige slacks and a light blue polo shirt, looked down at himself and then up at Norcross, "You didn't tell me to dress for night combat."

"Hold up, Estimo!" Norcross turned toward the kitchen and yelled. "Roger, you ready for your walk?"

Roger came into the living room, "I'm out of here." He walked over to Maggie, kissed her on the cheek, and turned for the door. She patted his rear-end twice, like a fellow jock praising a stellar play.

Maggie, Norcross, and Estimo sat down. Norcross laid out his plan.

Outside, banished from the meeting, Roger waited. He watched the shadow of a six-foot saguaro lengthen to near that of a par-five hole. The sun set before Norcross stuck his head out the door and called him back to the condo.

Chapter 52

The planning session broke up at 8:30 p.m. Roger watched from his front window as his guests piled into Estimo's rental Chevy. Norcross sat up front, Maggie and Manuel occupied the rear seats, Estimo drove.

* * * * *

They arrived in Nogales at exactly 10:17 p.m. Norcross had previously made arrangements for Maggie to be "on loan" to the FBI for a few days.

They drove to the entrance of the Border Patrol motor pool. Maggie hopped out and flashed her badge. The guard knew her but appeared suspicious, probably because she wasn't in uniform. She watched him pick up the phone and overheard him speak with a supervisor. Twenty minutes later, she drove out of the compound with a green and white decaled B.P. Ford Explorer.

She stopped beside Estimo's car. Norcross and Manuel got out of the Chevy and joined her in the B.P vehicle.

Norcross fastened his seatbelt and looked over his shoulder. He motioned for Manuel to attach his belt. The diminutive man complied. Maggie drove them along the dirt road to the spot where she had apprehended Manuel. She stopped, turned off the lights, grabbed her night vision goggles and jumped out. She opened the rear door for Manuel. Norcross slid over into the driver seat. "Good hunting," he whispered.

* * * * *

Estimo had a different assignment. He headed back north as soon as Maggie's truck had driven off. Less than ten miles from Nogales, he stopped at the Rio Rico Resort and Country Club. He checked in and made sure that the rooms he had reserved for Maggie Lopez and for Bob Norcross were in the system.

His next task was more difficult. He left his overnight bag in his room and walked outside to an area that appeared to be the employee parking area. Five of the twelve cars parked there had Mexican license plates. He noted their makes, approximated the age, and jotted down the plate numbers of five.

* * * * *

Maggie followed Manuel as he cautiously walked in the direction of the house where he had broken through the tunnel. Even in the limited light, she noticed his shaking hands. A few hundred yards away, she watched Norcross turn the Border Patrol SUV around. It was now pointing back toward Nogales with its high beams blazing. She could hear the faint sound of the engine running.

Manuel retraced his steps. The fear that enveloped him the night he had escaped from the tunnel returned. He recalled the man grabbing his foot, then dropping the rock on the man's head. He agonized over the fate of his digging partner, Pepe. A slight breeze passed across his face, momentarily cooling his sweating body.

Maggie was a step behind, her hand resting on her service piece. She had moved it from the middle of her back to her hip, where it would be more accessible. She swallowed hard, trying to settle her stomach. She was scared, too, but her training kicked in and she focused on the mission. She placed her hand on Manuel's shoulder. They stopped for a moment, and she put on her goggles, and scanned the area before them. Satisfied it was clear, she removed the goggles. They continued walking.

* * * * *

Javier, glad to still be alive, waited in the passenger seat of the black Buick along with José, his regular driver. They had just escorted Brogadas and Maliq to the Apache Cave restaurant.

As the two walked up the steps, Brogadas spoke. "This is the finest Mexican eatery in all of northern Mexico."

"That can't be!" Maliq paused for effect.

Brogadas turned and looked at him.

"That can't be because the best place to eat in northern Mexico is the Brogadas hacienda," said Maliq.

Brogadas laughed and slapped him on the back. "You made my blood boil for a moment. Well, they are one and the same. See? I own this place." He lowered his voice so that Maliq had trouble hearing him. "I do my laundry here." Maliq didn't understand the American phrase that would have made sense to anyone familiar with the drug trade, meaning that he mixed his drug profits with the restaurant's revenue. Maliq smiled as though he understood.

"We eat a good meal first. Then we make our inspection. Where would you like to sit?" Brogadas spread both his arms. The room was empty. Officially the restaurant had closed at 10:00 p.m.

* * * * *

Estimo approached the man behind the front desk of the Rio Rico Resort. He had already selected the newest Mexican registered car on his list. "Can you tell me if an employee owns that red Ford Ranger out back?"

The clerk was surprised by the question. "I can. Why do you ask?"

"It's a private matter I'd like to discuss with the owner."

"Did you hit it?"

"I may have. Could you ask the person to come to the lobby?"

Moving out from behind the counter, the man said, "He is here. It's my car." He frowned and placed a "Back in Five Minutes" sign on the counter and rushed toward the door, hurrying to catch up with Estimo who waited outside.

Under the portico Estimo reached out a hand and stopped the desk clerk.

"It's okay. I didn't hit it."

"Then why'd you say that?" The clerk looked confused.

"I wanted to talk to the owner in private,"

The clerk placed his hands on his hips. "What about?"

Estimo had practiced the line but he wasn't sure how it would be received. "I need to rent a car with Mexican tags so I can drive across the border to Nogales and bring my girlfriend here for the night. I don't have Mexican insurance on my car. I'll pay you well and leave you a deposit for the full value of the car. How much did you pay for it?"

The man stared at Estimo. After a long pause he said, "Twelve hundred dollar."

"You paid twelve hundred for that car?" said Estimo breaking into a smile.

"Yes."

"I'll leave you fifteen hundred, the keys to my car, and one hundred for the use. What do you say?"

"You're not planning to transport illegals or drugs?"

"Absolutely not! Just my girlfriend."

"Two hundred for the use," said the car's owner.

"Two hundred?"

"Yes."

Estimo extended his hand. "Deal."

"My shift is over at six."

"The car will be back in the same spot by five."

"All cash! No checks!"

Estimo reached into his pocket and pulled out a wad. He fanned the money. "All cash."

* * * * *

Manuel saw the house first. The lights were on inside. He stopped and stooped down. Maggie leaned over him and studied the house. They were approaching it from the west side. She put on her night goggles and scanned the area in front and back. She saw the outhouse. "Wait here," she whispered.

273

Manuel flattened himself onto the ground and lay motionless. Only his eyes moved. Maggie bent over and cautiously crept toward the outhouse. She heard a toilet flush from inside the main house. Then motion lights flashed on; it became as bright as an airport runway around the entire house. She heard shouting inside, but couldn't understand what was being said. She ran behind a huge boulder next to the outhouse and flopped to the ground, service weapon in hand. She closed one eye to protect her night vision.

* * * * *

The car that Estimo had "rented" was only eight years old and the owner had kept it in near perfect running order despite the 59,000 miles on the odometer that had turned over once or maybe even twice. The tires had worn thin, but it was still the best of the five in the lot.

He drove away with a soft Mariachi ballad playing on the radio. Elated with his "car rental" success, he hummed along with the recording. *"Cu cu rru Paloma. Cu cu rru ... ya... no... llor ... es.* at the last word, Estimo heard a bang and the car leaned to the right.

The bumble, bumble sound kept time with the music as the front tire went flat. He brought the car to a stop. He changed his mind about liking the song and gave a hard twist on the radio knob. It broke off and fell to the floor. He prayed that there would be a usable spare and jack in the trunk.

* * * * *

Norcross yawned. He lowered the SUV's backrest as far as it would go and closed his eyes for a moment. He didn't hear the ten illegals who had scaled the Nogales wall a short hundred yards from his position and moved right behind his vehicle.

* * * * *

Maggie squinted into the blazing lights with one open eye. A man in silhouette was standing outside the house. He looked in her direction and then walked to the far side of the house, away from where Manuel lay hidden. A second man stood just outside the doorway and looked around. He yelled to his friend alongside the house.

"Probably a coyote, the four-legged kind." He laughed at his own joke. "I'll turn off the motion lights. They were supposed to be off until after midnight when Brogadas and his guests come through." The first man came back to join him and nodded. Both went back inside.

Maggie waited five minutes and crawled over to the outhouse. She opened the door and stepped inside. She placed her hand on the bench-seat and gently lifted up. It gave. She peered down and saw the top of a rope ladder. She released the seat. *This was one end of the tunnel, an outhouse that didn't smell, sitting next to a building that had inside plumbing. Tada!* Maggie backed out the door, which was complete with a quarter moon window.

A huge hand clamped over her mouth. Then an arm bulging with muscles encircled her chest. Her feet left the ground. She saw stars above her, and then felt the earth hard on her back.

She lost her breath as three hundred pounds landed on top of her. His beefy hand pulled her shirt and bra up, exposing her breast.

The attacker looked down and grinned, displaying rotten teeth that probably had never seen a brush, let alone a dentist. His sickening sewer-breath repulsed her. She struggled to turn her head to the side.

He kept his left hand over her mouth hard and with his right reached for her belt buckle. She squirmed from side to side and tried to reach for her weapon but her arms were pinned.

"You look good enough to eat," the man said softly as he brushed against Maggie's ear with his bulbous, wet lips. Unable to remove her belt, he reached for her exposed breast. His enormous hand completely covered both breasts. He squeezed hard. Maggie clamped her teeth. She couldn't cry out. The hand covered her nose.

She struggled to breathe.

Chapter 53

First came the special guacamole appetizer. "My guy prepares this delight better than any other chef. He starts with fresh chunk-chopped avocados then mixes them with super-hot jalapenos … adds fine ground garlic … tops with fresh-squeezed lime juice." Brogadas was bragging to Maliq as he as he made chopping, grinding, and squeezing motions. "Eat. Eat, please."

The home-baked corn chips, lightly salted, were uniformly shaped triangles, perfect for dipping. Brogadas hated misshapen or broken chips. The wait-staff hated them even more—an imperfect triangle meant immediate dismissal.

When the entrée arrived, the aroma from the pork empanadas served with fresh charred pineapple salsa, chipotle aioli and diabla sauce sent Brogadas into ecstasy. He closed his eyes, inhaled deeply and said, "This is better than sex, my friend."

Maliq privately disagreed, but laughed politely.

Maliq ate the same dish, made with lamb. Brogadas had been informed that the Muslims, like the Jews, had an aversion to pork.

Although Maliq enjoyed the meal, he exaggerated his satisfaction for the benefit of his host. When a fresh fruit plate was served for dessert, Maliq, already stuffed, nibbled on only a half-dozen grapes. Brogadas ate everything on the plate. A rare Turkish coffee completed the feast. Maliq sipped his cup appreciatively.

Maliq was dying for a smoke but held off. Instead, he palmed the roll of Tums in his pocket. They would be needed soon. He already felt the jalapenos simmering in his esophagus.

It took nearly two hours to finish the meal. Brogadas patted his enormous abdomen then asked, "Ready to go, my friend?"

Maliq used his napkin to pat a coffee drip off his chin. "Yes."

Brogadas began to rise. Two waiters hurried over and pulled back the chairs for the lone diners.

Javier and the driver were standing at the curb with the doors of the car open wide.

With Brogadas and Maliq in the back seat, the driver headed toward the Ortega house, where the newest gateway to America began. The tunnel was ready for inspection. Javier shivered every time he approached the house. Ever since he had dispensed with Paco for letting the Guatemalan get away, Javier could not rid himself of the thought that he too remained a marked man.

* * * * *

Maggie heard a thud. The man on top of her groaned, his body went limp. She pushed with all her strength and managed to squeeze out from underneath him. She fought for fresh air, at the same time grabbing her weapon, which had fallen from her waistband. She sat up and coughed. Manuel looked down at her. He stood over her attacker, a ten-pound rock still held chest high in both hands.

Maggie pulled her bra back into place and her shirt down. Manuel looked away as the moaning man tried to rise, then slumped back onto the ground. Manuel lifted the rock over his head.

Maggie shook her head, no. She got up and motioned for Manuel to drop the rock. Together they ran back toward the tree line where they had hidden before. She pulled him down, aimed her weapon toward the house, and waited.

"Alberto!"

Manuel stiffened.

A man at the back door of the house yelled again. "Alberto."

"I'm here." Maggie's attacker managed to sit up.

The guy at the door walked over to where the Buddha-sized man rested.

Maggie put her hand on Manuel's shoulder. She could feel his body shaking. "Stay down Manuel," she whispered.

She watched and listened as the man from the house stood over his fallen partner. "What happened to you?"

The big man staggered to is feet. "I tripped. Hit my head on a rock. I'm okay now."

Maggie smiled. The big gorilla was not going to tell anyone about letting a snooping, pint-sized, hot bitch get away from him.

The attacker picked up something off the ground as he rose up. It was her night goggles. Maggie stiffened. "Ah, shit!" Manuel had learned a new English word.

Quietly she led Manuel back toward Norcross.

On the hasty walk back to the vehicle, Maggie thanked Manuel for clobbering her attacker. She would have cautioned him not to mention the encounter with the bad guys but knew that he wouldn't, even if he spoke enough English to be understood.

* * * * *

Norcross was snoring softly when Maggie banged on the window. He jumped. "Jesus Christ, Maggie, you scared the shit out of me."

"Sorry, Bob, but we're in a bit of a hurry."

Norcross unlocked the doors. Maggie and Manuel jumped in back. "Downtown Nogales, driver," said Maggie.

Norcross drove to the meeting place with Estimo. He hoped that Estimo had obtained the wheels required for the next stage of the night's operation. He shook his head at the scare Maggie had given him by knocking on the window. "Maggie, that excursion took too long. Timing is everything. I was just about to come after you," he lied. "Did you run into trouble?"

"No, we didn't. I passed a group of illegals on the way back. Did you have any trouble?"

"No. Sure they came from my direction?" Norcross couldn't admit that he never saw them.

278

"Maybe not." said Maggie.

*****

The SUV approached the Burger King lot. Maggie saw Estimo behind the wheel of the old, beat-up, Ford Ranger. It was 12:01. The new day had just begun and she was already beyond tired. Norcross and Estimo must be just as exhausted, she thought. Norcross steered over to the Ranger and parked. Maggie and Norcross hopped out. He stretched. Maggie brushed herself off. Manuel remained in the SUV.

"How'd it go?" asked Estimo.

Maggie answered as she walked over to him. "Great, we found it. Tell you more later. Manuel and I better get started."

She noticed a worried expression on Estimo's face.

"Anything wrong?"

"Maggie, the tires are bad," he said. "I had a flat and changed it. The spare is worse than the one that went flat."

Displaying more bravado than she felt after her encounter with the gorilla, Maggie hiked up her pant leg and stuck her thumb in the air. "Manuel and I can always hitch a ride."

"Look out for potholes. The roads must be bad over there." Estimo held the door for her. She called Manuel. "Over here." Manuel got out of the SUV and climbed in the front seat next to her.

Norcross leaned over Estimo and added his caution. "Be careful, Maggie. Don't take any wild chances. It's not necessary, since we now know where the tunnel exits on this side."

Maggie climbed behind the wheel. "Don't worry. Manuel will protect me."

Norcross and Estimo shot a glance at the short, thin, frail-looking man. Each face showed the unspoken thought, *Oh, sure!*

Maggie started the truck, rolled down the window, waved, and drove off. When she got to the border checkpoint, she recognized the female who was hustling cars across the border. Seeing the Mexican tags, the woman yelled at Maggie to move faster. She did so, without ever coming to a complete stop.

The sign read: "Welcome to Nogales, Sonora–the Mexican Frontier." It was repeated in Spanish.

Nogales on the American side was a ghost town at midnight on a weekday. The Mexican side was just revving up. Many under-aged tourists and some University of Arizona students came here to drink. Some Americans looked for drugs and hookers. Most found what they wanted and avoided trouble. For a border town, it was much safer than Tijuana and didn't compare with the murders and lawlessness of everyday life in Juarez and Nuevo Laredo.

Manuel could not remember the name of the restaurant, but said he thought that it was named after some Indian. Maggie ran down the famous chiefs for him: Sitting Bull, Geronimo, Cochise, Crazy Horse. He couldn't remember. She recalled that some tourist had spoken of a really good Mexican restaurant across the railroad tracks, away from the bustling central part of town. It seemed worth a try. She drove over the tracks and down a dark, deserted-looking street. The Apache Cave's neon sign turned off as Maggie rounded the corner. Manuel tapped Maggie on the shoulder and pointed. They had found the restaurant where Javier had eaten and bought Manuel the unforgettable take-out meal.

Manuel fidgeted in his seat then he jumped. *"Ay, eso es!"* This is the place. *"Es el restaurante!"* The house is very near here … down this street and to the right … I think. Do we have to go there? I am very much afraid now."

"Calm down, Manuel. All I want is to drive by. We won't stop even for a minute."

Maggie drove past the Apache Cave and turned right as Manuel directed. She went two streets farther and hung a left. The street she had chosen was empty of pedestrians and they saw only two parked cars. Up ahead on the right, they both recognized it at the same time, the black Buick.

Maggie drove by slowly. She had memorized the tag number Carlin had given her. It matched. Manuel slid down to the floor as Maggie passed. The driver of the Buick stood on the curb leaning against the front fender.

They had located the house, the entrance to the tunnel. She noted the street – Calle Navojoa.

"We go home now? Please, we go home now?" said Manuel.

Maggie nodded. "Yes, Manuel."

280

As she went by three men were just leaving the building. They all looked in Maggie's direction, with more much interest than she liked. She guessed one must be Javier. The really big man had be Brogadas, she thought. The third man stared the hardest, with a look that increased her discomfort. She shivered and picked up speed. In the rear view mirror she saw the driver say something to Javier. She didn't need to be told what he said but imagined: *That truck passed here too slow. Nobody gets lost on this street.*

Taking Manuel's advice, she stepped on the gas and shot toward the border checkpoint. She didn't see the pothole until it was too late. The tire blew with a sound like a shotgun blast.

She felt certain the men getting into the Buick must have heard it too. Manuel's knees bounced hard against the floorboards, his head hit the dash. He looked up at Maggie and spoke in perfect English. "Shit!"

Maggie looked over at him in disbelief. As she had imagined earlier, Manuel now acquired his fifth English word.

Chapter 54

Maggie drove on the flat until the rubber shredded off and the truck hobbled along on its rim. She knew she couldn't outrun the Buick. As she neared the congested strip-club section of town people began to stare.

She didn't want to be stopped by the police, so she pulled into the first spot she found and parked. Manuel was out of the truck before Maggie. He waited on the sidewalk. Maggie reached him, took his arm, and ducked into the nearest club. Nobody in the club paid any attention to them because all eyes were locked on a scantily clad young female patron dancing on the bar. She wore a tank top, no bra, and a micro denim skirt that she hiked higher and higher in time with the cymbal beat of the "bump-and-grind" provided by the band's drummer. Maggie steered Manuel toward a back door. Manuel peered over his shoulder at the dancer until she was out of sight. Maggie focused straight ahead.

The alley led to a busy street packed with revelers looking for the perfect place to party. Maggie and Manuel melted into the crowd. Maggie dropped Manuel's arm, worried that they didn't look like a match. "Stay right behind me," she told him. She kept walking toward the border, but followed the least crowded streets. When they reached the checkpoint, she hesitated. She would pass easily, but Manuel had no papers and could be stopped.

Maggie looked around. She spotted the Hotel Colonial de Nogales. "Wait here, Manuel. Look in shop windows but don't wander too far."

She walked inside, booked a room, and without inspecting it went back for Manuel. He was nowhere in sight. Her heart sank when she spotted the black Buick. It was parked directly across the street from where she had left him. She felt exposed standing on the curb, so she began to back around the corner. She backed into a man who was walking fast. Maggie stumbled. *"Perdoname Senora. Perdoname!"* The man grabbed her shoulders to prevent from her from falling.

"No, it was my fault," she said in English.

"No, I go in big hurry. Excuse me," he offered in halting English.

Maggie nodded. "I'm okay."

She recognized him. It was the driver, José.

Maggie turned and began walking normally. She closed her eyes and took a deep breath. She wanted to look over her shoulder to see if José was still looking in her direction, but she didn't. She turned the next corner and stopped. She bent over to catch her breath.

Out of the corner of her eye, there was José again. He had doubled back. He crossed the street and kept walking away. If he was looking for Maggie, he had failed to see her. She continued around the block and went straight to her hotel room. She didn't see Manuel along the way.

Sitting on the edge of her bed, she brought her fist down hard on the mattress. "Dumb, dumb, dumb heading straight for the border. Naturally that's where they'd be looking for us."

She heard a knock at the door and jumped off the bed.

"Who's there?"

No answer. *"Quien es?"* The door did not have a peephole. She tried English. "Who's there?"

Through the door she heard, "Don' shoot, toilet paper, shit."

She unlocked the door and jerked it open.

Manuel stood there grinning.

She pulled him inside, relocked the door, and hugged him. For the first time, he hugged her back.

Maggie sat Manuel down. She wanted to discuss their options. But there came another knock at the door. *"Severiso de quartro,"* Room Service, said a male voice. Manuel jumped up. He whispered in Maggie's ear. "I know this voice. It is José." Maggie knew the voice too. She had spoken with him only minutes ago.

Her eyes raked the room for an escape route. The balcony was the only way out. She led Manuel to the rail. It was only a short drop to the carport canopy. She hopped over the rail, hung down, and dropped. Manuel followed her.

She crawled to the edge. It was an even shorter drop to the roof of a row of shops. At the edge she found a downspout and tested its rigidity. It felt solid. She climbed over and shimmied down the remaining eight feet. Manuel was right behind her. A few pedestrians saw them climb down and laughed as they walked past. They must think two lovers just got caught in a hotel room by a jealous husband or wife, thought Maggie. Good–just what we wanted them to think.

Back on the street again, Maggie headed for the red light district. As they neared, she looked at a troupe of young girls hanging on the corner. Some appeared only in their teens. Maggie approached the oldest-looking hooker in a group of six huddled together. She whispered in her ear. The woman laughed, and cupping her mouth whispered back. Maggie said something else to her that Manuel couldn't hear.

"Okay, fifty American" said the hooker. Maggie handed her the cash. The hooker grabbed Manuel by the arm and led him across the street. Maggie followed.

The hooker led them into a small, one-room efficiency apartment. It smelled of stale beer, pot, and leftover food. She began to take off her blouse before she had fully closed the door.

Maggie looked at Manuel. He was transfixed. He couldn't have blinked if he had wanted.

* * * * *

Javier thought his boss seemed anxious when he dropped Brogadas and the Arab back at the Apache Cave. Brogadas instructed both him and José to return to the port of entry area and

284

look for the red truck and its occupants. If Brogadas was anxious about something, then Javier had better be anxious too.

He was.

It was easy to find the red Ford truck with the flat tire. The police tow truck already had its front end up, ready to remove it. Javier jotted down the tag.

Brogadas and Maliq waited in a small anteroom just off the restaurant's closed main dining area. A waiter brought more of the Turkish coffee that had been served at dinner.

"My friend, I apologize for the delay and the apparent trouble tonight. I'll have a new car brought to us in a few minutes."

Maliq sipped his coffee. "I understand these things."

"If the red truck had not passed so slowly we would have ignored it. But since it did we had to check it out."

"I understand," said Maliq.

Brogadas lowered his voice. "It is better to know now if the tunnel has been compromised, and not later when we are transporting important cargo or you and your men."

"Yes, of course." Maliq was cordial, but he had been on guard ever since Javier handed over the night vision goggles found at the base of the outhouse on the U.S. side. When none of Brogadas' three men could explain the find, Maliq knew that all was not going well.

The sighting of the red truck had convinced him that using the tunnel for entry into the U.S. was no longer a viable option. He'd have to change his plans. Maliq maintained a polite smile but he grimaced at the thought of changing plans at this late date.

Brogadas guessed Maliq's thoughts from his expression. On the whole, he was relieved that his decision to hide the escape of one of the tunnel diggers from Maliq would not burden him any longer. A more urgent matter now claimed his full attention. He needed to move as much of the Afghan heroin as possible through the tunnel, starting tonight.

The second car arrived, and Brogadas led Maliq to it. The driver would take Maliq back to the estate where his men rested. Brogadas would remain in town to await the report from Javier and José regarding the people in the red truck. Then he would order the immediate movement of the heroin now stored in the tunnel.

* * * * *

285

Norcross checked his watch for the third time. It was almost 4:00 a.m. He looked at Estimo. "Okay, I'm worried, how about you?"

Estimo sat up straight in the driver's seat of the Border Patrol SUV and looked back at him. "I've been concerned since about three. I didn't want to worry you."

"Yeah, me too. What'll we do now?"

"Call in the National Guard. That's what I wanted to do ever since I learned about this sorry situation."

"Good idea," said Norcross. "How well do you know Madam Governor?"

Estimo got out of the truck and peered through his open window. "If that's supposed to be funny, it's too late for funny." He walked over to the edge of the Burger King parking lot and looked around. Seeing no one, he relieved himself.

Norcross joined him. "No, not trying to be funny. Sorry. I was just trying to calm myself. You got to admit though, the Guard isn't a bad idea."

Estimo pulled up his zipper and waited for Norcross to finish. They both walked silently back to the truck and got back inside.

"I've got it!" said Norcross.

Estimo jerked his head around to stare at Norcross, "I'm listening."

"Let's just take this baby and go over and look for them."

Norcross already had the engine started. Estimo grinned. "Now you're thinking like James Bond. I love it! *Var-mo-los mur-cha-cho.*"

Crossing the border in a Border Patrol truck proved unexpectedly difficult, especially since neither of Norcross or Estimo were dressed in border patrol uniforms. After many calls back to Customs it seemed that no one wanted to be responsible for approving the unusual request at such an early hour. Finally, Estimo produced his CIA identification and the Red Sea parted. The gate was barely up when Norcross hit the gas.

The Mexican side was now almost as quiet as the American. Some Mexicans were up and heading for early jobs across the border. The party animals were by now sleeping off their evening carousing. The U.S. BP truck attracted little attention except for a woman peering around the corner of a pharmacy who Norcross thought looked a little like Maggie. She waved frantically at them.

"That's her!" Estimo made the positive ID.

Quickly Norcross made a wide "U" turn, running up on both curbs to accomplish the maneuver without backing up.

Maggie clung to Manuel like a cheetah with a cub in its mouth. She ran to the BP truck and flung open the back door. She pushed Manuel inside then jumped on top of him.

Shots shattered the morning calm.

The rounds smashed out the rear window and ripped away the passenger mirror. Norcross gunned the engine. The truck flew up the street and past the orderly line of vehicles waiting to cross into the U.S. The Customs agents heard the shots. They watched as the BP truck crashed through an unused gate.

Norcross sped through so fast that none of the border agents had time to react. However, they did hold up all regular traffic due to the confusion. Now that the cow had left the barn, the border would be closed for five hours. Nearly every Mexican would be late for work today.

Norcross pulled up to the Burger King parking lot, and everybody but Maggie jumped into Norcross' rental car.

Maggie drove the BP truck back to the motor pool and explained to the dispatcher that she had crashed the gate and had been shot at by drug runners. She would have to file another accident report and let the people way up the line sort out the strange events. She anticipated there would be disciplinary action against her and Estimo. The matter would be settled in Washington.

Maggie feared that she'd be relieved of her FBI detail and placed on indefinite administrative leave. She would be right.

Norcross drove first to the Rio Rico Resort. When Estimo appeared in the lobby it was almost 5:30 a.m. He approached the clerk at the front desk.

"May I have my car keys please?"

The man handed them to Estimo.

"Where's my truck?"

"Keep the $1,500, the Mexican Police confiscated it and you don't ever want to ask about it. Don't go back for the tag either.

Shaking his head in disgust the clerk said, "I knew something was wrong when you didn't return by five."

"Here's an extra fifty for a cab." Estimo, with a controlled smile, handed the money to the stunned-looking man and walked out before he could ask any more questions.

It only took Estimo forty-five minutes to drive the eighty miles to his hotel, where he flopped, fully clothed, into bed.

Norcross drove to Roger's house, where he dropped off Manuel. He and Roger helped the exhausted Manuel to the sofa. Norcross didn't offer Roger a report, except to say that Maggie was okay.

"Where is she? What happened? When can I see her?"

Norcross raised his hand. "She'll tell you what she can."

Roger stood in the doorway. He was just as frustrated and anxious as he was before Estimo had arrived.

* * * * *

Maggie finished her report by 7:00 a.m. and drove herself home. She played a Shakira tape as loud as she could stand to keep herself awake. She was asleep by eight-thirty. She didn't call Roger.

Chapter 55

Maggie woke up at 6:30 p.m. hungry.

Estimo woke up at 7:15 p.m. starving.

Norcross woke up at 7:30 p.m. famished.

Carlin arrived at Roger's at 7:45 p.m. with pizza and beer to share with Roger, Manuel. Carlin was looking for an update. Roger was too. Nobody had called.

"Can you believe it, Carlin?" said Roger. "I haven't spoken to Maggie since they left here last night. Manuel can't tell me anything."

The phone rang. Roger answered. It was Maggie.

"Maggie, how are you? What happened? What's going on?"

Carlin could tell from just half of the conversation that he wasn't getting answers to his questions. After a minute of silence Roger said, "Okay. Goodbye."

Roger looked at Carlin. "Nada. Nada. I got nothing."

"Told you before," Carlin reminded him, "you're a lousy reporter."

Roger shook his head and called Manuel, who was still asleep on the sofa. Manuel took a seat at the table and eagerly reached for a slice of pizza. He looked rested but troubled.

The three men ate in silence.

The phone rang again. Roger answered, then hung up, and reported. "That was Norcross, he'll be here in an hour with Maggie and Estimo. He asked you to stay."

* * * * *

At the Brogadas estate, Maliq quieted his men who were gathered for a briefing in the mammoth breakfast area of the main house. "Gentlemen there must be changes in our plans. We must move the date up to the day after tomorrow evening. We will all go together with the Mexican coyote and his illegals." He explained that those scheduled for other routes were to forget about them. They would leave at eight in the evening. They would have to endure a two-day walk in the desert. Maliq then pointed to Amir, "José will prepare you for the trip. He is still in charge of the group walking with the illegals. José, your group grew from three to nine. Take over."

Amir nodded to Maliq. "Thank you, Miguel." He then repeated the instructions that he had already given to his initial group: what to wear, what to take, and how act. He reviewed how much water to take and when to drink. He covered what foods to take and what not. He spoke for over an hour. He warned them about rattlesnakes and *la cholla* – the jumping cactus that supposedly could send its barbs at you even from a foot away.

Maliq commended Amir on the presentation and then told them to get some rest. "After tomorrow night," he warned, "it will be a while before you sleep in a real bed again."

* * * * *

Roger cleared the kitchen table and made a pot of coffee for the caffeine addicts. He and Manuel would get their buzz from Cokes.

Everyone arrived at around the same time. Roger's kitchen became crowded, and he suggested they move to the living room. Manuel went upstairs with his soda and a bag of chocolate-chip cookies, a gift from Carlin.

Norcross chaired the gathering. "This is about the most dangerous thing that I have ever done," he began. "We can all end up in jail for a long, long time." He looked at each one. "Anyone

290

who wants to leave, now's the time. Maggie ... Roger ... Carlin ... Estimo?"

Each indicated with a nod that they intended to stay.

"The meeting of the 'Tucson Five,' will now come to order," said Roger.

Maggie shook her head but smiled wryly. They might very well end up known by some such moniker, she thought.

Norcross shook his head too. He didn't smile. "Some of you may know that I stopped at FBI headquarters in Phoenix a few days ago. I tried to obtain safe federal custody for Manuel and failed. I called Washington and asked for support with my efforts here and was turned down flatly." He paused for a long moment. "I tendered my resignation."

The room fell silent. Maggie had never dreamed that the meeting had gone so bad.

"The bureau has not yet accepted it, so for the time being, I'm in limbo."

Estimo stood up and looked around. "I asked for additional support from the CIA and guess what? I also got turned down and my superiors know a great deal more than the FBI about these bad guys and their plans. So I'm acting on my own as well."

Suddenly everyone got it. They were all outside the law and on their own.

After everyone had a moment to reconsider the option of leaving the group, Estimo glanced around the room. No one spoke or moved. Estimo took a deep breath. "Okay, Maggie." he said. "Tell us what happened last night." Maggie gave a full report about events on both sides of the border."

She spoke for thirty minutes. When she finished the men sat stunned.

Finally, Roger said, "Maggie, if I'd had known ..." He didn't finish the thought.

"Roger, not now," said Norcross.

Norcross looked at Maggie, "I need to apologize to Manuel."

"So do I," said Estimo.

Carlin looked to the CIA agent, "Based on everything we now know, Estimo, what do you think the Arabs are up to, and when do you think they'll cross into the U.S?"

"There's no doubt in my mind that they want to assassinate the nine names on their list," Estimo answered. "The *when* is a tougher question."

"What list?" they all asked at the same time.

"It's a list of names of prominent people from business, television, and the movies. I turned it over to the CIA with my report, but I noted all of them. For the moment, I see no purpose in naming names."

Norcross chimed in. "I agree."

The others mumbled their concurrence.

Carlin asked, "How can we find out how they plan to cross, and when?"

Maggie spoke. "One way was the tunnel, but after last night I don't think they'll try to use it."

Everyone nodded.

"The alternative is to cross with a pack of illegals, with or without Mexican military support."

"I think they'll use the Mexican military," said Roger.

Carlin shook his head. "I'm not so sure."

"Why not, Carlin?" said Norcross.

Carlin paused and leaned back in his chair. "There's been far too much border action for their military to risk another fight. Remember, they attacked Maggie in January, and we believe that they participated in supporting one drug lord's attack on another in March." He took a deep breath, "Besides, President Fox will visit the U.S. in a few weeks. They wouldn't risk another border incident just before his visit."

Norcross nodded. The rest mumbled again.

"If Carlin's right, that leaves traveling with a coyote and a pack of illegals," said Estimo.

"We still don't haven't answered, when and where?" said Roger.

Estimo wondered out loud. "How can we find out?"

"I know how."

All eyes turned toward Maggie.

"They'll come with the best guides in the business. So they'll probably enter through Sasabe and travel the Devil's Highway."

The others looked at one another.

Maggie continued, "All we need is one confederate at *la ladrillera.*

"The what?" asked Estimo.

"The brickyard," Maggie said. "But it's not really a brickyard any more. It's the name used for the jump-off point through Organ Pipe and the Devil's Highway. It leads to U.S. highways Eight and Nineteen."

"Okay. How can we find a confederate who'll tip us off when the Arabs are ready to jump off?" asked Estimo.

"Well, I'm on admin leave. I could do it." said Maggie.

The reaction was instantaneous and not what she expected.

"No way!" said Carlin

"You're crazy!" Norcross told her.

"Forget it Maggie!" said Estimo.

Roger shouted. "Maggie, I won't let you do this!"

Maggie stood, a wicked look in her eye. "It's settled then. I'll travel down to Sasabe and pretend I'm a scared and lonely crosser. When I see the nine OTM's I'll travel to *la ladrillera*, contact you when I know when they're ready to cross. How's that for a plan?"

Everyone stood, talking, shouting, and screaming at the same time.

"Quiet! Norcross managed to yell louder than anyone. They all looked at him, then over to Manuel who had just ventured into the living room to see what all the commotion was about.

When the room went silent Norcross asked, "Maggie, what's an OTM? Maggie looked at Manuel and pointed at him, "He's one. 'OTM' means 'other than Mexican.'"

"Oh," said Norcross, sitting down. He paused. "Maggie has offered a plan. Does anyone have an alternate?" They all sat down, including Maggie.

The room fell silent again.

"Coffee, anyone?" asked Roger.

Chapter 56

No one had a better idea; no one could talk Maggie out of going. Still, there were a few things she needed to do before she headed south. She wanted to visit Margarita again, with Manuel, the child's uncle. Carlin made the arrangements. Maggie had to beg Norcross to let Manuel leave Roger's place. He was concerned that Manuel's illegal stay in the U.S., courtesy of the FBI, might trigger some official reaction. Maggie eventually won him over. How much more trouble could "The Tucson Five" get into than they already faced? Her argument was indisputable.

Carlin picked up Maggie and Manuel at Roger's and drove to the Arizona Child Protection Agency. The meeting was set for noon. The service was delighted that Mr. Ward had found a relative of Margarita's living in Tucson. This might solve the problem of the foreign child's status in time for the May disposition hearing.

Mrs. Santiago greeted the visitors at the front door and escorted them to Supervisor Boca's private office. Mrs. Boca was on vacation. The three huddled together on a overstuffed sofa and waited nervously for Santiago to bring in Margarita.

The door opened and Margarita flew into the room. All stood up. She went straight to her uncle Manuel. He picked her up in his arms. No words were spoken. Tears flowed. Maggie moved over and touched the child's back. Margarita responded. She put one arm around Maggie. More tears, more quiet minutes. Carlin pulled gently on Maggie and Manuel and led them back to the sofa. They sat with Margarita in the middle. The child smiled. She alternately hugged both of them with her thin, frail arms. Maggie watched Carlin wipe a tear from his eye as he walked out of the room.

The visit with Margarita had gone better than Maggie had anticipated. The child was more talkative, had gained weight, and appeared to be working through the loss of both parents.

* * * * *

After Carlin dropped Maggie and Manuel back off at Roger's, Maggie went to the thrift store and purchased the oldest, most worn-looking jeans she could find. She also grabbed a man's western shirt. Then she went home, put them on, and went outside, walking to the desert wash behind the apartments. When she was sure no one was watching, she laid down and rolled around in the sandy dirt. Now the outfit was almost ready for her trip. Having intentionally purchased jeans that were too long, she rolled up the pant legs three times, then unfolded the right one and sewed a pocket into it.

Estimo had warned her that if anyone caught her with a satellite phone she would be murdered. Murdered by the *guias,* the coyotes, or the Arabs–each would kill her without hesitation. She placed the satellite phone Estimo had given her in the pocket and sewed it closed.

While she was sewing, the phone rang. Still thinking about Estimo's warning, she sprang off the sofa and grabbed the phone. "Hello."

"I d-d-o-n-t t-a-l-k s-o g- g-o-o-d b-u-t I a-m s-t-i-l-l a g-g-r-e-a-t l-o-v-e-r."

Even with the halting speech, she recognized the voice. She screamed into the phone, "Marty! Marty, I swear, I swear, I was just thinking about you."

"S-u-r-e. I b-b-e-t."

"No, really, I'm sitting on my sofa and I was thinking about you and how much I could use your help right now. But forget that – how *are* you?" For the second time today, she had tears of happiness in her eyes.

The serious head wound made it difficult for her old patrol partner to talk, but he hadn't lost his sense of humor. She was thrilled to learn that he was back to work, a desk job for now. He had heard that she was on administrative leave and sought details. "I'll need to about my situation in person." She told Marty that she'd come right over. She also wanted to ask if he'd help with her latest planned clandestine operation.

She arrived at Marty's place just as he pulled into his driveway from work. They spent an hour filling each other in on what had transpired with each over the past months. Maggie ended by telling him that tomorrow she was going undercover into Mexico.

It was near midnight when she got up to leave.

"Be very careful Maggie," he warned. "Your life will be in danger every minute you're over there."

"Thanks, Marty. I promise. One last question, my friend, how well are you getting along with the governor these days?"

He smiled. "Guess you'll find out soon enough."

* * * * *

Maggie purposely didn't shower, so she'd smell as bad as all the other illegals. With scissors in hand she looked into the mirror and decided, "It's gotta go." She snipped and cut away until she couldn't grab any more. Then she took an electric razor and gave herself a number three buzz-cut.

The knapsack rested on the kitchen counter, packed with all her essentials. She removed all her jewelry and re-counted her pesos. She had sewn a hundred dollar bill in her left pant leg for emergencies. The $1,500 U.S. for the coyote was in her right coat pocket zippered shut.

In the morning she'd pop in the brown contacts. She hoped that with the loose-fitting jacket over her, she just might pass for a boy.

Sonora, Mexico

At dawn, Norcross picked up Maggie and drove her to Nogales. Estimo was with him and he talked all the way, filling her with as much knowledge about undercover work as he thought she could absorb. Norcross reviewed the plan of action once she located the jump off point for the Arabs to cross into American. She was to call when after they had stepped over the line.

At Nogales, she caught the first bus to Santa Ana. The small dusty town wasn't much more than a bus stop in the desert. She waited four hours before catching the bus going north to Altar. At Altar it was 6:00 p.m. when she boarded the last bus to Sasabe. She didn't want to linger around Sasabe too long or she would arouse suspicion. A migrant only stayed in Sasabe a day or two then jumped a shuttle up to *la ladrillera* for a late night hike to America.

She had to find a place to sleep. After walking up and down the sad-looking main street, she located a hotel, although it offered no sign as such.

"Do you have rooms for rent?" She lowered her voice but didn't try sound like a man. A teenage boy sweeping the floor answered. "Come back when you are ready for bed. We have plenty of rooms tonight.

"How much?"

"One hundred pesos for private, sixty to share with one other, twenty for dormitory."

"Can I leave a deposit for a private room?

"No need they'll be many."

"Okay, I'll be back."

She noticed a restaurant directly across the street. It had outdoor seating that would allow her to observe almost the whole town. She'd be able see if a bus showed up with sixty migrants that might head for her hotel and grab all the rooms. She didn't share the boy's opinion that this would be a slow night.

Traffic on the road was constant. With every bite of her taco she swallowed a mouthful of dust. She had to purchase water by the bottle. There was no free water in Sasabe.

She had almost finished her meal when a modern, private, luxury bus parked in front of the hotel. Although only nine migrants got out and went into the hotel, Maggie knew she'd have to find a new place to sleep tonight. She also knew she'd be leaving for *la ladrillera* tomorrow.

As she was paying the bill she saw the bus driver looked over at her. In fact, he was staring. She bent over and pretended to tie her shoe. A chill shot down her spine as she realized the driver was José. She got up and slowly walked away. Her mind was churning as she turned right off the first street she reached. Maybe she should try to get to *la ladrillera* tonight. Maybe this town wasn't big enough for her and her prey. Maybe she should just call it quits – while she was still alive.

She couldn't help herself. Contrary to Estimo's warning, she peeked around the corner. She watched José get out of the bus and walk over to the restaurant she had just left

She heard a terrible racket behind her. She froze.

Three children flew past her and ran across the street. She turned. She didn't see any adults following them, someone who might have questioned her snooping. Minutes later she saw José get into the bus munching on a burrito. He drove off. She was breathing easier now. It appeared that José had not recognized her. She watched as the bus was out of sight. The Arabs were apparently going 'native' from here on. No more luxury transportation. No more civilization for them or for Maggie. From now on, they would experience, firsthand the true life of a migrant heading north.

Maggie found a van driver and asked him for a ride. He explained that the last regular runs to *la ladrillera* were over for the night. He would take her in the morning for ten pesos. Then he reconsidered and said tonight, fifty.

She'd probably have to sleep under the stars. There were no hotels, motor lodges, or flophouses at *la ladrillera*. Despite this, she decided to go right away. The quicker she left Sasabe the better.

Chapter 57

Maggie slept out in the open on what had been the back seat of an old bus, the carcass of which was rusting just above her. She awoke at daybreak having slept surprisingly well. A few vehicles drove in and dropped off migrants, but the rush wouldn't come until after dark. She got up and wandered around the perimeter, avoiding the few men and one woman who huddled near the only structure, a shack occupied by Senor Torres, the camp organizer. She had met with him last night, given him a thousand dollars, and asked him to find her the best guide he could. Now he came out of the shack, saw her walking by and called her.

"Gitano."

She had not give Torres her name but had told him to call her "gypsy."

"Yes."

"Come here."

Maggie approached him. "For just another six hundred American, I can guarantee you the very, very best guide going out tonight."

"What is his name?"

Torres laughed. "I don't know his name but you can call him, "Cortez." He thinks of himself as a hero and a conqueror. He is helping Mexicans reclaim the southwestern *Estados Unidos* for themselves.

"Cortez?"

"Yes. He is the best. They write songs about him. It is true."

299

"I'll let you know later," she said and walked away.

"Don't wait too long, his group fills up fast." He yelled at her as she walked away.

Maggie knew that $1,500 was the highest rate going. The extra hundred must be for him, she thought. She decided to give him the extra five hundred and try to pay his bribe with some of the pesos she had stashed. She wanted to save her last hundred dollars for some possible later emergency.

At noon she returned to the shack and negotiated the deal she wanted. It cost her an extra thousand pesos.

A group of guides drove in at 7:00 p.m. Torres introduced her to Cortez, who told her to wait at an assembly area just behind the shack. Five other migrants were already sitting on the ground there. She stood apart from them, and leaned against the far corner of the building so she could see out front.

At eight she spied the nine Arabs. They got out of a van and assembled near the rusted bus hulk. She closed her eyes. She was relieved that they were not part of her group and that they were definitely going across tonight.

Maggie's group had grown to fifteen. No others were added to the Arabs' nine. At 8:00 p.m. the camp began to stir. Migrants began to getting up, adjusting their packs, and collecting their gear. The murmuring became loud.

Maggie had overheard the buzz that three groups were crossing tonight. Maggie's group, the Arabs, and one other that might number as many as twenty. Torres stood in the middle of the assembly. "Quiet! Listen up but stay in your group," he pleaded. "The first group out will be this one." He pointed right at Maggie. "The group will be led by Juan."

There were three guides standing next to Torres. Juan left Torres' side and walked toward Maggie's group. "Cortez will lead second that group." Torres' pointed to the Arabs. Cortez walked over to Maliq. They shook hands. Maggie guessed that it had been prearranged earlier for Cortez to lead the Arabs and she had been screwed out of an extra five hundred dollars, plus the pesos by the thieving, bastard Torres.

Torres ordered Juan to escort his group to the open trucks. He explained that each group would leave an hour apart. "You should not have contact with any other group. *Buena suerte,"* He wished them good luck.

Maggie trailed behind her group as they walked past the Arabs to an awaiting shuttle ride to the border. She listened to them talking. They all spoke with the same accent she had heard on the tape. She eyed the Arabs–especially their leader, who looked quite handsome standing in the soft moonlight. When he looked back in her direction, she looked away. *He could never ID me from that quick glimpse on the steps of the tunnel house.* At least that's what she hoped.

At that moment she noticed a man fall in behind her. He had not initially been sitting with her group or standing with the other guides. She'd have to keep an eye on him. She also watched two other men walk over to the Arabs' group. Were they more guides, or guards? Maggie wondered.

She was the first to climb into the back of the flatbed truck. A rickety rail provided support as the group, packed like cattle, was expected to stand for the short ride to the border. Maggie was squeezed up against the cab. The men closest to her knew that she was the only female in the group and they jostled for a position next to her. She turned her back to them and looked out over the cab. She felt hands on her ass.

She bit her lip and remained silent. She knew it would only be a few minutes ride and she couldn't chance an incident. She squeezed her legs together as one hand tried to slip between them. The truck stopped at a flat, sandy parking area located just on the Mexican side of the border. The men closest to her pushed forward and jump off the back quickly before she turned around.

Maggie jumped down and without looking at any one in particular she said, *"Passivo cabrones!"* She said it loud enough for all the men in the group to hear. She felt better after challenging the masculinity of those who had taken advantage of her on the truck. A ripple of sneers greeted her put down.

The only visible clue that they were at the border, two wooden posts, fifty yards apart with strands of a trampled wire fence hanging off. She looked up. A bright halo surrounding a three-quarter moon, made it far to light for her to remove her phone. She'd have to sneak off alone later.

Roger, having the only four-wheel drive, drove Norcross, Estimo and Carlin to the spot where Maggie had indicated the migrants' route would most likely follow. He found a shallow wash and parked. It was a hundred yards east of the actual trail on the Devil's Highway. They were approximately fifteen miles north of the Mexican border. Maggie had estimated that the first group would pass that point around midnight. Roger turned the truck around and parked. It was 10:15 p.m. He broke out snacks and drinks. Estimo left on a reconnaissance mission to locate a vantage point closer to the trail. He found a perfect spot that provided a clear view looking south of a major trail along the Devil's Highway. It was well hidden in underbrush and rocks. He surveyed the area to his front. The spot was well hidden from the trail.

The laser of a Bushnell Yardage Rangefinder scope found the back of Estimo's head. It remained there for just over a minute.

Estimo turned around and crawled away for the lookout position. Once below the ridgeline he stood up and walked back to the others hanging around Roger's truck, eating and drinking. The scene reminded Estimo of football tailgate party. "Sorry to interrupt your fun but I found the perfect lookout."

"Want a Coke?" asked Roger.

With an edge to his voice Estimo responded. "No, and it would behoove you to keep the noise down and post a guard to our front. This is not a picnic. Someone may get hurt out here if we don't watch our step." Even in the pale light, they could see the red coloring rise in Estimo's cheeks.

Roger stiffened. He knew Estimo was right. He had already witnessed the killing of one, no-nonsense, well-trained CIA agent. Norcross apologized. Carlin volunteered to take the first shift to the front.

Estimo handed Carlin night vision goggles and a radio. "Remember our job is to report and run. Contact with the migrants is to be avoided if at all cost."

Estimo showed Carlin how to hold down the mic when he wanted to talk. He ordered Roger to stay by the truck now designated the command center and handed him a radio too. Relay any messages from Carlin to me. I'll be back up on the hill. We'll rotate every hour. Norcross, why don't you take the first rest?" As Estimo finished handing out duties, he stopped and cocked his head. "Hear that?"

They all listened for a moment then nodded in agreement.

It was the unmistakable throbbing of a truck engine.

Estimo grabbed his radio and goggles. He ran back to the lookout. Carlin left for his post, walking back the way they had come. After twenty yards he dropped down, put on his goggles, and looked around. He put the radio to his ear. Estimo's voice crackled, "There's a Border Patrol truck now parked right in the middle of the trail about seventy-five yards below our lookout. I don't see anyone. Stay alert. It could be the bad guys with one of our truck."

The laser returned to the back of Estimo's head.

After an hour Norcross walked up to where Estimo was positioned. "My watch. Get some rest now. Carlin and Roger have already switched jobs."

Estimo handed him the radio and satellite phone. "Keep the phone in your pocket. It will vibrate instead of ring. Let's hope Maggie calls soon."

"Any sign of whoever drove the Border Patrol truck there?"

"No. But stay alert."

Norcross paused. "Estimo?

"Yeah."

He was going to tell him that he and the others needed the kick in the butt earlier. Instead he said, 'Rest well. I feel we're going to need you later."

Estimo walked back to Roger's truck.

The laser settled on the back of Norcross' head.

Chapter 58

Maggie knew she was boxed-in. The extra guide to the rear, she figured, was there to prevent anyone from falling behind. She was next to last so she nonchalantly moved ahead of three other immigrants before they became strung out single file.

The pace, fairly fast on the flat open desert, would slacken on the hilly slopes just ahead. She could see the trail narrowing and the desert growth closing in. She had to duck under a mesquite tree that had played nurse to three four-foot saguaros. The saguaros led to a row of healthy creosote shrubs and hundreds of crucifixion thorn trees that would gash many of the arms of the careless.

She steered wide of a jumping chollas but her shin attracted the spike from a prickly pear cactus. She led out a yelp. Her cry caused a ripple of giggles up ahead. The trail split around a screw bean mesquite.

Maggie wanted to pull the satellite phone from her pant leg and call Estimo. She estimated the Arabs were about to cross the border. Her guide had turned left at a fork in the trail. When Maggie reached the intersection she dropped back from the man in front of her and slowed her pace for a minute. She then walked quickly, appearing to close the gap but deliberately creating space from the migrant right behind her. She rounded a curve at the top of a slight rise, and as the trail dropped below she jumped into the thick underbrush to her right and crouched behind a three-foot boulder.

She held her breath and listened for the four migrants and the trailing guide to pass.

She felt blood trickle down her upraised arm before she felt the pain.

She looked at her palm where a two-inch needle had broken off a fishhook cactus and had stuck there. The hand began to throb. Wiping off the blood on her pants, she took out pocketknife, ripped open her pant leg and removed the phone. She pressed star—send.

"'G-man,' here."

She had expected to hear Estimo, but it was Norcross who answered. He used his code name. Estimo had given one to each of them.

"'Magpie' here. At fork. Party went west. All alone. Will alert when foreign bodies approach." The map Maggie had left with them would show her exact location.

"Magpie. Out."

She then backtracked along the trail. When she reached the fork she hid once again in the rough growth. She pulled the cactus needle out and wrapped her hand with panties from her backpack. She rested her head on her backpack and dozed off.

She was awakened by an engine noise that sounded like a model airplane in her semiconscious state. Then she realized it was a military Humvee, the same sound she heard the night she and Marty were attacked. She struggled to her feet. She strained into the darkness until she saw the red nightlights. It was coming right at her.

She ran out to the trailhead. She stumbled and fell, picked herself up and continued until she found a crevice. She jumped down and reached in her pocket for the satellite phone. It wasn't there. In her haste she had left it on the ground.

Maggie listened hard. There was more than one vehicle. Then the engines quieted to an idle. They had stopped at the crossroad. The engines revved again. Judging by their sound they were headed up the eastern trail, away from her. As the noise receded, she crouched and slowly crept back the trail, ready to jump aside at the slightest sound.

She raced back to her earlier resting place. Frantically she searched the area for the phone. She dropped to her knees and felt all around. She found it next to a dead thorny branch. She nicked her hand again.

The engine noises were now far off in the distance. Maggie went back to the fork and examined the ground on the eastern trail. She saw the tire tracks of the Humvees, overlain by numerous boot and footprints. The Arabs were apparently walking behind the vehicles. It looked like Roger had been right after all. The Mexican military were escorting the Arabs.

* * * * *

Estimo rejoined Norcross at their lookout.

The laser moved from the back of Norcross' head to the side of Estimo's head before he dropped down beside him. The spotter now had two targets.

"I can't rest any more," said Estimo.

Norcross shifted slightly to make room for him. "Happy for the company."

His satellite telephone vibrated. Norcross retrieved it and answered. "'G-Man' … Understand … 'Spyman's here too, will relay message. Out."

Estimo put his arm on Norcross. "What'd she say?"

"She saw two military vehicles leading the Arabs and headed this way."

"Is she still at the fork?"

"Yes."

Two hours later, Estimo heard the engines … growing louder … and louder. Suddenly they stopped.

First came flashes. Next the ear-popping clatter of fifty-caliber machine guns. Tracers and fire pierced the darkness, brightening the entire area. Norcross and Estimo covered their heads and ducked down low.

The spotter shifted his view to the source of the machine gun fire.

Suddenly the gas tank of the burning border patrol truck exploded. Flames shoot thirty-feet in nearly every direction. The surrounding vegetation blazed hot. The smell of burning rubber reached Norcross and Estimo. Roger and Carlin heard the commotion and ran forward to see the firefight. They flopped down next to Norcross and Estimo.

Estimo shouted. "Let's get out of here!" Estimo took a last look as his team started down the embankment toward Roger's truck. He watched the two Humvees swing around the burning Border Patrol truck, followed by a dozen helmeted soldiers.

As Estimo rose up to leave he was startled to see Norcross just standing, with his jaw dropped. Estimo grabbed him by the arm and pushed him toward Roger and Carlin who already were well down the hillside.

"Can you believe this?" Norcross shouted to no one in particular. "Mexico has just fucking *invaded* the United States."

Chapter 59

The spotter beam shifted to the two Humvees silhouetted against the flaming Border Patrol truck. The eyeball behind the scope blinked when the two Humvees split open like paper boxes under exploding hand grenades. The pounding didn't stop after incinerating the Humvees. Mortar rounds continued to hail down on the Mexican soldiers standing behind them..

Maliq and his men twenty yards behind the Humvees and the Mexican troops stopped their forward movement. The Arabs had dropped to the ground when the fifty-calibers opened up. Maliq was seething. This had to end badly, he knew. He had wanted to go with an unescorted group, but Brogadas had insisted. Most likely he had wanted to make up for the loss of the tunnel as an option for crossing.

When the mortar fire lit up the Humvees and scattered the troops, Maliq yelled to his men. He got up and retreated back along the trail. His men followed.

* * * * *

The full-bird, National Guard colonel put down his range-finding scope and ordered a cease-fire. He radioed for his troops flanking the trail to move in and take prisoners. His orders were not to shoot unless fired upon. Through his scope he observed the Mexican's throwing down their weapons and standing with their hands in the air as their vehicles burned. The surrounding brush caught fire.

Maliq missed the Mexicans' surrender. He and his men were already on the trail headed back toward Mexico.

"Hu ... hu ... halt!"

Maliq wheeled around, wondering where the shout came from.

The command came from Marty Fallon.

And it had the opposite effect. Maliq and his men scattered quickly in all directions. However, twenty border patrol agents were waiting on both sides of the trail. One Arab after another ran head on into an armed agent. They gave up without a struggle. Another ten agents pursued the few fleeing Arabs who had slipped through the trap.

* * * * *

Maggie heard the firefight and rushed up the trail.

She didn't see the man running blindly in the dark until he crashed into her. Being the smaller of the two, she was thrown onto her back. The man stumbled and fell to the side. Quickly, they both got back on their feet. They looked at each other, both with a glimmer of recognition.

"In a hurry?" asked Maggie.

Maliq glared at the woman for a second. Then he lunged at her, his arm high above his head. A sliver of moonlight glistened off a thin blade. Maggie leaned back, but the knife nicked her cheek. She cupped her hand over her face and lashed out with a karate kick. Her foot landed smack in the center of Maliq's crotch. He reeled back, bending over to absorb the pain. Head down and moaning softly, he slashed out blindly with the blade.

Maggie took aim and kicked again. Her foot caught his hand. The blade shot into the blackness.

His mouth contorted in pain. He lifted his head and eyed Maggie, speaking in perfect English. "Someday soon – I kill you! You American bitch!"

Maggie glared back.

Maliq turn and ran down the trail.

309

Maggie's foot felt like it was being squeezed in a vice. She looked down. Her shoe had come off during her second karate kick and her right foot was bloody and swollen. She sat down, placed her hand on her cheek to stop the bleeding, and waited for help.

Two National Guard, A-10 Thunderbolt II, Warthogs screamed low and fast just above the tree line. "What a beautiful sound," Maggie mumbled to herself as she watched the planes' lights and tail-fire arch overhead. They disappear beyond her line of sight leaving behind their engines' roaring echo. Behind the jets came the familiar thump-thump of a border patrol Black Hawk helicopter. It stayed and circled overhead.

Maggie watched as six border patrol agents neared her position. She yelled. "Over here!"

Marty was the first to reach her.
"You ... l-l-l-look ... l-l-l-like ... sh-sh-sh-shit."

Maggie grabbed his leg for support and tried to pull herself up. He reached down for her, grabbed under her arms, and lifted. They were eyeball-to-eyeball in an instant. "Well–you look like an angel."

She threw her arms around his thick neck. "Glad to see you, partner, and a special, special thanks to your *gov-ah-nator* sister and the National Guard."

"Told you she'd come through with her private little Army."

Marty kissed her on the cheek and released her. She stood on her one good foot.

A medivac helicopter set down in a nearby clearing. Maggie hobbled over to it, leaning on Marty. Medics loaded four stretchers with wounded Mexican soldiers. Then they helped her up into the craft. The cargo door slammed shut and they soared off.

* * * * *

Estimo had called the border patrol to alert them of suspicious activity on the Devil's Highway. He was surprised when they said that, "We're already on it."

Roger, Carlin, Norcross and Estimo had made it back to Route 19 as the medivac chopper flew overhead. Maggie talked on the satellite phone to each of them saving Roger for last.

"I'm fine, just a few minor scrapes. Don't make a big deal out of a little cut. Now listen, Roger. I understand that a good story about tonight's action might get you a promotion."

"Possibly." he answered.

"Well, I'll give you the whole story but there's a catch."

"What's that?"

"I'll only give the interview in my bedroom to a naked reporter."

She heard him laughing.

"There's a limit to what I'll do for a story," he joked. "Let me think about it."

"Don't take too long," she teased back. "There are hundreds of reporters who'd like this offer."

"You're tough. Okay, okay. I'll do it."

Maggie hung up.

Roger looked straight ahead and drove. He said nothing to his passengers. His broad smile spoke for him.

At last Roger had a source willing to talk about action on the border. Some jobs were better than others. Some jobs shouldn't be called jobs.

Ah, the life of a reporter, he mused.

* * * * *

Maggie lay on a stretcher as a medic wrapped her foot. She closed her eyes and imagined a naked Roger sitting on the edge of her bed taking notes.

The combination of exhaustion and morphine took over. Her eyes remained shut tight as the chopper bounced once, then settled onto the helo-pad atop Tucson General.

She awoke six hours later in a hospital bed. She remembered a dream. She smiled. Then she giggled.

Chapter 60

Osama leaned against an oversized cushion and beckoned a servant to bring food. The roasted lamb and rice reminded Maliq of the remarkable meal his Mexican host, Senior Brogadas had served. The two ate in silence. When they were nearly finished, Osama spoke, "Are you well, my son?"

"Yes, in fine health."

"And you?" Maliq nodded in Osama's direction.

"I, too, am in good health."

Maliq inquired about Osama's family and they talked a great deal about the weather. After the meal, servants presented a bowl of water to each and they washed their hands. An offering of cologne, which they splashed on top of their heads, concluded the evening meal ritual and the business portion of the meeting could begin.

"Now tell me about your travels, my son." Osama again leaned back onto his favorite silk cushion emblazoned with the name of Saladin in Arabic across all four sides.

It took Maliq over an hour to relate everything that had transpired since leaving Afghanistan in January for Mindanao. He ended with his departure from America on the first flight out of Denver to Mexico City on September 11.

"As you know already, out of the nine, only Abdul, Amir and I made it to our targets' homes. I assassinated the actress, Bonnie Becker in Aspen, Abdul killed billionaire Magabucks McDonald in Las Vegas and Amir was killed trying to enter Senator

McGuire's home in New Jersey. Maliq closed his eyes. "I beg your forgiveness for my failures?"

Osama snapped his head upward and clicked his tongue. "No. You did not fail." He reached across, grabbed both of Maliq's hands and squeezed hard. "You accomplished so very much and we learned valuable lessons. No more talk of failure."

Maliq looked up. Osama relaxed again on the opulent cushion. "Now, I suppose you have questions?"

Maliq smiled and bowed his head slightly. "Yes." He leaned forward. "Was my mission a diversion for the airplane attacks?"

"No, absolutely not. We wanted to demonstrate that we could strike America throughout their country and in many different ways. We particularity wanted to eliminate the news anchors so their voices would not be heard on our day of triumph."

Maliq shook his head. "Then, we did fail. We failed!"

Slowly Osama raised himself up. When he was at his full height, he glared down at Maliq. "Do not say that again." His lips tightened and he shook his finger in Maliq's face. After a long pause, he sat back down. Maliq stared at the floor. Osama noticed Maliq's' troubled expression.

"Listen," he said to Maliq.

Maliq raised his head up and looked into his leader's eyes.

"What you did was even more important than knocking down the towers and smashing their Washington military headquarters. You proved that we Arabs can assimilate into Mexican culture and walk across the border along with the immigrants. You established a pipeline. Already hundreds are learning Spanish here in Kabul and will soon follow in your footsteps to Mexico. Later hundreds more will follow. Then..." Osama's voice trailed off, "Enough about that later." Neither man talked for a while.

Maliq spoke up. "May I go back?"

Osama paused. "I shall think on it. Later you will tell me about the border crossing difficulties in more detail. Now you should rest. I believe that we should leave this area soon. We have awakened the devil, and he will surely attempt to revenge his loss. Their president already speaks of a new crusade. May Allah protect us."

Osama stood first to show the meeting had ended. Maliq rose and the men embraced. Maliq bowed. "Praise be to Allah," he turned and started toward the exit. Osama reached for Maliq's hand and walked with him to the open tent flap. He watched Maliq walk away with head down and shoulders hunched over – a man whose mind was in turmoil.

Osama considered for a moment, shrugged his shoulders, and decided to grant Maliq his request.

* * * * *

By Special Order of a grateful President, lawyers from the CIA, FBI, U.S. Border Patrol, the Arizona Governor and Senator Maguire's offices were instructed to make the many miles of red tape strewn about and ignored by the "Tucson Five" disappear. By 2011, most had but not all.

Washington bought the story that a drug lord had purchased the Humvees and dressed his men in "borrowed" uniforms. Mexico would never attack its most respected neighbor to the north. Never!

Afterword

Shortly after moving to Tucson in 2000, I learned firsthand what it was like living near the Mexican border. I heard for the first time, the term, "illegal alien." I perhaps saw them, or at least, the trails they left behind in the desert. Maybe one made up the beds at the resort where I maintained an office. Maybe my wife and I actually hired one, Maggie, to help us organize our new house when we moved in. She was the sister of the car rental agency employee. It never crossed our minds to ask for papers.

I thought a lot about the risks, the fears, the basic instincts that must drive a man or a woman to leave one's home, travel by foot across a blazing desert, and into an unknown life. Imagine the risks? There's the risk of being robbed, raped or mistreated by a guide or fellow traveler...risk of capture by the border patrol...risk of being held for ransom...risk, of even death. Why? Why do they do it by the thousands year after year?

They do it with hope for a better life, for a job...opportunity to make a little money to send back to Mexico...a better home and future for their children, and for many, many reasons related to basic needs. I believe that I could have been one of them, if I were in their impossible situation.

Then came 9/11.

For me, that changed the border issue from one of slowing or stopping illegal immigration of undocumented workers to one of stopping potential terrorists. I fathomed that most people could not tell an Arab from a Mexican, if the Arab lost the beard, kept the mustache, and arrived at the border speaking fluent Spanish.

Now I wonder, what if hundreds, if not thousands arrived in the U.S. alongside the undocumented workers? I also imagined the potential assistance and protection that could be afforded by the drug cartels.

What terror would we face then?

A cry went out after 9-11 concerning border security but little has changed over the past years. More agents have been added, a few more miles of fence constructed but basically, I believe, the border remains wide open.

Armed with my theory and a good laptop, I began this novel for an audience of one—Senator John McCain. I had been warned by a senator's aid that I would never get a copy into his hands.

I wrote the book anyway.

As to facts gleaned, from the *9-11 Commission Report*, the original plan of Khalid Sheikh Mohammed was for ten planes leaving from many different cities with targets in Los Angeles and Chicago as well as Washington, DC and New York City. Osama bin Laden rightly considered the plan too ambitious and suggested it be limited to four aircraft leaving from east coast cities with east coast targets.

This novel concerns a fictional plan to spread terror beyond the east coast at the same moment the Islamic terrorists were hitting the WTC twin towers, the Pentagon, and the failed, surmised target of the White House.

Charles Redner
September11, 2012

Made in the USA
Charleston, SC
10 January 2015